THE DEVIL MAKES THREE

THE DEVIL MAKES THREE

LUCY BLUE

Charlotte, NC
FALSTAFF
BOOKS
WWW.FALSTAFFBOOKS.COM

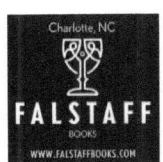

Cover Design by Lynne Hansen

This story is dedicated with love and respect to the memory of Ms. Daisy Mitchell and to librarians everywhere.

PUBLISHER'S NOTE

The Devil Makes Three contains scenes of racial violence that may be disturbing to some readers.

PROLOGUE

When Ontreas Clark burned down the Saxon County Courthouse, everybody who cared knew why. His case had been called the day before for trial first thing the next morning, and for once, Deputy Solicitor David Duncan had a rock-solid file. Ontreas and three co-conspirators had robbed Smitty's Drive-In, and somebody had brandished and fired off a gun. Two of the others had already pled out, and both of them had named Ontreas as the shooter. The fourth man had never been found, identified, or even acknowledged as real by the other defendants. Ontreas was facing a full ten years with no parole and no probation; this would be his third strike—his third conviction for a violent crime. His public defender advised him to pack a toothbrush. Jury trial or not, he was going to jail.

So, he burned down the courthouse. Or so everybody thought. It made a stupid kind of sense, Duncan said the next day, sipping sweet tea and eating a basket of hot wings at the Allavance Grill with Sheriff Buster Smoakes and Colby Knox, the newly hired Fire Chief who was mentally spiffing up his resume even as they ate. All the paperwork was in the courtroom for the week; the indictments, the evidence files, the sentencing sheets filled out and ready. Burning it all had probably seemed like the only way out to a meth-addled three-time loser like Ontreas. "Bless his heart," the assistant solicitor had mumbled, taking a bite of her salad.

They found him in the backyard of his grandmama's house that same night, less than three blocks from the scene of the crime, sitting on a rusted metal glider next to the clothesline and sipping cheap malt liquor from a can. "Where y'all been?" he asked when he saw the lawmen coming toward him with their guns drawn.

"You going to have to come on with us now, Ontreas," Deputy Travis said. "We don't want no trouble."

"Ain't going to be no trouble." The dangerous felon put down his malt liquor and stood up. Behind the cops and beyond his grandmama's house, he could see the smoke rising like a nest of thick black snakes across the orange sky. "I'm going down the road tonight?" he said as they cuffed his wrists behind him.

"To Columbia, yes, sir," the deputy said. "For a long, long time, I suspect."

"That's all right." In the distance, something exploded, sending sparks into the sky. "As long as I'm leaving here."

He had done a good job. The fire had started in three different places—the courtroom just past the metal detectors, the clerk of court's office in the records room for plats and deeds, and the mailroom in the basement. The old brick and plaster building acted like a chimney; pretty much everything was lost. Luckily the clerk had just six months before gone on the state computer system, so all her most vital records were saved. But local historians bewailed the loss of three hundred years' worth of mossy, handwritten documents and ledger books, long stored in acid-free boxes in the bare earth cellar of the clerk's office at the foot of a brass and cast-iron spiral staircase that the clerk always said was going to kill somebody someday.

Three days after, Ontreas was sentenced at a folding table set up in the empty derelict of a bankrupt furniture store downtown.As he was sent down the road for the next thirty years, a crew of graduate students came up the same road to assess the damage and salvage what they could. They packed the crispy, crumbling ruins into fresh, clean boxes and sighed over what had been lost.

Somehow nobody noticed the jagged ruin of a two-liter propane tank that had exploded in the flames in the farthest, dimmest corner of the cellar, or the narrow tunnel dug into the earthen foundation behind it, or the ancient iron strongbox inside, its lid thrown open and torn askew in the blast. Nobody squatted beside it or shone a flashlight inside. Nobody spotted the crude clay figure of a man blackened by smoke and broken cleanly in two.

So nobody saw the Dark Man coming.

1

Jacob had finished his first pint and started on his second by the time his ex-wife arrived. Seated in a corner booth, he watched with pleasure as she made her entrance, a crisp, exasperated Englishwoman in an ivory-colored raincoat. There was a bit of comic bother with her umbrella, a terse exchange with the barman, then she saw him.

"*Gloria in excelsis*," he said, rising to kiss her cheek. "Here at last."

"Are you aware how many pubs in Dublin are called Kavanaugh's?" she answered, waving her smartphone at him. "Luckily, the driver knew the one near a cemetery." She was perfectly made up; no one would have suspected the two of them were the same age, both closing in on fifty. His face, always thin, had taken on hollows under the cheekbones and deep crinkles around the eyes, shadowed even more deeply now that he'd given up sleeping. But Gloria's skin, from a distance at least, looked as fresh and dewy as a girl's. She returned his kiss in kind. "I knew that must be the one."

"I could have come to London," he said, pulling out her chair.

"Not really. You're the famous man of letters, after all." She sat down. "I'm merely an accountant."

"You've never been merely anything." He sat back down and signaled to their waitress. "You look stunning, by the way."

"After the ferry in the rain? I hardly think so." She caught him smiling and smiled back. "Stop teasing me."

"You know I wasn't." The waitress had come over. "Will you have a pint?" he said, raising his glass.

"Dear God, no." She looked the girl over with suspicion. "I don't suppose there's any chance of a decent glass of wine."

"Every chance and better than decent," he promised. He ordered her a respectable sauvignon blanc, and the serving girl went away with a smile.

She slipped out of her coat and settled back in her chair. "All right then, tell me. What's this about? Maggie's concerned, you know."

"What?" he asked, surprised, over a sip of his stout. "Maggie is?" Maggie was their daughter, a student at Oxford.

"She tells me you haven't been sleeping." She crossed her arms , but her eyes remained kind. "What's wrong?"

"Nothing is wrong." He and his daughter exchanged emails almost every day, but he didn't remember mentioning the nightmares. "I didn't ask to see you to talk about that."

"What, then?" The waitress placed Gloria's wine on the table. She took a sip and gave the girl a tiny nod and smile. The girl smiled back and winked at Jacob over Gloria's head before she walked away.

"You're my business manager." Jacob said. Gloria had managed his finances back when he'd had almost none. It had seemed only logical to ask her to continue when he had millions, divorce or not. "I'm about to spend a lot of money in America, and I didn't want you to be alarmed."

"What are you buying?" She took another sip. "An American?"

"Nothing like that." He knew she lived in dread of his remarrying, though he couldn't imagine why. She herself had remarried twice since their divorce and was now very happy, according to Maggie. "I'm going to buy a house." He took a deep swallow of his drink, the strange thrill that came over him every time he said it out loud coming over him again. "And some land—a plantation actually, in South Carolina."

"A plantation?" He had managed to surprise her. "Jacob, you can't be serious."

"I am." He smiled, enjoying her shock.

"Why on earth--?"

"I'm not sure." He had been weighing how much or how little to tell her since he'd made up his mind to do it. "I dreamed about it," he said, deciding to give her the full, unvarnished truth.

"Oh, for God's sake."

"Just listen." He stared at the dregs of his stout. "I started having these dreams... nightmares, really. I thought it was a new book trying to come through." He felt her sympathetic look without having to look up and see it. He had been blocked so long, it had become his habitual affliction, like traumatic blindness or a severed limb. "I started taking down notes whenever I woke up, and it worked. The dreams became steadily more vivid. I could see this place. I even drew out the floor plan."

"You said these were nightmares," she said. "What happened in them?"

"It doesn't matter." He saw no need to frighten her with descriptions of the screams in the darkness or the blood that soaked his hands. He flashed her a smile. "Scary stuff. My specialty." He could see from her eyes that she wasn't convinced. "The point is I woke up one morning with the name of the place in my head. Briarwood." He finished his pint.

"So now you think you should buy some place like this plantation in your dream."

"No." He shook his head. "On a whim, I decided to do a search for the name online." Whim was precisely the wrong word, though he had used it several times already to describe the feeling that had driven him to his editor, his research assistant, and to the real estate agent in South Carolina. Compulsion would have been more accurate. "And it's real," he said. "Briarwood is a real place." He grinned. "And it's meant to be haunted."

"Oh, Jacob," she said. "Some estate agent must have seen you coming. It hardly sounds like an uncommon name."

"It wasn't a real estate listing I found." Remembering, he felt the same shock and dismay he'd experienced that morning when he first found the pictures on the Web. It had been like discovering someone else had already written his masterpiece. "It came up on one of those amateur ghost hunter sites. Apparently, a mass murder was committed there before the American Civil War." He tried to email the creator of the site but got no response. Looking closer, he found out that the site hadn't been updated in more than a year.

"And I swear before Christ, Gloria, it was the same place." He had felt sick looking at the pictures, badly framed, dark, barely focused. The photographer had obviously been trespassing in the dead of night, probably with nothing more sophisticated than a smart phone. But Jacob had been sure it was the same place.

"You write horror books," his ex-wife pointed out, bringing him back to the present. "I'm sure you saw a documentary about these murders at some point."

"I'm sure you're right." This was the cover story he had already decided on; it made so much sense. But he knew it wasn't true. That one website was the only reference to Briarwood he had found in a month of looking on his own and three weeks working with Viola, his talented research assistant. There were no documentaries about Briarwood, no books, no mentions in the half dozen regional histories he had found. There was only a single website and his own fractured dreams.

When he called the history department of the nearest university, no one on staff had ever heard of Briarwood or the murders. Then a graduate student called him back to say his fiancée was from Saxonville, the town nearest to Briarwood, and had heard the story. As it turned out, the fiancée's aunt was the secretary/receptionist at a real estate agency with an ancient listing for the property.

"The house has been vacant since the murders in 1837," he told Gloria. "But the property has been on the market since the 1950s."

"How convenient," she said. "Jacob, really."

"I haven't absolutely decided to buy it," he lied. "If I get there, and it's all a scam, I'll come back at once, and you can say I told you so."

She took his hand across the table. "At least take someone with you." She had been his wife for fifteen years, his closest friend for twice that long. She knew him well enough to be concerned about more than his bank account. "Maggie has a holiday coming up."

"No." The very idea of Maggie at Briarwood made his blood run cold.

"Then I could go, I suppose." Gloria suggested.

The look on her face made him laugh.

"You in South Carolina?" He ought to have said yes just to see her there.

"I just don't want you to get carried away in some mad... " She trailed off, and he caught a glimpse of real fear in her eyes before she looked away.

"Have I gotten as bad as all that?" He squeezed her hand. "Gloria?"

"You look appalling," she said, pulling her hand away. "You're obviously not eating.""Of course I eat." He resisted the urge to reach for his glass. "I just need a change of scenery, I think. And I won't deny I'm intrigued." Why had he called her at all, he suddenly wondered. He could just as easily have sent her an email before he signed the check. Did something in his subconscious want her to talk him out of going? "Local legend contends the murders were supernatural in some way."

"Naturally," she said, sipping her wine, oblivious to her own joke.

"If nothing else, I should get a passable non-fiction book out of it." He had filled the gap since his last novel with two such projects, spinning his wheels. "Either way, it doesn't matter." He picked up his drink. "It's already decided. I'm going."

She smiled. "I never doubted it for a moment." She pushed her empty glass away. "When do you leave?"

"Tomorrow." His hands shook. For a moment, he wanted desperately to reach for her again, to grab her by both hands and beg her to save him. But from what? "I'll fly into Charlotte, North Carolina, then rent a car and drive the rest of the way."

"Dear God," she said, obviously picturing an uncharted wilderness full of hillbillies. "Do you know where you'll be staying?"

"I'm booked into a bed and breakfast that's meant to be charming."

"Oh, Jacob."

"It will be fine." He took her hand and kissed it. "I promise I'll be fine."

2

Serena had come home to Saxon County two years before because she'd had no choice. Once upon a time, she believed she would do great things, but the world taught her better. Now she just survived.

That Tuesday, she woke up at seven a.m. in the bed her late husband had slept in as a child. She ate toast and drank a smoothie while standing at the kitchen sink. Her mother-in-law fixed bacon and eggs for her father-in-law, and he sat at the table reading the morning paper. The three of them chatted, exchanging pleasantries and discussing the news of the day, nothing she could have remembered later if she'd thought to try. She told them she was leaving for work, and Claudine, her mother-in-law, told her to have a blessed day. She said she'd try and told them to do the same.

"You be careful, sugar," her father-in-law, Henry, known as Rooster, called as she walked out the door.

As she got into her car, her eyes happened to fall on her keychain. It was a thick, clear plastic rectangle encasing a stylized portrait of an African goddess. Her late husband bought it for her at a gift shop in New Orleans on a long weekend away. "She looks like you," he had said, and she had laughed.

The name of the goddess, Oshun, was printed in gold script across the portrait, a beautiful woman with an elaborate braided hairstyle who held a little round fan poised against her chin. Serena had looked up the name on the internet and read a few website articles about the *Orisha*, but she wasn't really interested. She'd been raised Baptist and wasn't in the market for any new gods. She was a historian, not a mythologist. She kept the keychain because it was a gift from Trey, and usually she didn't notice it at all, any more than she noticed she had five fingers on each hand.

But that morning, she saw it. She stared at it, her mind wandering for several seconds. *Mama,* she thought, a word that rarely passed through her mind. *Mama had one like this.* Then she broke the trance and put the key in the ignition.

She pulled her car into the parking lot of the Briarwood Community Center half a minute behind Miz Rae, the branch librarian, just as God and Miz Rae intended she should. She helped her boss unload a monster-sized pumpkin from the trunk of her ancient Cadillac. They put it on the porch next to the library door. "Get that old scarecrow out of the storeroom," Miz Rae said when they went inside. "And did you get those leaves?"

"Yes, ma'am, I did." She put her mid-morning snack in the refrigerator and turned on her computer. She checked the book drop—a James Patterson hardback and three cowboy movie videos. Kirk Benson had been by.

She spent the rest of the morning decorating while Miz Rae sat at the front desk. She dusted off the scarecrow and stapled down a hank of his yarn hair that had gotten yanked loose the year before and fluffed his floppy felt hat to cover the spot. She put him on the porch beside the pumpkin. While she was out on the porch, she chatted about the weather and the relative dangers of trick-or-treating with a homeschool mom while Miz Rae dealt with the woman's wild-ass children inside. She pasted colored paper leaves on the glass doors leading from the community center proper to the library, making swirls across the glass.

At noon, Miz Rae's best friend, Miz Regina, turned up with lunch for the three of them—white Styrofoam plates from the Columbus Day hot dog and bake sale at the Briarwood Baptist Church with Styrofoam cups of sweet tea. Serena put up the "Be Back at 1:00" sign, locked the library doors, and joined the older ladies in the back office.

They ate at the work table in the back, and Miz Rae made Serena and Miz Regina laugh until they cried, talking about the people at the church. "You bad, Rae," Miz Regina said, wiping her eyes with her paper napkin. "You know you so bad."

"I'm just telling the truth," Miz Rae said without cracking a smile, but Serena saw the twinkle in her eye.

At 12:45, Serena had just traded her little bag of barbecue potato chips for Miz Regina's slice of lemon poundcake when the back door from the parking lot suddenly opened.

Tom Stewart, the director of the Saxon County Library, had let himself in with his key. "Afternoon, ladies," he said. "Don't let me disturb your lunch."

"You can't disturb us," Miz Regina said. But of course, he could. He was a man, and he was White, and technically he was the boss. His arrival changed everything. Miz Rae grunted in a way he was welcome to interpret as pleasant.

Tom was nice enough; they all liked him fine. But he was the boss, even though Miz Rae had worked for the library for forty years. She had worked at the main branch in town when Tom and Serena had each gotten their first library cards. When the library board passed over her to give the director's position to Tom and his graduate degree, they had opened this branch at the Briarwood Community Center and made Miz Rae branch manager as a way to smooth things over. Mostly it had worked. Tom acknowledged the branch as her special queendom, and Miz Rae didn't make waves. But he knew, she knew, and Serena knew he would always be that White boy the board had given Miz Rae's big job to.

"What are you doing working today, Tom?" Serena asked. "I thought county council decided to close down everything in town for the holiday."

"Oh, we're closed," Tom said. "We don't work hard like y'all do."

The Saxon County Council, all Republicans, had decided they were all aggrieved on behalf of Christopher Columbus and would make a big show of recognizing his holiday. Miz Rae thought that was foolishness. She kept the Briarwood branch open and put "Happy Indigenous People's Day!" up on the big sign out front.

She also stayed open all day on Saturday instead of just the morning with the help of high school volunteers (Serena had Saturdays off), and she refused to allow public use computers. Tom left these issues to her best judgment, and they both slept better because of it. "Carol Ann Sweatt called me at home."

"Oh lord," Miz Rae said, immediately sympathetic. Carol Ann was a real estate agent and the chairwoman of the library board, a go-getter from Atlanta who thought the whole county belonged to her and her husband, the president of the bank. "What does she want now?"

"Y'all will never believe it," Tom said. "She sold the Briarwood place."

Both the older ladies cried out in shock. Miz Regina turned over her tea. "You can't mean it," she said, grabbing it up before the lid came off.

"The old Briarwood plantation?" Serena said. "I didn't even know it was for sale."

"It's always been for sale," Miz Rae said. "But didn't nobody ever believe there'd be somebody fool enough to buy it."

"I couldn't believe it either, but that's what she says," Tom said. "Serena, you'll never guess who she says bought it."

"Who?" Serena said. Miz Regina wasn't looking well, she noticed.

"Jacob McGinnas."

This time it was Serena who gasped. "You're kidding!"

"Who is that?" Miz Regina asked Miz Rae.

"That writer who writes all those horrible books about monsters and demons and I don't know what all ungodly mess," Miz Rae said. Miz Rae's own reading tended toward Maya Angelou, Jane Austen, and Agatha Christie, with the occasional biography thrown in. "You might know it'd be some kind of fool like that."

"Carol Ann is supposed to be meeting him over at the Briarwood house this afternoon," Tom said. "She wanted me to come and bring him copies of everything we had on the house and the murders."

"You need to go out there and tell him he's crazy," Miz Regina said. "Don't nobody need to try to stay in that house."

"Is it really haunted?" Serena asked. She had moved away from Saxon County when she was seven years old. Her husband had been the real native, but she knew about the murders.

"Ain't no such thing as haunted," Miz Rae said, fixing Tom with a baleful glare that dared him to dispute her. Tom was a semi-professional paranormal investigator. Miz Rae was a Baptist.

"I don't think the trust that owned it has ever let it be investigated," Tom said. "Maybe if he buys it, McGinnas will."

"That's probably *why* he's buying it." Serena was a huge fan of Jacob McGinnas's books. She'd been reading him faithfully since she was a teenager. "Maybe he'll write a book about it." She had liked his last two non-fiction books, but she yearned for a new novel.

"Carol Ann seems to think that's the attraction," Tom said. "I thought I remembered there being a whole file of stuff in the local history room at the main branch, but I couldn't find it. So then I thought since this branch is closer to the actual site, it might have gotten moved out here."

"I'll go look," Serena offered, getting up.

"I don't think we've got anything," Miz Rae said, also getting up. "You're going to have to talk to Miss Creighton about that."

Miss Florence Creighton was the former director of the library. She had held the post from the Monday after she graduated from the Winthrop Training College in 1922 until her forced retirement due to advanced dementia four years before. She was the one who hired Miz Rae in 1960, staring down a segregationist board with her watery blue eyes and daring them to tell her she couldn't. When she was forced to retire, the present-day board had brought back Tom, who had worked at the main branch as the local history librarian for a year and a half before he went to grad school. Miss Creighton now lived in a rest home in the mountains and was, by all reports, withered as a raisin and entirely out of her mind.

"Let's just look," Tom said, giving Serena a glance. "You never know."

But Miz Rae was pretty much right. All they found in the tiny walk-in utility closet that functioned as the archives for the branch was a single thin folder in the vertical file with a photocopy of a newspaper article Tom himself had written ten years ago when he'd been the local history librarian.

"This is good," Serena said, reading through the first few paragraphs. "I didn't realize you were such a good writer."

"Yeah, well, that was back when I had time to practice." He took the article from her. "I know there was more stuff, though. I used it to write this in the first place."

"Maybe somebody borrowed it and forgot to bring it back." Serena couldn't stop herself wondering if Tom had neglected to put it back himself. He was a great guy but the classic absent-minded academic. His wife, Evie, swore they'd need a second house soon just for his books and papers. The missing file could be stuffed in a box in his attic with a bunch of comic books. "What are you going to tell Carol Ann?"

"That we'll keep looking, I suppose." He closed the file drawer. "Go to hell, if I could tell her what I want to tell her."

Serena smiled. "Which you absolutely cannot."

"Which I absolutely cannot." He looked at his watch. "And I've got to go."

"I'm sorry, Tom." The door was open, and out in the library proper, she could see Miz Regina was still there, standing at the desk with Miz Rae. The two of them were huddled together like they were planning a heist. "Hey, can I come with you?"

He looked surprised but not unhappy. "Yeah, if you want."

"I've always wanted to see that place." Miz Rae was watching them, she realized. She pretended to be listening to her friend, but she was really watching over Miz Regina's shoulder. "And you know what a big fan I am of Jacob McGinnas."

"Come on and go, then," Tom said, grinning. "I can use the help."

3

Jacob had intended to rent a sensible car at the airport, something with good gas mileage and just big enough to hold him and his luggage. He'd never been a particularly avid driver, and his daughter was constantly on about carbon footprints. But, somehow, when the cute redhead at the rental counter had said, "Oo, a Mustang just came in; don't you want it? It's black," he had heard himself say why yes, yes he did indeed.

Now he was at the wheel of a roaring, gas-guzzling beast, bashing down the broad, straight American highway out of the city at an entirely ludicrous speed. Johnny Cash rumbled ominously on the stereo, and the satellite navigation was set to the longitude and latitude of Briarwood Plantation, the only way it knew how to find it. He had lost his mind, apparently; he probably looked absurd. But he felt fantastic. Not even a sudden gathering of thick, gray clouds across the sky as he drove dampened his mood.

The closing on the property was set for the next morning. But the real estate agent, an exhausting woman named Carol Ann, had agreed to meet him at the property that afternoon as soon as he arrived so he could have proper look around. "I'm so excited," she had said on the phone in her honey-thick accent. "I've never been inside the house, you know. I don't know anybody who has."

If he hadn't had the sat nav, he would have been completely lost. He turned off the interstate onto another four-lane road, then four miles later onto a twisting country lane that seemed to lead to nowhere forever. It wound between yellow-green cow pastures and bare, black skeletal orchards and vast, flat brown fields dotted here and there with white—actual wads of cotton. "Lawsy, Miz Scarlett," he muttered to himself. "I don't know nothing 'bout buying no plantation."

He finally came to a tiny sort of village with green signs that identified it as North Creek. But a white frame church was called Briarwood Baptist according to its light-up marquee out front ("Come Expecting!" it exhorted, whatever that meant), and an ugly new glass and brick building was labeled the Briarwood Community Center. The jaunty scarecrow guarding their steps made him smile.

But the sat nav said drive on. He passed out the other side of the tiny town and back into the countryside, thicker woods now with skeletal autumn trees overhanging the road from either side. A little more than a mile past North Creek, the sat nav beeped and said, "Turn left in five hundred feet." At first he thought there must be a mistake. Then he saw a narrow gap in the trees and a rutted, red dirt road barely wide enough for his car. As he turned, branches of scrub and cedar scratched the car's flanks. There was no gate, but starting about a hundred feet up the drive, he started seeing the ruins of brick columns at regular intervals on either side as if there had once been a fence of some grandeur.

Half a mile in, the drive curved sharply to the left and broke free of the taller trees. He stopped the car and took his first long look at Briarwood.

The house stood at the top of a hill with what must once have been a magnificent sloping lawn laid out before it. Now it was covered with the same kind of scrub pine and underbrush as lined the driveway, but the effect was still quite striking, like something out of a movie. The house itself seemed remarkably intact. From his vantage point at the foot of the hill, he could almost believe it was still habitable. The white paint was worn gray, but the lines of the structure seemed solid.

It was much bigger than he had expected, a Greek revival rivalling the massive country estates rich Englishmen had once built in Ireland. With its massive columns and round east wing, it looked more like a public building than a family home, some great parliament or temple more than a farmhouse. Looking up at it, he had to remind himself to breathe, and his heart pounded. Imagine the labor that went into that, he thought. Slave labor, like the pyramids, no doubt. But he didn't feel righteously indignant; he felt sad, almost angry. How dare anyone abandon such a beauty, whatever might have happened there? How could they have left her to die and disintegrate alone?

The drive forked at the top of the hill. The path leading to the back of the house was completely overgrown, and a rusted farm gate hung on newer, shiny chains across it. The other branch looked fresher, as if the brush might have been cleared from it once or twice in the past decade. Jacob drove slowly around to the front of the house, the V8 engine in his rented beast rumbling like a dragon's snore. He parked in front of the steps and got out.

The dry grass was as tall as his hips and brittle with autumn frost where it was shaded by the house's shadow . Up close, Briarwood was no less grand but much more obviously deserted. He saw no path worn through the grass, no footprints in the thick, mossy mud caked on the steps. He could have been the first human to approach the house in centuries—the first living thing, for that matter. The high grass and scrub should have been a haven for mice, rabbits, even quail, but he didn't hear a sound or see a single stir of movement. The whole place was as dead still as an empty tomb.

So why was the front door standing open?

He stood at the foot of the steps, leaning forward to peer through the shadows. The clouds had thickened; it was as dim as twilight on the porch. "Hello?" he called. No answer. He was half an hour early for his appointment with the real estate agent, and there were no other cars parked out front. Anyone inside would have had to either fight the gate and brush to pull around back yet leave no sign of their passing, or else hike in from the road on foot.

He walked up two steps, his work boots leaving clearly discernible footprints in the mud. "Is someone here?" Between fluted Corinthian columns, the open doorway yawned at him in silence.

He crossed the porch with purpose, boots clomping. The thick wooden door was massive, at least eight feet tall. It seemed to be intact, and the lock was unbroken. No one had forced it open. He touched it lightly, and it swung back further, hinges squealing like a cheesy sound effect.

He stepped into the vast empty cavern of the front hall. Directly in front of him was a grand, curving staircase, and more columns were set in perfectly straight lines leading up to it. Floor to ceiling windows lined the front wall. The shutters on the outside were open, but he didn't see a single pane of glass that was broken or even cracked; every window was perfectly intact. Each was hung with great velvet drapes, sagging and blackened with age and dirt, but also still intact, and gray light filtered between the heavy panels. The floor was bare wood and strewn with dead, crumbled leaves over a thick coating of dust—again, no footprints.

Double doors stood open to his left as he turned back to the staircase. In the shadows beyond, he could make out a long dining table still covered with a cloth. Moving closer, he saw a massive sideboard still set with an elaborate silver service, black with tarnish but otherwise untouched. Who would just abandon such a thing? Why hadn't it been picked clean? Looking at it, he realized his mood had turned. A feeling of dark oppression seemed to have gathered around him like the clouds outside, pressing down on his psyche like a moldering pillow might be pressed over his face.

He had felt this way before. On their honeymoon, he and Gloria had gone to Spain. Touring the dungeon of a castle where heretics had been walled up to die, he lost himself completely, sobbing uncontrollably and fighting off anyone who tried to touch him. Poor Gloria had been covered in scratches and bruises by the time she'd managed to drag him back outside into the light.

What could have possessed him to come here now?

He had decided to go back outside and wait for the real estate agent when he noticed the footprints on the stairs. Someone had tracked some dark liquid on the pale wood, something dark brown, almost black, like paint . . . like blood. Moving closer, he kicked away a thicker scattering of rotten leaf matter and saw the prints led away from a larger, darker stain on the floor of the hall just at the foot of the steps . . . blood soaked deep into the wood.

"Bollocks," he muttered aloud, but the hair on the back of his neck prickled, and his flesh turned cold. Surely it was a fake, a prank, something staged for a camera or to frighten some dupe in the recent past. No real bloodstain could have lasted so long, could it? The wood would have to have been completely saturated. But mass murder with an ax could do that. And if the story he had read of Briarwood's abandonment was true, who would have been left to clean it up?

Without stopping to think any further, he followed the prints up the staircase, trying not to notice how perfectly his boots matched them as he walked. As he climbed, the prints faded out from full shoe shapes to smears to mere smudges at the top that led a few steps down the hall to the right. The man with bloody feet had climbed the stairs for a reason.

His heart ached, and tears stung his eyes. Wallpaper hung in tattered ribbons on the walls, and the floor was scarred in two straight lines down the middle where a carpet runner had been ripped up. The smell of dust and rot was closing in on him and making him feel sick. He imagined he could smell the blood; surely he *must* be imagining it.

He followed the smudges to the right and then around the corner; he seemed to know exactly where he was going. He turned a glass doorknob at the end of the hall and went into a bedroom at the front of the house. The drapes in here were silk, some pastel color gone gray with age and neglect, and the shutters were open. Going to the window, he looked out over the second-floor gallery and down on his rental car parked below. It looked so solidly vulgar, so real, it made him smile. Gloria had been right. He'd been crazy to come here, mad to think of buying such a place. When the real estate agent showed up, he'd tell her he had changed his mind. Just as he made the decision, he heard the sound of motors coming closer, two cars coming up the drive. It was fate.

He was just about to turn away from the window and head back downstairs when he smelled something else. When he smelled *her*. Over the damp, ancient rot of the house, he smelled clean white cotton warmed by the summer sun. Soap, and the lightest hint of lavender, and clean, sweet skin underneath. He felt the warmth of a woman's presence, soft hands touching his back. He braced his hands on the window frame, holding himself up. His knees had gone weak. The feeling of despair he had felt before dissolved like a mist in morning sunlight, and wild joy seized his heart. There was life in Briarwood, not just death. He wasn't mad to come here. He belonged here. *She* had called him to come.

A battered, late model hatchback pulled into the yard, followed by a shiny white Cadillac SUV. The Cadillac opened first, and a woman who could only be his real estate agent got out, a fit, tastefully dressed, middle-aged blonde with sunglasses perched on top of her head in spite of the cloudy weather. A man got out of the hatchback, a rumpled, tweedy sort of fellow with overgrown hair and a wrinkled blue shirt. The real estate agent greeted him with energy; he responded with a shrug, passing her a manila folder.

The passenger door of the hatchback opened, and another woman got out. Jacob felt himself smiling. She was beautiful. She was Black and young, no more than thirty, with a gorgeously curvy body under jeans and a sweater that were both just a little too tight. She looked up at the house, and he gasped when he saw her face. "Sweet darling," he murmured, utterly smitten. Her eyes were huge, and he had never seen such luscious, perfect skin. Whoever she was, she was worth the trip to America all by herself.

They had seen his car and were headed for the porch. He went to meet them, and the strange sensations Briarwood had inspired in him were all but forgotten.

4

Serena had always imagined Briarwood as some version of Tara, but she'd never dreamed it would be as big as it was. It looked like something out of a painting or a horror movie, too grand and awful to be real, but familiar, too.

"Hey Tom," she said as they got out of his car. "What movie did they film on that porch? Some horror movie from the Eighties, I think, or maybe a miniseries? Something I saw on TV."

"Nothing that I know of," he said as Carol Ann's car roared up beside them. Mr. McGinnas must have already been inside the house; a rental car was parked in front of the steps. She felt a pleasant little thrill and smiled. Of course, he'd be driving a Mustang. "As far as I know, nobody's ever even taken a picture of it. The trust that owns it won't allow it."

"Isn't it gorgeous?" Carol Ann said as she got out, all the bells on her Cadillac dinging. "Can you imagine living in a place like this?" She'd been talking to Tom, but now she noticed Serena. "I mean, it was awful, of course, the way it was built and how they kept it up and running. But still, it must have been beautiful in its day."

"It's beautiful now," Serena said. "And awful, too."

"I wouldn't want to live in it like it was," Tom said. "Master or slave, you'd still be shitting in a bucket. Carol Ann, have you told this man there's no toilets in this place, and the kitchen is in the back yard?"

"I'm sure he realizes it will need some work to make it livable," she said. "Did you bring the information I asked for?"

"I brought what we had," he said. "And I think I can fill in the gaps if you want. Are you wanting to tell him about the massacre?"

"Ordinarily, I'd say no," she said. "But I think that's why he wants to buy it."

As they talked, Serena had wandered up the mossy steps, drawn into the shadows of the porch by an almost painful feeling of nostalgia. She was sure she had seen this place before. So she was the first one to see Jacob McGinnas when he walked out the front door.

"Hi." Smiling in person, he was more handsome than in his always-serious book cover photos. But he looked older, too, and thinner, with crinkles at the corners of his eyes and strands of silver in his jet black hair. "I'm Jacob."

"I'm Serena." She shook the hand he offered and smiled back, and a shiver of mutual attraction passed between them, or so it seemed to her. That was strange, too. She hadn't felt any such thing since Trey died, not for anyone.

"Mr. McGinnas, hi," Carol Ann said, coming up the steps like she was charging a beach. "I'm Carol Ann Sweatt; we spoke on the phone."

"Call me Jacob, please," he said, giving Serena another smile before he let go of her hand to shake Carol Ann's.

"So nice to meet you, Jacob," Carol Ann said. "That's Serena, and this is Tom. They're from the local library. Tom is the director and our resident historian and ghost expert. I asked him to come so he could give you some background on the house."

"I just wanted to tag along so I could meet you," Serena said. "I'm a big fan of your books."

"Thanks; that's lovely." He was soft-spoken with a lovely Irish accent. "And thank you, Tom. I'd love to hear about the house. I hope it's okay I just went in. The door was open when I got here."

"It's fine, of course," Carol Ann said. "But I don't know why the house would be open. This should be the only set of keys." She pulled a huge ring of old-fashioned keys out of her purse.

"Well, it wouldn't be the first time," Tom said. "Locks that won't stay locked are one of the observed phenomena of this house." Serena noticed his Southern drawl had gotten more pronounced, the way it always did when he gave a lecture or told ghost stories. "Nice to meet you," he said, shaking Jacob's hand.

"Let's all go in and have a look," Carol Ann said. "I'm dying to see what it looks like on the inside."

"Have you really never been in?" Jacob said.

"No, never," Carol Ann said. "I inherited this listing when I bought the real estate business, but I've never had a chance to come out."

"My God," Serena said. "Look at it." It really was like walking into a movie, one she'd seen a long time ago but still dreamed about.

"It takes your breath away, doesn't it?" Jacob said. "Come look at the dining room. It's like it hasn't been touched."

"It probably hasn't been," Tom said. "The entire Montgomery family was killed in the massacre, and almost all the slaves were either tried and hanged or moved off to other plantations."

"Tried and hanged?" Serena said. Jacob wasn't kidding; the dining room table was still set for a meal, with silver chargers and candlesticks tarnished black. "I thought one White guy did all the murders."

"He did," Tom said. "Or at least we think he did. The problem was, he killed pretty much every White person at Briarwood—Caleb Montgomery, the man who built the place, his wife, Ellen, their sons, Caleb Junior and Halsted, their daughter, Alice Rose, a daughter-in-law, June, and the family minister, a Mr. Holloway. Seven people in one night—maybe in less than an hour.

"How is that even possible?" Jacob said. They were all looking at the table. Serena counted the chairs and plates, trying to imagine where they all must have been sitting and how it might have happened. There were nine places set, an uneven number. Wasn't that supposed to have been bad luck or bad form or something? "You're talking about four adult men and three women," Jacob went on. "All killed in a single night by a single man. Why didn't any of them run?"

"That's what some of the people in town said," Tom said. "How could one man with an axe kill seven people? And one did run, Halsted's fiancée, Naomi. She was the only witness, but she couldn't tell them much."

"An axe?" Carol Ann said. "He used an axe?"

"When the locals showed up, Ezra Woodbine was in one of the upstairs bedrooms covered in blood, still holding an axe," Tom said. "When they asked him what had happened, he said, 'I killed them all.' And when they found the bodies, they believed him."

"Let's open up some of these drapes," Carol Ann said. "We need some more light in here."

"Naomi is the one who brought the townsfolk here," Tom said, going to the window. "She was found running down the public road toward town screaming her head off. Even after she was found, she kept on screaming, no words, just screaming and pointing back toward Briarwood."

"Was she hurt?" Serena asked as Tom opened the rotting velvet drapes and weak daylight fell across her face.

"Not a mark on her," Tom said. "But she never spoke another coherent word, and she died before morning, supposedly from fright."

Jacob opened another set of drapes. "Who was this Woodbine?" The light behind him made him look even taller and more like a handsome wraith.

"He was an Englishman who was here visiting," Tom said. "His family owned cotton mills back in England, so he was probably here on business. But several friends of Alice Rose Montgomery testified that he and Alice Rose were engaged to be married, that the special occasion at dinner that night was supposed to be the announcement of their engagement."

"I still don't get why some of the slaves were hanged," Serena said. She tried not to notice that none of the rest of them seemed bothered by this point. She ought to be used to it by now, this unconsidered acceptance the White people in Saxon County and the rest of the South had of the evil in their past. But it twisted in her stomach every time. "Did Woodbine murder any of the slaves?"

"That's another thing that's weird," Tom said. "In one account written by an assistant to the coroner, the body of a young African woman was discovered brutally beaten." He took the file back from Carol Ann and consulted the article inside. "He wrote that Woodbine 'violently protested his innocence of her murder.' But none of the other accounts mention her at all."

She's why he did it, Serena thought. *He killed them all for her.*

"Where were the rest of the bodies found?" Jacob said. He had come to stand close to Serena, and he touched her shoulder for just a moment, a comforting, protective gesture.

"In the drawing room on the other side of the hall," Tom said. "Let's look."

"You know, all the glass in these windows is original," Carol Ann said as they followed Tom. "I wouldn't even know how to value something like that."

"Sure you would," Jacob said. "The asking price is on the website." Serena laughed, and he winked at her.

The pocket doors to the drawing room were closed. Tom tried to push them open, but they wouldn't budge. Jacob went to help, and together they shoved them back as the rusted hardware screamed.

A wet, rotten smell of decay poured out of the doorway as soon as it was opened. They heard the dry scuttle of what sounded like thousands of insects or mice. "So much for that priceless glass," Jacob said. The shutters over the windows and the French doors in this room were hanging from their hinges, some in broken pieces, and every pane of glass was shattered.

In the dusty daylight, the tiny creatures they heard could barely be seen scurrying into hiding, bringing the shadowy corners to life. The drapes hung in tatters, and all of the furniture, chairs, sofas, and tables seemed to have been upended. Books and bric-a-brac lay strewn and broken all over the floor. A mirror over the fireplace was shattered. And everywhere on everything were dark stains that could only be blood—on the upholstery, the rugs, the wallpaper, even soaked into the woodwork.

"We'll get an exterminator in here, of course," Carol Ann said, her voice barely shaking. "A good glazier and clean-up crew, and you'll never know anything ever happened. This room could be beautiful again so easily."

"I'm not so sure," Serena said. Looking at the room, she expected to feel the thrill of a haunted house, but she felt more than that, a weird excitement so intense, she saw lights in front of her eyes like the onset of a migraine. "You can just see it, can't you?"

"You can," Jacob agreed. From the moment he had walked out on the porch, he'd been watching this beautiful girl, this Serena. He had to keep reminding himself not to stare. *Behave yourself, you dirty old bastard,* he reminded himself. But he would have sworn his fascination was grounded in something more than just her beauty; he met pretty girls all the time. Looking at her, watching her react to Briarwood, he felt the same tingle of recognition he'd felt in his very first nightmares about the plantation. Standing beside her now in the open maw of this rotting tomb, he was reminded of the feeling of peace that had come over him upstairs, the scent of clean, sun-warmed skin and freshly-ironed cotton.

"Nobody came back here to clean up?" she asked.

"I don't think they did," Tom said. "I remember when I was first doing research on it about ten years ago, I couldn't even get anybody to tell me who owned the land."

"It's a trust," Carol Ann said. She pushed her way between Jacob and Serena. "Tom, help me close these doors." Jacob put a hand on the door as if to stop them, then backed away.

"Who's in the trust?" he asked as the doors were closed. "Relatives of the Montgomery family?"

"Presumably yes, when it started, but I don't know," she said. She was exactly what he'd expected from her voice on the phone. She could have driven her monstrous SUV straight out of an American TV show about a sassy Southern go-getter with bleach-blond hair and nerves of steel. But Briarwood was obviously giving her the creeps. "I don't think there are any Montgomerys left, but I haven't really looked. The trust has an attorney in town. And there's a whole big file of old papers at his office that he'll be turning over to you if you buy the property."

"How's that for a tease?" Jacob said, laughing.

"Hell, I might buy it just for that," Tom agreed.

"You could never afford it," Carol Ann snapped. Tom flinched, and Serena's eyes widened. "Jacob, have you been upstairs at all?" the estate agent went on, softening her tone.

"I have," he said.

"Is it safe?" Serena said.

"Oh yeah," he said. "It looks solid as a rock."

"Oh, it would be," Carol Ann said, leading the way to the stairs. "These old heart pine floors stand up to anything. They're like iron."

Upstairs, some of the rooms were stripped bare, but some still had beds made with full linens and rotted pillows. Jacob thought that if they opened the drawers in the dressers, they would find the clothing of the dead still carefully folded, awaiting their return.

Their last stop on the second floor was the bedroom he had explored before. This time it just felt like a musty, empty room, but his eyes were drawn back again and again to Serena, standing at the window where he'd stood before.

"I'm still not clear on why those slaves were hanged," she said, looking out over the front of the house. The edge of anger he could hear in her voice was as seductive as her beauty. There were depths to this woman that could drown him.

"That was so long ago," Carol Ann said. As they'd toured the upstairs, she had slowly regained her good humor. "I doubt anybody remembers."

"There's actually a short mention of it in the original newspaper write-up of Woodbine's trial," Tom said. "I don't have it in front of me, of course, but I remember it. Apparently, some persons unknown told the authorities that Woodbine was actually an abolitionist and the murders were meant to be the start of a statewide slave uprising."

"Was he an abolitionist?" Serena asked.

Yes, Jacob thought but didn't say. He wasn't sure why he'd thought it. Had the website mentioned this?

"I don't think anybody ever bothered to find out," Tom said. "Six male slaves were hanged the same day as Woodbine, but their names weren't recorded. The rest were sold off with the proceeds going to the town as restitution for court costs."

"Dear Lord in heaven," Serena said.

"One report I read said one slave woman who was of invaluable assistance to the authorities was given her freedom," Tom said. "At least three hundred others were sold."

"That would have been a huge amount of money," Jacob said.

"Not necessarily," Tom said. "They were sold for pennies on the dollar to other farmers in the county. Let's put it this way. Before Woodbine's massacre, Briarwood was the only farm within thirty miles in any direction that could call itself a plantation, and Caleb Montgomery was the only legally designated planter, meaning the only one in this part of the state who owned more than twenty slaves. Within a year afterward, there were seven. I suspect most of the people of color in Saxon County are descended from people who lived at Briarwood."

"But no Montgomerys," Serena said.

"Nope," Tom said. "They would have either taken the names of their new masters or taken new names of their own choosing after the Civil War. And by the way, the town probably did turn a bit of a profit. The county courthouse, fire station, and the original library building were all built that same year. In a weird way, Ezra Woodbine was one of the founding fathers of Saxonville."

"That's a gruesome way to think about it, Tom," Carol Ann said. "I don't know anything about the slaves that were here, but I know the property has never left the possession of the original Montgomery Trust. And the full three hundred or so acres of the original plantation are intact except for the rights of way for two state roads that run through two corners of it. There was some work done on the grounds sometime back in the Sixties, but I don't know what."

"Putting up those gates, I would imagine," Jacob said.

"I bet Miz Rae knows," Serena said. "What do you bet, Tom?"

"I wouldn't be a bit surprised," Tom agreed.

"Miz Rae is the librarian for the branch out here at the community center," Serena explained. "She's my boss."

"I saw the library as I was driving in," Jacob said. "Nice scarecrow."

"Thanks," she said, smiling. "I put him out myself."

"We've got one more floor to look at," Carol Ann said. "According to our listing, there are several small rooms in the attic that were probably used as servants' quarters."

"But no bathrooms," Tom joked.

"Thank you, Tom," Carol Ann said. "That's very helpful."

"It's all right," Jacob said. "You don't have to show me any more. I love it." A chill passed through him, making him feel queasy. Then he made eye contact with Serena again, and when she smiled, it passed. "I'm going to buy it."

"Wonderful!" Carol Ann said. "Let's write up the offer."

Jacob let Tom take Serena to walk through the rest of the house while he and Carol Ann filled out her stack of forms. The two librarians came back down the front stairs just as they were finishing up. "It's very, very dark up there," Serena said. "And creepy as hell."

"Mr. McGinnas, would you ever consider letting a paranormal investigations team come in and do a survey?" Tom said. "I have some friends who would dearly love to get their equipment in here."

"Ghost hunters?" Jacob said. "I don't know. I'm not sure what I think about all that stuff. I prefer my scares a little less scientific."

"Miz Rae says they're courting demons," Serena said, giving Tom a nudge. "But I think it would be fun. If y'all do it, I want to come and watch."

"It wouldn't be any big thing," Tom said. "No cameras for TV. We just investigate and report our findings to the property owners."

"They're very professional," Carol Ann agreed. "They did our house in town before the remodel. Of course, they didn't find anything, but I'm still convinced it's haunted."

"We'll see," Jacob said. It was getting late. Even with the shutters open, it was almost too dark now to see the bloody footprints on the stairs. No one else had mentioned them, Jacob noticed. "Thank you for coming out to give me the history, Tom."

"You're very welcome." From his smile, Jacob could see Tom was disappointed. "Come on, Serena. I better get you back to the branch before Miz Rae thinks I let the haints get you."

"Tell Miz Rae I'm coming to talk to her," Jacob said, following them out on the porch.

"She might not like it," Serena said. "She thinks your books are wicked and that if you buy this house, you're crazy."

"She's right on both counts," he said. The sky was turning Halloween orange as the sun began to set. "But I'm coming anyway."

She laughed. "Then I guess I'll see you then."

He stood on the porch and watched them drive away, barely hearing Carol Ann chattering on behind him.

5

That night Jacob had no trouble falling asleep in his four-poster at the bed and breakfast; he was jet-lagged and exhausted. But he opened his eyes at four in the morning and found himself wide awake. He lay there for an hour, watching the shadows the lace curtains made on the wall from the streetlight just outside and listening to the innkeeper's fat cat pace like a sentry up and down the hall. When the grandfather clock downstairs wheezed once and chimed five, he surrendered and got up to go for a run.

Saxonville's town square was eerie and quiet in the dark before the dawn. A fifteen-foot obelisk of stacked granite and concrete stood at the center of the canyon of crumbling storefronts, topped with a pyramid of concrete cannonballs. A tarnished brass plaque proclaimed this great phallus a monument to the glorious dead of the War Between the States, placed there in 1910 by the Daughters of the Confederacy. A wreath of barely-faded plastic flowers leaned against the base.

As Jacob read, he heard a noise from behind him, a squeaking, clanking rhythm repeated at a deadly pace as if the ghost of one Confederate might have returned in irons. He turned and saw a makeshift rickshaw coming up the hill, a child's red wagon attached to an ancient, rusted bicycle with a long, dragging chain. The bike was peddled by a tall, thin man with the long, gray hair and bushy beard of a prophet. Jacob first took the figure in the wagon for a dwarf or a small child, but as they drew closer, he saw she was an old woman with no legs, white-haired and wizened as a dried apricot. She wore a baseball cap and a black heavy metal tee-shirt over neon pink sweatpants tied in knots where her knees ought to have been. As Jacob watched, she flung a rolled-up newspaper and clocked the door of the Chamber of Commerce dead center.

Jacob stared, and they stared back. Then the old woman smiled. "You want a paper, honey?" She had only two teeth that showed, canines like fangs. "Fifty cents."

"All right." He dropped two quarters into a pink palm as smooth and shiny as her face was wrinkled. She held out a paper.

"Have a good day." She held the paper a second too long as he took it, her grin widening as she let it go.

"You, too." The man was still scowling as he pedaled away, but the woman waved, and Jacob waved back.

Halfway down the hill were the burned-out remains of a courthouse built on the lines of a low-rent Greek temple, with columns and arches burned black. Spotlights on the lawn were still pointed at this ruin and still lit, their hot beams steaming in the morning mist. Standing directly in front of one of these so close it must have burned him was a man with skin so black that he looked like an ebony idol. His arms were outstretched, his eyes closed, and he was smiling. At his feet sat a collection of plastic grocery sacks full of rubbish, and the pocket of his ill-fitting sport coat bulged with the shape of a bottle of liquor.

"Don't you worry, Mister Ezra," he said, making Jacob jump. "Ain't no use no how." He laughed, but his eyes stayed closed, and Jacob saw a thin, white foam of saliva on his thick, chapped lips. "What gonna come gonna come."

I'm dreaming, Jacob thought, feeling relief. Suddenly it made perfect sense, the gray-white crone with her papers and this laughing Black god. It was all a dream. He laughed himself.

The man's eyes snapped open. "Don't you laugh, Mister Ezra." One of his eyes was lazy, with a drooping lid and clouded over with a cataract; the other was bloodshot, the white the color of old vellum, the iris tobacco brown. "You start to laughing, you might not never stop." He smiled. "But never you mind." He reached out and put a pudgy, calloused hand on Jacob's arm, and Jacob recoiled. "You go on back to your bed now and sleep while you can." He closed his eyes again. "What's coming gonna come."

A perfectly ordinary-looking car pulled up to the stoplight at the corner, rumbling, solid, and real. Jet lag, Jacob thought, turning his back on the vision in the spotlight that might or might not have been a man. Just jet lag. He waved to the driver of the car and was relieved to see him wave back. Then he turned and headed back to the bed and breakfast.

By the time he made it to the lawyer's office to close the deal on Briarwood, he had almost forgotten his nightmare pre-dawn stroll. The closing took place in a cluttered conference room/library with a pair of stuffed mallard ducks in flight climbing one wall and a numbered Civil War print (Confederate, of course; the field council of Robert E. Lee) on another. The signing of documents was managed by a pleasant but harried paralegal who shuffled the long pages like a blackjack dealer in Vegas. Her boss, a lawyer in shirt sleeves, drifted in and out of the room at intervals like he wasn't quite sure what he was meant to be doing. Carol Ann was there, of course, brisk and caffeinated, bullying the paralegal and asking Jacob if he needed coffee and how he liked his bed and breakfast. She was like a game show contestant waiting to start the final jackpot round.

The Montgomery Trust was represented by another lawyer who arrived late, a striking strawberry blonde. "Amanda Flynn," she said, offering her hand to Jacob. She wore a crisp and achingly stylish dark suit and heels, but her long, gleaming locks wouldn't have looked out of place on a beauty pageant contestant, nor would her bright pink lipstick. "I'm so sorry to be late."

"Amanda, how's your daddy doing?" Carol Ann asked.

"He still has his good days," Amanda said. "He is so sorry he can't be here to meet you, Mr. McGinnas. He wanted me to ask what county in Ireland you hail from."

"Dublin born and raised, Miss Flynn." She had what used to be called a "whiskey voice" that sounded like it might have been more cultivated than natural. "Your family is Irish, I take it."

"On my father's side, yes, from County Tipperary," she said. "But of course, we've been here since the 1800s."

"Amanda's father, Jack Flynn, is chairman of the board of trustees," Carol Ann said. "But he's had some health problems, so Amanda is stepping in. She has his power of attorney."

Miss Flynn's smile should have frozen the other woman's blood. "He said to tell you how pleased he is that you're buying Briarwood," she said.

"And how pleased is that?" Jacob said, smiling back. He couldn't stop himself from picturing how all that strawberry blonde hair would look spread out on a pillow.

"Very," Miss Flynn said, but he wasn't sure he believed her. "It's been abandoned and empty far too long."

The lawyer rushed back in like he'd been pushed by a windstorm. "Oh good, Amanda, you're here," he said, peering at her over his glasses. "Let's get started."

Signing all the documents took more than an hour. Jacob barely glanced at any of them. Gloria would have been incensed. But when the lawyer said they were finally done, he did have a question. "Carol Ann mentioned there was a box of documents that came with the house," he said. "When do I get that?"

Miss Flynn gave the real estate agent another look to strike the spirit dead, but Carol Ann didn't seem to notice. "Amanda should have all of that," she said, tucking her commission check into her bag. "Can he just pick it up at your office, Amanda?"

"I'll have to see if I can dig it up," Miss Flynn said. "I doubt Daddy has seen it since it was turned over to him back in the Fifties. It's probably up in our third-floor file room at the law firm. I'll look when I get back to the office."

"Amanda, what do y'all want to do about this check for the trust?" the lawyer said, looking up for a moment from his file.

"Just send it certified to the trust address," she said, standing up. "I'll get Daddy to sign for it himself."

Jacob stood up, too. "Miss Flynn, I'm very anxious to get a look at those documents." He gave her his full Irish charm, brogue to dimples. "Can I come with you now and help you look?"

She laughed. "I don't think we're insured for visitors on the third floor," she said. "It's a disaster area. But I'll tell you what. I'll go over there now and see if I can find it, and I'll meet you at the Allavance Grill for lunch."

"It's right on the square," Carol Ann said, putting on her sunglasses. "You can't miss it. I'd go with you, but I've got to get to the bank."

"All right then," Jacob said. "It's a date."

6

The waitress at the Allavance Grill put in Rooster's order as soon as they walked in the door. "What do you want to drink, honey?" she hollered across the restaurant at Serena.

"Sweet tea is good," Serena called back. Her father-in-law had eaten his lunch here every weekday for at least thirty years, rain or shine, working or idle. The only deviation from his usual routine her presence inspired today was for him to head for a private booth in the back instead of his usual seat at the Black old coots' table. Two of these long tables ran side by side, equidistant from the front door and the cash register, one Black and one White. There was no sign to indicate this segregation, only custom and the comfort of the men themselves, which had established this protocol so long ago nobody remembered when it wasn't so. There was much friendly calling back and forth between coots Black and coots White, much pausing and shaking of hands along the narrow frontier between the tables. But when they sat down, they never mixed. Some of these men, ancient and wrinkled and soft as old dollar bills, had been sitting in their seats since the door opened for breakfast at six a.m., and they would sit there until their wives or daughters came to collect them when lunch closed down at two.

As Serena followed Rooster, the coots of both tables turned their heads as one to watch as if she were parading down the runway of a beauty pageant or a strip club. She and Rooster both pretended not to notice. If she'd been another young woman, not his dead son's wife, Rooster would have watched her, too.

The waitress brought their tea as they were sitting down. "What are you going to have, honey?" she asked Serena, pulling a pen from behind her ear. Like all the waitresses at the Allavance, she was White, middle-aged, and looked worn down to the bone. "Do you need a menu?"

"No, I'll just have the special." Friday was fried fish, hush puppies, coleslaw, and a choice of "vegetables" which included both cherry gelatin and cottage cheese.

"And bring her some banana pudding, too, Ella," Rooster said. "She's having a hard day."

"Thanks, Rooster," Serena said as Ella went away. "I hate I had to come to you and Claudine for this."

"Stop worrying about that," Rooster said. "What else were you going to do?"

"Nothing," she admitted. "There wasn't anything else I could do." She had gone to the credit union that morning expecting to get an addition on her loan in a matter of minutes. She hadn't even called Miz Rae to tell her she'd be late to work. But when Stacy, the Loan Officer, had called her back to her office, the news had not been good. She wasn't authorized to give Serena any more money, and her boss had said no.

"I don't understand," Serena had said, feeling the familiar cold tingle on her scalp and nausea in her gut. "I've had a loan here for three years, and I've never missed a payment. I did this same thing six months ago, and y'all begged me to take twice as much as I'm asking for now."

"Your credit score has changed," Stacy said. "Have you defaulted on something else? Had a lot of late payments on utilities or medical bills, something like that? My screen doesn't show exactly what the problem is, but if you want to wait, I can try to get you a printout of your credit report."

"That would be nice, thank you." She didn't want to say thank you; she wanted to knock this woman's teeth down her throat. But that wouldn't be prudent. "But what can we do about this loan now?" She had to have the money. She'd had no choice but to pay to have her car fixed; she had to be able to get to work. But now, she had to make her monthly payment to the IRS, or she could go to jail.

She could tell Stacy wanted to ask her to just go away, but she knew she wouldn't; she was as locked into this dance as Serena was. "Is there somebody who could co-sign for you?" she said. "We can try that."

So she had called Rooster, and he had come. And even though his contracting business cycled hundreds of thousands of dollars through this same credit union every year, they made him wait in the lobby for an hour while Stacy and her unseen boss probed his personal credit history.

While they waited, Serena read through her own credit report and found the problem—an old cell phone bill from Las Vegas. She hadn't even known this phone existed; Trey had probably used it for work. Odds were good she wasn't liable for the debt, that after she spent a few hours on the phone explaining her situation to another series of faceless voices, it could be erased. But for right now, the damage was done.

Eventually, Stacy came out with a thumbs up and fresh smile, and they'd signed all the papers. She'd gotten her money and written her check to the feds, and dropped it off at the post office. Now Rooster was treating her to lunch before they both went back to work.

They were just starting to eat when Jacob McGinnas walked in. He wore jeans and a black sweater, but couldn't have created a bigger stir in pink robes and a flaming tiara. Nobody said a word; in fact, all conversation stopped in a wave of silence that rolled across the restaurant as every head turned. "That's that writer, Jacob," Serena told Rooster.

"The one bought the Briarwood place?" Rooster said.

"That's the one." As she said it, Jacob caught sight of her and waved. When she waved back, he smiled and started towards them, and the buzz of talk around them recommenced. "I guess you're going to meet him."

"Serena, hi," Jacob said. He looked happier today, excited. But there were still dark circles under his eyes like he hadn't slept well.

"Hi, Jacob," she said. "Meet my father-in-law, Henry Decatur."

"Mr. Decatur," Jacob said, offering his hand. "Jacob McGinnas." Their fellow restaurant patrons were still taking turns staring, but Jacob didn't seem to notice.

"Call me Rooster," Rooster said, shaking his hand. "Everybody does."

"Rooster," Jacob repeated. "And I'm Jacob, of course." It had been a long time since any man's smile had made Serena's heart flutter, but this one did. She felt a sharp stab of guilt but pushed it away. "May I join you?"

"Sure you can," Rooster said. "Serena, honey, scooch over."

She laughed. "Yes, sir." Jacob slid in beside her, warm and smelling like the crisp autumn air outside. "What are you doing here?"

"I had my closing on Briarwood this morning," he said as Ella returned with her pad in hand.

"What'll you have?" she asked with the big, friendly smile Allavance staff put on for outsiders and tourists.

"That fish looks good," Jacob said.

"Oh, it is," she assured him. "It's our Friday special. Everybody loves it."

"I'll have that, then," Jacob said. "And a beer. Whatever you have on tap."

"We don't sell alcohol," she said, her smile dimming a bit.

"Iced tea then," Jacob said.

"Sweet or unsweet?"

"Sweet," Serena answered for him. "And drop him fresh fries, please."

The waitress gave her a bit of side eye, but Jacob didn't say anything. "All righty, then," Ella said. "Be right back."

"Don't count on it," Rooster muttered as she walked away. "So Serena said you bought the Briarwood place."

"I did," Jacob said.

"I've just got one question for you," Rooster said. "Were you born crazy, or did it just come upon you all of a sudden?"

"Rooster!" Serena said, but Jacob laughed.

"You think I made a mistake?" he asked.

"I just can't think why you'd want it," Rooster said. "You'll have to pour at least a million dollars into it to make it where anybody could even think about living there. There ain't no way in the world you'll ever get that kind of money back out of it. It's hell and gone from everywhere; ain't nobody who could afford it ever going to want to move to Saxon County."

"Except me," Jacob said.

"Except you," Rooster agreed, laughing.

"Rooster is a contractor," Serena said. "He knows all there is to know about the houses around here and what they're worth. A lot more than Carol Ann Sweatt."

"Aw, now, y'all give Carol Ann too hard a time," Rooster said. "She's all right."

"Uh huh," Serena said, rolling her eyes. "I bet she was in her glory at that closing."

"She did seem excited," Jacob said. Ella was back with his food. He shifted in his seat, and his knee touched Serena's. "Thank you," he said as Ella walked away. "I'm supposed to be meeting a woman named Amanda Flynn here. Do you know her?"

"Oh yeah," Rooster said, turning his attention to his plate.

"Not well," Serena said. "What are you meeting her for?"

"Her father is apparently chairman of the board of trustees for the Montgomery Trust," Jacob said. Rooster snorted, pushing a morsel of macaroni and cheese on his fork with a hush puppy. "What am I missing?" Jacob said. "Is Jack Flynn an asshole?"

Rooster laughed. "Jack Flynn is THE asshole," he said. "And his daughter might be worse. What are you meeting her for?"

"She's supposed to be bringing me a box of old papers that come with the house," Jacob said. "Apparently it's in storage at their family law firm."

"Tom's dream stash," Serena said. "Watch your back; I think he might strangle a kitten to get his hands on that."

"I'll bear that in mind," Jacob said. "This fish is good, by the way. What is it?"

"The sign says flounder," Rooster said. "But any fool worth killing knows it's perch. Sure enough, Jacob, do you mean to live in that old place?"

"Yeah, I think I do," Jacob said. He had been pleased past all reason to see Serena when he'd walked in. He'd been less pleased to hear her call Rooster her father-in-law. His imagination needed her to be single. But she wasn't wearing a wedding ring, he noticed, and no husband had been mentioned. And the longer he talked to this Rooster, the better he liked him. "What do you think I should do to fix it up?" he asked. "How should I spend my million dollars? Where should I start?"

"With a gas can and a book of matches?" Rooster joked. "No, it's a piece of history, good or bad. Serena was telling me the bones still look real good, and if the bones are good, everything else can be fixed." He sat back in his seat and took out the cigarette he would light on his way out the door. "You know what I'd do if it was mine? I'd find me an architect down in Charleston that specializes in restoring those old fancy houses they have down on the Battery, and I'd get him to come up here and look at Briarwood and draw me up some plans. In the meantime, I'd hire me a project manager who knows this area and how to get things done, and I'd put him in charge of the actual work. Then I'd go to Jamaica and wait for him to call me and tell me it's done."

Jacob sipped his tea, ice cold and sweet as soda pop. "Sounds good to me," he said. "When can you start?"

"Me?" Rooster laughed. "No, no," he said, shaking his head. "You don't want me."

"Why don't I?" Jacob said. "You're a building contractor, aren't you? Didn't Serena just give you a glowing recommendation?"

"You talk to Jack Flynn or Carol Ann Sweatt," Rooster said. "They'll be more than happy to tell you who you need to hire."

"I don't want to ask them. I'm asking you." Both Serena and Rooster looked uncomfortable, he realized. "Unless you're not interested, of course." Gloria would have told him he was mad to engage a contractor he'd barely met whose work he'd never seen. But from the moment he'd made up his mind to have Briarwood, he'd been acting on pure instinct, and his instinct told him Rooster Decatur was the only man for the job.

"Oh, I'm interested," Rooster said. "I'd be crazy not to be."

"Can you do the job?"

"Oh, hell yeah," he said. "But Jacob, you got to understand where you're at." Serena was staring at a morsel of food on the end of her fork. "A job like that will put a lot of men to work in this town. There's going to be people who will want to be sure it's the right men."

Jacob had grown up in Dublin, but his grandfather had been a shipbuilder in Belfast during the worst of the Troubles. He thought he understood. "It's my house and my money," he said. "As far as I'm concerned, the right men are the ones who'll get it done right and fast without putting me in the poorhouse. Do you think you can find them for me?" Serena hadn't looked up, but he saw a smile flirting with the corners of her mouth. "Do you want to try?"

Rooster put his cigarette back in the pack and the pack back in his breast pocket. "Maybe I do." He extended his hand across the table. "I'll have to talk it over with my wife," he said as they shook.

"Of course."

"But you go on and find your architect." He winked at Serena. "I'll give you an answer by tomorrow evening."

They went on to make small talk about the beautiful autumn weather and Jacob's books and the people he'd met in town. They were all three laughing at Rooster's description of his first meeting with Carol Ann when Amanda Flynn walked in. "Your lunch date is here finally," Serena said. The lawyer obviously didn't see him; she was walking back and forth across the restaurant.

"That's some ass, ain't it?" Rooster said.

"Rooster!" Serena said, smacking his hand across the table. "Be ashamed!"

"He's not wrong, though," Jacob agreed.

As if she'd heard him, Amanda turned and caught sight of him at last. She seemed a little taken aback to see him sitting with Serena and Rooster, but she recovered her smile and came over. "Oh good, you went ahead and ordered," she said. "Hey Rooster. Hey…I'm so sorry; I don't remember your daughter-in-law's name."

"Serena," Rooster said. "How are you, Miss Flynn?"

"I'm well, Rooster, thank you." She was looking at Jacob and Serena. "I didn't know y'all were already friends."

"Me and Tom Stewart rode out to Briarwood with Carol Ann when she was showing Jacob the house," Serena said, looking right back.

"Did you find my papers?" Jacob said.

"I did," Amanda said. "That's what took me so long. I've got the box in the trunk of my car right now."

"Fantastic," Jacob said. "Won't you join us?"

"Me and Serena have to get on back to work," Rooster said, standing up.

"I've got to go, too, I'm afraid," Amanda said. "I've got to get Daddy his lunch."

"Then I'll just go settle up," Jacob said, also rising. "Rooster, here's my number." He handed over his card. "I'll be waiting on your call."

"I'll call you," Rooster said. "Serena, honey, you keep your seat. I'm just going to pay the check."

"Please, let me," Jacob said. "I invited myself to your lunch; it's the least I can do."

"Thank you kindly, then," Rooster said.

"Yes, thanks," Serena said, getting up. "It was good to see you. And you too, Amanda."

"You too," Amanda said with her beauty pageant smile.

When they were gone, Jacob paid the check while Amanda got a plate of fish to go. He held the door for her and followed her out to her car, a bright red convertible roadster that looked brand new. She opened the boot to reveal a stained and tattered cardboard filing box. "There it is," she said. "It looks like there might have been some water damage at some point. I hope there's something in there you can still read." She stepped back and let him pick it up. "What are you hoping to find anyway? I assume this is for a book."

"No idea." The box smelled nasty, like mold and rot and something worse, a rancid, chemical smell. Holding it was like carrying a freshly disinterred corpse. "I suppose I'll know when I find it."

She smiled. "I suppose you will." As soon as he'd stepped back out of the way, she slammed the boot lid shut. "Good luck!" Without further pleasantries, she got in her car and drove away.

7

Jack Flynn had hosted a poker game every Friday night that wasn't Christmas for the past thirty years. His last night on earth was no exception.

"All right, Jack, I'll ask," Kirk Benson said, tossing his ante in the pot. "I ain't scared."

Kirk owned every gas station in Saxon County that didn't belong to Indians or Koreans; every one of them had a big "American Owned and Operated" banner hanging over the door. None of the six men at the table were bothered by this, and only one was amused. "What the hell happened with Amanda and that doctor we've been hearing she was going to marry for the past year and a half?"

"You heard already," Jack said, frowning at his cards. "He took that job up north, and she didn't want to move."

"Bullshit." Kirk and Jack played football together in high school back when all the players had been White. He took liberties with Flynn the other four wouldn't dare. "My daughter Wrenn said she saw them in the parking lot of the Moultrie Inn having a hell of a fight more than a week before anybody heard a word about any job up north."

"And we can all guess what Miss Wrenn was doing at the Moultrie

Inn," Jack said. "Any of you boys happen to see her that night?" Jack could take liberties, too.

"She said Amanda was squalling like a possum in a snap trap, saying she'd kill him dead," Kirk pushed on undaunted as the others laughed. "What were they fighting about?"

"Two cards," Jack said to the dealer.

"Three for me," Frank Sweatt said, tossing in his discards.

"I'll stand," Kirk said. "So what about it?" The other three men folded. "What'd he do to piss her off and make her call off the wedding?"

"I called off the damned wedding," Jack said, tossing in his bet. "And what he did was his anesthesiologist. His male anesthesiologist."

"I knew it," Kirk said as the others hissed and groaned in appropriate horror. "Did I not tell y'all that doctor was funny?" He looked around the circle in triumph. "How many times did I say it?"

"You think a man's gay if his clothes match," Chuck Kennedy said. Chuck was a doctor himself, the chief of medicine at Saxon County Hospital, and to his wife he called Kirk Benson a "pinkneck." The others laughed at this new remark, even Kirk. "I suppose you blame me, Jack, for Joe Smith." Smith was the jilted gay physician whose clothes had presumably matched. "Since I introduced him to Amanda."

"No, I blame our friend Frank," Jack said. He lay down his hand, four queens. "His damned wife was the one who kept pushing them together."

Kirk swore a mighty oath and tossed away his full house, nines and sevens.

"You know Carol Ann," Frank said, showing his pair of tens. "She loves to play matchmaker." Jack chuckled, raking in the pot. "But she had no idea he was light in the loafers, and neither did I."

"None of us did," Chuck assured him. "Well, none of us but Kirk, and his gaydar must be tuned better than ours."

"Fuck you, Doc," Kirk said, smiling around his cigar.

"Carol Ann's already got a new prospect all picked out for Amanda," Frank said. Jack Flynn made him nervous as a sore-tailed cat sometimes.

"Is this one queer, too?" asked Pink Collins—State Senator Pinckney Collins, a legacy Democrat with a Republican heart. Money from four of these six men had helped keep him in office the past fifteen years.

"That writer, Jacob McGinnas, the one who bought the old Briarwood Plantation," Frank went on. "Carol Ann said he's planning to spend a fortune fixing it up, and he's single."

"Lady of Briarwood," Chuck said. "That ought to suit Amanda."

"Tell Carol Ann she's batting a thousand," Jack said. He felt sharp, more his old self than he had in weeks. He'd definitely use the pill tonight. "That one's not queer; he just likes—." He used a word for Black women that shocked even this audience—or everybody but Kirk, anyway. During his long law practice , Jack had been scrupulously careful in the word he used to designate the most profitable majority of his client base—colored in the Fifties, Black in the Sixties, African-American when that came into fashion. He had retired just as people of color started to catch on and had never heard POC. Now in his twilight years, he had returned to the truth of his heart, inscribed there in childhood. This was presumed to be harmless.

"Amanda went to meet him for lunch at Allavance, and he was already sitting in a booth with that Rooster Decatur and his daughter-in-law, the pretty one who works at the library up at North Creek. McGinnas and the lovely widow were apparently quite cozy." He belched. Damned Pink had brought hot wings, his weakness; he couldn't resist them, even knowing the heartburn they'd give him later. He didn't notice the look his guests exchanged at the mention of Serena.

"That's all right," he went on. "I wouldn't want Amanda married to a writer, rich or not, or trying to live out at Briarwood." Any mention of the old plantation left a nasty taste in his mouth. Trust that idiot Sweatt to bring it up. "You're all as bad as a bunch of old women, gossiping about my daughter," he said. "What's it to any of you who she marries?"

"Nothing, Jack," Chuck said in a soothing, bedside manner tone. But they all knew this was a lie. Amanda Flynn wasn't just the most potentially wealthy heiress in Saxonville and the town beauty. She was the only child of the last Flynn, director of the Trust. When Jack was gone, and it wouldn't be long now, if she didn't have a husband, she'd have to take the job herself. Truth be told, she'd been doing it for years already. No woman had ever been director of the Trust; no woman ought to have the stomach for it. "Let's just play cards," Chuck said.

"I tell you what, though," Kirk said. "That Decatur girl is a honey. I wouldn't mind a taste of that myself."

"Kirk, good God," Chuck said, sharing a glance with the man opposite him.

"Pardon me, Doc," Kirk said, cracking open another beer. "Does it make your wife feel better, knowing your receptionist is White?"

"Shut up, Kirk," Jack said, but he smiled. "Deal the cards."

The men played until midnight, as was their custom. Jack took twice as many pots as any other player. He was sure he hadn't played so well in decades. The beer flowed freely, and each of the other players excused himself more than once to see a man about a horse. Each of them passed unseen by the downstairs bedroom Amanda and Joe Smith had set up for Jack in what had once been his study. Any of the five could have gone into the bedroom and tampered with the medications lined up on his bedside table like bottles behind a bar with no one the wiser. His Black chauffeur/handyman was in his own room upstairs with headphones on his head watching expensive Japanese porn purchased with Jack's platinum card. His Black night nurse didn't arrive until midnight. She refused to be in the house during poker games, and she was too discreet and too efficient for Amanda to dare insist. Any of the poker players would have known after watching Jack take his second pot exactly which pills should be poisoned.

As the party broke up, Chuck helped the chauffer transfer Jack from the leather chair where he'd played to his wheelchair, and Pink Collins lingered to watch. "Do you think he'll live there?" he asked. "McGinnas. Do you think he'll really end up living at Briarwood?"

"I hope he does," Jack said. His back was killing him, and the colostomy bag against his thigh was full of shit and unpleasantly warm. "I hope it eats him alive."

The night nurse changed the bag and made him clean and comfortable, answering all his remarks with a soothing "umm-hmm" like he might have been a babbling child. She tucked him into the hospital bed, elevated so he could watch TV, and made sure he had the remote, her bell, and a fresh glass of ice water close to hand.

"Good night, Mr. Jack," she said, switching off the overhead light to leave him in the soft glow of the bedside lamp and the TV. "I'll be back to check on you at three."

"Liar," he said. "You never come back before morning." He didn't know if this were true or not; he was always sleeping. But like all the old White people in Saxonville, he assumed the Black people paid to care for him were as lazy as they dared to be and secretly wished he were dead.

When she was gone, he took the sliver of little blue pill with half his glass of water. His closet case almost-son-in-law had gotten him the pills months ago before he'd been confined to bed and the chair, and he'd cut each one into quarters. "Any more will kill you, Jack," he'd told him as he dropped the slivers back into the bottle. "Your heart will give out."

His nurses had seen the pills, of course, and so had Chuck Kennedy. But seeing Smith's name as prescribing physician on the label, they had each in their own moment determined the matter to be quite out of their hands—let the sin be on Joe's head.

The effect of the pill was almost immediate, and he closed his eyes and masturbated vigorously. This unseemly ritual was his most treasured point of pride. He might not be able to walk to the toilet or remember his mother's maiden name anymore, but he could still spill his seed, even if it were only into his own pajamas while thinking of the wide, white-polyester-covered backside of his nurse.

The effect of the poison was slower and more subtle. It took hold a few moments before the old man's final climax, a thousand tiny blood vessels exploding in his brain at once. The pain was blinding but mercifully brief. When the night nurse came in at three, she found him dead, his eyes and mouth open and dry, his penis still clutched in his fist. She left him that way and called Chuck Kennedy. Chuck called the coroner from home and met him at the house.

"Well," the coroner said when they pulled back the covers and made their discovery together. "I reckon he died as he lived."

With his dick in his hand and other men's money in his wallet, Chuck thought. "Don't be vulgar," he said aloud. "Just fix it." The coroner was also Saxonville's most prominent mortician. "And make sure Amanda never knows."

8

By Halloween, the lawn at Briarwood had been cleared of all its brush and weeds. The winter grass seed spread under a blanket of hay was just beginning to sprout. The front drive had been leveled and widened enough to accommodate big construction trucks between the curving canopy of oaks, and tons of gravel had been laid to tame the red clay mud.

Inside the house, all the nineteenth-century furniture and fixtures had been appraised, catalogued, and put into storage by Reese Middleton-Smith, the antiquities and restoration expert from Charleston whose work had been featured many times on PBS. Even the broken, bloodstained chairs from the parlor had been photographed, wrapped in bubble wrap, and tucked away in a rented warehouse in Charlotte fifty miles away with everything else.

None of the original finishes in the house proper had been altered or removed, but basic repairs had been made for safety to the front steps and staircases. A temporary power system for the construction crews had been set up on the front lawn, wired all the way out to the highway mains. On the morning of the 31st, a crew of half a dozen maids from Charlotte came in and scrubbed down everything in the front entrance hall and dining room as best they could. When they told Jacob the bloodstain at the foot of the stairs was beyond their technology, he just smiled. "Leave it then," he told them. "It adds to the atmosphere." His audience would expect him to scare them silly; with Briarwood's help, he wouldn't disappoint them.

The Halloween night reading had been Tom Stewart's idea, a benefit for the library. Jacob resisted at first; the whole thing had felt a bit camp. Then the translation of some of the papers he had found in the Trust box came back, and he'd suddenly yearned to do it. He couldn't wait to see their faces when they heard.

Industrial spotlights on steel frames flooded the front hall with an unnatural pinkish glow, and he made his entrance down the grand staircase from total darkness above. "Good evening." Two hundred or so people sat on folding chairs between the peeling columns, a packed house. "I'm Jacob McGinnas. Welcome to Briarwood." A scattering of nervous laughter broke out with a wave of polite applause. "And happy Halloween."

The crowd was mostly young college students, as Tom had predicted, making a road trip from one of the universities nearby. But he spotted a few familiar faces. Tom and a pretty redhead who must have been his wife sat at the end of the front row, and Amanda Flynn was halfway back, wearing a black turtleneck sweater and a bemused, cat-like little smile.

"The flyers all said I'd be reading from my own works. So I'm sure you're expecting the standard selection of moldy oldies." A few people called out suggestions. "But actually, with your kind indulgence, I'd like to read you something new—or rather, something much, much older." He didn't realize he was searching the crowd for Serena until he found her. She sat in the very back row at the very edge of the light. He smiled; she smiled back and gave him a little wave.

"I found this in a box of old papers that was passed on to me by the Montgomery Trust when I purchased this house." He held up the original cracked and molded leather journal. "My research assistant examined it, and she confirmed it dates from the 1560s, more than two hundred years before the house was built. It's written in French, but she sent me a translation. If you'll allow me, I'll read you the juicy bits."

Saturday, October 31, 1562

My companion continues to force his attentions on Chitsa, the savage woman we have taken as our guide. He is a brute and a vulgarian—he sings obscene songs and makes blasphemous jokes, and the more I ask him to stop, the harder he tries to vex me. But I require this very brutality if we are to survive this wilderness separate from our companions until help arrives. Nor do I harbor any tender sympathy for this native creature. I saw the ways of her people only too clearly back on the island at Charlesfort and know them to be little more than animals. But I find her cries of protest beforehand and weird songs and weeping after these episodes disturbing. How is a sane man to sleep? I will be glad when he tires of such sport or finds better and more willing company.

Wednesday, November 18, 1562

It has begun to snow. My companion insists that this is proof we have traveled as far north as the first settlements of our countrymen and will find others of our kind soon, but I know this to be folly. We have traveled by foot less than a month from the coast, and the stars are wrong. But I keep these truths to myself to spare his hopes as long as possible.

Sunday, November 29, 1562

Christ and His Holy Mother have smiled on us at last. After four days of ice and rain, we have found sanctuary, a stone structure in the midst of this wilderness. It is very old, a sort of round den half-dug into the earth, but the walls are intact. To fashion a roof of branches was the work of a single afternoon. I write this in more comfort than I have known since our party left the ship. Night has fallen, but for the first time in many months, I sit before a fire laid upon a real stone hearth. Our clothes have dried, and we are warm, and the fire provides good light, though I still squander a candle to write this.

My companion found rabbits in the woods and has made us a decent dinner. There is a creek nearby which provides wholesome water. We are thinking of waiting out these rains in this spot before continuing our journey, and it is in my mind to stay here the rest of the winter. I do not know what savage might have first constructed this hovel; the hearthstones are carved with ugly, stick-like writing I do not recognize. But it is our salvation.

The only one who does not rejoice at our good fortune is the Indian woman, Chitsa. Poor fool, she knows nothing of such comfort as a stone dwelling and will not willingly come inside. She refused to assist us in making the roof, pretending not to understand what was wanted, and as we worked, she sat on the frozen earth in the rain and wailed like some wild creature. So piteous were her cries, even my companion was moved to comfort her. When the roof was done, he spoke to her quite gently, entreating her to come inside. She refused and hid her face with her hands. She would not look at him even when he struck her. When he returned from his hunt, she cleaned the rabbits and prepared them for the pot. But when she tried to build a fire outdoors like an idiot child who could not feel the rain, he lost all patience. He picked her up and carried her inside. She screamed and fought to leave the house like an animal desperate to escape a trap. He was forced to bind her and cook the stew himself, then pour the food into her mouth with a spoon. And all the while she wept, entreating him in the gabble-babble of her savage tongue. As I write now, she is watching me, still bound, lying beside him as he sleeps. "What do you fear so?" I ask her, but she does not even try to understand.

Tuesday, December 1, 1562

The snow and ice have returned. After much debate, we have determined to winter here where we have shelter and game and water are plentiful. It was a mutual decision, and we are both content. My only worry is how we will manage our tempers living so close for such a long time. I suggested that since she is so unhappy in this place, we could release Chitsa to return south to her own people or find others of her kind near here.

"Who will warm my bed this winter?" he said. "You? Is there something I should know, my friend? Should I be watching my back?" I became angry, I

must confess, but he only laughed. "No, no, my friend. I will keep the savage. She smells like a dog, but at least she has her proper parts." A strange light came into his eyes that I have never seen before even in our worst, most desperate days back on the island. For a moment he looked like a lost child about to weep. "Besides, there is no one else."

Friday, December 4, 1562

My companion was wrong. There are others in the woods. We can hear them screaming in the night, terrible laughter and shouts in a language none of us can understand. All the world outside our tiny hovel is now covered in ice, and we can hear footsteps on the frozen leaves. We have fashioned a stout door of logs with leather hinges, and sometimes it seems someone is pacing right outside. But if we open the door to confront them, we find no one. My companion has wasted much too much ammunition firing his musket into the woods at nothing. At first, I thought the sounds must be animal or the cracking of branches under the ice. But even I have had to admit that something or someone is laughing at us. There is malice in the sound.

I had the idea that Chitsa could go out and speak with them. She is much calmer now that she has become accustomed to living indoors, and of all of us, she seems the least bothered by the noises from the woods. My companion has begun to teach her some rudimentary words in French—to pass the time, he says—and he seems to understand some snatches of her native babble. He communicated my plan to her, that she should be our ambassador. Perhaps we could even trade with these others, he suggested. We could need supplies before the spring, and we still have some small treasures that might tempt them.

"Not Chitsa," she said, touching her chest with her fist. She said another word we didn't know, waving both hands in the air as if to suggest some large, fearful shape. "Not Chitsa."

"Just tell them we mean them no harm," I said.

"Not French," she insisted, touching each of us in turn with the clenched fist, then herself. "Not Chitsa." She made the other sign again, looking not at me but at my companion, and said the other meaningless word.

"You'll try," my companion said. He grabbed her around the waist and

carried her to the doorway, ignoring how she struggled and protested in her own tongue. He kicked the door open and shoved her outside.

At first, she only sprawled there, weeping, on her knees, gabbling more nonsense. Then slowly, she rose and faced the woods. She called out in a clear, strong voice like I had never heard from her before, and though I couldn't understand a single word, a shiver ran down my spine. She spoke for some few minutes without stopping, and the laughter from the woods went silent.

She had picked up a rock as she knelt. Now she raised it to her forehead and cut herself just at the hairline, spilling blood down her face. "Come!" she cried out in perfect French. "Come! Come! Come!" My companion rushed outside and scooped her up, roaring and cursing. He beat her savagely then dressed her wound, but at no time would she look him in the face, and she never made a sound. Just now, as I lit this precious candle to write, I saw her watching me. Our eyes met, and she smiled.

Wednesday, December 16, 1562

My companion is gone. Last night we had quiet for the first time in more than a week, and though I was meant to be on watch, I confess I fell asleep. I awoke in the darkest hour of the night to a dying fire and the sight of my companion standing over me, loading his weapon. When I questioned him, he said, "Do you not hear it?" Only then did I realize the taunting laughter and shouting had returned. I had grown so accustomed to the maddening racket, I no longer noticed it.

But then I heard something else—my companion's name. Whoever was in the woods was calling him out. I swore an oath, calling on the Blessed Virgin.

"It is those devils from the ship," he said. "They have tracked us here. They mean to murder us and take the girl." Chitsa was sitting by the fire, staring into the flames. The wound in her forehead has scabbed over, but it is still a horror. She did not smile or frown or make any sign she had heard.

I tried to reason with him. It was madness to imagine that our former shipmates, if they lived, could have traveled so far and found us in this wilderness. But he refused to listen and threw me off when I would have held him by force. "Stay with her," he ordered me as if I were the peasant and he the master. "Protect her if you can."

That was many hours ago. I watched him cross the clearing and saw him disappear into the dark woods. The calls and laughter stopped. The only voice I could hear was his, calling out taunts of his own. He was the strongest by far of the sailors at Charlesfort; if he had been right and it had been the others of our party, he could have beaten them easily. Chitsa came and stood beside me, and together we saw the light of his torch disappear. We heard his musket fire.

Then nothing.

At daybreak, I went out to look for him. I bound the girl's hands and tied her to the doorpost, and she didn't protest. She seems neither happy nor sad nor even frightened anymore. With my sword in hand, I searched the woods all around the clearing then traced the creek for nearly a mile. But I found no sign.

Thursday, December 17, 1562

I have lit all my candles. I fear I will not need them long.

When I returned to the hovel, Chitsa did not seem surprised to see I was alone. Nor did she attempt to question me about what I had found. "You let go," she said, shaking her bound wrists. "Chitsa go."

I could not think of any reason to refuse. Perhaps my companion had been right about the purpose of our tormentors; perhaps they only wanted the girl. If I let her go to them, perhaps they would leave me in peace.

I expected her to flee as soon as her bonds were cut, but she didn't. She went to the creek and bathed herself despite the bitter cold, then came back to the hovel with another clay pitcher of water. I followed her and watched all of this, but she took no notice of me.

The floor of the hovel is hard-packed red clay. The girl poured her water out on the floor and made a thick, red mud. She stripped out of her garments with no pretense of shame and sank her fingers into the mud. As I watched in horror and revulsion, she painted herself all over with it, from the top of her forehead to the tips of her toes, even the folded shadow between her legs, staining all of herself red as if she had been dipped in blood.

She scooped up another handful of the gory filth and held it out to me.

"Help," she said, pointing at her bare back with her other hand. "You help." I turned away from her, bile rising in my throat.

By nightfall, she was done and back to sitting by the fire. She was still naked. The mud had dried but glowed red in the firelight. She was like some pagan idol formed of clay. I prepared supper and offered her food, but she refused. Indeed, she made no sign she heard me at all.

When the sun was gone completely, and the moon had risen, I heard it—the voice of my companion singing one of his horrible songs. At first, I was glad; I thought he had been spared and was coming home. But the song came no closer, and the look on Chitsa's face as we listened turned my soul to ice. She was smiling, and even under the bloody clay, she was more beautiful than any woman I had ever seen. But in her eyes, I saw malice and hunger, such evil as I have never known. She moved to rise, and I raised my knife as if I would defend myself against her. She laughed. She said something in her native tongue, but I couldn't tell if it was meant to be a warning or a curse. And still the terrible song went on outside, slurred and twisted out of tune.

She went to the door and opened it. I wanted to stop her, but I was paralyzed with fear. She stepped outside, and I scrambled on my knees to follow as far as the door to watch.

In the moonlight, she was even more beautiful. The wind was like ice, but she never shivered. Her evil spell protected her from cold. She stopped at the edge of the clearing and called out.

The thing I cannot name stepped into the light. I knew its face, but trust in me, it was not the man I knew. It was not a man at all. It turned to look at me and smiled, baring bloody teeth. I thought I would faint, but even this mercy was denied me. Chitsa opened her arms, and the thing came to her, falling as a lover at her feet.

I turned away and closed the door. I fastened the latch then nailed it with a spike. I piled the logs for the fire in front of it, then our packs. I lit every candle.

I can hear them, laughing and singing together. Soon they will come for me.

9

Serena almost hadn't come to the reading. She hadn't had anyone to go with her. She'd known none of her friends from church or old friends from school would have the slightest interest in a reading by Jacob McGinnas, and Miz Rae had said she'd rather eat dirt. Her mother-in-law Claudine's reaction had been even worse; she'd been against even Serena going. "The only good thing they could do to that place is burn it to the ground and haul off the pieces," she had said when Serena invited her.

Rooster wouldn't go either; he and Claudine had fought long and hard when he'd come home and told her about the job as project manager for the restoration. Money had won out in the end, but Claudine still wasn't happy about it. Serena could see her point; every time Carol Ann Sweatt came into the library to crow about Briarwood being restored to its former glory, Serena wanted to throw up. But she'd always wanted to hear Jacob read, and this might be her only chance. And besides, if she were really honest, she'd admit how much she just wanted to see him again, even from a distance. She promised herself this was a silly game she was playing with herself. She wouldn't act on this attraction; if the opportunity to act on it came up, she'd be horrified. But when he caught her eye from the podium and smiled, her heart skipped a beat.

She liked his Frenchman's story; it was deliciously scary and perfect for Briarwood. But she kept getting distracted as he read and losing the thread because she liked just watching him so much. She loved his voice and the lilt of his accent and the way he put on the tiniest bit of French seasoning in the dialogue. He looked up from his pages a lot, engaging the audience with dark, mischievous eyes, and every time he did it, she smiled. He was having such a lovely time, scaring them all to death. When the story was over, there were several seconds of breathless silence, the only sounds the wind outside and the buzzing of the lights. Jacob raised an eyebrow, and she laughed as the crowd broke out in applause.

He read another couple of his stories, and everything went over well, but nothing else hit as big as the Frenchman's diary, even his most famous work. After the reading, he offered to answer questions from the crowd, and the college kids were ready; some of them had even written their questions down on little cards so they wouldn't forget. Jacob was laid back and gracious and funny, and the crowd all seemed to love him. "Mr. McGinnas, where was that journal found?" one of the boys asked. "Was it here on the Briarwood property?"

"I don't know," Jacob said. "As I said, I found it in a box of old papers that was given to me when I took possession. Nothing had been labeled or catalogued. The Montgomery Trust might know more. Miss Flynn?" All eyes turned to Amanda Flynn as he pointed. "Miss Flynn is the director of the Trust."

"I'm so sorry, Jacob," Amanda said, not sounding sorry in the least. "I've never seen or heard tell of that journal before tonight. It's a good story, though. I might have to break down and read one of your books."

Jacob laughed. "I plan to do a full investigation of the history of Briarwood," he said. "Maybe you can start with that."

"Well, I think that's wonderful," Carol Ann Sweatt burst out without raising her hand. If people were talking, Carol Ann was going to have her say. "The house already looks two hundred percent better.

When you're done, are you going to open it to the public? There's a fully-restored plantation house down near Charleston that is just exquisite; Frank and I have been there several times. People rent it for events and weddings; I think they even have their own catering staff who dress up in period costumes." Beside her, her husband Frank was turning purple. "Something like that would be wonderful for Saxon County."

"I'm sorry to disappoint you, Carol Ann," Jacob said. Serena was pretty sure he'd glanced back at her. "I'm not really interested in making Briarwood a tourist attraction. I certainly can't imagine why anyone would want to get married here." Some of the college kids snickered. "I plan to live in the house for now, as soon as it's habitable. I want to write here." There were murmurs of approval from the crowd. Carol Ann looked like she'd just tasted something nasty. Amanda Flynn was looking at her watch.

"If I did open it to the public someday," Jacob continued, "it would be as an African-American history museum and memorial. Just from what I've seen so far in the records and heard from local historians, I know terrible things happened here, and I don't just mean the murders."

Other people had questions. Serena thought of a few herself, details about his books she'd been wondering about for years. But once he'd mentioned the museum, she'd stopped listening or thinking about anything else. Her degree was in applied history; she'd been an assistant curator at the Nevada State Museum in Las Vegas before her husband Trey died. Surely nobody else in Saxon County was more qualified to run a museum of African-American history at Briarwood.

Looking around the hall, she didn't see the past or the present but an exciting, meaningful new future, not just for herself but for Briarwood and the people of Saxon County. She could imagine the school buses parked along the driveway and lines of happy children, Black and White and every other color, learning about the horrors of the past, not as a scary story but the truth so it could never be repeated. For the first time in years, she could imagine herself doing something, wanting something, caring if she lived or died beyond a single moment. She could have a purpose again. She might still have a life. Lost in this vision, she didn't realize Jacob had finished until she heard everyone else start to applaud.

The Loving Patrons of the Library had set up a reception for afterward, wine and cheese and punch and little orange cupcakes decorated with black plastic spiders. Serena got herself a plastic cup of red wine, but she didn't intend to linger. Jacob had been completely swallowed up by Carol Ann and the rest of the White ladies of the Historical Society as soon as he left the podium, and Tom Stewart was hovering on the edge of the pack with his ghost hunter buddies right behind him. She was just about to find a place to abandon her drink and sneak out when someone touched her arm.

"Hey Serena." It was Tom's wife, Evie. "Come be bad with me." Tom blended in well with the fine folk of Saxon County, but his wife stuck out like a flamingo in a chicken coop. She was a tiny little thing, curvy right up to the edge of plump, with hair dyed a shade of red not found in nature. Just then, her smile made her look like a mischievous imp. "I want to go exploring."

"What do you want to see?" All the doors leading off the hall were closed, and an off-duty sheriff's deputy was stationed on the stairs.

"Just the library. Tom said it was awful." She had taken Serena by the hand and was leading her toward the front door. They had met a few times before and been friendly, but they were hardly hand-holding friends. But that was Evie; affectionate and open as a child and just as inappropriate. To hear Tom tell it, she drove him crazy, but he obviously adored her.

"It was disgusting." Serena had to admit, she wanted a closer look, too. "But I think they've cleaned it all out."

"Still, though." Blue port-a-johns had been set up on the front lawn, and people milled back and forth and lingered in little clumps on the steps. "Tom said the fire marshal was going to make them leave the French doors unlocked," Evie said, dragging Serena around the corner of the house, out of the light. "Do you have a flashlight on your phone?"

"Yep," Serena said, taking it out. "Let's go."

The front hall where Jacob had done his reading had smelled like pine oil floor wax. But the dark parlor still smelled rotten. "Tom said it was horrible in here when y'all came through before," Evie repeated, running the beam of her tiny flashlight over the walls.

"It was." Serena ran her own light around the baseboards, looking for bugs and rats. All the furniture had been taken out, and the rugs were taken up, so their voices echoed in the empty room. They could hear the sounds of the reception as a sort of watery echo on the other side of the wall. "You could hear all the roaches and mice scurrying as soon as you opened the doors." The broken windows were covered with fresh, yellow plywood, sealing them in tight.

"Oh my God." The other woman trained her light on the floor and picked her feet up high with every step. She was a professional dancer and ran a children's dance academy in town. "Nasty." She splashed light over a cracked plaster wall that was splattered with a dark stain. "So in here was where he did it."

"Some here and some in the front hall." Serena couldn't remember where she'd heard this. Tom or Jacob must have mentioned it. But in her mind, she could see Ezra Woodbine dragging the men in here one by one, their bootheels catching on the rug.

"Holy shit." She sounded deeply impressed. "Did you hear Carol Ann talking about turning the place into a White supremacy theme park?"

Serena snickered. "Yeah, I did." She liked Evie better and better. "Did you see her face when Jacob said he might turn it into a museum?"

"That was awesome. I hope he does it." The glass had been removed from the shattered mirror over the fireplace, leaving the empty frame. "You could totally run it for him."

"Why?" Serena said though she'd had the same thought herself. "Because I'm Black?"

"Because you've got a degree in applied history." Evie ran her fingertip over the mahogany face of a cherub carved into the mantelpiece. "But being Black probably wouldn't hurt."

Serena bit back the apology that wanted to fall out of her mouth. "I didn't know you knew about my degree," she said instead.

"Oh yeah," Evie said. "That's part of the standard Tom Stewart 'What the Fuck are We Doing in This Fucking Town, For Fuck's Sake?' monologue."

Serena laughed and Evie continued. "Chapter five, verse three." She put on an excellent impression of Tom's voice. "'Serena Decatur has a degree in applied history from the University of South Carolina, and what's she doing? Stamping books and putting up bulletin boards out in North Fuckwad because I can't pay her a decent salary or bring her to town.'"

"He did not say that."

"He says it all the time. He's all about opening a local history room and putting you in charge of it, but the board won't hear it."

"Wow." She'd never heard a word about any of this. Surely if she'd known, Miz Rae would have mentioned it. "I would have thought Carol Ann would be all over a local history room. She's all the time talking about bringing in tourists." She was standing where there'd been a pink satin settee before, split in two like a fence rail and stained black with blood. She didn't realize she had seen it so clearly or committed it so much to memory, but thinking of it now made her scalp crawl.

"I know, right?" Evie wiped her hand on her shirt. "Apparently, she was all for it when Tom first brought it up. Then at the next board meeting, when it came up again, she had changed her mind." She swung her flashlight up to the ceiling. "Oh wow, look at that." The pinpoint of light crept slowly over a band of painted angels flaking away to dust. "Tom's about to die to get in here with his ghost hunting kit."

"Jacob didn't say no." Saying his name made Serena feel better. She liked the way it felt in her mouth, calling him Jacob because she knew him. But it wasn't enough. He wasn't here. "Does Tom really believe in ghosts?"

"Oh, yeah." The voices from outside really did sound like they were drowning, damned souls lost in the deep. "And I'll say this," Evie said. "If there are real ghosts anywhere, they'd be here."

"I hear that." The first time she'd seen this room, it had affected her strangely; she'd felt a weird excitement that had made her feel dizzy, made lights flash in front of her eyes. This time, she felt like she was buried alive. The air felt thick and poisonous, pressing against her skin. Listening to the echo of the crowd outside, she realized they didn't sound like ghosts at all. She and Evie were the ghosts, trapped here in this room.

Suddenly she felt exhausted, like just lifting her foot to take a step would be more than she could do. She was breathing fast, she realized, tiny, shallow breaths like a mouse pinned under a cat's paw. She trained her light on the heavy sliding doors and wondered how they'd ever find the strength to get out. *Help,* she thought, but she couldn't make her mouth say the word, couldn't draw a deep enough breath to scream. *Don't let me die in here.*

"It feels weird in here," Evie said, and she was breathing too fast, too. "I don't like it."

The doors slid open, and the light and sound from the reception flooded in. Jacob was holding one door; Tom was holding the other. "There they are," Jacob said.

"I should have known," Tom said as Evie ran to him and hugged him. "What's the matter, ladybug?" he said, laughing as he hugged her back. "Did the boogeyman get you?"

"It's pretty creepy in here," Serena said. Now she felt dizzy and sick to her stomach, and her skin was clammy with sweat. But Jacob was smiling at her, so she made herself smile back. "We were sneaking. Sorry."

"Don't be," he said. "But let's turn on some light." He plugged one extension cord into another, and a tall construction lamp buzzed into life. Pinkish-orange light spilled into the corners, lighting up the cobwebs and the dust bunnies and everything else.

"Y'all stripped out everything," Tom said, letting go of Evie to come inside.

"It's all in storage," Jacob said. "I haven't decided what I want to do with this room yet. What do you think, Serena?"

"Gut it." She was starting to feel better now; in fact, she felt a little silly for getting so freaked out. But she hadn't forgotten that feeling like being smothered. For a crazy moment, she had almost run to Jacob the same way Evie had run to her husband. "Strip out the floors, knock down the plaster, take it down to the skeleton and start over."

"No," Tom said. "You can't do that."

"Sure he can," Serena said. "You'll never get the bloodstains out of that plaster or the wood floor."

"So cover it up," Tom said.

"No," Evie said. "You can't just cover it up and pretend it's not there. You have to face it and get rid of it." She realized they were all staring at her. "At least that's what I'd do."

"Do you think that would do it, then?" Jacob said. "Would that get rid of the ghosts?"

"I don't believe in ghosts," she said. "Like Miz Rae says, I'm a Christian." She smiled. "Sorry, Tom."

"I agree with Serena," Evie said. "Whatever might be in here, get rid of it."

Tom smiled and put his arm around his wife. "We're about to have a bunch of looky-loos in here," he said. "We should close this up and go back to the party."

"Tom's right," Jacob said. He put a hand on Serena's back to steer her toward the door. "Let's get a drink."

When they went back out in the hall, half a dozen college kids were waiting for Jacob with copies of his books in hand, and Carol Ann pounced on Tom and led him and Evie away. "I'll be right with you," Jacob told the autograph seekers. He walked with Serena to the bar and poured her a fresh drink himself.

"I shouldn't," she said. "I've got to drive home, and you've got all those people waiting."

"Did you like the story?" he asked.

"I did," she said. "Did you write it, or did you really find it like you said?"

He laughed. "Don't you trust me?"

"I do," she said. "But it does sound like you." She looked at her drink, away from his searching eyes. "You like to punish the bad guy."

"I do when I know who he is." He touched the back of her hand that was holding the cup. "Stay until after and talk to me about it."

"I really can't." But she wanted to. She set down her drink. "I need to get home. My mother-in-law will be worrying about me."

"What about your husband?"

"He's dead," she said. Her lips curled in a smile; how horrible was that? "He's got no more reason to worry about me."

"So you do believe in heaven," Jacob said. "But not ghosts."

"You got it." She offered her hand. "It was good to see you again, and the story was great."

"But you don't believe it's real." He took her hand and held it without shaking. "I hope you're right about the ghosts." Nobody but Trey had ever looked into her eyes the way he was looking at her now. She felt her skin flushing hot. "You're wrong, but I hope you're right."

"You write ghost stories for a living, and I like those a lot." She pulled her hand free. "Isn't that enough?"

"I guess so." He took a step back. "For now, at least." Someone was calling his name from behind her. "Tell Miz Rae I'm still coming to see her."

"I will," she said. "We'll see you soon."

10

A little less than a week later, Jacob went to the library in a shiny new RV. As he turned in, he noticed the scarecrow he had admired the first time he drove past the Briarwood Community Center had been replaced with shucks of dried corn that made him think of burning witches and wicker men. The day he'd first come to Briarwood had been blue-sky beautiful; today the world looked gray. The parking lot was empty except for an ancient white Cadillac, and he pulled the RV into the deeper shadows of the bare pecan trees at the back of the lot.

The glass library doors were decorated with cardboard cutouts of turkeys and apple-cheeked pilgrim men and women who looked like they'd burn a witch as soon as look at her. A little bell tinkled as he went through the door.

"Be right with you," a woman's voice called from somewhere in the stacks. The tiny library seemed remarkably well-stocked for its size. Most of the room was crowded with row upon row of well-stuffed bookshelves, and a periodicals rack just inside the door held both *The New Yorker* and *The Christian Science Monitor* alongside *Southern Living* and the local rag. Two beautifully aged oak tables with matching chairs were set up directly in front of the modern-looking circulation desk, and he saw not a single computer.

"Just passing through?" The owner of the voice he'd heard came out of the stacks brandishing a feather duster. "I saw your ride when you pulled in."

"You must be Miz Rae." She was much more attractive than he'd expected from Serena and Tom's descriptions and much younger, no more than a few years older than himself. He extended his hand. "I'm Jacob—"

"I know who you are." She ignored his hand and walked right past him. "I know you from your accent."

"Right." He followed, bemused. "Did Serena tell you I was coming to talk to you?"

"She did." She put the circulation desk between them. "I don't know why, though." Both Serena and Tom had made her sound formidable, a dragon lady in cat's eye spectacles, and her tone was certainly all business. But he got the distinct impression that he frightened her. "I don't see where we've got much of anything to talk about," she said with a defiant tilt of her chin.

"I was hoping you could tell me more about Briarwood," he said, pressing on despite her manner. "Serena says you know all there is to know about this part of the county."

"I don't know a thing about that place you haven't heard already," she said. "And if I did know, I wouldn't tell you."

"Ma'am, have I offended you in some way?" he said.

"Sir, you have not." She folded her hands, beautifully manicured, slightly arthritic, a single beautiful pearl and ruby ring, obviously genuine, on her right hand, no wedding band on her left, and placed them on the desk. "I've read your books, Jacob." He was surprised she used his first name. "The last man on this earth who needs to be at Briarwood is you."

"Now, Miz Rae, come on," he said with a smile he didn't quite feel. "How can an educated Christian woman like yourself believe in ghosts and goblins?"

"How can a man who writes those books not?" Their eyes met, and though he wanted to laugh, he couldn't. She wasn't joking, and she wasn't wrong. "It's not ghosts or goblins I'm worried about," she went on. "I'm not like Tom Stewart; I know there aren't any human souls left up there to haunt that place. When God's people die, we go to hell or heaven; there ain't no other choice. But there are spirits in this world, and there is evil, and you know it as well as any man alive. And you want to play with it. You think your money will keep you safe, or maybe you think you're too smart to be fooled."

"Fooled by what?" he said, still pretending to be amused. But inside, his stomach churned, and his hands started to sweat. He felt like a child caught doing something dark and wicked, some proof of a failing in his character he needed desperately to hide.

"You know what," she said. "And if you don't now, you will before you're done." In the quiet, they heard another car pulling into the parking lot outside. "That will be Serena coming back with lunch." She surprised him again by putting her hand over his. "You say you want me to tell you something. Let me tell you this. If you really want to fix Briarwood, if you want to honor and comfort the poor souls who suffered and died there, burn it down."

Her palm was cool and dry, and her eyes were tawny green behind her glasses. "Tear down the pieces and burn it again, and all the trees around it. Fill in the wells and springs and streams, and scrape down the earth to the clay, then salt the clay so nothing ever grows there again. Then with all the money you saved not restoring that horror house, build a wall all the way around it ten feet tall and five feet thick with broken glass and barbed wire and electric shock and anything else you can think of that will keep the foolish out. Lock the gate and throw away the key. Then you can look your Lord in the eye on the day of judgement and say you did what you could do to fix Briarwood." They heard Serena's car door slam. "Or just run back home to Ireland now as fast as you can go." The bell over the door tinkled. "But either way, leave poor Serena alone."

From the RV in the parking lot, Serena expected to find a couple of Yankee tourists bending Miz Rae's ear about their family history, not Jacob leaning over the circulation desk holding her hand. "Hey y'all," she said, locking the door and turning around the sign. "Is everything all right?"

"Fine," Miz Rae said, straightening up and gently pulling her hand away. "What'd they have at Perry's?"

"Spaghetti casserole and liver and onions," Serena said. Perry's was the gas station/hot bar halfway back to town where she'd gone to get their lunch. "I just got you some fries and a milkshake."

"How much of that nasty casserole you reckon they throw out every week?" Miz Rae said as she headed for the back. She no longer seemed aware that Jacob was there. "I don't know why they keep making it."

"Hey Jacob," Serena said. He smiled and moved in for a hug, so she smiled and hugged him back. "Is that your RV outside?"

"It is." He didn't seem the least bit bothered by Miz Rae's ignoring him, and when Serena followed her to the back, he followed Serena. "How do you like it?"

"It's huge!" Serena set out the bags of food on the work table. "Miz Rae, did you see this thing Jacob's driving? It's bigger than a doublewide trailer."

"I heard him driving it in," Miz Rae said, unpacking her French fries. Serena saw her hands were shaking—what could they have been talking about? "Y'all go on back out front if you want to talk. I'm getting ready to listen to my stories." She turned on the radio Miz Regina kept tuned to the TV band for the soaps.

"Yes ma'am," Serena said, more mystified than ever. She'd been hearing Miz Rae make fun of Miz Regina about those stories for as long as she'd been working there, and whenever Miz Regina wasn't with them, the first thing Miz Rae said was, "We don't have to listen to that trash today, thank you, Jesus." Obviously, then, she wanted Jacob out. "I'm going to walk out front and let Jacob show me this new ride of his if that's all right."

"Whatever you want to do." She was fiddling with the volume like she was suddenly fascinated by an ad for disposable diapers. "Don't let your lunch get cold."

"No ma'am," Serena said. "Come on, Jacob."

"Enjoy your lunch, Miz Rae," Jacob said. She loved the way he sounded saying "miz" with that Irish accent. "It was lovely to meet you finally."

"You, too, Jacob." Whatever was bothering Miz Rae, it wouldn't have damaged her manners. "You be careful in that monster."

He was smiling, bemused. "I will."

Inside, the RV was much nicer than any doublewide trailer Serena had ever seen, with teak paneling and leather upholstery and granite countertops. "I am given to understand by the dealer that Keith Urban and Nicole Kidman own one just like this," Jacob said when he'd given her the tour.

"Fancy." Even the tiny bedroom was luxurious, a king-sized bed in a closet. "What made you decide to buy this?" She turned her back on the bedroom and closed the pocket door behind her. "Are you going on a trip?"

"No, no," he said. "But I've had all I can stand of that bed and breakfast." In the small space, he seemed even taller than usual, towering over her. "They've finally gotten water and sewer lines run at Briarwood, so I've asked them to put me a hook-up in the front yard. I can park this there for as long as it takes to finish the house."

"You're going ahead and moving onto the property?" He wasn't crowding her at all, but he still seemed really close. "Does your phone work out there now?"

"It does not." He sat down in one of the plush captain's chairs around the little table, and suddenly she could breathe. "Your father-in-law has already pointed out to me if I fall and break my neck, I'll die alone." She laughed, and he smiled. "But I'm not scared."

"I would be, I think." She sat across from him. "I know it's silly, but when Evie and I were in that parlor on Halloween, I didn't like it. It felt wrong." He stretched out a hand to her, and after a moment, she took it. "Have you…felt anything in the house?"

Jacob liked having her in his home. He liked the way her soft, smooth hand felt in his. "I have," he admitted. "I haven't told anybody about it, but that first time I went inside, it scared the hell out of me. I thought I was having a heart attack."

"What happened?"

"Nothing, really," he said. "Like you said, it just felt wrong. I had seen that bloodstain at the foot of the stairs, and I could have sworn..." The footprints he saw had since disappeared.

"What?" Her eyes were wide.

"It was just dirt on the stairs, but it looked like footprints," he said. "I followed them upstairs, and I felt sick. I had decided not to buy the place at all."

"But you seemed fine when we showed up," she said.

"I did," he said. "I was." Sitting close to her now with the smell of her breath and her perfume all around him, it was easy to remember. He didn't think he'd ever enjoyed just looking at anyone as much as he did looking at Serena, not even Gloria in the early days when he was first falling in love. But that was madness, surely. He was a man in his forties, not some smitten kid. "But I felt something else, something lovely," he said. "A presence." *A woman,* he thought but didn't say. *A woman who wants me there.* "It felt very warm, very inviting."

"Did you see anything?" she asked.

"No," he said. "Whatever it was, it was like it was behind me. I stood looking out the window, and I felt this warm, beautiful presence telling me I should stay." He smiled. "And then I saw you."

Smoooth, Serena thought, amused. Something about this clumsy line made him seem more familiar, more human. "Pull the other one," she said aloud. "You're making that up."

"I'm not, I swear," he said, laughing, and she wondered how a man with such a wicked and sexy twinkle in his eyes could write such scary books. "The very moment I was deciding to stay at Briarwood, I saw you and Tom drive up."

"Uh huh." She stood up. This felt too natural, too right. "I better go inside before Miz Rae comes out here to get me."

"She might bring a shotgun when she comes," he said. "She warned me to leave you alone."

"She did not!"

"I promise you she did." He stood up, too. "I think she mistrusts my intentions."

She couldn't help but smile. "Well, you are kind of shady."

"Oh really?" He took a step toward her. "How's that, then?" If he wasn't using that sexy Irish accent on purpose, he should have been. Either way, it was working a treat.

"Oh, I think you know." She hadn't flirted with anyone since the night they'd told her Trey was gone for good, and her skin now tingled all over. She wouldn't have been surprised to see sparks dancing on her fingertips. But how was that possible? How could her first attraction after the love of her life be for a White man who was so much older? When he took her hand again and drew her closer, the motion felt inevitable, a choreographed dance she was bound by nature to perform. But when she tasted his mouth as it touched hers, the intimacy startled her, and she pulled away.

Jacob let her go at once. "I'm sorry." He wasn't, but he didn't want to frighten her.

"No, don't." She put her hand on his chest with her fingers slightly curled, holding him there and pushing him away at the same time. "It's not that I don't..." He watched her searching for the words and finding the cliché. "It's complicated."

He sat back on the edge of the table. "Do you want to explain it?"

"I don't know." He reached for her hand again, and she let him take it and fold it against his heart. "My husband died...and I live with his parents. And you're famous...and White." She felt the heat of him through his thick, black sweater. She didn't know how to bring her fantasy of this writer she had admired into this living, breathing man. And she couldn't forget her husband; she could almost feel him standing behind her like a ghost. "And you just appeared and bought the local haunted plantation I've been hearing about all my life," she went on, pushing the feeling away. She snickered. "And my boss doesn't like you."

"Am I allowed to say none of that matters?" His skin was so white that even freshly-shaved, his black beard showed through as a shadow, and the vein at his temple showed blue.

"Doesn't matter to you."

"Doesn't have to matter to you."

"That's easy for you to say." And that was the other thing, wasn't it? What would the good White ladies of the Loving Patrons of the Library say if she and Jacob got involved? She pulled her hand free and stepped back. "I have to go."

"I just want to see you." He didn't stand or try to stop her.

"I want to see you, too." She wanted to do more than see him. She wanted to surrender, to be swept away, for the fantasy to be real. She wanted to be an imaginary woman who took a rich White lover and lived easily ever after. But only a fool could believe that story could be true, and she'd lost the freedom to be foolish. "You will see me. I'm not going anywhere." She stopped on the steps down to the door. "I like your new house."

"Thanks." He still didn't move, but he smiled. "I'll see you soon."

11

In addition to the RV, Jacob had bought a used car—a hybrid—to ease his conscience. On Thanksgiving morning, he was gassing it up for the first time in two weeks when Amanda Flynn pulled up to the pumps. "Good morning," he said as she got out. "Can I help?"

"I've got it, thanks." He had never seen her dressed so casually before, a skintight ladies version of an American football jersey over equally skintight jeans. But he'd never seen her wearing so much make-up, either, and her hair was perfectly styled. When she reached for the gas pump handle, he saw her nails were tipped like talons and painted bright garnet to match her jersey. "How did you escape Carol Ann's Thanksgiving dinner extravaganza?" she asked. "I know she must have invited you."

"I said I had a previous engagement." His tank was full. "Is that where you're going now?"

"God, no." She was bending over just a wee tad too far to fill her tank, making him think of commercials for motor oil back home. "I'm skipping town entirely." It was barely noon, but her speech was slightly slurred. "I'm going up to Charlotte to a sports bar to watch the big game and audition prospects for the weekend." She smiled, and her garnet lipstick made her mouth look both irresistible and appalling. "Care to come along and put your bid in early?"

"I won't say I'm not tempted." And he was, so much that certain parts of him ached with it. There was a darkness in this girl he found almost painfully alluring. "But as I said....previous engagement."

"Previous engagement," she said with him.

"I'm having dinner with Tom Stewart and his wife," he said. An evil impulse struck him. "Care to come along with me?"

"Thank you, no." She finished pumping her gas and hung up the handle. "I don't really fit in with the Democrats." She brushed a lock of blonde hair back from her cheek. "Will Serena Decatur be there?"

"I don't know." He felt a sudden heat in his face, and that annoyed him. "Evie didn't mention it."

"Uh-huh..." She got into her little red sportscar. "Y'all have fun."

"Amanda, wait." He put a hand on her window frame and leaned down. "I don't think I've had a chance to tell you how sorry I was to hear about your father."

She laughed. "Oh honey, please," she said. "The old man got off easy." She waved and rolled up her window as he straightened up, then she drove away.

Tom and Evie lived in a shabby Craftsman cottage in the closest thing to a multicultural neighborhood Jacob had seen since he'd come to Saxon County. As he pulled in behind a shiny black van, a woman in a sari and a hunting jacket stood in the driveway next door saying, "Be careful!" as her husband lowered a turkey into a deep fryer.

In the front yard on the other side, half a dozen small Black boys played American football under the supervision of a pair of dads holding cans of beer. As Jacob got out of his car, one of the boys scored, breaking free of the pack and dashing through a gap in the hedge into Tom and Evie's yard. He broke out into an elaborate victory dance, and Jacob applauded. He waved to the dads, and the dads waved back.

Inside, everyone was gathered in the kitchen, finishing up the feast. The black van belonged to Tom's friend, Jason Hargett, the self-appointed paranormal investigations expert. "I promised Evie I wouldn't ruin Thanksgiving bugging you about this," he said five minutes to the second after he and Jacob were introduced.

"And yet here we are," Evie said, giving Jacob a wink.

"But I cannot tell you how much I want to get some equipment into that house," Jason went on. Evie and Jason's wife, Suki Ann, did the actual cooking, working their way through a bottle of wine while the men drank beer and watched—Tom had put an ice-cold Guinness in Jacob's hand as soon as he walked in the door. Jacob chose to appreciate this as a thoughtful gesture and cracked it open. The TV in the living room was blaring "Jingle Bells," played by a marching band, but nobody seemed to be terribly interested.

"What kind of equipment are we talking about, then?" Jacob said. Jason and Suki Ann wore jeans and t-shirts like Tom and Evie, but their van outside looked brand new, and very fresh, very expensive-looking tattoos covered every inch of visible skin on Jason's arms. He reminded Jacob more of a roadie for a rock band than any kind of scientist.

"Just the basics to start," Jason said. "We'd do a walk-through first with EMF detectors and a couple of good thermal cameras. Then we'd set up motion detectors, digital EVP recorders, and three hundred-sixty-degree camera rigs in the hot spots." He was built like a cinder block wall, with the close-cropped hair and wild eyes of a true believer. "And we'd have a team on-site, spread out with handheld cameras and recorders."

"But what's this whole operation for?" Jacob said. "Are you writing a book or making a movie? Is it some sort of internet thing?" He thought about the website that had first pointed him from his dreams to the reality of Briarwood. It wasn't hard to picture this Jason as its author, skulking around in the dark.

"No, sir," Jason said.

"No," Tom echoed.

"We don't have any interest in trying to make any money off your name or Briarwood," Jason said. "We won't even share our findings if you tell us not to." Jacob was reminded of friends back in Ireland who had joined the priesthood and the IRA. Jason had that some sort of intensity in his eyes, the same twitching in his hands as he talked about his quest.

"Then what's the point?" Jacob said.

"We just want to know," Tom said before Jason could answer. "If there's something there, we want to see it."

"Mr. McGinnas, until a year or so ago, I was a United States Marine," Jason said. "I served in Afghanistan and Iraq, and I saw people die in ways that might even give you nightmares." The light in his eyes had gone flat, and all expression had left his face, as if his features were incapable of expressing how he felt as he remembered.

"Trust me, I have nightmares all the time," Jacob said.

"I just want to know if...*that* there's something else. Something... after..." Jason said.

"I think I can understand that," Jacob said. "I just don't know that the answers you're looking for are at Briarwood. Or if I'd want them found if they were."

Evie had been listening to them talk as she mixed up some sort of breadcrumb and celery concoction in a big bowl with her bare hands. But Suki Ann had turned completely away from them to peel apples and gave no indication she heard a single word.

"Isn't it always better to know?" Tom said.

"Spoken like a historian," Jacob said, smiling. "But I'm a novelist."

"I hear the game starting in the living room," Evie said. "Why don't you boys go in and watch and leave Jacob in here with us girls for a bit? We'll butter him up for you."

"I'm not saying I'm against the idea," Jacob said. "I've already been giving it some thought."

"You keep thinking about it," Jason said. It was obvious from the slump of their shoulders that both men were disappointed, but they both managed to smile.

"Holler when you need me," Tom said, kissing Evie on the cheek.

"Suki Ann, are you all right?" Evie asked the other woman as soon as the men were gone.

"What's wrong?" Jacob asked.

"Jason just gets so crazy about this stuff," Suki Ann said. "Evie, I am so sorry. He promised he wouldn't say anything, but I don't think he can help himself."

"Jason's got PTSD, which I'm sure you already guessed," Evie said, dumping the sludge in her bowl into a casserole dish. "He's a great guy, the sweetest guy alive, and I think the things they asked him do —" She broke off, looking at Suki Ann. "I don't think killing people came easily to him," she finished.

"Most of the time, he's fine," Suki Ann said. "The ghost hunting stuff is just a fun hobby. But ever since Tom told him about that house, he's been obsessed."

"And Tom knew he would be; that's why he told him," Evie said. She rinsed and dried her hands, then hugged her friend. "I should have known they were plotting an ambush. I don't blame Jason, and I'm certainly not mad at you."

"Suki, do you want me to say yes?" Jacob said. From the next room, he could hear both men yelling at the television.

"I don't know," Suki said. "I don't know what's better or worse for him, finding something or going and not finding something, or you just shutting him down completely." She was a very pretty girl with her own elaborate tattoos that showed at her wrists and throat. "I wish I thought if you said no, he'd just give it up and stop thinking about it."

"But he wouldn't, and neither would Tom," Evie said, going back to her casserole.

"Have they done a lot of investigations?" Jacob asked. "Have they ever found anything?"

"They did an investigation at an abandoned slave cemetery and saw some orbs," Suki said. "And Tom convinced Jack Flynn to let them set up on the third floor of his law firm for a couple of nights last summer." Evie snorted, pouring turkey broth over the mush. "They recorded some EVPs—"

"Electronic voice phenomena," Evie said.

"And this girl, Naomi, who works with them, said she felt some stuff," Suki finished, watching Evie. "She's supposed to be a sensitive, like a psychic."

"Uh-huh," Evie said, patting the wet sludge with the back of a wooden spoon.

"Wow," Jacob said. "Will Naomi be joining us for dinner?"

"She will not," Evie said, putting the casserole in the oven.

"Evie and Naomi don't socialize," Suki said with a sly grin.

"I'm pretty free and easy; I don't have a lot of rules," Evie said. "But if you try to fuck my husband, you're not welcome for Thanksgiving dinner."

"I'll bear that in mind," Jacob said, giving Suki a wink that made her smile. "Honestly, I don't have any particular objection to them coming into Briarwood." He had never been entirely convinced by the scientific approach to the paranormal; from what he'd seen, most of it seemed more like projection and wishful thinking. But he liked Tom and Evie, and he felt an immediate sympathy for Suki Ann. Jason was a little scary, a great character—he could already see him showing up in a book someday.

"It's entirely up to you," Evie said. She was now scattering miniature marshmallows on another casserole dish full of mashed sweet potatoes. "If you're not comfortable with it, they'll just have to get over it. They're big boys; they'll manage." She went to the doorway and called into the living room. "Baby, are you still going to carve up this bird for me?"

"Whenever you get ready," Tom called back.

"Ten more minutes." She put the sweet potatoes into the oven. "If you do decide to let them, we'll have to call Serena," she said. "She told Tom she wanted to come investigate, too."

"When would we want to do it?" Jacob said.

"Evie, you are bad," Suki said. "Look out, Jacob. Evie is a terrible matchmaker."

"On the contrary," Evie said. "I am a wonderful matchmaker." She tasted the gravy and smiled. "We could do that first walk-through tonight."

Serena had been invited to the big Decatur family Thanksgiving at Rooster's mother's house in the country, but she had politely declined. "Are you sure?" Claudine asked her as she packed up her pecan pies. "I don't think you ought to be all by yourself on another holiday."

"Claudie, honey, leave her alone," Rooster said. "She'll probably be glad to have the peace."

"I'll be fine," Serena promised. "Y'all go on and have fun."

"You want us to bring you back a plate?" Claudine said. "We'll bring you back some pie at least."

"*We will* bring pie, and you *might* get a bite," Rooster corrected, walking out the back door with the basket.

"You need to start getting out," Claudine said when he was gone. "Christmas this year for sure." She had put a smooth, sweet-smelling hand to Serena's cheek. "You promise?"

Serena hugged her. "I'll try."

They were barely out of the driveway before she was running a bath. She had a perfectly adequate stall shower in the bathroom just off her bedroom, but Claudine had a soaker tub with jets and lights and candles set around it—a gift from Rooster on their thirtieth wedding anniversary. Serena was officially welcome to use it whenever she liked, but she only felt right about it when her mother-in-law was gone.

She deep conditioned her hair and covered it with a cap, then slid into the bath. She hadn't had the house to herself since Easter—on the Fourth of July, Rooster and Claudine had hosted the barbecue here, and she'd hidden in her room all day, pleading migraine. She didn't dislike her dead husband's family; far from it. But she couldn't spend a whole day under the microscope. Specimen: Trey's widow. Trey, who everybody had loved and admired; the high school football star who'd gone to the Citadel on a scholarship; the Air Force officer; the family success story; the one who'd gotten out. The one who'd gotten himself shot in the head by a drug dealer on a dark, desert highway in Nevada, leaving his wife behind to face his debts and a family who barely knew her.

If she had a family of her own, things might have been different. But her parents had been killed in an accident when she was seven years old. She ended up packed off to her father's Aunt Lillian, the only family member who would take her. When she turned eighteen, what was left of her inheritance became her own, and Aunt Lil had pretty much kicked her out. She went to college on her own dime and never looked back, met Trey at a party the summer after graduation and followed him west. Aunt Lil still lived barely thirty miles away, but they rarely spoke.

She sank into the bubbles up to her chin and turned up the jets with her toe. If she'd had the money, she would never have come back to Saxon County or even to South Carolina. She dreamed sometimes of the places to which she might have escaped: New York or Los Angeles, maybe even Tokyo or Paris. But there was no money after Trey, not even enough to survive on her own in Las Vegas.

So she'd come home and put herself away in his parents' spare bedroom like another one of Trey's old football trophies, gathering dust. "What are you waiting for, honey?" Claudine asked her sometimes. After two years, even Trey's mother would have been glad to see her find somebody else. The only one who never tried to fix her up was Miz Rae at the library. But Miz Rae had been waiting for something and gathering dust for quite some time herself, or so it seemed to Serena.

As the hot water played around her body, her thoughts strayed to Jacob McGinnas kissing her in his little rolling palace, and her fingers roamed over her stomach. But she pushed the memory out of her head and shaved her legs instead.

When she got out, she rinsed her hair in the sink and decided to roll it—she hadn't had curls in ages, and for once she had the time and the big mirror to do it. She had just gotten the last lock wrapped around a perm rod when her telephone rang. Cursing the telemarketer she expected, she wiped her oily hands on a towel and answered. "Hello?"

"Hey Serena, it's Evie." She could hear Tom's wife smiling. "Did I get you up from dinner?"

"No, it's fine," Serena said, wracking her brain, trying to think what Tom's wife could want on Thanksgiving. "What's up?"

"We've got Jacob talked into letting Tom and his buddy Jason go ghost hunting at Briarwood," Evie said. "Don't you want to come?"

"Jacob is with y'all?" She felt a sharp stab of jealousy. Evie was infamous for her matchmaking; heaven only knew what kind of heifer she'd dragged up from the barn for Jacob. Probably that slutty Naomi girl Tom was always talking about.

"Yeah, Tom talked him into coming for Thanksgiving," Evie said. "Can you get away?"

"Claudine and Rooster are gone," Serena said. "But I just rolled my head." *Now?* she thought, exasperated. *It has to be now?*

"Just pull it out of the rollers and put it in a ponytail," Evie said. "Or tie a scarf around your head; you're gorgeous enough; it won't matter."

Spoken like a White girl. "When are y'all going?" she asked.

"Probably in about an hour. We're still eating dessert," Evie said. "Me and Tom will come pick you up."

"No, it's okay," Serena said, mentally calculating. She could probably get her hair dry with Claudine's bonnet dryer. But an hour was shaving it close. "I'll meet y'all out at Briarwood."

"Awesome," Evie said. "I'll tell Jacob you're coming." She sounded positively bursting with mischief. "He'll be thrilled."

12

By the time Serena finished getting ready, the sun was going down. She was nervous all the way out of town, expecting at any moment to see Claudine and Rooster coming back the other way. She had left them a note, and she was a thirty-year-old woman; she could go where she liked. But she still felt better when she'd made the turn toward North Creek and knew she was in the clear.

Jacob was waiting for her down at the gate, a tall, thin scarecrow silhouetted against the purple twilight sky. Something about this image made her shiver, so much so that she almost stepped on the gas and kept driving. Then he waved, and she saw his smile, and the premonition passed.

"Happy Thanksgiving," he said, leaning in as she rolled down her window. His car was parked just inside the open gateway, blocking the drive. "There's no lights yet, so I thought I should guide you in."

"Thanks." He'd let his beard grow since Halloween, and the flecks of white made him look older but sexier, too. "I'm sorry it took me so long to get here."

"Not to worry; you haven't missed much. I think they're still setting up their equipment." She'd put a hand on the window frame, and he put his hand over it, warm and big and barely calloused. "Come on. Follow me up."

The RV was parked on the front lawn, a big, shiny chunk of modern reality to slap the face of the broken plantation charm. The unpainted hulk of the house was silhouetted against the last dying rays of twilight, lit by nothing but a couple of gas lanterns on the porch and the pale glow of more lanterns in some of the windows.

"Watch your step," Jacob said, offering her a hand as she got out of her car. "The ground is really soggy from all the trucks." She wore high-heeled boots, and she told herself this was why she kept hold of his arm as they walked across the muddy lawn and up the steps. But she could feel her resolve weakening, her doubts melting away.

"I offered to turn on the work lights for them," he said as he opened the front door. "But Jason said they might interfere with the original energy. Have you met Jason?"

She laughed. "Oh yeah."

Inside, a few more gas lanterns were scattered around the front hall, one at each doorway and one at the foot of the stairs. "I think he just wanted to preserve the ambiance," Jacob said, picking one up.

"Where is everybody now?" She could hear voices and footsteps echoing through the big, empty house, but she couldn't place where they were coming from.

"Setting up EMPs and DVRs and ABCs and 123s and Christ only knows what else," he said, laughing. "You should see the tons of crap they carried in here; it's like a spy film." Jacob liked that she had come, liked that she'd been late, liked that she was still holding his hand. She was wearing her hair loose in its natural ringlets tonight, and he very much liked that, too. "They're all very excited. Some woman named Naomi has already fainted twice."

She laughed. "I bet Evie is loving that." From somewhere above them, they heard a shriek then another woman's laughter. "It's like a haunted house, isn't it?"

"It is a haunted house," he said. "But I don't know that you can find what's haunting it with a tape recorder." She had been very clear the last time he saw her that she didn't think they should be together, and he had never been one to push. But here, in this light, in this house, she was very nearly irresistible.

"Should we go try to find them?" she said.

"We should." He laced his fingers with hers, and she didn't object.

"You need to show me the room you said you felt the ghost in," she said as he led her up the stairs. Footsteps echoed on the bare wooden floors above them—the others were in the attic. "Do you remember?"

"Of course I do." He picked up a lantern with his other hand. "It's right down here." Rooster and his crew had accomplished a lot up here. The floors had been sanded smooth and yellow-white, ready for their new finish. Thick paper runners ran the length of the hall, taped down to make a walkway. Instead of mold and dust and rot, the hallway now smelled of fresh wood and paint and linseed oil; warm, inviting smells. But in the lantern's light, menacing shadows still danced on the walls, and the floors still creaked underfoot. Jacob imagined that under the sweet perfume of progress, he could still smell the stench of decay.

He opened a freshly-painted door. "In here," he said. "I was standing right there at that window."

She let go of his hand to go look. The room was bare, swept clean, the drapes and shutters removed. Through the sparkling, hand-blown glass, he could see the wavering image of the rising moon, a swollen orange crescent crawling up the branches of the trees. "Look at that moon," Serena said, touching the glass. "Isn't it beautiful?"

"It is." He put a hand on her shoulder, and felt her shudder. He turned her to him, and she didn't resist. Her eyes glowed green in the lantern light, cat's eyes, and she smiled. "Just say no," he said.

"I don't want to say no." She put her hands on his chest and gripped his shirt front. For a moment, he felt the cravat at his throat, felt sun-warmed skin through a thin cotton dress under his hands instead of Serena's thick sweater.

Then he kissed her, and she was just Serena, beautiful, brilliant Serena, and he loved her, wanted her completely. They sank together to the clean, bare floor bathed in cold, blue moonlight, warm, aching bodies entwined. The old house creaked and moaned around them as they came together at last.

The paranormal investigators didn't find much despite Naomi's hysterics, just a few cold spots and some EVPs they could play back and analyze later. But over the next twelve hours, after Jacob McGinnas made love to Serena Decatur for the first time in the old man's room, the following things all happened:

Tom and Evie Stewart made a baby.

Ontreas Clark, the armed robber and amateur arsonist who burned down the Saxon County Courthouse, hanged himself in his cell.

In Palm Springs, California, a White orthodontic surgeon who had never known he was adopted from South Carolina as an infant in the 1960s, stopped his luxury sedan on an almost empty freeway and dragged the Black woman stopped in front of him out of her SUV, and bludgeoned her to death with a golf club from his trunk.

Miss Florence Creighton, former director of the Saxon County Library, suffered a massive stroke in her room at the Methodist rest home.

Jason Hargett, paranormal investigator and former Marine, dreamed he was in the desert in Afghanistan, cutting open babies with the hunting knife his grandfather gave him for his thirteenth birthday. Inside every baby he found more babies, like seeds inside a pomegranate, glistening with blood.

Amanda Flynn, attorney at law and chairman of the Montgomery Trust, drugged and robbed a running back for the Carolina Panthers she had just met in a hotel bar. She beat him bloody with a wooden coat hanger from the hotel closet after he was unconscious. She threw away his watch but kept his cash.

An antiques dealer in London was shot and killed by an unknown assailant in an alley in the middle of the night. The attack was presumed to be a mugging, but police found his wallet in his coat.

Frank Sweatt, president and general manager of the Saxonville National Bank, took several items from the safe hidden under his desk chair in his man cave/office at home. One of these items was a pistol, which he loaded and held for an hour as his wife slept in the next room and the HDTV played on. Several times he cocked the hammer, and twice he pressed the barrel to his forehead. But when the news came on, the weatherman promised good golfing in the morning for the first time in a month. He put everything back in the safe and went to bed.

Laurel Heath, Saxonville's homeless crazy with a home, stood in the glow of the spotlight that still shone on the lawn of the county courthouse in front of the burned-out hulk and sang all five published verses of "The Battle Hymn of the Republic" ninety-seven times through with no discernible loss of volume or visible sign of fatigue.

And in a shiny RV on the lawn of the Briarwood plantation, Jacob McGinnas and Serena Decatur slept entwined in Jacob's king-sized bed, warm-blooded mammals curled up in their den and hiding from the dark.

13

Serena woke up in the dark and couldn't remember where she was. She had been dreaming something scary, but it faded from her memory as soon as she opened her eyes. She reached out of the tangle of blankets with her dominant left hand and touched a cool, smooth metal wall. She reached out with her right and touched Jacob. She recoiled with a gasp, then she remembered. She reached out again and touched his chest: warmth, heartbeat, breathing, covered in silky-fine hair. She could hear him breathing, not quite snoring. *Sweet Jesus,* she thought, *what have I done?*

Her eyes had adjusted; she could see the RV bedroom now, the outline of the curtained windows. She slipped out of the bed as quietly as she could, and Jacob didn't stir. By the time she was dressed, gray light crept in around the curtains, and she could see his face.

In the dim light, his pale skin almost glowed; he was an alien, a stranger. But he was familiar, too, the way his hair fell over his forehead, the curve of his jawline, the blue veins in the back of his beautiful hand on her pillow. *This is crazy.*

She found her coat and her keys and slipped out.

On the Briarwood lawn, she could have been the last living woman on earth. It was cold and misting rain, and the grass was brittle with frost. Crows screamed overhead and from the tops of the trees. And over it all loomed Briarwood, old gray wood patched with shining yellow, her windows like wide, staring eyes, a dead witch half made up.

She shifted her keys into a weapon in her hand like she hadn't since she moved back from Las Vegas and hurried toward her car. Rooster and Claudine must be worried sick about her. Worse, they must surely have guessed where she was and what she had done.

She was reaching for the door handle when she heard footsteps right behind her and felt breathing down her neck. She turned with a little shriek, striking out with her keys, but the figure wasn't close at all. A man stood halfway across the lawn as if he'd just come out of the forest. She tried to cry out, but her mouth had gone dry. In the dim light, he was hard to see, a figure of shadow standing in the open. But she could see he was smiling. "*Voila ma fille*," he said in a deep but lisping voice as if he were missing teeth. "*Elle est venue*." He wore thick, dirty layers of leather and rags with a shapeless red hat; some sort of historical costume.

"I don't know you," she said, but she doubted he could hear her; her voice came out a rasping whisper. "Go away."

"Don't know me?" His shape melted into a shadow, but she would have known his voice anywhere. "Since when?" The shadow moved closer, slithering over the grass then rising up into a man again. Her dead husband, Trey.

"Not real." A lump rose in her throat; she was trembling so much, she could barely stand. "I'm dreaming."

"No, baby." He looked as solid now as her own hand in front of her face. "You are waking up." He was only a few steps away from her now, and she could see his eyes...staring and dead like the last time she'd seen him, and blood soaked the collar of his shirt. He was reaching out for her, and she opened her mouth to scream.

Her cellphone rang from the pocket of her coat. She grabbed for it, looking away from the thing pretending to be Trey. She swiped to answer, ready to scream for help. But when she raised her eyes again, he was gone.

"Hello?" Miz Rae's voice came from the phone in her hand. "Serena, are you there?"

"Yeah…" She put the phone to her ear. "Yes, ma'am."

"Did I wake you up?"

"No, ma'am. I'm awake." *Just stressed and spooked,* she thought; she must have been just seeing things. She felt guilty and freaked out about Jacob; of course she'd seen Trey. *And the Frenchman from Jacob's story?* she thought. *Why did you see him?*

"I need you to meet me at the library," Miz Rae was saying. "I need you to take me somewhere."

"At the library out here at Briarwood?" Serena said.

"Out here?" Miz Rae said. "Serena, where are you?"

"Yes, ma'am," she said. "I can meet you. What time?" If she went home to change, she'd need time to explain to Claudine where she'd been.

"I'm here now," Miz Rae said. "Can you hurry?"

"I'll be right there," Serena said. "Give me ten minutes."

Miz Rae stood beside her Cadillac in the library parking lot when Serena pulled up. The sun was just breaking over the horizon behind her, burning red through the trees. "I need you to drive," she said. "We'll take my car."

"Miz Rae, where are we going?" Serena said as she got out. She was having an extremely weird morning. She had never seen her boss dressed in anything but a suit or sweater set for work or a dress and hat for church, but today she wore jeans and a t-shirt from a church picnic from twenty years ago.

"We've got to go up to Boone to the Methodist rest home," Miz Rae said, climbing into the passenger seat of the Cadillac. "Miss Creighton has had a stroke."

"Oh no." She got behind the wheel; the car was already running. "I don't think I've ever driven to Boone." She'd never driven Miz Rae's Cadillac before, either. To her knowledge, no one ever had except Miz Rae and the man who took it off twice a month and washed it.

"The address is already in the GPS," Miz Rae said. "Just drive."

"Yes, ma'am." She had pulled over into the parking lot of Perry's gas station between Briarwood and the library just long enough to text Claudine that she was all right and on her way to meet Miz Rae. Now her phone beeped with an incoming text. "I guess you're wondering how I got here so fast," she said. Miz Rae wasn't likely to have anything good to say about her spending the night with Jacob, but she'd be good practice for facing Claudine.

"Not really." Miz Rae pulled the CD set for the latest James Patterson thriller out of her purse. "Let's just listen to a book." Without waiting for Serena to answer, she put in the first disc.

They stopped twice on the way up, once at a drive-thru for biscuits and coffee and once at a gas station to fill up and pee. At the rest area, Serena checked her messages.

From Claudine, she had gotten one word: *ok*.

From Jacob, she had gotten: *Where did you go? Is everything all right?*

To Claudine, she responded: *On my way w Ms Rae to see Ms Florence Creighton. She had a stroke. Will call later when we know more.*

To Jacob she replied: *I'm fine. I have a work thing. Will call when I get home. Sorry.*

Claudine responded almost immediately: *Y'all be safe.*

Jacob took longer; Miz Rae was on her way back to the car when his text arrived: *Don't be sorry. I'll talk to you tonight. I miss you.*

She smiled and texted back: *I miss you, too.*

Driving in, the Methodist rest home looked like an upscale mountain resort, cabins around a lake, small condo towers with faux-rustic exteriors further back, then what looked like a hotel. This was where Serena parked, and they went in through glass doors discreetly marked "Hospice Care." A nurse met them at the reception desk and led them down the hall.

"She's having a bad morning," the nurse said to Miz Rae, the two of them walking side by side as Serena trailed behind. "The paralysis is minor, but her mind has gone down a hundred percent overnight. She doesn't remember where she is or how she got here. She can't tell us what year it is." She spoke to Miz Rae like the two of them knew one another and had spoken many times before. "We're hoping seeing you will help her relax."

The room was light and airy with pretty curtains and flowers on the desk. But the poor little old White lady strapped down to the bed was cutting up like she was being electrocuted through the mattress.

"Let me up from here, you bitch!" she screamed as soon as she saw the nurse. "I don't know you! I don't belong here! I don't care what they say, I am not crazy!"

"Hush now," Miz Rae said, going to the bed. "It's all right. Nobody thinks you're crazy." She put one hand on Miss Creighton's shoulder as if to keep her still and stroked her hair with the other so gently it shocked Serena. She thought Miz Rae was a good, kind woman, but had never seen her show such tenderness to anyone before.

"You're going to be all right," Miz Rae said as the old woman sank back and stopped fighting.

"Please," Miss Creighton said, starting to cry. "Please just let me have my baby."

"Hush now," Miz Rae said again, her own voice cracking. "Don't start all that."

"I'll take good care of her," Miss Creighton said. "I can keep her safe, I promise. We'll go far away from here."

"Hush…shhhhh…"

"I love her so much. She's my baby, not yours. I would never let anybody hurt her."

"I know you wouldn't." Miz Rae was crying now, a frightening sight. "I know." She clasped Miss Creighton's hand in both of her own. "But it's so late, honey," she said. "It's so late, and the baby's sleeping." She looked back at Serena and jerked her head toward the curtains. "And we're so tired," she went on as Serena closed them. "Aren't you tired, honey?"

"So tired," Miss Creighton said. "But I want her. I won't let you keep her from me anymore."

"All right, honey, if that's what you want," Miz Rae said. "You can take her first thing in the morning."

"Yes." The old woman relaxed.

"Sleep now, and I'll pack her things in the morning, and y'all can go." The nurse smiled at Serena. "Just go on to sleep."

"I want my picture," Miss Creighton said. "Let me hold my pocketbook."

"It's right there in the drawer," the nurse said to Serena, pointing to the bedside table. In the drawer amongst the hairbrush and toothbrush and hand lotion and tissues was an old black and white photograph of a young Black man holding a baby Black girl.

"This?" Serena said, handing it to Miz Rae.

"Here it is," Miz Rae said. She unfastened the restraint on the old woman's tiny wrist and put the photo in her hand. "Now you go on and get some rest."

"She's beautiful, isn't she?" Miss Creighton said, her eyes closing. "Just like her daddy."

"Hush now." Miz Rae stroked Miss Creighton's hair until her breathing evened out in sleep.

The nurse patted Miz Rae on the shoulder. "I'll be at the desk if you need me."

"Wow," Serena said when she was gone. "Miss Creighton had a baby? A Black baby? Or is she just confused?"

"She is confused," Miz Rae said, sliding the photograph from the old lady's hand and sitting in the chair pulled close by the bed. "But of course she had a baby." She stroked Miss Creighton's marble-white hand. "She had me."

"Oh." Serena sat down, too, so hard her chair scraped and made an ugly noise. "Oh God, I'm sorry." She had noticed the lightness of Miz Rae's skin more than once, but that was Saxon County. She never would have guessed her mother was White.

"Nobody much knows about it anymore," Miz Rae said. "They're all gone now—Daddy and my grandmama. That's who she thought I was just now, my grandmama."

"What happened?" Serena said. "Unless you'd rather not say."

"If I didn't want to say, I wouldn't have started." She sat back in her chair and looked at the photograph. "When my daddy came back from Korea, he wanted to go to college. But he knew he'd never pass the entrance exams. His people had been farmers in Alabama; he'd only ever finished eighth grade, and he already had a job working in the mill. He went to the library and met Miss Creighton, the spinster White lady who was the librarian. He told her what he wanted, and she helped him. They used to meet in secret so nobody could get the wrong idea. He'd work his shift until four o'clock every day, then go home and take a bath. Then he'd come to the back door of the library at six, after Miss Creighton locked up, and they would study together. She taught him four years of high school sitting at the circulation desk. She had a friend who was a librarian at a college, and she got old entrance exams from her so he could practice.

"And she got pregnant," Serena said.

"They fell in love." She said it like she could barely believe it, like it was a fairy tale come true. "She believed in his mind, and he wanted her body, and neither one of them had ever had that before."

"That's sweet." Serena remembered Miss Creighton behind the circulation desk when she was a little girl before her parents died, a withered crone in long, dark skirts and bright red lipstick. She tried to imagine her falling in love with the man in the picture. "It's romantic."

"It was," Miz Rae said. "She said it was. But it was also 1956. They weren't married; they couldn't even get married, not in this state. And she was pregnant." She shook her head. "Her family sent her out to California to stay with her aunt until the baby was born, and my grandmama went with her as her maid. She said the whole time she was waiting, she prayed I would be born looking White. She had the idea she could convince them to let her keep me if I was White. But I came out looking like this."

"Oh Miz Rae..." The older woman was dry-eyed now, but Serena felt tears forming.

"My grandmama brought me back and told everybody I was her cousin's child," she went on. "But all the old folks knew the truth."

"But what about your daddy?" Serena said. "Didn't he have a say?"

"He wanted to move to Canada so they could get married," she said. "He even found a job up there with a mining company. But she wouldn't go."

"Why?" Serena said.

"She said it was because she couldn't leave her job," Miz Rae said. "He didn't believe her; he thought she just didn't want to marry him. But I do. Her family has been in charge of the library as long as there's been a library in Saxon County."

"What did he do?"

"He went north and went to college just like he planned. He became a civil engineer for the city of Baltimore. He died when I was in college."

"And your grandmother wouldn't let him take you."

"He didn't ask." She had no expression on her face as she stared down at the photograph. "He married somebody else and had another family. I only ever saw him twice."

Serena's own parents had died in an accident when she was a child, but at least she could remember them loving her and wanting her. "It sounds like your mother loved you," she said. "Did you know—?"

"That the little White lady at the library was my mama? God, no. My grandmama wouldn't let her see me, wouldn't even let her send me a birthday card."

"That sounds so cruel."

"No, Serena," she said, shaking her head. "It was the only way to be safe—for me to be safe, Miss Creighton to be safe, my grandmama and the rest of her family to be safe. You don't know what things were like back then, what the Creighton family was like. As long as they could pretend I never happened, I was fine. But if I had become an embarrassment, if there had been a scandal?" She shook her head again. "Grandmama was a hard woman, but she was smart. She did what she had to do."

"How did you find out?" Serena said. She had woken up that morning freaked out because she'd spent the night with Jacob, but that felt like manufactured drama compared to this.

"I shouldn't have been able to afford to go to college," Miz Rae said. "But a week after I was accepted, a second letter came from the lady who was the head of the library science department saying I had a full scholarship if I wanted it. I hadn't decided on a major yet, and I had always liked the library, so I said thank you very much."

"Didn't that seem strange to you?"

"Of course it did. But all my life I had felt like the Lord was looking out for me special. Even though I was this abandoned child, even though my grandmama had no money to speak of, every time I really needed something, things would work out where I got it."

"And it was her."

"And it was her," she said. "The week after I started college, the head of the department invited me to come to tea at her house to meet the lady who had endowed my scholarship. And it was Miss Creighton. I knew her from the library at home, of course, but I hadn't had any idea she even knew my name. She said she had been watching me all my life, and she thought I had a lot of potential. We became good friends. I wrote to her every week, just like I did Grandmama. Then when I graduated, she made the Board offer me a job. That made Grandmama furious. She wanted me to go north and get away from Saxonville. But I wanted to work for Miss Creighton."

"When did she tell you the truth?" Serena asked.

"Not until she got sick and knew she would have to retire," she said. "We had just found out Tom was coming and that I'd be running the branch out at Briarwood. She told me not to be upset, that I would be better off. She said she was glad that burden would go to somebody else, that she prayed my whole life that I could get away from it somehow. I thought she was talking out of her head. We had always talked about me taking over for her someday, and she had always seemed to like the idea. That's when she showed me this picture. I recognized it; my grandmama had kept one just like it on her mantelpiece. And that's when she told me the truth."

"Wow," Serena said. "I don't know what to say, Miz Rae. I can't even imagine what that must have felt like."

"Relief." Her tears had started again. "I love her, Serena. I always loved her. To find out that I was hers, that she had always loved me… it was a precious gift."

"I am so sorry." She couldn't help herself; she got up and hugged her.

For a few seconds, Miz Rae allowed it. "Now, now," she said, pushing Serena away. "Why don't you go see if you can find us some coffee?"

The hospice center didn't have a cafeteria, just a vending machine putting out a brown liquid that was coffee in nothing but name. She took the Cadillac and drove out to the highway to a chain coffee shop and got herself something cold and sweet and Miz Rae a large coffee, black.

When she got back to the room, Miss Creighton was awake again, and Miz Rae was bending over her. "Baby girl, you have got to get out," the old woman said. "He took it all anyway, didn't he? Let them have it." Her speech was much more slurred now than it had been before, but she sounded much more lucid. "Forget the library, forget Briarwood. Just go."

"Hey Serena," Miz Rae said, looking back at her—kids at the library always said Miz Rae had eyes in the back of her head. "Miss Creighton, you remember me telling you about Serena?"

"Hey Miss Creighton," Serena said, putting the coffee down on the desk to join them. "How are you feeling?"

The old woman's blue eyes showed no hint of recognition, and she didn't smile. "Fuck them, Rae," she said, clutching Miz Rae's hand in a fist that looked like talons. "You hear me? Fuck them all."

"Now, you don't need to be worrying about all that," Miz Rae said.

"That damned Pink will be in my business before I'm cold," the old woman went on. "You just let him have it. You pack up and get out. That's what I should have done." Through all of this, she stared straight at Serena. Now her eyes went wide. "You've seen him, haven't you?" she said. "I saw him, too."

Miz Rae had already gone to the door. "Nurse!"

"Seen who, ma'am?" Serena said.

"You know who." Her hands fluttered on the blanket like dying birds. "I never really believed it." The hard, lucid voice was gone; she sounded weak and frightened. "I never even read those papers. I didn't want to know." She gasped, grabbing for Serena's wrist, and her eyes rolled back in her head.

"Get out of the way!" Miz Rae said, pushing Serena aside. "Go get that damned nurse!"

"I'm here," the nurse said, pushing past Serena, too. "Now you know she has a DNR. Senator Collins—"

"Don't even tell me about Pink Collins," Miz Rae said. "She's in pain, damn it! Make her not in pain!"

"Yes, ma'am." The nurse gave the old woman a shot, and Miss Creighton sank back into her pillows with her eyelids mercifully closed. "It won't be long now," the nurse said in a tone she obviously meant to be soothing. "You want me to call the doctor?"

"It's all right," Miz Rae said, sinking back down in her chair. "We'll wait." Serena handed her the coffee she'd brought. "Praise Jesus."

The nurse left, and Serena started to move away. Miz Rae caught her hand and squeezed it, holding it to her cheek before she let go.

14

Jacob stirred slightly when he heard Serena's voice outside the RV. A tiny part of his brain wondered who was with her, but he was sleeping so soundly, his body wouldn't move. Then he heard her car start and stopped struggling, sinking back into sleep. He didn't wake again until some time later when he heard another, larger engine rumbling closer. He sat up and peered out the window—Rooster's truck. He watched the contractor get out, grab his toolbox, and head up to the house. He felt a little guilty knowing he had slept with this good man's daughter-in-law the night before. But where had she gone to, anyway?

He got his phone and texted: *Where did you go? Is everything all right?*

He waited for an answer, but none came.

He put on some coffee, got dressed, and poured two cups.

He found Rooster on the side porch with the recently restored French doors laid out on a pair of sawhorses. "Good morning, young man," the contractor said.

"Good morning to you," Jacob said, handing over one of the cups of coffee—after two months, he knew how Rooster took it; this was a ritual between them now. "I didn't expect to see you today."

"Yeah, I let the crew have the holiday," he said. "But I wanted to go on and get the new locks on these doors." He sounded as cheerful and friendly as ever, but there was an extra note in his tone, a plastic edge of fake heartiness. "I understand you had the ghost wranglers up here last night."

"We did," Jacob said. "I did, yes. Did Serena tell you?"

"She left us a note yesterday saying that was where she was going." He put down his coffee and went back to hand-chiseling a notch for the lock. "Did y'all find any spooks?"

"I haven't heard the final report yet, but I doubt it," Jacob said. "I'm sorry, Rooster. She left early this morning. I don't know where she went."

"She's with her boss, Miz Rae," Rooster said. "She texted Claudine right after sunup. She didn't tell you?" He didn't look up from his work.

"Not a word." The other man said nothing. "Do I need to apologize?" Jacob said. "Have I overstepped some boundary?"

"No, no, Serena's a grown woman," he said, still not looking up.

"I care for her a lot, Rooster," Jacob said. "This isn't just…I wouldn't ever…" He shook his head, trying to clear the fog of thoughts Serena inspired. How to explain that being with this woman he barely knew felt like his life's first moment of clarity? Like for once he was exactly where he was meant to be, doing exactly what he was meant to be doing? "I love her," he said, because wasn't that what true love meant?

Rooster shook his head, smiling, amused. "That's good, I guess." He squatted down and blew sawdust out of the notch "Does she love you?"

Jacob laughed. "You're asking me?" The phone in his pocket beeped—an answer from Serena: *I'm fine. Have a work thing. Will call when I get home. Sorry.* "Does that look like she's pining for me to you?" he asked, showing it to Rooster. "I'm over my head, man."

"All right, all right," Rooster said. "I don't need details." But he was still smiling. "I ain't going to pretend to be happy about it. But I ain't going to shoot you." He switched to a finer chisel. "My wife, on the other hand. She might be a different story."

"Is she upset?" He heard a car driving up from the road—Tom's car, he saw as it rounded the bend.

"She ain't talking," Rooster said. "And that ain't never a good sign."

Tom pulled up behind Rooster's truck and got out. "Good morning." He was dressed for a hike and as cheerful as Jacob had ever seen him.

"Good morning." Jacob waited for him on the porch, and Rooster kept working. "Rooster was just asking me, did you and your friends have any luck last night?"

"We won't really know until we check all the tapes," Tom said, shaking Jacob's hand then offering the hand to Rooster. "Morning, Mr. Decatur."

"Morning, Thomas," Rooster said, pausing to shake.

"Naomi thought she felt something," Tom went on. "But Evie would tell you Naomi always feels something."

"She did mention that," Jacob said. "What brings you out this morning?"

"I was hoping you'd let me walk around the property a bit," Tom said. "I keep thinking about that Frenchman's journal. He wrote that they found a stone structure near a water source. We ought to be able to verify at least that much of his story."

"You want to find it?" Jacob said. "You don't think I made it up?"

"No," Tom said. "I mean, I didn't."

Rooster chuckled over his chiseling.

"Did you?" Tom asked.

"I did not," Jacob said. "And thank you. Your faith in my integrity is as rare as it is reassuring."

"You know he's pulling your leg, right?" Rooster said.

"I swear I'm not," Jacob said. "I found that journal in the papers that came with the house. Somebody might have faked it, but it wasn't me." He had never considered that the cursed shelter from the Frenchman's story would still be somewhere on the property, but

Tom was right. If it was real, it must have been. "There is a creek that runs through the property," he said. "I've heard it when I run."

"You run out here in these woods?" Rooster said. "By yourself? Are you crazy?"

"I always keep my phone with me." That was a lie, and even if it hadn't been, phone service at Briarwood was a joke.

"Do you mind if I try to find it?" Tom said.

"Not at all. I think it's a great idea," Jacob said. "But I'm coming with you." He finished his coffee. "Come on, Rooster. Come with us."

"Me?" Rooster said. "No, no. There ain't nothing I need in them woods."

"Aren't you curious?" Tom said.

"Not especially," Rooster said. "Well..."

"What?" Jacob said.

"I will say this." He put down his chisel. "All my life I've been hearing about this place, about how it's supposed to be cursed or haunted and how anybody who comes here ends up cursed, too. But I've been working out here for months now, and all I see is a rundown old house and some grown-up woods. It's just a place like any other place." He held up a hand to Tom. "And I know you say different, but I don't believe in all that mess. I believe when we die we might go to heaven or we might go to hell or we might not go anyplace at all. But I don't believe we just stay anywhere, not even Briarwood." He shrugged, smiling. "So maybe I ought to go look around after all."

"Maybe so," Jacob said.

"If nothing else, I can put Claudine's mind at rest. She thinks the boogeyman lives up here somewhere." He reached for his gloves. "Hell, why not? Let's go."

Jacob expected the creek to be little more than a trickle, and within sight of the house, it was. But as they followed it deeper and deeper into the thick underbrush and towering pines, it broadened and deepened, spilling over rocks and down deep red clay gorges. "Look at that!" Rooster said, pointing as a silver fish surfaced over a waterfall. "This thing is full of fish."

"Nobody's fished here for almost two centuries," Tom said. "Nothing but other wild animals, anyway."

"The first week we had a crew up at the house, we saw the biggest raccoon I ever saw in my life," Rooster said. "He kept coming up, trying to get in the garbage cans, and I swear to you, he had no fear. We'd holler at him, and he'd just look at us like we were on his nerves and go right back to working on that lid. Some of the boys wanted to get a gun and shoot him, but I couldn't see any point in that. We just got some better garbage cans with heavier lids, and he stopped coming around."

"A raccoon will catch and eat a fish," Tom said.

"Hell yeah, he will," Rooster said. "A bobcat will, too, and a coyote. I wouldn't be surprised if you had a bear up in here somewhere." He grinned. "How you liking that RV at night, Jake?"

"I haven't seen any bears yet," Jacob said. "But there are definitely deer. I scare off at least half a dozen when I come out every morning."

"Oh yeah," Rooster said. "They just love that new winter grass we planted."

"Fish and deer," Tom said. "This really must have seemed like paradise to those Frenchmen."

"I'm surprised you don't have redneck boys sneaking in here to hunt and fish right now," Rooster said.

"They won't come here," Tom said with an impish grin of his own. "Hadn't you heard? This place is haunted."

They both laughed, but Jacob didn't find it all that funny. "Do either of you smell that?" The cold wind that rattled through the trees carried a stench that grew stronger as they followed the stream. At first he thought he imagined it, but now that they had stopped, he was sure it was real.

"Smell what?" Tom said.

"Something's dead somewhere around here," Rooster said. "Been dead a while from the stink."

"Oh yeah," Tom said. "Yeah, I smell it." He laughed as if he were embarrassed. "I thought it was just me."

"Probably a deer some coyote didn't finish eating," Rooster said.

"It smells like a crypt," Jacob said. "There's a place in Spain, a charnel house…" He broke off, laughing himself. "So yeah, something dead."

"If you boys are scared of haints, I've got plenty to do up at the house," Rooster said.

"Haints are my specialty, remember?" Tom said.

"Mine, too," Jacob said. "Let's go a little further."

"How far is it to the highway, anyway?" Rooster said as they set off again.

"Miles yet," Tom said. "The Briarwood property is huge." The stream was widening out again, and the half-frozen banks were springy underfoot. And the smell was getting stronger.

"What is that?" Rooster said, pointing ahead. They could see the sides of a brick structure through the trees. "Another old barn or cotton dock, maybe?" The property around the house was dotted with the ruins of plantation buildings built of this same brick.

"This far away from the house?" Jacob said, leading the way.

They came out of the trees into a clearing. The building was a plain brick box built directly over the stream, three stories tall. "Y'all know what that is?" Rooster said. "That's an old cotton mill."

"That's not possible," Tom said. "The first mills weren't built in Saxon County until after the Civil War. And Briarwood has been sealed up since the 1830s."

"That's as may be," Jacob said. "But aren't these tire tracks?"

"Well, I'll be damned," Rooster said. The overgrown yard around the mill was cut neatly in two by a rutted path in the red clay mud marked with tire treads. "Some ol' boy has been bringing a truck up in here or a jeep. A car wouldn't make it."

"Is it just me, or is the smell coming from inside there?" Tom said.

"Oh yeah," Jacob said.

"You know what it's got to be, right?" Rooster said, sounding a lot less confident than he had before. "Boys have been coming in here poaching after all and leaving their mess in that mill. There's probably twenty years worth of rotten deer carcasses with no heads piled up in there."

"Maybe so," Jacob said, but he didn't believe it. Ever since they'd come into the woods, a strange feeling had been growing over him like a second skin, not fear but fury. Briarwood belonged to him. How dare any other predator kill there? But since when did he think of himself as a predator? He felt a stabbing pain in his temple; the stench was starting to give him a headache. He shook his head, pushing back the pain and the thought that inspired it. "Let's have a look."

The wide main door stood half-ajar on rusted iron hinges. When Jacob swung it open, the stench of rotten flesh slammed into them, physically knocking them back. This was no ancient crypt; this was still fresh enough to smell juicy. Even with his lips pressed shut and jaw clenched against it, Jacob could taste the rot like slime on his tongue. He put a hand over his mouth, gorge rising in his throat. His flesh crawled as visions of maggots squirmed in his imagination, and he felt faint.

"That is nasty," Rooster said, still at the back of the group where he couldn't see.

"Oh my God," Tom said, his voice rising into a sob.

Jacob stood frozen, and stared.

The inside of the mill looked half-finished, with its second story no more than a skeleton framework of raw beams and rafters. And hanging from the beams like hams in a smokehouse were what looked like dozens of human corpses.

"Sweet Jesus," Rooster said as he pushed past Tom and saw.

Jacob crossed himself for the first time in decades. "What the hell is this?" he said. Some of the hanging corpses were little more than dry skeletons. Others were still in active decay. All of them, as far as they could tell from the flesh remaining, were Black.

"Can't you guess?" Rooster said in a voice as deadly as the stench. He moved deeper into the horror, pushing past Jacob. Tom started to retch, stumbling behind him.

"Get out," Jacob said, catching him before he fell. "This is a crime scene. Call the police." Tom nodded and ran for the door. Jacob followed Rooster.

"No haint did this," Rooster said. He was standing in the center of the slaughterhouse, surrounded by the hanging dead. His face was blue-black in the ugly, filtered light. "This was men." From the clothes on the corpses, it was obvious this horror had been going on for a very long time. The skeletons wore nineteenth-century buttoned trousers and the rags of full-cut shirts. Some were in suits, some in work clothes. Some were still intact enough to show signs of torture; some still had half-rotten faces contorted in pain. "So many," Roster said. "God damn them…look how many!" He turned to Jacob in fury. "Do you see this?"

"I see it." What else could he say? "Tom is calling the police."

Rooster—Henry, he reminded himself; this man's name was Henry—made an ugly, scoffing sound and turned away. Then his face changed, crumpled from anger into grief. "No…" He ran into the shadows, pushing hanging dead men aside like gruesome curtains, making Jacob dodge to follow him as gorge rose in his throat.

He found him with his arms wrapped around the legs of a corpse that could have been the newest, a young man in track pants and sneakers. The flesh of his bare chest and back was flayed to the bone and hung in dry ribbons, but his face was still recognizable. "No," Henry kept repeating, clutching the dead man, trying to pull him down. "No no no no no—"

"Henry, stop!" Jacob said, grabbing him.

"Don't you touch me!" Henry roared. He punched Jacob in the jaw so hard Jacob staggered backward, seeing stars. "I'll kill you, you cracker son of a bitch!" He collapsed to his knees on the ground. "This is my son!"

"Oh dear God," Jacob said, falling to his knees, too. "Sweet Christ in heaven…" Henry howled in grief, and Jacob wept with him, helpless to do more. His son…Serena's husband? But no, Serena's husband had died out west. In the distance, he heard the wail of sirens. "We'll find the men who did this," he promised. The rage he had felt before was nothing; suddenly he was blind with fury. How dare they? "They'll pay," he promised Henry. "All of them will pay."

15

The Saxon County Sheriff's Office did the best they could. When Tom's initial call to 911 went through, they dispatched a single patrol car to find out what he was raising so much hell about, and the officers stopped at Perry's Gas and Grill on the way to pick up a hot dog each and put a call in to Kirk Benson.

But as soon as he hung up with 911, Tom called his old college roommate, a sportswriter for a newspaper two counties away. And when he saw that single cop car coming up the drive, Jacob called the lovely young woman from the Charlotte TV news who had interviewed him at Halloween. And once Rooster had spoken to Claudine on the phone and made her aware that their second son, Davon, had been found dead, he called their minister, Reverend Holloway, who had connections at both the NAACP and the Southern Poverty Law Center. Davon had been missing since a year before their oldest, Trey, Serena's husband, had died in Las Vegas. They had known in their hearts Davon must be dead. He wouldn't have simply vanished without telling his parents why. But they held out hope.

By the time Kirk Benson called Pink Collins and interrupted him in the middle of making final arrangements for his dead Aunt

Florence, there was nothing Pink could do to "calm things down." In less than an hour, Briarwood was crawling with reporters, activists, and state and federal law enforcement officers who owed precisely nothing to the Montgomery Trust.

"Sorry boys," Pink told Kirk and Frank Sweatt and Chuck Kennedy on a conference call. "There ain't a damned thing I can do to slow this thing down now. I'm as fucked as you are."

"Not quite," Kirk said with admirable calm. "But you can be the one to call Amanda."

An hour later, the entirety of the Briarwood property was declared a crime scene. Jacob, Tom, and Rooster had each been questioned, and their vehicles thoroughly searched, including Jacob's RV. They were told to leave the premises along with the reporters and activists. The victim's advocate for the State Law Enforcement Division out of Columbia walked Rooster to his truck and made sure he had a card to call if he needed anything, and the special agent of the Department of Justice Regional office in Charlotte who was provisionally in charge shook Jacob's hand and promised to keep him informed. Tom stood under the pecan trees alone, just watching, waiting.

The whole circus relocated to the parking lot of the Briarwood Community Center. Jacob made his RV, WiFi hub, and satellite phone available to Reverend Holloway and his friends and himself available to any reporter who wanted to interview him outside. Most of them posed him so their cameras picked up the parade of police cars, fire trucks, and ambulances passing back and forth along the two-lane highway behind him, lights on but sirens off, coming and going from Briarwood.

Against her husband's specific instructions, Claudine arrived at the community center just as the sun was going down. Though they had never met, Jacob recognized her immediately and broke off in mid-sentence with the pretty news anchor he had called first to go meet Claudine as soon as she parked. He shielded her from the reporters and led her to the RV and her husband.

"Serena is on her way home," she told him as he opened the door for her. She put a hand on his arm. "She should be here soon."

"I'll watch for her," Jacob promised. "I'll bring her straight inside." Tom had already explained to him that the dead man in the mill was not Serena's late husband, Trey, but his younger brother, Davon.

As soon as Claudine and Rooster saw one another, they both burst into tears. Jacob closed the door and left them to their grief.

Soon after, from where he stood under an oak tree smoking a cigarette, Tom Stewart saw Serena's car pull into the back side of the parking lot. She looked frazzled, but calm, and beautiful as ever. As Jacob crossed the parking lot to meet her, Tom went to his own car. He drove straight home. Evie was already sleeping; this wasn't the first time he'd come home late. He kicked off his boots and crawled in bed beside her still fully clothed. She stirred, and he made a little soothing noise, taking the remote control out of her hand and setting it aside before he curled in close.

"Baby?" She wriggled free and turned to face him then put a hand over her nose and mouth. "Jesus God, baby, what is that smell?"

He tried to answer, to tell her it was nothing, that he'd explain tomorrow, to push it all away just one more night. But when he opened his mouth, a horrible noise came out, a sob from the bottom of his soul that went on and on, hitching for breath but not stopping. He felt like he was being turned inside out, and he thought he might be sick again. But all that came out was howling, a hurt dog in a trap.

"Tommy, what?" She was touching him, pushing his hair back from his forehead, crying herself, obviously terrified, and that made it worse. "Tommy, tell me what happened."

But he couldn't say it, not to her. He grabbed her and crushed her close, rocking her as he cried.

16

Serena saw Jacob coming toward her as soon as Miz Rae pulled into the parking lot. "You go on," Miz Rae said. Claudine had called and given them the broad strokes while they were on their way back from the mountains. "Whatever you find out, you can tell me all about it at work on Monday." For the first time since Serena had met her, Miz Rae looked every day of her age, hollow-eyed and worn to the bone.

"Are you all right?" Serena said. "Can I call somebody to come stay with you?"

"Regina's already at the house," she said. "Just go on now. They'll be waiting for you." She patted Serena's hand. "Tell Claudine I'll be praying."

"I will." She got out just as Jacob reached for the door handle. He waved to Miz Rae as she was pulling out, and she was shocked to see Miz Rae wave back.

"Hello, love," Jacob said. He didn't hug her, but he did squeeze her hand. "Henry and Claudine are in the caravan with the minister. I told them I'd watch for you."

"Thanks." He started to steer her toward the RV. "Wait…" She couldn't face Claudine yet. Her voice on the phone had been horrible enough, a flashback to the night she had called her from Las Vegas to tell her Trey was dead. "Can we go in the library for a minute? I'm still not all that clear on what's going on. I need to get my bearings."

"Absolutely." He still held her hand. "If you have a key."

She led the way into the community center and locked the door behind them then led him through the dark library to the office at the back before she turned on a light. She closed the blinds and locked the door, then slammed herself into his arms.

"It's all right, darling," he said, holding her and stroking her hair. His accent was more pronounced when he was moved; she had noticed it in bed the night before. "I'm so sorry." She wrapped her arms around his waist and pressed her cheek against his chest. "Were you and your brother-in-law close?"

"I only ever saw him once, at me and Trey's wedding," she said. Davon and Trey had been close as boys, and they talked on the phone at least once a week. But Serena had never been part of that. She was part of Trey's new life. His life away—away from his family, away from Saxonville. When Devon had disappeared, she knew it shattered Trey . But he barely talked to her about it. He had shut her out, and she had let him. "Claudine said there were other bodies," she said, making herself pull away.

"The last count I heard was sixty-one," Jacob said. "But because some of them are so old, there could be more that have fallen apart. The copper in charge, Special Agent Harris, said they'd have every available ambulance working all night to move them all."

"Sixty-one?" She felt her knees dissolving and reached for him again, and he guided her down to a chair.

"I couldn't believe it," he said, also sitting. "I've written things like that, seen them in my mind, but never…I couldn't begin to describe what it was like." His hands shook, and she put hers over his.

"You will, though," she said. "Eventually." They looked like they were praying together, facing one another knees to knees. "And all of them had been lynched?"

"Harris said it was far and away the worst hate crime he's ever seen," he said. "And it's obviously been going on for a very long time—there's no telling how many people were involved."

"Do they think it's the Klan?" she said.

"I think so, yes," he said. "But he said it's unusual for any Klan chapter to be organized and disciplined enough to maintain something even close to this without getting caught." For the first time she noticed how pale he looked, with deep, dark circles around his eyes. "As awful as it is, finding your brother-in-law among the victims gives them a starting point in their investigation. They know who he is and exactly when he disappeared."

"Whoever killed him is still in Saxon County." She felt cold and sick and throbbing with such anger she could barely see. "God, Jacob, this place...this horrible place."

"I know, darling—"

"You don't. I mean..." She pressed his hands then let him go. "You're sweet, but you don't know. You can't. I can't, or I couldn't, and I'm right in the middle of it, and Rooster and Claudine and Trey...he was so glad to get away from here and so scared he might have to come back." She got up; she couldn't sit still anymore. "I saw him."

She had all but decided to never tell him or anybody else about the ghost she'd seen that morning. She'd been feeling sleepy and guilty; it couldn't have been real. But now it spilled out. "This morning out at Briarwood, I saw a ghost."

"What are you saying?"

"When I was leaving this morning, when you were still asleep, I saw a ghost come out of the woods." She crossed her arms across her stomach with her shoulders hunched high. "He was solid. I thought at first he was a tramp who had wandered up from the road. Then I realized...the way he was dressed...he was the man from your story, the one who raped the Native American woman. Except you didn't write that story, did you?"

"I did find that journal and get it translated," he said. "But I don't know if it's really authentic. How could you be sure that's who you saw?"

"It wasn't him, not really," she said. "It was something else, something that wanted me to see it and see what it was. It looked like the Frenchman, then it changed." Tears spilled from her eyes, surprising her. She hadn't known she felt like crying. "It turned itself into my dead husband, Trey."

"Sweetheart …"

"It was coming toward me, talking to me, reaching for me, and I was so scared," she said. "But maybe it didn't want to hurt me."

"Serena, sweetheart, your Trey didn't die at Briarwood, did he?" Jacob said.

"My husband died beside the highway between Las Vegas and Los Angeles" she said. "If what the friends of the man who supposedly shot him said was true, he was dealing drugs on Nellis Air Force base where he worked. There's only one reason I can think of why he might have been doing something so stupid. And that's because he couldn't pay his debts and he couldn't find any way out for us except to come back here to Saxonville. He would rather have risked his life and his honor or even gone to prison than do that."

She had broken out in gooseflesh. He reached for her, but she dodged away; she couldn't stand for him to touch her. "This place is evil, Jacob. It's always been evil, and I knew it, sort of. There are always little micro-aggressions everywhere you go, little things people say and do and don't do. But it's worse here. You aren't ever allowed to forget here, not even for a minute. You always know they hate you."

"Who hates—?"

"White people, Jacob," she said, pronouncing each syllable as if he were a stupid child. "When you're Black, you know they think you're shit—" He opened his mouth, and she held up her hand. "I swear to God, if you say not all White people, I will kill you." He nodded, sitting back down. "You find a way to get used to it. You tell yourself it doesn't matter what they think or that it isn't really as bad as you know it is because what choice do you have? You have to live, right?" She sank back down in her chair. "But then something happens like today, and you remember. Do you know where I was today?"

"Henry said you went somewhere with Miz Rae," he said.

"I went to be with her while she watched her mother die," she said. "Her old, sick, lonely, spinster, White mama who could never be with the man she loved or raise the child they made together because she was White and he was Black and the baby was Black, and her White family just could not have it, and she was scared to leave them. That old bitch lived and died alone rather than let anybody know the people she loved were Black."

"Serena, darling, that isn't me," he said like it mattered, like he was what she was talking about, like the two of them together was the point and not just a fluke outside the system.

"And now I hear about this lynching shed, this factory for hanging and torturing Black men that has been just sitting out here all this time. Who are these people doing this killing, Jacob? Who could be that evil and just keep going on with their lives like nothing is wrong? How am I, how is any Black person in Saxon County or anywhere else supposed to live? How do we ever feel safe? How can we not want to kill them all, get them before they get us?"

"So leave here," he said. "Leave Saxon County, leave this whole horrible country."

"And how am I supposed to do that?" she said. "You think I live with my in-laws because I like it? I don't have any choice—even living with them, I can't pay my bills. How am I supposed to just pick up and leave? And what would it accomplish if I did? It wouldn't change anything."

"Leave with me." He took her hands again, and she let him because she was just so tired. She couldn't fight him, too. "Briarwood is a crime scene now; heaven only knows when I'll be able to go back or when the crews will be able to get back to work on the restoration. And even if I could go back, after what I saw today, I couldn't stay there. I don't know if I'll ever be able to stay there again."

"You're leaving?" she said. "You're going back to Ireland?"

"I'm going to Spain. I have a house there near the ocean, a tiny place, but the views are like heaven." He touched her face, brushing a curl back from her temple. "I have to get away from here, angel. I have to try to write."

"Did you know you were leaving last night?" she said.

"No, God, no," he said. "Last night…everything is different now. Almost everything." He pulled her into his arms. "Come with me, Serena, please. I can't bear to leave you behind."

"Jacob, last night was lovely, but it was…weird," she said. How could she explain to him what being with him meant? Real or not, that ghost had known its business, coming to her as Trey. "I mean, I don't know about you, but I don't just do stuff like that. And now this, everything that's happened today." She splayed her hands across his chest, holding on to him and holding him away. "Did you hear what I said before? I saw something. I saw a ghost."

"I did hear you, love, and I believe you." He took her hands and kissed them before folding them between his own. "That's part of why I think we need to go. Not forever, just…we need a break." She could see how scared he was. His hands shook, and pure terror filled his eyes. "Come with me to Spain. You can read, do research, walk on the beach. Give yourself a break for once. Let me take care of you."

"But you don't know me," she said. "Not really. And I don't know you. How can I trust you—why would you want me to trust you to just carry me off and take care of me? That's not real, Jacob. That's a fairy tale." But it was such a beautiful fairy tale. If they went away, she wouldn't have to face the gossip of Saxonville or Claudine's disappointment. She could rest, finally; rest and heal and let him love her. Wasn't that what she'd always wanted? But what would happen when he stopped?

"You do know me, and I know you," he said. "We've known one another since the moment we met on that broken-down porch on that horrible, haunted house. I love you, Serena. Come with me."

Did she love him back? It seemed stupid that she might, childish, but she felt something, a pulling, yearning ache for him, a burning desire to trust him. "I do love you, I think," she said, pressing her cheek to his chest. "Can you let me think about it?" The dream of the museum rose up in her mind, of having a purpose, a mission. After discovering this horror, shouldn't she want that even more? But she was so tired, so scared, all she could think was how sweet it would be to feel safe.

He squeezed her tight. "Of course." She turned her face up to his, and he kissed her. "Ready to see your family now?"

She took a deep breath and let it out. "Not remotely. But yeah, let's go."

17

Jacob lay beside Serena, sleeping again in the nest of the RV. Everybody else had gone. The parking lot of the Briarwood Community Center was deathly quiet except for the hum of the cars and ambulances still passing sporadically back and forth to Briarwood. Jacob had given charge over his dead man's mill to others, and now he was determined to run away. Serena might even go with him, she said, back over the ocean. And the Dark Man who watched them felt despair.

But Saxon County, as always, served him well. Four pick-up trucks skidded into the gravel parking lot, horns and country music blaring, Confederate battle flags flying from the beds. The hooded men inside hooted and shrieked with delight. They spilled their beer into the dirt and called for Serena by name.

The cross was already soaked in pitch, and the ground underneath the gravel was soft mud. Planting it was a job of minutes, even for this drunken crew. The cross was lit before Jacob was fully awake.

Serena saw it first and screamed, grabbing for Jacob as she peered through the blinds. He woke up, confused and frightened, but his first thought was to protect Serena. "It's all right," he told her, reaching for his jeans. "Call 911."

Then the first Molotov cocktail hit the side of the RV. The window over the bed exploded, and the curtains burst into flames. More bombs were exploding and spilling fire from every side. The RV filled with smoke in less than a minute. Serena saw a darker shadow on the smoke even in the chaos, and she froze. Then Jacob grabbed her, scooped her up, bed sheet, blanket, and all, and ran for the door

He burst out of the tin can house screaming not in fear but in pure, burning rage, and the Dark Man leapt from the ground to the treetops with joy, knowing his moment had come. Jacob shoved Serena behind him toward her car.

"You dare?" he roared, advancing naked on the Klansmen in their sheets. The young ones gaped in shock, but the old one pulled his hood back down over his face. He jumped back behind the wheel of his truck and slammed it into gear as Jacob picked up a smoldering bomb one of them had dropped and threw it. The amorphous shape of the Dark Man shrieked and gamboled through the treetops like the wind as the bomb exploded on Kirk Benson's hood and his truck swung out of control. The young one in the passenger seat, his grandson and namesake, leapt free as the truck crashed into the burning RV, but his robes were on fire. Jacob laughed, an old god standing naked bathed in the light of the flames.

The dark shape swept down from the treetops and streamed into his nose and ears and laughing mouth. Jacob and the Dark Man looked at Serena, so beautiful, their goddess, and they loved her, raged for her. And they were one.

Serena watched the white, hooded robes of the man behind the wheel of the burning truck catch fire, then she saw his face—Kirk Benson. Then he was burning, melting like a horror from a movie, too awful to be real. She was screaming, but Jacob was laughing.

"Stop it!" She shoved him, trying to snap him out of it. The second Klansman rolled on the ground, screaming, trying to put out the fire on his robes. Without thinking, she threw the blanket wrapped around her over him, trying to stifle the flames.

"Help me!" he kept screaming with his voice still muffled by the hood. "Jesus, please help me!" The other three trucks raced away, skidding past a green ambulance as it turned into the parking lot—one of the meat wagons from the state morgue. A state police car was right behind it, and she could hear more sirens in the distance coming closer.

"Don't touch him!" Jacob roared. He moved her bodily out of the way and snatched the smoldering blanket off the Klansman. "Who are you?" He snatched off the hood and exposed a weeping teenage boy.

"Kirk's grandson," Serena said. She had helped the boy research a school paper on Frederick Douglass for Black History Month the year before. He had always called her "Miss Serena."

"Who are the others?" Jacob said, kneeling over him. He should have been ridiculous, a skinny, naked White man with gray in his beard, but he was terrifying, even to Serena.

The men from the ambulance had reached them. "Sir, step back," one of them said, touching Jacob's bony shoulder.

"Not until he says their names," Jacob said, bashing the horrible boy's head against the dirt.

"I'll tell you," Kirk the Third was blubbering. "I'll tell you everything. Please don't let me die."

Police cars and a firetruck were pulling into the lot. The RV burned so high now, the pecan trees above it were starting to catch. "Jacob, stop it," Serena said. "We have to move."

"Here, miss," the second ambulance driver said, covering her with another blanket.

"Don't touch her!" Jacob said, lunging at the man. Then he froze, and his face went pale. "Serena?" He clutched at his heart and staggered.

"Help him!" she said. In the distance, she saw the state cops holding back the local cops and waving the firetruck through. She caught Jacob and hobbled with him, trying to hold him up. "I think he's having a heart attack!"

"It's all right, miss," the paramedic said. "We've got him." He lowered Jacob to the ground and went to work on him with a stethoscope while his partner stayed with Kirk the Third. The firemen were spraying Kirk's burning truck, and a fireman in a flame-retardant suit was trying to get him out. Over the paramedic's shoulder, she could see Jacob's face.

"It's okay, baby," she said. "I'm okay. Everything's going to be fine."

He smiled at her, and for a moment, she thought she saw his eyes turn red. Then he turned his head, and the illusion disappeared—it must have been the reflection of the flames.

A second crew of paramedics appeared with a gurney and lifted him onto it, while the first guy put an oxygen mask over his face. "Serena!" she heard him say from behind the mask.

"I want to go with him." she said.

The first paramedic looked around at the cops and fire and chaos. She didn't doubt that he knew, like she did, that she was the star and possibly only witness to what had happened, that everybody would want to talk to her. "Sure thing," he said. "Come on."

18

Gloria arrived at the Saxon County Medical Center eighteen hours after receiving Serena's call. The sidewalk out front was crowded with fans and reporters waiting for word on Jacob's condition and the attack that had caused it, and police blocked the hallway to his room. As she tried to explain who she was and fumbled through her carryon bag for her ID, a young man in a wrinkled blue suit walked up. "It's all right, Aaron," he said to the policeman who had stopped her, flashing his own badge. "This is Mrs. McGinnas."

"The ex Mrs. McGinnas," she corrected. "But yes. Who are you?"

"I'm David Duncan, the deputy solicitor," he said, offering his hand. "The prosecuting attorney for the case against the men who attacked your ex-husband." He glanced at the policeman who was obviously pretending not to listen. "But let's go on inside. I know Jacob is wanting to see you."

Jacob was sitting up in bed looking pale but alert. A beautiful Black woman of no more than thirty perched on a chair beside him. It had to be Serena.

"There she is," Jacob said, breaking out in a smile, and Gloria felt tears burning her eyes.

"What have you done to yourself?" she said, hugging him. She expected him to feel fragile, but his arms around her felt strong. Even in a hospital gown with an IV in his arm, he looked healthier than he had the last time she'd seen him in Dublin.

"Just a touch of heart attack," he said. "Gloria, this is Serena Decatur. Serena, meet Gloria, my boss."

"If she knows you at all, she knows that's a lie," Gloria said as she shook Serena's hand. "Lovely to meet you, Serena. Thank you so much again for calling."

"I knew you'd want to know," Serena said. Her voice was as pretty as her face, with a subtle Southern accent. "And I knew Jacob was going to want to see you as soon as he woke up."

"Y'all, I hate to interrupt, but I've got to get back to the courthouse," the attorney said.

"Yes, David, please," Jacob said. He seemed less like an invalid than a king holding court, as at his ease as she had ever seen him. "Gloria, love, David's just come from a preliminary hearing in the magistrate's court. What happened?"

"Me and the FBI boys were able to talk the magistrate out of all the warrants the locals wanted against you," David said.

"Warrants against you?" Gloria echoed.

"Oh yes, ma'am," David said. "The sheriff insisted on bringing charges of deadly assault against Jacob for throwing the Klan boys' bombs back at them. But the magistrate agreed that was foolishness."

"I should hope so," she said. "What sort of place is this?" Jacob patted her hand.

"But when Kirk Benson finally dies, I'm sure they'll try to stir it back up again, hoping for a murder charge or at least manslaughter," David went on. "So just be prepared."

"That's outrageous!" Gloria said. "Who is Kirk Benson?"

"The old bastard we think was the ringleader," Jacob said. "His truck caught fire, and he was badly burned." She noticed Serena turning her head and looking away, but Jacob still seemed fine, as if they might have been talking about an incident in one of his books. "He's here in this same hospital, isn't he, David?"

"Upstairs in the ICU," David said. "But he's not likely to last the week."

"What about the others?" Serena said.

"The magistrate upheld the federal warrants and issued state warrants for Kirk the Third, his daddy, and the three other men we arrested," David said. "We know from your statement that there was at least one other carload, and the feds are still looking for them."

"Do you think they'll find them?" Jacob said.

"Hard to say," David said. "We still don't know if they were more locals or people from out of town. And now that they aren't in immediate medical danger, the ones we have aren't talking."

"You said the feds are looking," Gloria said. "But not the local police—and you said the sheriff wanted to arrest Jacob."

"Yes ma'am," David said, turning a little red around the collar of his white shirt. "One of the men we arrested, Kirk's son, Junior, is a sheriff's deputy himself. So there's some bad feeling about the case."

"Bad feeling?" she said.

"Calm down, darling," Jacob said. "David and the FBI are doing their best." Again, he was acting like this travesty was no more than a plot point.

"When will the ones you have in custody be tried?" Gloria said.

"They'll go before the grand jury next term," David said. "They're all still locked up right now, but Amanda was able to get a bond set for them. Half a million dollars each. To be honest with you, I wouldn't be a bit surprised if they make it. Kirk's got more money than the Pope in Rome, and Frank Sweatt was at the hearing with his checkbook already out."

"Frank Sweatt is the local banker," Jacob explained.

"But I don't think we'll have any trouble getting them indicted," David said. "The grand jury convenes in three weeks, and hopefully by then the feds will have rounded up the rest of them."

"Three weeks!" Gloria said.

"Things don't happen quite as fast in the real world as they do on TV, Mrs. McGinnas," David said. "And to be honest with you, I doubt we'll be in any big hurry to put them on the trial docket even after they're indicted. There's evidence the truck that burned up was at the crime scene at Briarwood Plantation. Kirk and his bunch might very well have been mixed up in all those killings. That's going to be the big priority for the feds, and for me, too. We won't want to try them for anything until we know what all we're looking at."

"And meanwhile these animals are roaming free," she said. "Will Jacob and Serena be able to testify from London?" Jacob had called her before the cross burning and told her he intended to bring Serena back to the UK with him, and from the look of them now, they were still very much together.

"We'll talk about all that later," Jacob said, patting her hand again. She sat perched on the edge of the bed; with Serena in the chair, the two of them looked like handmaidens. "Is there anything else we should know, David?" Jacob said.

"I think that about covers it for now," David said. "We'll keep officers here with you at the hospital until you're released, and if y'all need anything, just call the office."

"We will," Jacob said. "Thank you."

"Hang on, I'll walk with you," Serena said. "I promised Miz Rae I'd come out to the library when I could. You'll be all right with Gloria here, won't you?"

"I'll be fine," Jacob said. "David, can someone ride with her?"

"No," Serena said. "I'll be fine, too. I'm not scared." From her tone, Gloria thought perhaps that was a lie. "I'll be back soon."

"Just be careful," Jacob said, taking her hand.

"I will be." She kissed him—a little hesitantly, Gloria thought. "It was nice to meet you, Gloria."

"You too," Gloria said. "I'm sure we'll talk again soon."

When she turned back from watching them go, Jacob was watching her, smiling. "All right then," he said. "Let me have it."

She moved to the chair. "I'm sure I don't know what you're talking about." He seemed so well, she didn't know if she should be relieved, annoyed, or frightened. When Serena had called and told her what happened, she'd nearly had a heart attack of her own. Flying over the Atlantic, she had been certain she would land and hear that he had died. She had composed checklists on her phone, tasks to complete, contacts to make, talking points for the horrible call she would have to make to their daughter, Maggie. But now he sat before her, pert as cock robin, deviltry dancing in his eyes.

"Serena," he prompted. "She's too young for me."

"By a considerable margin," she said. "But you don't need me to tell you that. And I must say, it's a small point to make in light of everything else." She longed for a cigarette, but of course in this American hospital, she couldn't light up. "Tell me about this touch of heart attack you've had, please."

"Sweetheart, it was the stress of the moment," he said. "They checked me out and found no damage to speak of to the heart."

"But you had open heart surgery."

"Which isn't nearly the horror it sounds, not anymore." Her own father had died of heart failure after multiple surgeries, so he knew how worried she would be. Was he downplaying his condition to spare her? "They put in a stint because of a tiny bit of blockage in one artery. But honestly, it's nothing. If I hadn't had these burns on my arms and the cuts on my feet, they would have sent me home by now."

"How did you cut your feet?" she said.

"Didn't Serena tell you?" he said, laughing. "We were sleeping when it happened. I ran outside barefoot—naked, as a matter of fact." He was still laughing, but she stared at him, aghast.

"It wasn't funny at the time," he said, sobering a bit. "But when I think now how I must have looked..."

"Jacob, those men could have killed you both," she said. "I'm sorry, but I don't find any of this the least bit amusing." She suspected Serena didn't either. The poor girl had obviously been crying when she'd called, and she'd looked none too steady before she left the hospital, brave face or not. "And one of them is all but dead himself from what Mr. Whatever-His-Name-Was said." She knew his name quite well—David Duncan—and she would have him thoroughly investigated before they left.

"Don't ask me to weep any salty tears for Kirk Benson," Jacob said, his smile snapping into a scowl.

"No, of course not," she said. "My point is, this is serious. I think the sooner we can get you away from this horrible place, the better. You and Serena both."

"I'm not leaving," he said. "I'm going back to Briarwood."

"Jacob, when we talked before this happened, you said—"

"I know what I said," he cut her off. "But Briarwood is mine. I'll be damned if they're going to run me off it."

"Oh, please. Don't come over all Irish." She was scoffing, but the look in his eyes frightened her. He reminded her of how he'd been just before they divorced at the first peak of his success, so angry and bitter she'd felt bruised just being around him. "You've been here all of two months. It's not as if you have any real connection to the place."

"That's where you're wrong." His hand was trembling, she suddenly noticed. He had always had such beautiful hands. "I've been writing, love." He smiled. "And it's good. Maybe the best I've ever done."

"That's wonderful," she said. "But surely you can write anywhere now that you've started. Take Serena, go to the house in Spain."

"No," he said, shaking his head. "I'm staying here. It has to be here." His hand clenched into a fist. "It will all be all right, sweetheart. Briarwood is mine."

19

The parking lot of the Briarwood Community Center was packed. Serena had to drive off the pavement onto the grass under the pecan trees to find a place to park. The FBI were in the process of setting up a field office inside, and Jacob's RV was now its own special crime scene. She did her best to not look at it as she drove by. But Miz Rae's Cadillac and Miz Regina's hatchback sat parked right by the front door.

Heavy plastic covered the bookshelves in the library, and agents in white shirts and ties were setting up computer stations on Miz Rae's prized oak reading tables. Miz Regina was packing up the historical artifacts from the glass case near the front desk—arrowheads, commemorative crystal goblets, crumbling vanity press volumes of local poetry, a letter from Eleanor Roosevelt. As Serena walked up, she was wrapping an arrowhead in tissue paper.

"Good morning," Serena said, smiling.

"Hey, honey." She taped the hand-typed index card label to the tissue: "Authentic Catawba Arrowhead Found at Creighton Farm, Circa 1910," and tucked it into the cardboard box with the rest. "Rae's in back packing up her desk."

"How are you, Miz Regina?" Serena said. "Are you excited?"

"Scared to death," she said. "You know I haven't ever been any further north than the Biltmore House. But Rae's niece seems like a sweet girl." Her smile was brave, her gaze determined. "I think we'll be just fine."

"I know you will." Tom and the library board had expected Miz Rae to put up a fuss when they wanted to close the Briarwood branch and turn it over to the FBI, but she surprised them by announcing that she was retiring, effective immediately, and moving to Baltimore. And of course Miz Regina was going with her.

Serena found her now sitting in her rolling desk chair in the back office with her back to the door. "Did they ever finish drilling holes in the floor?" she asked, sorting through a stack of business cards and tossing most of them into the trash can at her feet. "I cannot stand that noise."

"I think they're done with that part, yes, ma'am," Serena said. "Now they're popping out all the ceiling tiles to run more wires up there."

"Jesus wept." She was dressed for work as always in a pencil skirt and sweater set with discreet brown leather pumps, her gold-rimmed glasses perched on the tip of her nose. But there was a new brightness in her eyes, and her hands shook. "After all this mess is over, the Board will finally get to put in their computers out here, I reckon."

"Probably so." Serena pulled up a stool and sat down beside her. "I'm only going to ask you this one time, then I'll leave you alone about it." She took the older woman's hands. "Are you sure you want to do this?"

"Leave Saxon? Oh yes." She pulled her hands away. "My niece works at a college in Baltimore. She called me last night and said she thinks they might have a job for me in the library there." She tossed the rest of the cards into the trash and swept the small stack she'd been holding back into it, too. "I should have gone a long time ago."

"Okay then," Serena said, getting up. "Tell me what you need me to do."

"How is Jacob?" Miz Rae said.

"He's good." Hearing her say Jacob's name so casually sounded strange. But maybe after everything else, her reservations about him and Briarwood seemed like the least of too many evils. "They might let him go home tonight or tomorrow. His ex-wife got here. Gloria."

"And how is she?"

"Nice. Worried about him, I think." She started packing a stack of files into a box to give her hands something to do. "I think maybe she thinks I'm a gold digger."

"Is she right?" She looked up, shocked, to find Miz Rae peering at her through her glasses. "Are you putting up with all this mess because he's rich?"

Nobody would ever accuse Miz Rae of beating around the bush. Serena ought to have been offended, she supposed, but what was the point? She'd been asking herself the very same thing all night. "No," she said. "What choice do I have? I'm in it; I was there. Even if I wanted to leave him, I couldn't."

"Sure you could," Miz Rae said. "If that's what you wanted to do."

"That's not what I want." Every time she thought about the parking lot, she started shaking and felt faint. Even when she'd been able to steal a few hours of sleep away from the hospital, she hadn't been able to rest because of nightmares about Jacob naked and screaming, throwing fire. But what she remembered most clearly and calmly was how she'd felt when he'd fallen—bereft and terrified. She'd known in that moment that losing him would be the worst thing that could possibly happen.

"I love him," she said to Miz Rae now. "I'm sorry; I know you don't approve. But I do."

"I don't disapprove, Serena." Her eyes behind the glasses were sad but kind. "If you love him and he loves you, I think that's got to be something good. I mean, that's how it's supposed to be, right?"

"I guess so." She barely remembered her own mother, and the aunt who'd raised her had never been someone she could feel close to. And Claudine, dear as she was, was Trey's mama, not Serena's. Miz Rae had become the best mama she ever had. "I'm scared, Miz Rae. I'm scared of what's going to happen in court and what might happen to us if those boys go to jail and what might happen if they don't. I'm scared of what they found at Briarwood and what it means. I'm scared of all the ugliness they're going to find now that they know to look for it."

"I'm scared of all that, too," Miz Rae said.

"And just normal people stuff," Serena said. "I'm scared I'm making a mistake or that I'm doing something bad to Trey by being with Jacob. I'm scared Claudine and Rooster think I'm horrible."

"I'm sure they do not."

"I'm scared he's sicker than we realize and that he might die." Now that it was coming out, it was all coming out, all the fears she'd kept behind her lips, a poisonous string of pearls. "I'm scared he'll get tired of me and leave me. I'm scared of what he'll expect me to be if he doesn't." But she held back one little pearl, the worst and strangest of them all. *I'm scared that he doesn't seem scared any more.*

"You can be whatever you need to be, whatever you want," Miz Rae said. "You don't need me to tell you that, and you don't need Jacob to show you. You don't belong in Saxon, never have. Let Jacob take you back to Ireland if that's what you want, and forget all about this place."

"He won't go," she said. "He changed his mind. He says Briarwood is his, and he won't let them run him out. He even had a fight with the FBI man in charge. He told him when he's discharged from the hospital, even if that happens tonight, he's moving back to Briarwood, moving into the house. He called Rooster and convinced him to get a crew back out there to finish putting in the locks and turn on the water. He even called the guy who's storing all the furniture and told him to start moving stuff back in."

Miz Rae took off her glasses and stared at Serena, wide-eyed. "Lord Jesus," she said. "Jesus Lord, what is he thinking?"

"I guess they just made him mad," Serena said. Her mind flashed on the image of Jacob holding the Molotov cocktail, but she pushed it away. "I'm hoping Gloria can talk him out of it. She wants him to come back to England." Miz Rae had gotten up from her desk and opened a file cabinet. "What is that?"

"I went to Florence Creighton's house after I dropped you off the other night," she said. She had always referred to her mother as "Miz

Creighton" before, but that had changed, too. "There was a box of papers I knew Pink Collins would be after, and I wanted to get it first and burn it."

"What is it?" Serena said.

"The box was already gone," she said, pulling out a thick brown envelope. "But I knew she'd still have these hidden away. She loved them." She handed the envelope to Serena. "Letters. You know I told you her family had been the county librarians for generations. Apparently they've had a box of papers from Briarwood Plantation as long as there's been a library, and that envelope was in it. She showed it to me years ago, one night when we'd been talking about me talking over as librarian someday. She said they were love letters. Years later, when we were packing up her things to send to the home, the box was in the hall closet, but I saw the envelope of love letters in her dresser. I left it there, and it was still there the other night."

"Love letters to whom?" Serena said.

"I don't know and I don't care," Miz Rae said. "She offered to let me read them the first time she showed them to me, but I told her no. I didn't want to know anything about that old place."

"Why are you giving them to me now?" Serena said.

"So you can decide," she said. "If you read them, maybe you'll find something that will convince Jacob to go back to Ireland. Or maybe you'll want to stay."

"Some of those bodies they found date back before the Civil War," Serena said. "There might be something in these they can use to figure out who they were or who killed them." She opened the envelope, and a sweet, dusty smell of mold and old perfume drifted out.

"That, too," Miz Rae said. "Either way, I don't want any more to do with it. Read them, burn them, give them to Jacob, give them to the FBI. Whatever you decide, don't tell me. I don't want to know.."

"All right." She closed the envelope and put it down beside her purse. Jacob would be so excited. "What else do we need to pack?"

20

Serena made it back to the hospital just as Jacob was being served his dinner. "Hey baby," she said as she kissed him. "Where did Gloria go?"

"Back to Charlotte to check into a hotel," he said. "But she made appointments to talk to half the lawyers in the state plus the FBI tomorrow before she left. And she hired someone to go to IKEA to buy furniture for me to live with temporarily at Briarwood. She even called and talked to Rooster about the kitchen."

"He must have loved that." She took the big, brown envelope out of her purse.

"Actually, I think he did. They seemed to hit it off." He pushed his tray aside. "So what's that, then?"

"Miz Rae gave it to me." She pulled the tray back. "Eat your supper. You're trying to get your strength back, remember?"

"My strength is fine," he said, but he picked up his fork. "What is it?"

"Letters Miz Florence Creighton had stashed in her dresser drawer," she said, sliding them out. They felt as dry and delicate as rose petals pressed in a book. "She said they were love letters from Briarwood."

"Are you serious?"

"Apparently they were in a whole box of Briarwood memorabilia the library has been holding since the murders." She put the pile on his tray table. "The box was gone when Miz Rae went to the house to look for it, but she found these in the dresser."

"Who has the box?" he said.

"Miz Rae thinks Pink Collins must have taken it." She unfolded the letter on top. "Oh my God…"

"What is it?"

She read, "'To Mister Ezra Woodbine, Briarwood Plantation, Saxon County, South Carolina, from the Right Honorable Elizabeth Harley, Harley Park, Manchester, England.' Ezra Woodbine the axe murderer had a girlfriend back in England."

"Holy shit," he said, laughing. "Who'd have thought it? But you know, we don't know she was his girlfriend. She could have been a cousin or a maiden aunt."

"Miz Creighton told Miz Rae these were love letters." She held it out to him. "Do you want to read it first?"

"You read them to me," he said. "I can't wait."

July 5, 1837

Dear Mr. Woodbine,

I would remind you that I agreed to accept your letters as communications of friendship only, with no deeper or more intimate connection to be implied. While I am as aware as you of our fathers' hopes for joining my name with your fortune, I have not agreed to the match. And indeed, after reading your latest, I cannot imagine that I ever shall.

Your comparison of African slaves in America to medieval serfs and indeed the workers in your father's own mills is apt only insofar as they are people living in misery for the profit of others. But the serfs and mill workers are offered the illusion of choice, the hope, no matter how foolish, that their lives and labor are given in exchange for something of value and that they themselves have chosen to enter into this contract. They at least believe them-

selves to be better off than they would be without their employment, and the adults at least believe they can leave whenever they choose.

The slaves at this Briarwood you seem to so admire were ripped from lives of their own choosing in Africa and sold into a bondage they can never escape—or worse, were born into this bondage and have never known freedom at all. They own nothing—not their labor, not their children, not even their own bodies. You write of their quarters as a village. It is no such thing, sir. It is a stable, a paddock, a sty, and the people who live there, children of the Heavenly Father as surely as you or I, are treated as livestock. My father treats his fox hounds well, but would you care to be one? I know that I would not.

If I am indeed in your thoughts, you must make a better effort to think more clearly. If you sincerely wish that I will someday be your wife, you must prove your heart to be of stronger, finer stuff, unmoved by the golden trappings of wealth purchased through human bondage. If we are even to be friends, dear Ezra, you must not merely humor me in these convictions. You must understand them and accept them as your own.

I understand the duty you have to your father and his business. More than that, I commend you for it. But I could never love a man whose heart does not break for a slave. Be courteous to this Montgomery and his loathsome family as you must for the sake of your father's business. But if you mean to write me praise of them, you would do better not to write to me at all.

In great sorrow,
Elizabeth Harley

August 1, 1837

Dear Mr. Woodbine,

I am glad to read that chivalry has broken the seal on your conscience when reason, Christian faith, and simply charity could not. The exploitation of an entire race might be an economic necessity but the potential assault of a single attractive woman—

But I am being unfair. Forgive me, my love—no—I will not cross it out. I will not play the proper virgin, will not pretend to a disaffection I do not feel, not a moment longer. Truly, dear Ezra, you say I am your confidante, and you are mine. For all my scolding and all your jokes, you are the only soul on earth who has made the slightest effort to understand me or my beliefs, the only one who even pretends to share them. Perhaps the affection you have expressed for me (and which I have received with such poor grace it makes me blush to remember it) is no more than another duty you feel you owe your father, but I do not think so.

You know the state of Harley Park and of my father's fortune. You know how desperately the title my son will inherit requires your father's fortune to survive. And you know how little my affections and feelings truly matter. Gentleman that you are in character if not in title, I'm sure you would feel obliged to go through at least the pretense of wooing me to spare my feelings. But I can't imagine you would humor me so far as to pretend to share my radical views if you did not. I am possessed of as much vanity as any girl not cursed with some obvious deformity. But I do not imagine myself to be such a prize as that.

I dare say I seem mad to you or drunk. It's possible I'm making no sense. I do beg your pardon. But I feel as if I must choke on the hypocrisy of my life, particularly today.

My mother and I went with others of the Friends to a protest at the mill in Manchester. The conditions are horrible, as I'm sure you can imagine; tiny children crawling among the machines like little mice, snatched up in the works, beaten when they fall asleep or cry; people living like beasts to make money for men who have no more feeling for their suffering than they would a cockroach crushed under their shoe.

Men like your father.

Mama made a great show of standing up to His Lordship, my father, at breakfast, saying she and I would join the others at the protest whatever he might say. But in our fine, new carriage, we drove straight past the Woodbine Mill on the way, a place as cruel and full of horrors as any other mill in Manchester, certainly no better than the one we went to protest.

"Why do we not stop here?" I asked her. "Why have the Friends sent no letters to Mr. Woodbine? Why do we never block his gates?"

"You know very well why," she snapped at me. "Mr. Woodbine and your father are business associates, and he has been extremely kind to us."

"You mean he paid off Papa's creditors and bought us a new carriage," I said.

"Yes, Lizzie, I mean that," she said. I don't think I have ever seen such hatred in my mother's eyes. "And he has done those things because he believes you mean to marry his son. So prepare yourself to do so and stop giving your poor mother a headache."

Come home, dear Ezra, please. We can't let them turn us into what they are. You're quite right; Briarwood is not for you. Come home at once, and I promise I will marry you—on the docks if you like. Our fathers will be so pleased, they will leave us in peace and do their evil work without us.

We can go somewhere—Italy if you like, just as you always said you wanted—and wait for them to die. When they're gone, we can come back to England and claim enough wealth to do real good. We can close the mills; we can finance the abolitionist cause. You could even run for Parliament yourself. And in the meantime, we could be free of all the ugliness. We could be happy.

I do love you, Ezra. Please come home.

Yours as ever,

Elizabeth

November 22, 1837

Dear Ezra—

For weeks now I have been seized with a terrible melancholy, and whenever your name has been mentioned, I have struggled not to weep. After reading your last, I most grievously fear I know why. I blush hot and feel sick to remember the things I have written to you in my last. I ask you as the gentleman you are to destroy my letter and forget I ever wrote it. In return for this kindness, I shall try to put my own hopes and feelings aside to advise you as a friend. I only pray (I do not dare hope) that my letter might reach you in time.

Ezra, I beg you, please don't do this thing that you propose. It is not a shameful thing as some will say; indeed, your feelings do you great credit. I was too blind to see the depth of your passion. I doubted the sincerity of all your best instincts. Perhaps if I had not been so foolish and had trusted you and returned your feelings in kind when they were offered...but I cannot think of that. I will go mad.

But you must trust my judgment as your friend and believe me when I tell you, this course of action you describe can only bring pain. Not only to you and to your family and to all who love you, but to the very person you most wish to protect. While you are present in the reality of slavery and therefore know the truth of it better than I ever could, I have read the narratives and heard the spoken tale of many who have escaped. It is not an undertaking to be entered into with any emotion but the calmest, most sober resolve.

If you would help the cause, return to England and use your position and influence in ways that can do actual good. Do not throw away your life and the lives of all you mean to save in a fit of childish, unconsidered passion that can only bring disaster.

Leave this madness, dear Ezra, for the sake of the one you say you love. I beg you.

Yours forever,
Elizabeth

December 31, 1837

Fool! Fool fool fool fool fool! Fool you, and fool me—I loved you. God in heaven, I loved you, but I would not say—my foolish, damnable principles! Vanity, all of it, vanity and childish pride. If I had accepted you when you asked me, if we had married, you would never have gone to that horrible place. Or I would have gone with you, could have stopped you, stopped the madness that seized you—

Or could I? Was this evil meant? Was the sweetness that inspired it? If I had been with you at Briarwood, would you still have loved me? Would I have still been your soul's soft refuge? Or in that place, would I have been nothing at all?

I am writing to a dead man.
I am mad.
Your Elizabeth

When Serena finished the last letter, she was crying. "That poor girl," she said. "Can you imagine how she felt when she finally heard what he'd done?"

"I can," Jacob said, picking up the letter. "Poor lamb...I wonder whatever happened to her."

"It shouldn't be that hard to find out," she said. "Assuming she was real and this isn't all some made-up fantasy. Or somebody's idea of a joke."

"Do you think it's real?"

"I do." *I am writing to a dead man.* "It feels real."

"You realize this means you were right," he said. "Woodbine wasn't just a maniac on a killing spree. He was trying to start a slave revolt."

"When did I say that?" she said.

"The first day we met," he said. "The first time we saw Briarwood. Tom told us they hanged some slaves the same day they hanged Ezra Woodbine, and you said it must have been a slave uprising."

"Did I say that?" That day seemed so long ago; so much had happened since then. She couldn't be sure what she might have said. "I don't remember saying that."

"No?" He picked up another letter. "Maybe it wasn't you, or maybe I just thought it. The point is, this proves that was what actually happened." He read from the letter, "'Do not throw away your life and the lives of all you mean to save in a fit of childish, unconsidered passion that can only bring disaster.'"

"You think he told her he meant to start a slave revolt?" she said.

"I think it's obvious," Jacob said. "And sweetheart, think what that means for Briarwood. Think how important it is as a historical site."

"That's true." If he were right, Woodbine's attack on the Montgomery family was as big a deal as John Brown's raid at Harper's

Ferry and more than twenty years earlier. That taken with the lynched bodies Jacob, Rooster, and Tom had found on the property would make the site a hugely significant historical horror show.

"We'll find out the truth," he said. "We'll make it a museum, and you'll be the director. We'll make something good out of all this pain, together." It was her dream. It was everything she had ever wanted. All she had to do was stay at Briarwood.

He took her hand. "Yes? Do you want to?"

"Yes," she said, holding on tight. "I want to know the truth."

21

Serena didn't get home from the hospital until after midnight, but she heard raised voices as she unlocked the front door. She assumed Rooster and Claudine were up watching a movie. She rarely ever heard them argue and had never heard either of them shout. But the TV in the living room was off.

"You want me to be a coward," Rooster was saying in the kitchen. She saw them through the open archway on the other side of the dark dining room. "You want me to run away." Claudine sat at the table, her hands folded as if in prayer as her husband loomed over her.

"I want you to live," she said, obviously crying. "I want you to care more about your family than you do that damned house!"

"To hell with that damned house!" Rooster roared, making Serena flinch. "God damn it, Claudie, I am a man!"

"You are a dead man," Claudine said, shouting through her tears. "If you stay here, they are going to kill you the same as they killed Davon and all the rest."

"They arrested Kirk Benson's boys—"

"You think they're the only ones? You think if they sent all those boys to the electric chair a dozen more wouldn't rise up to take their place?" She raised her head as she spoke and spotted Serena, watching frozen in the dark.

Rooster looked where his wife stared and saw her, too. He opened his mouth as if to speak, then shook his head. Without another word, he grabbed his coat off the back of a chair and walked past Serena and out the front door.

"Claudine?" Her mother-in-law was getting up from the table. "Claudine, what's going on?"

She went to the sink. "How's Jacob?"

"Much better." She walked to Claudine, who started scraping dirty plates. She flipped on the garbage disposal, and Serena flipped it back off. "Claudine, what is it?"

She dropped the plate she held into the sink and gripped the counter's edge. "I can't stay here anymore. I have to leave." Her gaze was focused out the window into the dark back yard. "I am going to leave, and my husband is coming with me."

"Leave Saxonville?" Serena said. "But what about the investigation?"

"Fuck the damned investigation!"

Serena backed away in shock. She had never heard her mother-in-law say so much as a damn or hell when she stubbed her toe.

"What do you think they're going to find out that we don't already know?" Claudine continued. "Did aliens come down in a spaceship and murder my child? Was it the Mexicans? The Russians? They know exactly who did it already."

"That's why they're trying to find evidence," Serena said. "So they can convict Kirk and Junior and all the rest of them and find out who else was involved."

"Do you really think that's ever going to happen?" Claudine said, turning to her at last. "Do you think Amanda Flynn and the rest of them would ever let that happen? This is Saxon County, Serena. If they're looking for evidence, it's to find some way to pin it on somebody else, anybody else but a White man everybody knows."

"That's why Jacob called the FBI, and that's why we can't run away," Serena said. "We have to make sure they know we're watching, that the whole world is watching them now."

"Honey, they could not care less about the whole world, even less about you and me," Claudine said. "They are going to do exactly what they want to do the same as they always have and dare us to say a word against them. And if we stay here, we won't say a word because we know what's good for us, what will happen if we try to fight back."

"I can't believe that," Serena said. "I can't believe we haven't come any further than that, even in Saxon County."

"I know you can't." She sank back down in her chair. "You can't believe it, and Davon couldn't believe it, and Trey and Rooster—y'all all think you know better. You've been out in the world and seen places I don't know about. You've been in the Army or gone to college, and you've forgotten what this world, our world is. But I haven't. I might not know the world outside, but I know Saxon County."

"But Claudine, your home is here," Serena said. "Y'all have built so much here, this house and Rooster's business."

"Rooster's business is already gone," she said. "Your friend Jacob took care of that when he hired him at Briarwood."

"What are you talking about?" Serena said. "Briarwood is the biggest contract of Rooster's career, and he's done a fantastic job. Jacob is thrilled with the work he and his crew have done."

"Look in the desk," Claudine said. "Pull out that folder at the back of the bottom drawer."

Serena opened the desk in the corner where Claudine did the household accounts and found a fat, brown expandable folder.

"Read some of that," Claudine said. "Then tell me I'm crazy."

The file was packed full of hate mail. She flipped through page after page, feeling more and more sick. Some were handwritten on lined notebook paper with ragged edges; some were typed on water-marked bond. Some were printouts of emails from free accounts obviously created just for this purpose. But the underlying message in every one was the same.

On a child's notebook paper in purple ink: "Die, you job-stealing n------. I hope the house you and your slack-jawed monkeys are building burns down around that mick son of a bitch."

On pale gray legal bond from a laser printer: "As a native son, you have prospered in Saxonville, profited from the tolerance and patronage of your neighbors for decades. To monopolize an opportunity for the town that has made a place for you and your family for so long shows a level of ingratitude that leaves her city fathers breathless. We would be remiss in our duty as members of the community and betrayers of the friendship we have shared so long with you if we failed to warn you that these actions will not long be tolerated. There are those among us whose sense of justice outweighs their desire for peace. As a friend, I advise you to take whatever profits this enterprise has brought you and withdraw from the Briarwood project at once. If you do not, I do not dare imagine the consequences."

Printed out on Claudine's own printer from Rooster's business email address: "Abraham Lincoln was never a president here, and free blacks have no place at Briarwood Plantation. This insult to our heritage will not go unanswered. Get out while you have the chance. This town knows how to fix this problem, and if you force our hand, we will."

The last page in the folder was a drawing in crayon of a truck with Decatur Contracting written on the side parked next to a tree. The truck was on fire, and the tree was decorated with black stick men hanging like ornaments from every branch. The artist had used white correcting fluid to paint Xs in place of their eyes.

"Dear God in heaven," Serena said. "You have to show these to the FBI!"

"And what are they going to do?"

"Find out who sent them!"

"You know who sent them."

"But the FBI can prove it!" She couldn't believe they had kept this secret from her and from Jacob—some of the letters dated all the way back to October "We have to tell Jacob about this. He had no idea."

"Didn't he?" Claudine said. "Rooster warned him this would happen, didn't he?"

"He said some people might not be happy," Serena said. "But we never imagined anything like this."

"I know you didn't, either one of you." Claudine gathered up the folder.

"You have to take them to the FBI," Serena said as Claudine tucked them away out of sight again in the desk drawer. "You have to let them investigate."

"They're investigating enough already," Claudine said. "For all the good it will do." She locked the drawer. "I can't do it anymore. I can't keep on being afraid."

"I understand; I do," Serena said. But she didn't, not really. Even now, with the evidence spread out on the kitchen table in front of her, part of her wanted to deny it was real. She felt the same way she had the night she'd first heard about the murder mill. How could people be so hateful, do such evil, and still smile at her on the street? How could ugliness like this stay hidden for so long? But it had, and she had to face it. If she didn't face it now, it would just go on and on and never stop.

"Then come with us," Claudine said. "Forget about this White man and his plantation."

"I can't," Serena said.

"Honey, you can do whatever you want. You don't owe anybody anything. You can find somebody else to love you," Claudine said. "Somebody young and strong. You do not need this man."

"It isn't that," Serena said. "It isn't just that. Jacob is going to turn Briarwood into a museum. I'm going to help him."

"Sweet Jesus on the cross."

"Claudine, just think what that could mean," Serena said. "Think of all the good it could do. You say Amanda and the rest of them want to keep doing what they've always done, and nobody can stop them. This could stop them. If we drag the truth out in the light, they have to stop."

"They ain't never going to allow that to happen," Claudine said.

"I refuse to believe that," Serena said. "I refuse to be afraid of them." She took the other woman's hand. "I have to try. For Davon. For Trey." Both of them trembled in rage as much as grief. "You and I both know they lied about Trey. You know he couldn't have been doing what they said he did."

"Stop it, Serena," Claudine said. "Don't go there."

"This shit has got to stop," Serena said. "I have to do everything I can to make it stop."

Anger flashed in Claudine's eyes, then she pulled her into a hug. "You do it, then," she said, squeezing her tight. "I'll be praying for you."

"I know," Serena said, squeezing her back.

After a long moment, Claudine let her go. "It will be all right," she said, patting her shoulder. "Tell Rooster I went on to bed."

She wanted to argue, but Claudine had already turned her back and headed up the hall.

She found Rooster in the carport, sitting on a folding chair smoking a cigarette. "She tell you she's leaving?" he said as she came out.

"She did. She showed me those letters." It was cold, and she hadn't worn a coat. "I told her you have to show them to the FBI. Did you show Jacob?"

"No, no, of course not. Wasn't any use getting him all upset. It wasn't any different than I expected. I knew what would happen when I took that job." He tossed his butt and lit another, and she smelled the butane from his heavy silver lighter. "But I was just like you, sugar, you and Jacob. I told myself I could handle it, that it would just be a lot of talk. Then we saw that mill." She heard a tremor in his voice, and he stopped talking for a moment. When he spoke again, he was calm. "But your mother-in-law is right, sugar. There ain't no use showing the FBI. They won't care about all that."

"Those letters were written by the same people they want to arrest." She sat back on the bumper of Claudine's car, hugging herself for warmth.

"Probably some, yes." He smiled. "What do you think they can do, sweetheart? Arrest the whole town?"

"Jacob would want to know," she said. "He would want to do something about it."

"I know he would," he said. "If you want to tell him, go ahead." In the glow of his cigarette, she could see his eyes. "He told me he loves you." He didn't sound angry or sad, just resigned. "He'll take care of you after we go."

"You're going with her, then?"

"Of course I am. She's all I've got and all I need." She saw his white teeth as he smiled. "I reckon you'll be all right."

"They're going to find out what happened to Davon," she said. "Jacob won't let them just give it up. He's not from here. He wants the truth."

"He wants Briarwood," he said. "And he wants you. And he might think he wants the truth. But don't expect too much of him, Serena."

"He's your friend."

"He is. And he's your lover. And he's a good man, and he wants to do the right thing. But he's White, sweetheart."

"Don't say that," she said. "Don't say it like that." In her mind, she saw Trey's ghost again in the fields at Briarwood, reaching out to her, accusing.

"Don't ask him to choose Black justice over White security," he said. "He'll break your heart."

"No."

"Those men in that lynching mill are dead and gone. Davon is dead and gone." A bitter edge she almost never heard from him had come into his tone. "Jacob is alive. They're the past; he can't help them now. He wants his future with you."

At that moment in the third floor ICU of the Saxon County Hospital, Kirk Benson finally opened his eyes. He was the only patient on the ward, and the desk nurse was outside on the fire escape, smoking a cigarette. His room was dark but for the glow of monitors and the light from the hall, and silhouetted in the doorway stood the shape of Jacob McGinnas. But it wasn't McGinnas who spoke.

"You stupid cracker bastard," the dark man said through the Irishman's throat. "What were you playing at? All these years, all that killing—for what?" He was leaning in the doorway, arms crossed, dressed in a plaid bathrobe and bedroom slippers. "Did you think you were doing blood magic to keep me away? Did you think the witch's spell would fail if you didn't keep murdering her people? Or was it just about the money?"

Kirk's lips were burned like strips of crackling and sticky with ointment, and his tongue was raw and dry. But he tried to speak, to call out for the nurse.

"Be still, man. No one can hear." He came into the room, and though he couldn't turn his head, Kirk saw the man carried something long and thin and flexible dangling from his hand. "Whatever you meant to be doing, you failed." He stood over Kirk, his hair a wild black halo around his narrow, raw-boned face. "You're going to die." He raised the thing he held, a narrow leather belt. "Your seed are all going to die." He folded the belt into a strap and snapped it. "Your tribe will die in fire just as they deserve, and all the money will be gone." He snapped it again, and Kirk began to whimper, remembering his pa. "My queen will have her vengeance, and the witch is gone."

The heart monitor screamed as the patient's heart rate spiked dangerously high. The dark man touched it with one finger, barely glancing over his shoulder, and it stopped, the screen going black. "And I will rise," he said, bending close to whisper in Kirk's ruined ear. "And all of this world will be mine."

Kirk's body was so badly burned, even the weight of a bedsheet on his torso was too much agony to be borne. The first blow of the strap across his chest was the first fire that had put him here reborn. With the second, he saw stars before his eyes, and in spite of his dead lips and shredded throat, he screamed. If the nurse had left the door to the fire escape open, she almost certainly would have heard. But she was on her mobile phone arguing with her ex-husband about Christmas visitation with their son, and she had closed the door so no one else could hear.

When the leather struck his ruined flesh a third time, Kirk Benson breathed his last.

Half an hour later, Jacob McGinnas was sleeping two floors down in his own hospital bed, and the ICU nurse was back at her desk. The monitor in Benson's room sprang back to life, and every alarm went off. His heart had apparently stopped.

22

Kirk Benson had a proper funeral at the Holy Rock Baptist Church as if he'd died peacefully at home in his own bed. Amanda Flynn hosted a lovely drop-in afterwards where she served liquor and heavy hors d'oeuvres and displayed touching photographs of Kirk and her late father, Jack, as boys on the football field and Army reservists during the Vietnam War. Jack had been an officer. But the church for the service was only half full, and several members of the all-White congregation looked uncomfortable being seen there. The local news reporters gathered outside all called the occasion "somber" before hastening to mention that all but one of the pallbearers was under suspicion of murder by the FBI.

Jacob didn't attend the funeral. Serena convinced him it would be in poor taste. He hadn't been charged with having any responsibility for Kirk's death. David Duncan of the Solicitor's office was of the opinion that all dogs willing to lie still should be allowed to do so, and Amanda convinced her clients he was right. The idea of a civil case to be brought after the rest of the Benson clan was cleared was met with enthusiasm—the goddamned mick was made out of money, after all.

For his own part, Jacob didn't care. He was discharged from the hospital the day after Kirk died, and he moved back into his old room at the local bed and breakfast. He'd meant to move into Briarwood, but Serena and Gloria joined forces to talk him out of it. The fact that Rooster suddenly resigned as project manager had been another contributing factor—the indoor toilets weren't installed yet. So he called Carol Ann Sweatt and told her he needed a house in town. She found him what she called "a charming Craftsman" two blocks from the courthouse, and Rooster agreed to do an inspection as his last official duty before his resignation went into effect.

Jacob met him in the parking lot of the lawyer's office the morning of the closing. "All right, then, tell me. How bad is it?" he asked, meeting him halfway between his car and Rooster's truck and shaking his hand.

"It's all right," Rooster said. "The wiring was redone about ten years ago, so the air conditioning works. And the roof is good." He handed over a copy of his official report. "But if you end up staying there more than a year, you're probably going to want to get your plumbing looked at. I suspect your sewer line has some issues."

"Big issues like shit hitting the walls when we flush?" Jacob said.

"No, no, nothing like that," Rooster said, laughing. "Little issues like slow drains for your washing machine and your dishwasher in the next few years."

"We won't be there that long." He glanced through the report—thorough, concise, scrupulously honest, just as he had expected it to be. "I just wish I could convince you to stay on at Briarwood. Reese is fine, but he's not you." Reese Middleton-Smith, the antiquities and restoration expert from Charleston, had taken over the Briarwood project.

"I appreciate that," Rooster said. "But you know, Claudine's got her heart set on living at the beach." They had never actually discussed Rooster's reasons face to face. But Serena had told Jacob what both Claudine and Rooster had told her, and Rooster knew that she had. Jacob also knew that they had already signed a contract on a doublewide trailer in a nice RV and trailer park near a golf course in Garden City, a suburb of Myrtle Beach. "And I can't say I'm dreading sitting on my hind end fishing for a while myself."

"I hear that." Their eyes met in understanding, and they clasped hands again. "We'll take care of things here." *Your child will be avenged.*

"You just take care of yourself," Rooster said. "And Serena as much as she'll let you."

"You know that's not much." Serena planned to stay on at Rooster and Claudine's Saxonville house until it sold, and she wouldn't discuss where she intended to go when it did. But Jacob and the dark man had already decided. "But I'll try."

Carol Ann Sweatt roared up in her SUV at the other end of the parking lot. As she climbed out and came toward them, Jacob couldn't help but notice how much she'd changed since the first time he'd seen her. She was still perfectly dressed for her part in crisp capri-length slacks and a sweater set that looked brand new. But she had lost so much weight, her clothes looked boxy at the shoulders and hips. She wore twice as much make-up as she had before, but even so, her face looked sallow and drawn. Her once-perfect blonde bob was now pulled back in an unflattering headband that still showed dark roots. Whatever she might say, her life now was obviously less than perfect.

"Good afternoon!" she called in a fair approximation of her usual cheerful bellow. But the energy that had seemed like a force of nature radiating out of her before now seemed forced and fake. "How is everybody?"

"Not bad," Jacob said. "Henry was just telling me all about my new house."

"Isn't it beautiful?" she said. "A little gay couple had it for years and years until they moved back to California, and they did such a good job on it." She took off her sunglasses, and her eyes were sunken and deeply shadowed in spite of the make-up. "Rooster, did you tell him about the new roof?"

"I did," Rooster said. "I told him about that leaky toilet in the upstairs bathroom, too. When you replace that, you're going to have to replumb that pipe to bring it up to code. It's sitting too close to the wall."

"Oh, Jacob can afford it. Can't you, Jacob? He's made out of money." She shifted the straps on her huge, pink leather bag on her thin, fragile-looking little shoulder. "Shall we go on inside?"

"I'm going to leave y'all here," Rooster said. "Jacob, if you need me for anything, holler."

"You too," Jacob said. "When are you and the missus moving out?"

"End of the week," he said. "But I'll talk to you again before we go. Bye now, Carol Ann. Y'all take care."

Jacob could have sworn he saw tears in the woman's eyes. "You too." They stood together and watched Rooster walk back to his truck. "I hate this," she said. "Why did y'all have to find that horrible place? It is ruining this town."

"You think it would have been better if we hadn't found out all those men had been murdered in cold blood?" Jacob said. The man he had always been was horrified. But the man he was becoming was delighted.

"I think it would have been better if those horrible things had never happened," she said. "But since they did, yes, I would rather not have to know. Or not—I don't know. I don't know anything anymore." She gave him a ghost of her usual bright smile. "Let's go inside."

This closing was a lot less complicated than his last. The sellers were more than ready to see the last of Saxon County, and there were no mortgages or encumbrances. And Jacob was paying cash, so of course everybody loved that. One of the sellers was a fan, and Jacob autographed several of his books for him, including a first edition of Jacob's biggest seller.

After it was over, Jacob was eager to get away, but Carol Ann chased him down in the parking lot. "Wait, I have something for you." She motioned him over to her car and pulled two envelopes out of a box crammed full of them in her back seat. "An invitation to me and Frank's annual Christmas do," she said, handing one over. "We're late sending them out this year, and I wasn't sure of your mailing address."

"That's very kind, but I'll be going to Dublin to have Christmas with my daughter," he said, surprised and almost touched.

"Oh, no, it's not on Christmas," she said. "It's next week—just a cocktail party, drop-in kind of thing, nothing fancy. We have it every year. You've been here for months now, and so few people have gotten a chance to meet you."

"Thanks, really, but I'm not sure," he said.

"Well, think about it. We'd love to have you." She held up the other envelope. "And are you going to see Serena? This is for her."

"I will." He took it and saw Serena's name and address at Rooster's written in the same festive green calligraphy as his envelope.

"Tell her I said she is invited whether you decide to come or not," she said. "And I promise there will be other young people there, not just us old fogies. I know Tom Stewart and his little wife will come; they always do."

"I'll tell her," Jacob said, smiling. "Maybe we'll see you there."

23

Serena met Evie Stewart for lunch at a wings and beer joint in Hopewell, the college town twenty miles away from Saxonville. Walking in, she felt the blessed relief of strangers. Looking around the crowded room, she didn't recognize a soul. The hostess looked like a college girl, and she smiled all the way to her eyes. "Table for one?"

"I'm meeting a friend." Over the girl's shoulder, she spotted Evie waving from a booth near the window. "There she is."

"Great. I'll send your waitress back over."

"Hey," Evie said, getting up and hugging her before they slid back into the booth. "Is this okay? I know it's kind of loud."

"No, I love it." The restaurant was part of a chain that had been one of her and Trey's weeknight favorites in Las Vegas. "How was the doctor's appointment?"

"It was fine. We'll get to that in a minute." The waitress took Serena's order for a soda. "How was the library?" Evie asked.

"Not much help so far." Serena had taken the day off from work to come up to Hopewell and search the local university archives. "I found a couple of references to Briarwood in old newspapers from before the murders but nothing after and nothing we didn't already know.

"That's too bad." Tom's wife had called the night before and said she had a doctor's appointment in Hopewell and suggested lunch after. "Tom said Jacob's got his research goddess back in England looking for stuff, too."

"Yes, she's supposed to be working it from the Ezra Woodbine end." She and Jacob had shown Tom the Elizabeth Harley letters, and the librarian had been very excited.

"Is Jacob writing about Briarwood?" Evie said, sipping what looked like ginger ale over ice.

"He's writing something," Serena said. "He filled up at least one notebook while he was in the hospital, and I know he's been writing a lot since he got out." She had woken up in the middle of the night the past two nights in Jacob's room at the bed and breakfast to find him hunched at the tiny desk typing on his laptop.

"So, what's he writing? Has he shown you?" The waitress came back, and Serena ordered wings. Evie ordered a grilled chicken sandwich with no bacon and no cheese. "So?" she repeated when the waitress had gone.

"No," Serena said. "I haven't asked him. I don't want to be spoiled; I want to read it when it's finished. I've been waiting a long time for a new Jacob McGinnas novel." She watched Evie sip her drink again with a delicacy that was very much unlike her. "Are you okay?" she asked. "You're usually the one ordering a cheeseburger with a dozen hot wings on the side."

"I'm fine." Her blue eyes sparkled. "I'm better than fine. I'm pregnant!" They both shrieked and grabbed hands across the table.

"Oh my God!" Serena said. "Congratulations!" She was happy for Evie and Tom, so happy. But tears welled in her eyes. "Oh my God," she repeated.

"You're the first," she said. "Well, other than Tom—I called him from the doctor's office parking lot." She noticed Serena's tears. "Are you okay?"

"Of course, yes, honestly," Serena said. "Don't pay me any attention. I am so happy for you. This is a good thing, right? Were y'all trying?"

"We weren't really trying, but weren't *not* trying either," Evie said. "To tell you the truth, we've been not *not* trying for years now. I had pretty well decided it wasn't going to happen. But it's official. It did." Her smile was radiant. "And yes, it is a very good thing. Tom is so thrilled."

"That's wonderful, Evie. Seriously." She got up and went around the table to hug her. "What a lucky little baby."

"Yeah, right," Evie said, laughing as she hugged her back. "Poor little lima bean. We better start praying for them now."

"You'll be wonderful parents," Serena said.

"As long as we can keep the baby alive, we'll be okay," Evie said. "But you know I'm scared to death."

"Of course, you are," Serena said. The waitress came by, pitchers in hand to refill their drinks, but she shook her head, waving her off.

"But okay, you're a good friend, and I love you, and you're happy for us, and that's lovely," Evie said. "Now tell me what's up with you."

"Nothing," Serena said. "Well, everything, obviously, but it's not... we shouldn't be talking about this. We should talk about fun baby stuff."

"We've got months to talk about baby stuff," Evie said. "Who do you think's going shopping with me for everything? Tom? But I know you're going through hell right now—oh God! Should I not have mentioned the baby?"

"Don't be stupid. Of course you should," Serena said. "I need to hear about happy stuff, and I need to get out of my own head. Yes, bad stuff has happened, but I've been really lucky. It could have been a lot worse."

"True, but still." Her phone beeped with a text message; she silenced it and put it in her purse. "I still can't believe your in-laws are just leaving."

"They've got their reasons." How could she explain Claudine's terror to this girl who had grown up in the same small town without it? Why should she even want to try? "But it does put me in a weird position. I can't afford to live on my own."

"And you're not ready to live with Jacob," Evie said. "That I totally get. You guys haven't even known one another all that long."

"Exactly."

"Is Miz Rae really gone north for good? Because I know Tom would love to promote you to head librarian over at the Briarwood branch."

"He mentioned that," Serena said. "But with the FBI camped out there, who knows when that branch is going to reopen?" Suddenly she wasn't feeling all that hungry. "I don't know. I'm taking a couple of weeks off to go to London with Jacob for Christmas, so I guess I'll just see where everything stands when we get back."

"That's pretty exciting, right?" Evie said. "Have you ever been to Europe?"

"I went to Germany once with Trey," she said. "But yeah, I'm pretty excited. And Gloria, Jacob's ex-wife, has been nothing but nice, and she's really fun. And I really am looking forward to meeting their daughter Maggie."

"But it's still a lot to take in so fast," Evie said. "Particularly with everything else that's going on."

"Yeah, it is." She wanted to be a good friend who didn't make everything about herself, and at the same time she wanted to maintain some semblance of professional detachment from her boss's wife. And she really didn't know Evie all that well, and they didn't have that much in common. But she hadn't had a real conversation with a woman her own age in so long, it was hard to hold back. "And it's probably silly, but...I keep thinking about Trey." For one crazy moment, she considered even telling her about the ghost.

"That's not silly at all," Evie said. "He was your husband, and you loved him. And this is the first time you've even considered getting into a relationship with someone else since he died. It would be strange if you weren't thinking about him."

"I guess it would." Some of the weight of her guilt and confusion lifted from her shoulders like a magic trick. "You actually knew Trey, didn't you?"

"We went to high school together, yeah," Evie said. "We didn't run with the same crowd. I was a nerd, and he was a football star. But we had classes together, and he was always nice to me. I never saw him ever be anything but nice to anybody. And, God, he was gorgeous."

Serena laughed. "He was that."

"You know...okay, this is probably a horrible thing to bring up, and if you don't want to talk about it, tell me to fuck off. My feelings won't be hurt, I promise. But what happened to Trey? I know y'all were living in Las Vegas and that he was in the military."

"He was a first lieutenant stationed at Nellis Air Force Base." It was a horrible thing, and she *didn't* want to talk about it. But maybe she needed to. "And one night, he just didn't come home from work. The police and the Air Force started a search, and they found him and his car in the desert."

She had never had to formulate this event into a story for somebody else. The Air Force had told Claudine and Rooster what happened, and no one from her own family ever asked. "He had been shot in the side of the head. It looked like he had been trying to duck back into the passenger side of his car when they shot him."

"Oh my God," Evie said. "Serena, I had no idea he was murdered!"

"There was another man's body there, too," Serena went on. "Shot in the chest with a service pistol like the one Trey carried. They didn't find either gun at the scene." She clasped her hands on the table so tightly, her fingertips were turning purple. "The other guy was apparently a known criminal, drugs and guns and everything else. There's a lot to get up to in Las Vegas."

"But why would a man like that shoot Trey?" Evie said. "What were they doing in the desert?"

"The police picked up a couple of Deacon Hill's associates a couple of days later," Serena said. "That was the other guy's name, Deacon Hill. They said it was a drug thing gone bad, that Trey had been selling for them on the base and stealing."

"No way," Evie said. "That's not possible."

"They said he shot Hill then tried to run, and they both shot at him. They didn't even know which one actually killed him." She could still smell the lemon cleaner and puke stench of the room where she first heard this fairy tale, could see the Masonic tie tack of the cop who told it. "They charged them both with murder and sent them to jail. They had confessions and guilty pleas, and the case was closed."

"Serena, I knew Trey," Evie said. "I know you. I can't believe he would do something like that, and I know he'd never have been able to keep it from you if he had."

"I knew they had to be wrong," Serena said. "But after Trey died, stuff started coming out. He'd been telling me he filed our income taxes every year, but he hadn't. We owed tens of thousands of dollars in back taxes and penalties. We had a second mortgage I didn't know about on a house we'd owned for less than five years. Both our cars were leases. The car I'm driving now is the clunker I bought in college that was still in my aunt's garage back here in South Carolina. I worked for a museum that was run by the state, and I lost my job. And because of how the police said he died, I lost Trey's retirement. I had nothing. Less than nothing."

She had never talked about this before because she'd always been afraid she would fall apart, that the words coming out of her mouth would break down into sobs she couldn't stop. But she didn't feel fragile at all. She felt furious; she vibrated with the power of pure rage. "And of course, the police were investigating me, too, trying to say I was part of my husband's crime syndicate. They tried like hell to seize all the stuff I didn't really own before the banks and the IRS could take it. That was one thing the Air Force did for me. A JAG attorney who was friends with Trey stepped up to get the cops off my back."

"Serena, I had no idea," Evie said. "Dear God, there's got to be something we can do about this. You don't think Trey was really involved in any of this stuff, do you?"

"I don't know where all that money went or what he spent it on," she said. "But no, I know he couldn't have been selling drugs. I never saw or heard about a single shred of evidence that Trey knew those other men beyond his own dead body being found where they found it. He had no drugs in his system when they did an autopsy, and nobody at Nellis was ever charged with buying from him. But the thing that made me sure was his phone. They never found his phone. I asked for it; he had pictures on it I wanted. The cops said it wasn't at the scene, that the guys who shot him must have stolen it. But why would a Las Vegas drug dealer steal a four-year-old cellphone?"

"They wouldn't," Evie said.

"They wouldn't," Serena echoed. "I tried calling the state attorney general's office about it—that was what the JAG advised me to do." *Mrs. Decater, I'm sorry, but I can't help you with that,* was what she had actually said. Her face, so friendly and concerned until the moment Serena suggested challenging the police version of Trey's story, closing off like a steel-barred door. *But the state attorney's office will probably be willing to take a statement from you.*

"But they wouldn't return my calls," Serena said. "Then the IRS started threatening to send me to jail. So I cut a deal with them and came home."

"That's so unfair," Evie said. "God, Serena...I wish I knew what we could do because that's so wrong. Maybe Jacob—"

"No," Serena cut her off. "I can't be asking Jacob to fight this for me. It wouldn't be right."

"I can see that. Do you mind if I tell Tom? Maybe he knows somebody. But if you don't want me to tell him, I won't." She looked genuinely distressed. She wasn't just being nice; she gave a shit. That was a revelation Serena wasn't quite sure how to handle, but it was good.

"You can tell him, but I don't think there's anything he could do. After two years, I don't know that there's anything anybody could do." She smiled. "Anyway, you asked."

"I did." She took Serena's hand across the table. "I am so, so sorry."

"Thanks." She squeezed the other woman's hand as the waitress turned up with their food. "Now please, let's talk about happy baby stuff."

24

After lunch, Serena went back to the university library archives. The archivist, Dr. Anthony "Call Me Tony" Criscione, agreed that it was odd that a family as wealthy and prominent as the Montgomerys had been at the time of the murders left so little trace in the public record. From papers she found in the box Jacob was given when he bought the Briarwood property, she knew that the house had been completed by Caleb Montgomery less than two years before he and his family were murdered there.

"That's probably the problem," Tony said. "They weren't in Saxon County long enough to make a mark. Have you tried searching the property records at the courthouse?"

"Most of the older stuff was destroyed in the fire," she said. "And what they managed to salvage is still in Columbia being processed."

"And God only knows how long that will take to sort out," he said.

"To have had the money to build a place like Briarwood, Montgomery would have had to have been a pretty successful planter already," Serena said. "If he was originally from South Carolina, that would most likely mean Charleston County, wouldn't it?"

"Charleston or Horry or Georgetown—somewhere near the coast," he agreed.

"I emailed the Charleston County Library archivist, but I haven't heard back," she said.

"Sandy's been out on sick leave, poor baby," he said. "Cancer."

"I'm so sorry. I had no idea."

"But she's responded well to the chemo, and I think she's back at work. But I'm sure she's way behind." He paused, considering. "Her assistant used to be an intern here. Let me email him and see if he's got time to look at what they might have for you."

"That would be fantastic," Serena said. "Thank you so much."

"No problem," he said. "We'll be closing down for Christmas break after today, but if you give me your email, I can let you know what he says."

"Perfect." At least her trip wasn't wasted.

"Have you tried looking up the 1830 census?" he said as she wrote down her email address for him. "That might tell you where they started."

"That's a really good idea." She felt a little stupid for not thinking of it herself.

"Let me give you our login," he said. "I'm getting ready to lock up and head out, but the library is open until five. The kids are all finishing up exams and leaving for the holidays, so you should have the carrels to yourself."

"Thank you." She could search census records in the quiet for an hour then head back and meet Jacob.

"Come on, I'll get you set up." He wrote the password for the US Census database on a sticky note, then walked her out of the archives into the canyons of the stacks. "You know, if Mr. McGinnas needs any help compiling or storing his collection, we'd be happy to oblige him," he said as they reached a nest of study carrels.

Serena smiled. "Thanks, I'll let him know." If Briarwood became the museum they hoped, they would have their own library and archives. But she saw no reason to dash this nice man's hopes. "And thanks again for all your help today."

"No problem," he said. "Happy hunting."

As she settled in and opened her laptop, she could hear the distant murmurs and rustlings of students in the distance, but they were out of sight, like ghosts. She logged in on the library's surprisingly powerful internet connection and brought up the database.

Criscione's suggestion paid off. The 1830 census listed a Caleb Montgomery, Sr., with two sons, Caleb Montgomery, Jr., and Halsted, plus a wife and a daughter unnamed, all living in Charleston County, South Carolina. She went back to the internet and did a general search and found a link to a Charleston historical society that specialized in weddings and marriage records prior to the Civil War.

She clicked through and did a search for Caleb Montgomery, Jr. To her shock, a listing popped up—an announcement from the society page of the local paper from 1834. Caleb Montgomery, Jr., had married a girl named June Louella Benson. His best man had been his brother, Halsted, and the bride's attendants had been a girl named Naomi Kennedy and the groom's sister, Alice Rose. The groom's uncle, the Reverend Thomas Montgomery of North Carolina, officiated the wedding.

"Miss Serena?" Standing at the far end of the nearest aisle through the stacks was Kirk Benson, III. He wore a university sweatshirt, and his arm was still bandaged from the burns. "Can I talk to you for a second, please?"

"What are you doing here?" She realized the ghost-sounds of the other students had gone; silence lay over the basement of the library like a thick quilt.

"I go to school here," he said. "Or I did. I think I'm going to take a semester off." He started coming closer.

"No!" she said, throwing up a hand like a traffic cop. She wanted to jump up from her chair and run, but she wouldn't. *I will not be afraid of this boy.* "I don't think that's such a good idea, Kirk." In the face, he still looked like the freckle-faced little Huckleberry who had come to her for help with his homework. But in body he stood more than six feet tall and outweighed her by at least fifty pounds.

"I understand." He stopped halfway down the aisle. "It's funny you being here, us running into one another here, though, isn't it?" He seemed to be trying on his smile like he wasn't sure he wanted to wear it. "I just wanted to tell you how sorry I am about what happened." He kind of snickered and blushed red under his freckles. "That was a terrible night, wasn't it?"

"Kirk, you need to go on now." She slipped a hand into her laptop bag, feeling around for her keys. She was at the middle desk of a group of three, and he was coming toward her again.

"You won't even accept my apology?" He sounded hurt, but his expression was angry. "Miss Serena, you know me. You've been knowing me and my family since I was a little boy. You know we're good people."

"I'm sorry, Kirk, but I don't know that," she said. *Why the fuck are you apologizing?* "I used to think you were."

"Shut up! God, why do you have to be such an uppity bitch?" She jumped up as he grabbed the chair from the desk between them, blocking her in. "You've got a rich, White boyfriend now. What do you want from us?"

"Son, stop it." The library felt very big and very empty. If she screamed, would anyone hear?

"Just tell them it wasn't us," he said, pleading like a child and snarling like a monster. "Tell them y'all made a mistake."

"I can't do that."

"You can!" He shoved the chair aside, and she ducked behind her own. In her right hand, she maneuvered her keys into a weapon and willed herself to be strong. "Tell the cops you lied, you stupid bitch, or next time, you're fucking dead!"

He lunged at her, and she struck at him, putting her whole body weight behind the swing. But just as her fist was about to make contact, he wasn't there. She felt a hot rush of wind like the breath of a furnace, and the boy flew backward. His lips drew back in terror as he was dragged over the fallen chairs like a rag doll. "Miss Serena!" he screamed, grabbing at the bookshelves, knocking books to the floor. Whatever had him bashed him hard against the wall, once, twice, three times.

"Stop!" Serena said, clambering over the chairs. "Stop it!" He struck the wall again, and his body went limp, his head lolling to one side. "You're going to kill him!"

She heard what sounded like a dragon's sigh, and the boy slumped to the floor. She ran to him, slipping and tripping over the fallen books. "Kirk!" She fell to her knees beside him and put her fingers to his pulse—he was unconscious but alive. "Thank God." She stood up and called out. "Help!"

A security guard came running from the direction of the stairs. "What happened?"

"He...he fell," she said. "He tried to attack me, and I pushed him." She couldn't explain; this woman would never believe her. "We struggled, and I think he hit his head. Please, call 911."

But the guard did seem to believe her. "Don't worry, miss," she said. "Everything is going to be all right now." She spoke into her radio, speaking very calmly and distinctly. "We need paramedics in the library basement. There's been an attempted assault, and the perpetrator has been injured." Serena slumped to the floor, and her legs almost tangled with Kirk's. "They'll be here soon," the guard said. "They'll know what to do."

They thought Kirk had been trying to rape her, she realized. "He knows me," she said.

"They almost always do."

In his room at the bed and breakfast, Jacob slumped over his desk, his body drained from the effort of protecting his beloved from so far away. His heart beat out of rhythm, and blood dripped from his nose on to his manuscript. He pushed it away gently but didn't have the strength to sit up. *Please,* he thought, speaking to the dark man who forced him to be strong and let him see and reach so far. *Just let me finish the book.*

When he could raise his head, he swallowed a pill with the warm whiskey in the glass by his hand. Half an hour after that, he was able to rise to his feet.

When Serena came home, he pretended to be surprised when she told him about the attack and protested that she hadn't called him at once. He called his attorney then sat on the closed toilet to talk on the phone while Serena had a long, hot bath, holding her hand as she soaked.

Later the attorney called back as they ate Chinese takeout in bed. He assured them that the Benson boy was fine now, just bruised and shaken.

"Do you want to press charges?" Jacob asked Serena.

"No." She reached for his hand again and rested her head on his shoulder. "I just want to forget it ever happened."

Later still he held her in his arms as she slept, the dark man cradling them both.

25

Serena helped her in-laws pack their rented moving truck in the sluggish freezing rain on Friday morning. She had just stowed another box of books and was picking her way back down the slippery ramp when a nondescript silver car pulled into the driveway. Agent Harris from the FBI got out on the driver's side, and David Duncan from the Solicitor's office was riding shotgun. "Rooster!" she called as Duncan got out and opened the back door. A woman completely swathed in an oversized hoodie got out. Her face was covered with a scarf.

"Good morning, Mrs. Decatur," Agent Harris said, coming over to Serena. He offered her his hand to help her down the last few steps. "Is the rest of the family at home?"

Claudine had come to the screen door. "What is it? What's happened?"

"Hey, Miz Decatur," Duncan said. He was ushering the hooded woman across the front yard like she might have been an invalid or blind and holding an umbrella over her head. "You reckon we could come inside?"

Rooster came around the house from the carport. "Y'all come on in out of the wet." He motioned Serena in first and put an arm around Claudine as they led the others into the living room. The walls were bare of pictures except the huge family portrait hanging over the fireplace that was bolted to the wall. The bookshelves were empty, the lamps and knickknacks all gone. The couch and Rooster's recliner sat there covered in plastic. The vacuum cleaner stood in the middle of the living room where Claudine had been vacuuming the carpet after taking up the throw rugs.

Agent Harris picked up a chair in each hand from the dining room and carried them into the living room for Rooster and Claudine. Serena perched on the arm of the couch. Duncan led his charge toward the recliner at the other side of the room, but she didn't sit down, and neither did he.

"I reckon y'all have some idea why we're here," Duncan said. "Do you know Wrenn Benson?"

"We've met," Serena said as the woman took off her scarf and hood. Wrenn was Kirk Benson's only daughter and Amanda Flynn's hometown sidekick, the kind of White woman who dressed uptown but talked like the trailer park. Today she was a hot mess, drawn and pale even with the spray-on tan, with dark circles under her eyes. "Why would you bring her here?"

"In my house?" Claudine said. "Oh my Lord Jesus ..."

"Hang on," Rooster said. "Just let them tell us what they came to tell us, then they'll go."

"Thank you, sir," Agent Harris said. "And Mrs. Decatur, I do apologize." From the look on his face, Serena got the idea this was Duncan's idea, not his. "We've had a break in our investigation of your son's murder. We're about to make arrests."

"Who?" Serena said.

"Y'all better not have brought this girl here to tell me her daddy had nothing to do with it," Claudine said.

"No, ma'am," Wrenn said. She sounded as bad as she looked, hoarse and exhausted. "It was my daddy who did it and my brother and two other boys who worked for Daddy—the same ones they already arrested for the other thing."

"Miss Benson is going into the witness protection program," Duncan said. "She has given us a statement and agreed to testify. We wouldn't be able to arrest your son's killers so quickly if she hadn't come forward."

Claudine leaned on her husband and clutched Serena's hand so tightly the bones were cracking. "What does she want?"

"I want to tell you I'm sorry," Wrenn said. "It's my fault." She seemed genuinely distraught. "Davon and I…we were in love, and my daddy found out about it, and that's why they killed him. I swear I didn't know. I kept telling myself that he had just gone away. I thought maybe they threatened him and scared him off. But when they found his body…" She hiccupped, and her bottom lip quivered like a child's. "Miz Decatur, I am so, so sorry." Her voice was like a child's, too, unnaturally high-pitched with a cloying sweetness that seemed obviously put on.

"How can you be so sure they did it?" Rooster said. He sounded calm, detached, like a lawyer on TV.

"Junior told me. I *made* Junior tell me," she said. "After Daddy…" She glanced at Serena. "After Daddy's accident, I made Junior tell me exactly what happened with Davon. And when Daddy died, I called the police. I know I shouldn't have waited even that long, but I was so scared of my daddy. Even when he was in the hospital, I was so scared of what he'd do."

Claudine let go of Serena's hand. "Exactly what did happen?" she said. "What did your brother tell you?"

"I don't think it's appropriate for us to go into all that right now," Duncan said.

"Then why bring her out here?" Rooster said.

"She wouldn't agree to testify unless we let her apologize in private to you and Mrs. Decatur first," Harris said.

"And you thought the best way to make that happen was to pay us a surprise visit in our home," Rooster said. His jaw was clenched so tight, Serena could see the muscle twitching, and Claudine put her hand over his.

"We didn't mean any disrespect, Rooster—Mr. Decatur," Duncan said. "We just knew y'all were leaving town in a few days and wanted to put all this behind you. Plus, we're moving Miss Benson to an undisclosed location until the trial."

"You don't really want to know," Wrenn said. "I couldn't stand to hear it all myself."

"I am his mother," Claudine said. "Tell me what you know."

Duncan looked a little panicked. "Miss Benson ..."

"She's right; she's Davon's mama," Wrenn said. "Don't worry; I'm not going to change my story." She took her hands out of her pockets to show nails bitten down to the bloody quick under Christmas red polish. "We had been....keeping company with one another for a couple of months when Junior saw us out together at the mall in Charlotte," she said, wringing her hands, lacing and unlacing her fingers. "He was mad at me that week because Daddy had paid for me to get rims put on my car instead of giving Kirk the Third money for a ski trip. So he took pictures of us together on his phone and showed them to Daddy." She swayed on her feet. "Could I sit down?"

"Do what you want," Claudine said. Like her husband, she sounded calm, detached. She wasn't looking at Wrenn; her gaze focused on the bare window that looked out on the front yard. But she was holding Serena's hand so tightly, it hurt.

Wrenn sank down on the edge of Rooster's recliner. Duncan hovered over her, but Harris stayed where he was behind Rooster's chair. "He didn't say anything to me about it at first," Wrenn went on. "He talked to a girl who manages one of his stores, Roxanne—she's a friend of mine. She told him that yeah, we had been going out. She called me after he left, and I tried to find Davon, but he wouldn't answer his phone. Sometimes if he was working or with y'all, he wouldn't answer me. He'd call me back later when it was safe. Then my daddy came home and..." She was staring down at her hands in her lap, and she shook her head. "You don't care what he did to me. But he made it where I couldn't try to call Davon anymore."

Serena felt sick, but the girl was right; she didn't much care. And from Claudine and Rooster's faces she could see they cared even less. "That's when they went after Davon?" she said.

"I guess, yeah," Wrenn said. "Junior swore to me he thought they were just going to try to scare him. He swears he had never seen that place before. But when they got to Briarwood, Daddy made them chain Davon to the back of the truck."

"Made them?" Claudine said.

"They dragged him through the woods," Wrenn said. "Daddy said they had to put his blood on the ground."

"Jesus," Rooster said, his calm cracking at last. "Jesus God in heaven."

"Then they hung him up in that mill," Wrenn finished. "And they killed him." The tears finally broke. "And I loved him; I swear I loved him, and I'm so sorry."

"There, there, that's enough," Duncan said.

Claudine let go of Serena's hand. She leaned her forehead against her weeping husband's chest over his heart for a moment, her lips moving silently. Then she stood up to stand in front of Wrenn. "I know what you want me to say," she said.

"I know you can't forgive me," the crying White girl said.

"I can't," Claudine said. "But that's what you're after, you and Mr. Duncan both. You want one of those scenes that restores your faith in Jesus. You want me to hug your neck and say there, there, baby, Mammy understands." Duncan blushed bright red, but the White girl's expression turned hard under her tears. "You want me to be a good Christian and say that none of this is your fault and that I forgive your family for what they did and you for leading my boy to the slaughter. You want me to take your hand and pray for you so you can feel clean."

"You think this was easy for me?" Wrenn said, leaping to her feet. "My daddy beat the shit out of me. He's been treating me like the town crotch for three years, him and all his friends. And now he's dead, and my life is over! I have nobody! Everybody who gives a damn about me is going to jail because I told the truth."

"And I could not give a damn!" Claudine shouted back. "You want me to feel sorry for you, Miss Hot Pants? You want me to feel bad because your piece of shit daddy beat your ass?"

"All right, that's enough," Duncan said, taking a step forward.

Rooster seemed to come back to life like he'd been hit with an electric shock. "Put your hand on my wife in my house," he said. "I dare you."

"Don't worry; he won't," Harris said, moving between them.

"Davon is dead," Claudine went on like she saw and heard no one but Wrenn. "He's been dead for years, and you knew. Don't try to tell me you didn't know. You might fool this cop and this cracker lawyer with that cock and bull tale, but not me. You knew my son was dead, and you said nothing."

"You can't prove that," Wrenn said.

"I don't have to prove it," Claudine said. "You know it, and I know it. Prancing around this town with Miss Amanda Flynn like the Queen of Sheba, racing up and down the highway in that car your daddy bought you." She staggered, and Serena caught her from behind.

"Get out of my house," she said. "You want me to thank you for telling the truth; fine, I thank you. And I will pray for you. But mostly we're going to pray for ourselves. I'm going to pray that someday I will let go of this hate in my heart for you and your whole family and this whole, Goddamned evil town for taking my child from me." She turned back to Rooster. They faced one another for a moment, then she fell crying into his arms.

Duncan looked like a child who'd just been spanked in church. "Mrs. Decatur, I am so sorry."

"Just go," Serena said. "Please, just take Miss Benson out of here and go."

"I don't understand," Wrenn said through fresh tears as they took her out. "I don't have to testify, you know."

"No," Agent Harris said. "You can go to jail as an accessory instead if you like." He nodded to Serena and hustled the others away.

"It's all right, baby," Rooster said, holding Claudine close. "It's going to be all right now."

"I'll go close up the truck," Serena said. "I think we're done packing for today."

"No," Claudine said, straightening up. "We are packing up and getting the hell out of this town."

26

Carol Ann and Frank Sweatt's white brick Georgian mansion was lit up like a Christmas-themed casino. "Hang on," Serena said, catching Jacob's arm and stopping him on the sidewalk. "I want to get Rooster a picture."

"It is quite a sight," Jacob agreed. His own new house was less than a block down First Street, so they had walked down for the party. Other guests hadn't been so sensible; cars lined both sides of the street. "I didn't realize this was such a big event."

"Oh yeah," Serena said, snapping pictures with her phone. "This is the big dress-up occasion of the holidays for the White folks. Carol Ann makes sure of it. It's her annual 'fuck all y'all' to the town." She looked stunning in a chic but opulent gold dress with sky-high heels. "She's not from Saxonville, and Frank didn't grow up here. They moved here from Atlanta about ten years ago when Frank's great-aunt Louella died and left Frank this house. She had been living in it by herself since the forties, and it had just fallen to pieces; it looked like a haunted house." She put her phone back in her purse and slipped her arm through his.

"Aren't you freezing?" He wore an overcoat, but she didn't even have sleeves. "Not that I'm complaining, mind you."

"I'm fine," she said, snuggling close. A group of people he didn't recognize walked by and stared at them then hurried on.

He kissed the top of her head. "Now tell me quick before we go inside, what about Carol Ann and her big, ugly house?"

"It's the oldest surviving private dwelling in Saxon County. It's probably fifty years or more older than Briarwood." More people passed in pairs and groups down the sidewalk. Some of them spoke and smiled, but most just hurried on without making eye contact. "When Carol Ann said she intended to restore it to its former glory, all the old cats in the historical society were just over the moon. Then she started ripping out walls and cutting down hundred-year-old magnolia trees, and they all fell out in a faint. I wasn't living here yet, but Tom says when she put in a swimming pool out back, they just about had a riot in the street."

"Oh dear," Jacob said.

"But of course, since Frank Sweatt can buy and sell pretty much everybody in this town who isn't named Flynn or Benson, the old guard eventually had to shut up and pretend to get over it."

As if on cue, a black town car pulled up to the curb beside them. A young White man in a blue blazer hopped out and helped an old White woman in an ancient-looking mink coat climb out of the back seat. "Serena," she said, pushing her escort aside with her cane to fold Serena in a hug. "Don't you look pretty?"

"Hey, Miz Kennedy," Serena said with a smile that barely reached her eyes. "Have you met Jacob McGinnas?"

"So nice to meet you," the old woman said, barely giving him a glance. "Serena, I was so sorry to hear your father and mother-in-law moved away. How are they liking the beach?"

"They seem to like it fine," Serena said.

"I'm so glad." She clutched Serena's wrist in one talon while her escort hovered behind her, smiling and looking embarrassed. "You tell Rooster I asked about him. Tell him I'll be glad of that new roof he put on my sunroom come January."

"I'll tell him," Serena said.

"Come on, Grandmama," the boy said. "We better get you inside."

"Merry Christmas," the old woman said, hugging Serena again.

"Yes, ma'am," Serena said. "You too." She took Jacob's hand as they walked away.

"Come on, love," he said. "Let's find ourselves a drink. Fast."

Walking in, Serena thought the interior of the house looked like a photo shoot from a magazine about genteel living in the New South. Under its holiday decorations—a smothering abundance of fake greenery and tasteful glitz—all of the rugs were Persian, and every wall was hung with art featuring dogs on point or ducks in flight or botanical sketches of magnolia blossoms. A huge photographic portrait of Carol Ann, Frank, and their son, Frank, Jr., a student at Clemson, dominated one wall of the entry hall right next to the ten-foot, professionally-decorated Christmas tree.

But pride of place over the living room mantle was given to the ugliest painting Serena had ever seen. It was a portrait of a young woman in a white wedding gown with an empire waist and cap sleeves, obviously from the early nineteenth century. The background was roiling black storm clouds and broken columns as if she had been posed in the midst of the apocalypse, but she didn't seem bothered. Her flat-eyed expression betrayed no emotion at all.

"Carol Ann," Serena said, catching their hostess as she passed. "Who is that?"

"Oh God, isn't it horrible?" Carol Ann said. "That's Frank's great-great-however-many-greats Aunt June. Her family apparently built this house."

"June what?" Jacob said with a weird little smile. He hadn't wanted to come to this party at all, but Serena had insisted. She was determined to show them she wasn't scared. She had emptied her checking account buying her dress and spent all day on her hair and make-up.

"God if I know," Carol Ann said. She was resplendent herself in a slinky red velvet jumpsuit and bare feet, and obviously already a little bit drunk. "Poor Aunt June, that's all any of them ever called her. But when we got the house, it was in the will that we had to keep her ugly picture over that fireplace. I swear she haunts this house. Look at her eyes." She put a hand on Serena's arm and pointed. "Frank's cousin told me once that somebody told her when she was a kid that the woman was dead when she was posed for the picture; that's why she looks like that."

"Sweet Christ," Jacob said, laughing.

"Tom Stewart," Carol Ann said, hooking Tom out of the throng around the buffet table. "Come tell Jacob and Serena about poor Aunt June."

"I wish I could," Tom said. "Hey y'all." He shook Jacob's hand. "Serena, don't you look nice?"

"Oh, come on," Jacob said. "You know exactly who that is. That's June Benson Montgomery."

"Oh my Lord," Serena said.

"That's Caleb Montgomery, Jr.'s wife," Jacob went on. "One of the ones killed by Ezra Woodbine on his murder spree at Briarwood."

"No," Carol Ann said, shaking her head. "No, it can't be."

"I guess it could," Tom said. "All those old families used to intermarry all the time."

"Holy shit," Jacob said, obviously delighted. "I bet they sketched her body after she was dead. That would have been too early for photographs."

"Jacob, no," Serena said. "That would be too awful."

"Look at her face," Jacob insisted.

"But why would anybody do that?" Serena said.

"Exactly," Carol Ann said. "It's sick."

"People back then didn't think about death the same way we do now," Tom said. "If they wanted to memorialize her, it's possible."

"Or claim kin to Briarwood," Jacob said.

Evie came over, looking very pretty and very pale in a black knit dress. "Hey y'all," she said, linking her arm through Tom's. "What are we talking about?"

"Don't ask," Carol Ann said. "Jacob's being a horror writer." She squeezed Serena's hand. "Y'all have a wonderful time."

"We will, thank you," Serena said, but Carol Ann was already walking away.

"Sorry, love," Jacob called after her, not sounding sorry at all.

"How are you feeling?" Serena asked Evie.

"Funny you should ask," Evie said. "Can I borrow you for a minute?"

"Of course." Serena handed her wine glass to Jacob. "We'll be right back."

"Okay, this is stupid, and I am really embarrassed," Evie said in a half-whisper as they walked away. "But there is a line at the downstairs guest bathroom, and I have got to go."

"We'll just tell everybody you're a pregnant lady who's got to pee," Serena said.

"No!" She slid her arm through Serena's and leaned closer. "I've got to do other stuff." Serena started snickering. "It's not funny," Evie said, but she was laughing, too. "I've got to drop a big old stinky load." Serena burst out in helpless giggles. "And I can't do it with half the town outside the door listening."

"What do you want me to do?" Serena said. "Stand outside spraying air freshener and singing Christmas carols?"

"That could work," Evie said, poking her in the side. "But it might be easier if you just sneaked upstairs with me and helped me find another toilet."

They ducked past the kitchen door and up the dark back stairs. At the top was a closed door that looked promising, but it opened on what was obviously Frank Sweatt's home office—big desk, big recliner, big flat screen TV. "Damn it," Evie said, starting to sound desperate.

"Hang on." Serena went inside and opened a second door. "I thought so. Come on in; Frank's got his own little half bath."

"Thank you Jesus," Evie said, sprinting past her. "Thank you, Baby Jesus; thank you, Mary; thank you, Joseph and the shepherds and the wise men..." She closed the door behind her.

"I'll just keep a lookout," Serena said. Noises that would not have played well downstairs came through the door, followed by helpless giggles. "Girl, you better light a match in there," Serena said, walking away.

"It is so gross in here," Evie said. "There's all these cartoons cut out of magazines of naked chicks playing golf. And oh my god..."

"What?" Frank's desk was fairly neat with stacks of files and papers and golfing magazines.

"He has his password for a porn site on a sticky note stuck to the wall," Evie said. "Right next to the toilet."

"Ewww," Serena said. She didn't mean to snoop; her eyes were just wandering over the desk.

"Ewww," Evie echoed. "What's he been doing in here?"

"You want me to answer that?" She realized she was reading her own name. On top of one of the stacks was an official-looking document outlining the performance of a stock portfolio, and her name was hand-written in purple ink in the margin. *Serena Ariel Sanders Decatur.*

"No, please don't," Evie was saying just as the hallway door opened.

Amanda Flynn walked in. "I thought I heard voices," she said. "What are you doing up here, Serena? What are you looking for?"

For a split second, Serena felt exactly the way Amanda intended her to feel—embarrassed, ashamed, even a little bit afraid. Then she got mad. How dare this bitch? "Merry Christmas, Amanda," she said with a smile. "How you doing in there, Evie?"

"All done," Evie said, coming out of the bathroom. "Oh hey, Amanda."

"Evie, would you excuse us for a minute?" Amanda said. "I think Serena and I need to talk."

"I don't think I will," Evie said. She took Serena's hand, lacing her fingers with hers like they were besties forever on the playground. "Anything you need to say to Serena, you can say in front of me."

"I can't think of anything we need to talk about at all," Serena said, squeezing Evie's hand. "Are you okay now?"

"Never better," Evie said. "Merry Christmas, Amanda."

"Serena." Amanda grabbed Serena's wrist as they tried to pass. "Take some advice from a friend. Do what your family did and get the hell out of Saxon County."

"I beg your pardon?"

"You can't fix the past," Amanda went on. "The roots run too deep. And if you keep pulling, you won't like what comes up."

"You better take your hand off of me," Serena said, trembling with rage. "I have no problem whatsoever kicking your ass right here."

The other woman's eyes widened in genuine shock. She let go of Serena's wrist and made a big show of wiping her hand on her dress. "Well, damn," she said. "This dress cost a fortune, and that grease stain won't ever come out."

"I'll bet Frank Sweatt will buy you a new one if you suck his dick," Evie said. "Didn't Doctor Smith teach you how to suck a dick before your daddy ran him off? I heard he was the best." Serena had never seen a woman turn as white as Amanda; she looked like she might faint. "Oh look," Evie said. "Here comes Frank now."

"Well, hey ladies," Frank said, looking confused. "Is everybody having a good time?"

"It's a lovely party," Serena said. "But I think Amanda wants to ask you for a favor." Still holding Evie's hand, she led her down the stairs.

"Oh shit," Evie said as they got to the bottom and erupted into nervous laughter together. "Thank god I had already made it to the toilet, or I would have made a terrible mess right there on Carol Ann's rug."

"I can't believe you said that!" Serena said. They were standing just outside the open kitchen door, and the caterers stared at them like they'd lost their minds.

"I can't either," Evie said. "It must be the hormones." They dissolved into giggles again. "Tom is going to kill me. That heifer's on the library board."

"You think I don't know that?" Serena said. She didn't feel like thanking Evie exactly, but she did hug her tight, and Evie hugged her back. "But why Frank Sweatt?"

"Oh honey, Amanda Flynn and Frank Sweatt have been fucking around for years," Evie said. "That's why Amanda and Carol Ann hate one another so much. And then when it turned out Amanda's fiancé, Joe Smith, was gay, that just made it that much worse. Because of course Carol Ann is the one who fixed them up."

"He really was gay?" Serena said. "How do you know that?"

"Tom told me," Evie said, looking a little nervous like she was afraid she'd said too much. "He heard about it at a poker game right after Smith left town." They stepped aside to let a waiter pass with a tray of canapes. "Speaking of Tom, he and Jacob must be wondering what happened to us."

"Jacob told me if I left him alone with Carol Ann, we were breaking up for good," Serena said as they headed back toward the living room.

Evie laughed. "I don't blame him a bit."

Jacob was with Carol Ann, standing in the living room in front of the fireplace looking up at the ugly portrait of the probable corpse of June Montgomery. But he didn't look as if he minded. He had his hand in the middle of Carol Ann's back and was turned to her, listening to what she was saying. From where Serena was standing, she could see his thin, handsome face in profile, and he was smiling. He leaned in closer to Carol Ann and said something obviously naughty, and Carol Ann threw back her head and laughed.

The fire in the fireplace suddenly sputtered, and sparks exploded out and caught the rug on fire. Several people cried out, and Carol Ann tossed her martini on the flames, making them leap higher. Jacob pulled her back as another man whipped off his jacket and started beating out the blaze. Nobody but Serena seemed to notice that sparks had flown up and ignited the painting.

"Jacob!" Serena said, pointing.

Her lover turned and smiled at her with his arm still around Carol Ann's shoulders. The old oil paint went up like gasoline; within moments, the entire portrait was burning. And dead June Montgomery stared blankly on. Other men raced to try to save it, but Carol Ann was laughing, and Jacob just smiled.

27

Serena had one more thing to do before she could leave for Dublin. She pulled into the gravel parking lot for Monét's Fine Florist at nine the next morning just as Monét herself was unlocking the front door.

"Come on in, honey," she called over her shoulder as Serena got out. "I've got it in the fridge."

Lights were coming on in the shop as Serena walked in. "I put it together last night," Monét called from the back. The showroom was crowded with arrangements and wreaths featuring a lot of red candles and silk poinsettias and sprigs of plastic holly. All the weather-resistant graveside standards were mounted high on one wall, stand-up sprays of plastic roses in pink, red, or purple, mounted on Styrofoam frames. Serena's favorites were the rectangles that looked more like birthday cakes than funeral wreaths, each one decorated with a child's old-fashioned toy telephone and the legend "Jesus Called."

"What do you hear from Claudine?" Monét said as she came out. She carried a long, low-profile spray of real Leyland cypress fancied up with artificial berries and red plaid ribbon. "Is she liking the beach?"

"I think they like it fine," Serena said. "Monét, that's beautiful."

"You like it?" the florist said. "I thought it might be a little plain, but I wanted something masculine."

"It's perfect," Serena said, writing her a check.

"That Leyland cypress should hold up until at least New Year's," Monét said. "You shouldn't have to worry about it until you get back from England."

"Ireland," Serena corrected. She was sure she heard both curiosity and reproach in the other woman's tone, but she chose to ignore it. "I'm going to Ireland."

"I know Claudine and Rooster are going to miss you this year," she said. "We sure do miss them at church."

"I know they miss y'all, too." She was about to pick up her arrangement and go when a Mercedes roared into the parking lot outside.

"Lord Jesus," Monét said as Frank Sweatt jumped out and came rushing to the door. "Give me strength."

Frank looked shocked to see Serena, and she was a little shocked to see him. Monét's Fine Florist was all the way out at the highway on the edge of town. White folks bought flowers at Foster's two doors down from Frank's bank.

"Hello, ladies," he said. "Merry Christmas." He was obviously trying to sound casual, but his neck was turning red above his starched white collar. "Miss Monét, do you have that thing Carol Ann ordered? She asked me to come by and pick it up."

"Something for Carol Ann?" Monét said.

"Yes, that plant she wanted," he said.

"Oh, right," Monét said, glancing at Serena. "Let me just get it."

"How is Carol Ann this morning?" Serena asked as the florist disappeared into the back. "Are y'all recovered from the fire?"

"Carol Ann has the insurance adjuster coming to the house this morning," he said. "I think the painting is about the only thing that can't be fixed."

"I know y'all are both all broke up about that," Serena said.

He looked taken aback for a moment, then chuckled. "Oh yeah, Carol Ann is grieving."

"Frank, while we're here, there was something I wanted to ask you." She hadn't decided consciously to explore this, but running into him felt like a sign. "Last night when Evie Stewart and I were in your office looking for a bathroom, I just happened to notice a piece of paper on your desk with my name on it."

"Your name?" He was already so flustered, she couldn't gauge how much new impact she'd made. "On my desk?"

"Like I say, I didn't get a good look at what it was." She was fighting the same instinctual embarrassment she'd felt the night before with Amanda Flynn, a childlike fear that she was or had been misbehaving in some way and deserved to be punished for it.

"I think you must have been mistaken," he said.

"Here we go," Monét said, coming out of the back room with a massive Christmas cactus in full, red bloom. "Is this what she wanted?"

"Yes, that's just the thing," Frank said. "Now how much do I owe you?"

"Two hundred dollars," Monét said without batting an eyelash. Inflation was a terrible thing; Serena had picked one up for Miz Rae the week before and paid less than a hundred.

"Lawsy," Frank said, taking out his checkbook. "My wife does love to spend money, doesn't she?"

"And did you want to pay on your account while you're here?" Monét said.

Frank kept his smile, but his blue eyes went cold. "Yeah, I reckon I better do that, too." He started writing the check. "That fire last night was something, wasn't it, Serena? Came right out of nowhere."

"Well, out of the fireplace," Serena said.

"Right," he said with a laugh. "Still, you just never know what's going to happen, do you?" He ripped out the check and handed it to Monét. "Sometimes things catch on fire for no reason and burn all the way to the ground."

"Thank you, Frank." Monét was obviously shaken and obviously trying to hide it.

"No, ma'am," he said, picking up his cactus. "Thank you. You ladies have a merry Christmas."

As soon as he was gone, Serena pulled out her cellphone. "I'm calling the FBI."

"What?" Monét said. "Why would you do that?"

"That man just threatened you," Serena said.

"Oh now, don't be silly."

"You know that he did," Serena said. "I'm calling Agent Harris. He's the one investigating Briarwood, and he can be here in less than an hour."

"Like I've got time to stop and talk to him about nothing when I'm so busy," Monét said, forcing a laugh.

"Monét—"

"Serena, stop it!" She grabbed the phone out of Serena's hand. "Just stop." She canceled the call and handed the phone back. "Just leave me out of your problems, all right?"

Serena took it. "They're your problems, too, Monét."

"Then let me handle them." She put Frank Sweatt's check in her cash register and slammed the drawer. "Y'all have a merry Christmas."

When Serena got outside, Frank's car was pulled up next to hers. "I just realized what you must have seen on my desk," he said. "Carol Ann and the Loving Patrons want to give all y'all at the library a little Christmas bonus this year, and I had to get your full name from her for your check."

Serena didn't believe this for a second. She also didn't know how to refute it. "How nice," she said instead, forcing a smile as fake as his. "I'll look forward to it." If he thought she was going to thank him, he was doomed to disappointment. "Merry Christmas," she said, turning her back and getting into her car.

Jacob had formed a habit of writing in the library at Briarwood. While construction went on around him, he hunched over a folding table in front of the old fireplace with earbuds playing loud rock'n'roll. Today he was swathed neck to ankles in his wool overcoat against the chill as the glass was replaced in the double-hung windows. He was typing on a laptop, transcribing from a notebook, but every once in a while he stopped and made a handwritten note in the margin. Sometimes the notes were written in his own familiar handwriting. Sometimes they were spidery runes no completely-living soul could have read. He had grown accustomed to this and barely even noticed.

He felt a presence and looked up to find one of the workmen standing over him. He took out his earbuds and smiled. "Hi Kyle. What can I do for you?"

"A package just came for you." Kyle was one of the new workers Pinckney had brought in when he took over, a graduate student from Clemson. He had come to Briarwood on an internship, intending to do research for his dissertation on the impact of slavery on eighteenth and nineteenth-century architecture. Pinckney had him stripping the paint from the columns in the hall.

"Thanks." Jacob took the package, a padded envelope sent from Las Vegas, Nevada. "Any big plans for Christmas?"

"We'll be driving up to my wife's family in Virginia tomorrow afternoon." He looked around the room and shuddered. "Mr. McGuiness, how can you stand to work in here? Doesn't it give you the creeps?"

"I write horror books," Jacob said. "I find it inspiring, I guess."

"I guess it would be." One of the glaziers closed a window with a bang, and Kyle jumped. "Sorry," he said, looking sheepish. "This whole place is starting to give me nightmares."

"Then it's good you're getting away for a few days," Jacob said.

Kyle laughed. "You obviously never met my in-laws."

"Oh dear," Jacob said, smiling.

"But I'm sorry. I'm disturbing you."

"It's all right." Jacob stood up, folding the package and stowing it in his pocket. "I'm going out to stretch my legs anyway." He smiled at the boy. "If we don't talk again, merry Christmas."

28

The cemetery at Briarwood Baptist Church was nearly a hundred years older than the church building itself. Trey's grave was in the newest section, on the other side of the highway that skirted the Briarwood Plantation property. His marker was a simple granite slab surrounded by empty space reserved for the rest of the family. Serena had already been asked which side of him she wanted, and she had arbitrarily chosen the right. Claudine had been making plans for Davon, and Serena didn't want to rock her boat. But she wasn't sure she intended to die in Saxon County. Even if she did, would it still be right for her to be buried beside Trey?

She put the greenery arrangement she'd just bought on top of the stone and draped the ribbon to frame her husband's name. "Merry Christmas, baby," she said. Before seeing his ghost the month before, she had never once spoken to her dead husband's tombstone. But these days, any reminder that he was anywhere other than haunting Briarwood was more than welcome.

"'You sure did treat me nice,'" she sang softly, laughing, knowing he would have laughed, too. "I'm going to Dublin with Jacob McGuiness. Just for the holiday, I think. I hope you don't mind." Most of her was sure that not only didn't he mind, he didn't actually exist anymore, at least not as the Trey she had known. But again, recent events made her doubt everything she believed about the dead and everything else. "Your mama asked me to tell you she and your daddy miss you, but they probably won't make it up here until after the new year." Claudine believed absolutely that he could hear them. She hadn't been kidding in the slightest when she made Serena promise to stop by. "Do you hear any of this, baby?" she asked him now. "Could you answer me if I asked you to?"

She could have sworn she felt a tremor in the ground under her feet.

Get a grip, Serena, she thought. "Baby, my nerves are just about shot," she said out loud. "You wouldn't believe the shit that's gone down in Saxon County the past couple of months." She thought of the stories he had told her. "But then maybe you would." He had talked about their old hometown sometimes at night as they lay in bed like he was telling her about his nightmares before he fell asleep. She could still remember the way his voice shook and the glowing ember of his cigarette in the dark. "But it's bad, baby, so bad. I'm trying to fix it, I promise. I want justice for the past, and I want to make it stop. And Jacob's trying to help me, I swear."

This time she couldn't deny it; she actually saw the ground shake. The dry grass shivered, and loose dirt danced on a bare patch of red clay at her feet. But it wasn't just Trey's grave that was shaking. All around the cemetery, the ground shuddered as if something huge moved underneath the surface, preparing to break free. "Stop it," she said, blood pounding in her temples as her knees went weak. A crack opened up in the blacktop of the road as she looked back toward the church. "I said stop!" she ordered.

The shuddering stopped as abruptly as it had begun. *An earthquake,* she told herself. *They say we're due for an earthquake around here; there are little tremors all the time.* But it hadn't felt like an earthquake. It had felt too deliberate and personal; an act of will, not chance.

"Serena?" She hadn't noticed the Reverend when she'd walked over, but there he stood, just a few feet away in the little patch they called the Prayer Garden. When this new section of cemetery had been cleared, some of the older ladies of the church had insisted this was needed, and they bullied their sons and husbands into creating it, arranging a few concrete benches and planters in a semi-circle in front of a black granite statue of Jesus. "Are you all right?" the Reverend asked.

Did you feel that? She wanted to ask. But if he had, surely he would have mentioned it. "Yes, I think I'm fine," she said. She touched the greenery on Trey's grave as if reassuring herself it was still there. "I just felt dizzy for a second."

"Come over here and sit down." The six-foot, broad-shouldered man of God wore a gardening hat and gloves. A big bag of potting soil leaned against one of the benches. "I'm just taking out the last of these poor old pansies."

"Thank you." She wanted to pretend she was fine, that she had imagined the whole thing. But her head was splitting and she felt sick. And the road still had a broken crack in it she knew it hadn't had before.

"Sit down and catch your breath." He went back to pulling up pansies as she sat down on one of the benches. She expected him to ask after Claudine and Henry or maybe even drop a few probing, pastor-like questions about her relationship with Jacob. But he didn't say another word, just kept on gardening, half-singing, half-humming a song as he worked. After a few minutes, she could breathe again, and she felt better.

She had never actually been inside the prayer garden before, so had never noticed the slab of gray stone roughly the size of a coffee table half-buried in the ground at the center of the circle. "Reverend, what is that?" she said, getting up.

"What is what?" he said, looking over his shoulder. "Oh, that. I couldn't tell you, I'm afraid. It's been here a lot longer than I have."

The grass encroached around the edges of the stone, but most of the surface was clean. A single word was carved at the center, but it was worn so smooth, she couldn't read it until she knelt down and traced the shape of the letters with her fingertips. "Maman," she read out loud.

"Beg pardon?" the Reverend said.

"That's what's written on this stone," she said. "Maman—like French for mother. Is this an old grave?"

"I expect so," he said, straightening up with a groan. "I declare, I don't feel old in my heart, but my knees say something different."

"Is this a picture?" she said, tracing another cluster of carved indentations under the word. She licked her finger to wet it and ran it over the stone, bringing out the details. "It's a woman." The little figure was simple but unmistakably female. In one hand, she held up a mask or a big, flat spoon.

"A fan," Serena said, sitting back on her haunches. "She's holding a fan." She took her keys from her pocket and looked at her keychain. The image of the goddess painted on it was much more detailed, but the shape of her fan was the same.

"Is that a fact?" He offered her a hand and helped her up. "I don't pay much attention to this stone, Serena. The old folks need their totems, and I won't try to argue with them." He looked over at the Jesus statue. "But I've got something else."

She smiled. "Of course. Thank you, Reverend."

He smiled back. "You feeling better now?"

"I am, yes." The women of Briarwood Baptist Church had put their prayer garden around this stone, not the Reverend's Jesus, and there had to be a reason why. But if he knew it, he wouldn't tell her. "Thank you, Reverend." She squeezed his hand. "Merry Christmas."

Jacob hiked almost to the property line. A few more steps into a clear spot, and he could have seen the steeple at the Briarwood Baptist Church. He took the folded envelope out of his pocket and removed the cellphone inside. Unlocking it was easy; he knew the passcode the same way he had known the name and phone number of the Las Vegas police detective who had it. The same way he knew she kept it hidden at her grandmother's condo "just as insurance." The same way he knew how much money to offer her to make her give it up. He knew these things the same way he knew to tell his research assistant Viola to keep digging until she found Serena's Christmas present in the storage house of an antique store in London.

He knew because the Dark Man had told him.

The background picture was Serena posing in a casino next to a man dressed as the Egyptian god Anubis. He smiled. She looked so young and happy. He opened the pictures folder and found the video.

At first, there was only darkness, the interior of a car at twilight. A Black man's hand fumbled over the lens, then he heard a voice in the background, "What the fuck is going on?"

The view switched outward to figures at a distance, coming into focus through a dusty windshield. Two cars were stopped on the other side of the road, half-in, half-out of the empty highway with a magnificent desert sunset in the background. One was a silver muscle car with a blue light flashing on the dashboard; the other was a black sports car with the doors hanging open. In front of the sports car, a Black man was lying on the ground on his belly, arms bent behind him, wrists handcuffed. A White man stood over him, pointing a gun at the back of his head. "Oh shit," he heard Trey say, his voice dry and hoarse.

The image tilted as he got out of the car, still filming. As the angle changed, the camera saw two more Black men standing behind the unmarked police car with their hands planted on the boot and another White man and woman in police uniforms with guns drawn behind them. The woman saw Trey and cried out just as the first cop shot the man on the ground. In a single fluid motion, the shooter turned toward the camera and fired again.

The camera bounced on the ground.

There was more, of course: a shot of Trey's hand as he died, fist clenching and unclenching. Terrible sounds, broken words, the cops and the other captives shouting, screaming, weeping. The part of Jacob that was still the man he had been wept as he watched and listened. But when it was over, he turned off the phone and dropped it on the ground. He stomped on it with his heavy boot until it shattered. Kneeling, he picked the pieces apart then dug a hole in the dirt with his hands and buried some of the pieces. Scooping up the rest, he walked several paces, then knelt and did the same again, then again, then a fourth time until all the pieces were scattered and buried, part of the Briarwood earth. His Jacob-self was horrified, but the Dark Man reassured him.

She's with us now. She doesn't need to know.

When Serena got home to Jacob's house in town that night, he was coming out of the shower. "There's my angel," he said, kissing her. "Did you do anything interesting today?"

"Not really." Part of her wanted to tell him about the cemetery, the slab in the prayer garden, and the way the ground had shaken. But he looked tired; there were shadows under his eyes. Less than a month ago, he had been having open-heart surgery. They were leaving in the morning to go to the other side of the ocean, a place far away, where they could both rest. She'd tell him about it later.

"Nothing," she said, giving him a squeeze before she stepped out of his arms. "How about you?"

"Not a thing," he said. "Let's open a bottle of wine."

29

Serena and Jacob arrived at Jacob's house in Dublin at seven-thirty in the morning on Christmas Eve. A car had met them at the airport, and a man looking fresh as the morning in dress slacks and a sweater met them at the back door. "Welcome home, Jacob," he said. "And merry Christmas."

"And to you, Trevor," Jacob said. "This is my friend, Serena. Serena, meet my assistant, Trevor."

"So glad to meet you finally, Serena," Trevor said, shaking her hand. "Jacob has told me so much about you—all wonderful, I promise."

"Nice to meet you, too." She had slept hard on the plane, and part of her thought she must still be dreaming. Jacob's home was beautiful, a Georgian row house beautifully refurbished. She expected Hugh Grant to wander in looking lovelorn any minute.

"I'll just see about the bags," Trevor said. "Maggie's flight left Gstaad right on schedule, so she should be here by tonight."

"Wonderful." Jacob took her hand and led her into a small dining nook off the massive kitchen. Big windows with views of the back garden surrounded her. *A solarium,* she thought. *This is an honest-to-God solarium.* The round table was set with china and fresh flowers, and a full English breakfast was laid out on the buffet. "Coffee?" Jacob asked her, pouring himself a cup.

"Absolutely." He seemed perfectly at ease in this environment, a completely different person from the man she knew. "Do you always live like this at home?"

"Like what?" He handed her a plate.

"Like Bruce Wayne." Her stomach turned at the sight of the black and white pudding and baked beans, but she took a scone.

Jacob laughed. "I'll show you my Batcave later." He filled his own plate to overflowing. "Most days, Trevor leaves me to feed myself unless I ask him for something."

"He lives here with you?"

"Of course."

"And while you've been in South Carolina?"

"He's been here keeping my life on track," he said. "Taking care of my professional obligations, making sure Maggie's bills get paid, keeping the house for when I decide to come home."

"So, really, you're not just a person." Back home, he had seemed perfectly ordinary and independent. She had almost forgotten that he had once been an idol inside her imagination, her favorite writer. "You're a brand."

"There's no need to be insulting," he said, laughing. "My books are a brand, but I'm still just me." He took her hand across the table. "I'm no different here than I was at Briarwood."

"At Briarwood, you were living in an RV," she pointed out.

"Yeah, but it was a really nice one." They heard Trevor come back in the back door. "Trevor, do we have anything else on for today before Maggie gets here?"

"Not today," Trevor said. "What time shall I wake you?"

Jacob's bedroom made her feel a little more relaxed. It was gorgeously decorated and reasonably neat, but there were books stacked everywhere and a massive TV mounted to the wall. She fell asleep beside him while he watched the news.

But an hour later, he was sleeping, and she was wide awake. She rolled toward Jacob and smiled. Her sleeping prince. His long, black lashes brushed his pale, almost translucent cheeks, and she couldn't resist leaning in closer and kissing his mouth. But he barely stirred.

She put on his bathrobe and her slippers and slipped out of the room. The house was beautiful but freezing. Just across the way was another bedroom with a canopy bed and walls plastered over with posters—Maggie's room, no doubt.

At the end of the hall, she found Jacob's study. Like his bedroom, it was cluttered everywhere with books, and every inch of wall space not covered by bookshelves was covered with art. A shabby-looking leather sofa was shoved into a corner with a small TV on a stand in front of it, and a massive, modern desk filled the big bay window facing the street. But at the center of the room stood a much smaller, much older, and much more delicate desk.

She felt drawn to it; without thinking, she went into the room and pulled the door closed behind her as if afraid she'd be disturbed. It was dark wood with a golden glow—mahogany, she thought—and inlaid with lighter wood in a pattern of stars across the polished top. The initials "EH" were worked in brass and attached to the center drawer between two wing-shaped pulls.

She swept a stack of books off a chair and dragged it over. She ran her fingertips lightly around the curving, beveled edge of the desktop, and every contour felt familiar. She felt as if this were her desk, as if she had lost it long ago and forgotten it but now remembered it completely. Her fingertip worried a slight imperfection on the underside of the edge, and she heard a tiny click.

She pushed back and found a panel on the underside bulging slightly. She found the edge with her nails and pried it open; packets of papers tied with ribbon showered out. She slid to the floor and gathered them up. Letters addressed to Elizabeth Harley, sent from Briarwood Plantation. "Oh my God..."

She scrambled up and over the back of the sofa, settling against the cushions. Tucking the stack into her lap, she opened one and read,

"September 22, 1837... My dear Right Honourable ..." She slid out the last page and read the signature. *"Yours ever in friendship, Ezra."*

"Oh my God," she repeated. Her mouth felt so dry, she could barely get the words out. "Jacob!" But she didn't want him to answer, she realized. These were the letters Ezra Woodbine had written back to England to his fiancée, Elizabeth. Somehow they had found their way to Serena. She tore off the ribbons like she knew nothing about the preservation of historical documents and found the dates to shuffle them into order. Then she settled back to read.

30

May 1, 1837

My dear Elizabeth,

At long last, I have arrived. Rather, I arrived last Tuesday in Charleston, last Friday at Briarwood, and now finally, I have leisure and solitude in which to write. My voyage, as you can see, was longer than expected but mostly uneventful. I will not waste paper detailing it and will move on instead to that which I know to be of interest to you—the running of an American plantation and the plight and condition of the American slave. But if you will spare a morsel of your concern for a thwarted but faithful suitor, know that I am safe.

Caleb Montgomery is the master of Briarwood and my host. He met me at the boat in Charleston with the younger of his two sons, Halsted, who is of an age with me. I am sad to report that rather than the whip-wielding, ravening beasts your Quaker mother's favorite writers are so fond of reporting, I found them both to be most amiable company and as refined as most of the men of our acquaintance at home, rather more so than my own dear father. But I will not pretend South Carolina is anything at all like England. Although Charleston is a city of considerable size and elegance, we made the two-day journey to the plantation on horseback through a wilderness. Our narrow, winding road followed the course of one river then another, and along it we encountered barely any towns and no more than a dozen or so new-made farms.

The house at Briarwood is itself brand new and built on a scale so grand as to be embarrassing—your dear mother would find it quite American, I'm sure. But there is a touching bravery to its grandeur and to Caleb Montgomery himself. He has come to this wilderness not merely to survive but to endure, not to find his fortune but to found his dynasty. In this, he reminds me much of my own father, and I confess I have developed a deep affection for the man even on such short acquaintance. I do not expect you to share my feelings, and no, it is not lost on me that this brave new king is building his empire with the labor of those far less fortunate.

I still share your abhorrence for slavery as an institution. But have not all great empires been so built, from the pharaohs to the Romans, from your own much-mentioned Norman ancestors to my own father with his mills? I do not seek such greatness for myself and could never have the stomach to so exploit my fellow man in the pursuit of such power. But civilization as we know it is built by such men. Without Alexander, we have no library. Without William the Conqueror, we have no William Shakespeare.

But I can see the frown on your lovely face in my mind's eye even as I write, so I will return to matters of kinder and less argumentative interest.

Upon my arrival, I was introduced to Mrs. Ellen Montgomery, a Scotswoman of some beauty and great energy. She is a staunch Presbyterian and inquired of me within a minute of our meeting where my religious loyalties lie. I do not believe my answer of Church of England satisfied her entirely, but I dread to imagine my reception if I had declared myself a Catholic. But in my eagerness to amuse you, I do the good lady an injustice. She welcomed me with grace and much kindness and said she hoped I would enjoy my stay.

I did not meet the rest of the household until dinner. In addition to Halsted, whom I met in Charleston, there is the oldest son, Caleb, Jr., who resembles his father so closely in both form and manner he might be the same man reborn. He is recently married and has just returned from a European honeymoon with his bride, June, who was eager to sympathize with me on the rigors of my voyage.

"I didn't dare swallow a bite from the moment we stepped aboard until my feet touched land in Charleston," she confided in an accent no London stage actress could ever hope to reproduce. But she seems a kind and pretty thing, and young Caleb dotes on her. I am told there is a Montgomery daughter as well, a young lady of sixteen named Alice Rose. But she is currently paying an extended visit to relatives in Savannah and not expected to return for at least a month. If I do not convince Montgomery of the wisdom of my father's scheme, I may never have the honor of her acquaintance.

"But Mr. Woodbine, what of the slaves?" I imagine you asking. Note, please, that even in my fantasies, I am not so bold as to imagine you calling me Ezra.

The slaves are everywhere. As in your own household, every family member is provided with a body servant, the difference being that here they are all African slaves. I myself have been lent the services of a handsome young man named Arthur for the duration of my stay. Domestic duties are all accomplished by slaves under the direct supervision of Mrs. Montgomery. They range in age from small boys charged with chasing farm fowl off the front lawn to a white-haired man with a back so stooped he must surely see behind him better than he does ahead. whose sole duty is to sit in a chair in the back hallway and polish boots.

None of these people appear to be in any immediate distress, but as with our own hired servants, I'm sure they have feelings, hopes, and troubles of which we, the ones they serve, remain oblivious. They all seem to be entirely devoted to Mrs. Montgomery and to be somewhat afraid of their master, but again, this seems little different from our own arrangements in England. Indeed, I suspect the housemaids here have an easier time of it under the rule of Ellen Montgomery than my own mother's do at home.

The house staff appears to be about a dozen souls, but this number is entirely dwarfed by the "field hands," who are apparently legion and managed by an overseer named Simon Flynn. After breakfast yesterday, Montgomery and his sons took me on a tour of the property, and I saw what must have been hundreds of Africans working in the fields, gardens, stables, and shops.

Like any great farm, Briarwood is a village unto itself with a blacksmith and carpenter and any number of other craftsmen. From my father's correspondence with Montgomery, I had a vague notion of the scale of agriculture carried out here. Still, nothing could have prepared me for the sight of so many human souls, male and female, working in absolute concert along row after endless row of cotton.

It is planting season, so each worker has his or her heavy bag of seed and boring stick and bends and pokes and plants and covers and straightens and steps and bends again—backbreaking work, I'm sure. They sing as they work, establishing a rhythm that ripples over the hillside like an ocean's wave. The effect is less like agriculture and more like a mill. The slaves themselves are like a great machine, with each individual no more than a single cog. Seeing this, I found myself in absolute sympathy with you and your mother's point of view. How terrible to be swept up innocent from one's home and transported across the sea to a life of such labor—the basest thief could not deserve such punishment.

Then I saw the conditions under which these people live. Last night after dinner, Halsted invited me to accompany him on a walk, and we passed through the slave quarters. My father's workers would think themselves passed on to heaven if they found themselves in such comfort, row after row of neat new brick cottages. It is as fine and prosperous-looking a little village as any in the English countryside, and the people who live there are clean and well-fed with all their needs provided for. There is even a church which Halsted said is quite lively and well-attended.

Their work is hard, but at least they are rewarded for it with a standard of living many a free man might envy. If they had remained in Africa, would they have so much? And many of them are the third or fourth generation of their line born in America. They have no more connection to their African origins than your great-grandfather had to France.

I do not pretend that the estate of slavery is not abhorrent on its face, but in practice, at least here, I find it less the horror you and your mother imagine and more like the feudal system of our own medieval past. These slaves at Briarwood are like serfs, contributing their labor to the cause of an overlord strong and rich enough to protect them from danger and provide for their survival.

Montgomery has shown me the site on the river where he proposes to build he and father's new American mill, and it is a good one. I asked him if he thought the surrounding countryside, rural and isolated as it is, could provide an adequate workforce. He told me that he intends to staff the mill almost entirely with slaves. He and my father have calculated the purchase of these slaves as a necessary expenditure in the establishment of the enterprise.

For your sake, I will make every effort to dissuade him from this course. I know the thought of so many more humans in bondage fills you with dismay. But from a purely practical viewpoint, the plan makes rather elegant sense. The greatest threat to the success of my father's mills in England has always been problems with the labor. As a gentleman planter, Montgomery already has the apparatus in place to address such issues—health, safety, cooperation, efficiency—if that labor is African slaves. I will have to use all my powers of persuasion and a great deal of imagination if I am to turn him against the plan. My own father may never forgive me.

So as you see, you remain utmost in thoughts.

Yours as ever,

Ezra

May 28, 1837

Dear Miss Harley,

I hope you can forgive my impertinence in writing you a second time before I have received a reply to my first. Indeed, I cannot imagine you have yet received any letter from me at all. But events have transpired here that have disturbed me greatly, and I can think of no other confidante who might understand why.

My father's business with Montgomery goes well, so well in fact that construction on the mill has commenced based solely on the plans I brought with me from England. Montgomery insists I must stay beyond the three months originally proposed for my visit. Indeed, he has suggested more than once that I might remain here indefinitely. I told you before I left England that I would refuse such an offer if it were made, that my heart will always belong to my own country—and to you if you will have it. Be assured, dear Elizabeth, to that I hold and with ever more conviction. I do not belong at Briarwood.

Last week Miss Alice Rose Montgomery and her grandfather, Louis, whom they all call "Grand-Pere" or "the Old Man," returned from their visit to Savannah. Miss Montgomery is a perfectly charming young woman of the willfully empty-headed type you so despise. She flirts with me outrageously, and her brother, Halsted, insists I am the reason she cut her visit to Savannah short.

As she is apparently quite popular with all the young men of the planter class in these parts, I find that highly unlikely. Since her return, she has been visited by half a dozen different potential suitors, most of whom have better fortunes than I. She did make an effort to collect me with pointed questions about my romantic entanglements or lack thereof. I told her that you and I have an understanding, and she told me that England is very far away. But as she barely reaches my shoulder and requires a slave to button her boots, I believe I can fend her off and keep my virtue intact long enough to escape.

Of more interest to me is the Old Man. He was obviously born in France and has the open spirit and perverse humor peculiar to that country. He is a cripple, paralyzed entirely on one side of his body, and one side of his face is drawn downward, giving him an expression that can seem either sinister or melancholy depending on the angle of one's view. But he is, in fact, quite kindly and cheerful. His infirmity appears to have in no way dimmed his spirit or soured his sense of humor. Unlike the rest of the clan, he has a keen interest in art and literature—the library here at Briarwood is entirely his, I am told, and the walls of his own room are lined with more bookshelves the rest of the family do not touch.

When we were introduced, he questioned me closely about my history and background, just as everyone I've met since arriving has done. (The people of this region seem to consider rudeness a virtue when delivered with a smile.) But unlike the others, the Old Man seemed entirely unimpressed by my father's success and hopes for my future and far more interested in my Oxford education. When I told him I had spent several months on the continent, he seemed delighted. Apparently, both Caleb, Jr. and Halsted had been offered a Grand Tour and adamantly refused it. When I told him how much I had enjoyed mine, particularly Italy, he said I must convince Halsted to go.

"Tell him about the girls," he suggested, making Mrs. Montgomery slam down her fan and leave the drawing room at once.

This alone would have been enough to intrigue me, and I have befriended the Old Man. But while he seems quite open and friendly, I have become increasingly convinced there is some mystery attached to his presence here, perhaps even something sinister. He rarely takes meals with the family, preferring to remain in his own room. Because the family calls him Grand-Pere, I assumed he must be Ellen's father. But that lady, with her staunch Presbyterian opinions and Scottish accent, resembles him not at all and exhibits toward him no outward sign of affection.

Rather, he is attended at all times by two slave women, an attractive Negress of middle age named Hester, and her daughter Ariel. They care for all his needs with great tenderness, and he seems to hold them in special regard, conversing with them in French quite affectionately. While the other house slaves are obviously under the authority of the lady of the house, Hester and Ariel are the particular property of the Old Man and do work for no one but him. They speak English; I have heard them talking to the other servants, who seem to bear them no particular ill will. But the Montgomery family takes no notice of them at all. They are never called upon to assist with any task, and indeed, after the first day of the party's return from Savannah, I have never seen them outside the Old Man's room.

Testing my theory, I made mention of them one morning at breakfast when one of the other housemaids who usually serves was absent, and Mrs. Montgomery looked at me as if I were mad. "Those two at table?" she said. "I think not." And the rest of the family looked at me quizzically, as if they weren't quite sure who I meant.

I am not certain I would ever have noted this peculiarity if not for a disturbing incident that stands in direct contrast to it. The family had enjoyed an excellent dinner after which Montgomery, his oldest son, and I had retired to the library to discuss plans for the mill. We didn't emerge until well past ten, at which time I assumed the ladies would have long since gone to bed. But I had just bid Montgomery good night and headed for the stairs when Alice Rose emerged from the shadows and caught my sleeve. She put a finger to her lips for silence and led me out through a side parlor onto the porch.

"Forgive me for being so bold, Mr. Woodbine," she said. "But I need your help." She seemed genuinely distraught. "Halsted has gone down to the quarters again, and someone has to fetch him home before Ma finds out."

"I'm sorry, miss, but I didn't realize the slave quarters were out of bounds," I said. "I went there with your brother myself only yesterday."

"That was in the daylight." Through the window, we saw the slave housekeeper (called Mammy by the family, so presumably a former nursemaid for the Montgomery children) turning down the lamps in the parlor, and Alice Rose drew me deeper into the shadows of the columns. "When you find him, you'll understand."

"When I find him?"

"Please, Mr. Woodbine." In the moonlight, I saw tears glistening on her cheeks. "If Caleb goes, he'll thrash him again, and Mama will know why. She'll make Papa send him away." She put her hand on my arm and looked up at me with eyes that would have touched the chivalry of a dead man. "Just find him and tell him to come home. He'll listen to you. He likes you."

As a veteran of the seedier corners of both Manchester and

Oxford, I had no fear of the slave quarters after dark. But I did not relish being a featured player in some family drama, either. "I'm sure he'll come home on his own when he's ready," I said, patting her hand.

"I know he won't." She moved closer and caught hold of my jacket, and her maidenly bosom pressed against my arm. "I'll let you kiss me if you go."

I tell you this not to make you jealous, Elizabeth—as if that were possible!—but to make you see how strange the entire experience was. This girl is beautiful by any standard, and under ordinary circumstances, seems as innocent and genteel as any society maiden you or I might know. But there was hunger and desperation in her in that moment that made her seem almost savage. If her intention was to turn my head, she failed miserably; rather, her performance inspired pity bordering on revulsion.

"I will go if you wish me to, Miss Montgomery," I said, extricating myself from her clutches as gently as I could. "Of course I will. You needn't...don't trouble yourself."

"Thank you." She drew back from me, and I couldn't tell if she was relieved or disappointed. "You should have no trouble finding him. Just ask the first Negro you meet." Before I could answer or say goodnight, she had turned away and gone back into the house.

As it turned out, I didn't have to ask anyone where to find Halsted. I heard him as soon as I entered the little village. He was on the porch of one of the cabins, singing, roaring drunk, with a frightened-looking slave wench clamped under his arm. Other slaves stood scattered around the yard, men and women in couples and three men holding musical instruments.

"Play on, goddamnit!" Halsted was shouting as I approached. "Dance!" He saw me and gestured in my direction with the bottle in his hand. "Dance for Ezra!"

The Negroes all looked at me with frightened, angry eyes, the men coiled fury, the women like statues. "Come home, Halsted," I said, blushing under their gaze. "Your sister sent me to find you."

"Which one?" he said, laughing. "Come, come, Ezra, look at this!" The girl he held was wringing her white head scarf between her hands, and her hair was loose and unbraided, a halo around her head. "Touch it!" He grabbed a handful of her hair, and she flinched, obviously biting back a scream of pain. "You think it will feel nasty, but it doesn't." He stroked her like a cat. "It's soft. Here, touch it!" He shoved the girl toward me down the steps, and she almost fell; I had to catch her in my arms to keep her from landing face-first in the dirt. She recoiled from me so violently, she nearly fell again. I steadied her by the elbow, then stepped back and let her go.

"It's late," I said. "Let's go back to the house before your father sends your brother after us."

But Halsted wasn't listening to me anymore. He was staring at something behind me. I turned and saw the younger of the Old Man's Negro nursemaids, Ariel, standing on the porch of one of the other cabins. Another slave was with her, and as I watched, he handed her what looked like money. But she wasn't looking at him or at Halsted. She was looking at me. I have been surrounded by the slaves of Briarwood since I arrived here; Arthur, my manservant, dresses me every morning. But until that moment, none of them had ever looked me in the eye.

"Evening, little sister," Halsted called. His voice quavered slightly behind his drunken bravado.

"You too drunk, Master Halsted," she said in a clear, strong voice that betrayed no trace of fear. "You do like this gentleman say and go on home to bed now."

Halsted's expression darkened. "You think I'll take orders from some wench?" He stumbled down the steps and started across the yard, fists clenched. Without thinking, I caught him, and for a moment, I was certain he would strike me. The other slaves remained paralyzed, wide-eyed with fear or shock, but the girl Ariel never flinched. In fact, she was smiling.

"Halsted, please." Please understand, Elizabeth, I like this young man. From the moment we met, nothing in his manner had hinted at anything but the most amiable of natures. If you met him in a ballroom at home, you would find him far more charming and attractive than you do me. But as I held him back from the girl, he seemed possessed by some wild demon. "Alice Rose is worried about you," I told him. "She asked me to bring you home."

He looked at my face, and it was as if he were just that moment recognizing me as if he were waking up from a dream. "Thank you, Ezra," he said. "It was good of you to come." All the resistance went out of him, and I led him back toward the house. As we crossed the lawn, I heard the slave musicians start to play. I confess I thought of the slave girl, Ariel, and wondered if she would dance.

Halsted went off to bed as gentle as a lamb, and the next morning, neither he nor his sister mentioned the night before. But I see these people more clearly now. For all their wealth and good manners, they are nothing like us. There is a savagery about them, a violence lurking just behind the mask. I mean to end my father's business here as quickly as I can and return to England. Briarwood is not for me.

Yours devotedly,

Ezra

Addressed to "The Right Honorable Elizabeth Harley"

September 22, 1837

My dear Right Honorable,

I have felt myself a cad for neglecting our correspondence for so long. But having now read your response to my first letter, I think it might have been better had I never written you at all. You are as intelligent and good-hearted as any girl of your class and station could ever hope to be. But you are a child.

All your meetings and speeches and pamphlets and picnics—if anyone turned up at one of your meetings with a pamphlet that described the horrors of slavery as it truly is, you would stone the man to death. My affection for you has always been genuine, Lizzy, and the part of me that loves you still would spare you the truth. No doubt you will find any number of amiable sheep as willing as I was to join you in your illusion, your pantomime of outrage. But I cannot.

Nor can I go on as I have done so long, allowing myself to be herded through the gates of a blind but comfortable life by my father, by convention, even, sweet girl, by you. I know that some day soon, all those who have known me will be shocked at the course I have chosen. Those who have loved me will want to know why. At times I have been bold and foolish enough to count you among these. And with your fine mind and warm heart, perhaps you can even understand.

Soon after the incident with Halsted I described to you in my last letter, one of Alice Rose's friends, Naomi, arrived for an extended visit. The excuse was that she had come to escape the heat and sickness of her family's own plantation in Charleston. But I believe she was brought in as a distraction for the youngest Montgomery son, and in this, she has excelled.

She is a very pretty girl with no more sense than a hen pecking corn. Alice Rose is a belle and a flirt; Naomi is an idiot. But Halsted seems entirely besotted. He has not visited the slave quarters after dark once since her arrival, and Mrs. Montgomery has quite exhausted herself devising amusements for "the young people," rides, picnics, even a ball attended by planter families from all over the state.

At each of these entertainments, I am trotted out as a conversation piece—the rich textile man's son from England—and significant looks and snatches of whispered conversation caught in passing have alerted me to my assumed place in this world. I am meant to marry Alice Rose. But I can assure you, your own changed affections notwithstanding, I shall not.

Amid all this tiresome fun and frolic, the Old Man fell ill, and I found my best refuge with him. I spent at least one quiet hour every day in his pleasant room reading to him. The curtains were drawn against the heat and blinding sunlight, and a small boy operated a huge fan on a shutter above us. I remain steadfast in my condemnation of slavery, but when the air is so hot it seems the breath of hell's own furnace, it is very pleasant to be fanned. In addition to the boy, we were at all times attended by Hester and Ariel. At first, they were shy in my presence, but within a week, they grew accustomed to me as they are to the Old Man himself and began to speak freely. I was happily surprised to find that Ariel was familiar with many of the books I read aloud. "Grand-Pere teaches me," she explained, casting down her wide green eyes. "Will you read more of the Shakespeare? He is my favorite."

"Mine as well," I told her, happy to oblige.

"Take care you do not miss a word, young friend," the Old Man said. "She knows the sonnets by heart and some lines from the plays."

"Take this, girl," Hester said, handing her daughter the chamber pot. "Wash it and bring the old master and his guest some tea."

The green eyes flashed, but she jumped up from her seat to obey. "Oui, Maman."

I confess I am hesitant to continue my tale from here. Indeed, if you had not chastised me so harshly and dismissed my lover's suit with such certain fervor in your last, I would spare you all further details. As a gentleman, I could do nothing else. But as we are not to be lovers, but rather cool friends who seek only to further one another's education and experience, I shall press on. Do not think I do so out of any ill feeling toward you. If I were to hate you for not loving me, I would be the worst sort of hypocrite.

If I seem angry, know that you are not the object of my rage. In truth, in recent days, my rage requires no specific object at all. I pretend I don't know why this should be, that my temper is no more than a mood or a symptom of the heat or a by-product of the other strong emotions that of late have seized me. But I fear I know that isn't true, fear this knowledge more than I have ever had sense to fear anything before. The world is so much bigger than we knew, Elizabeth, and deeper and darker. For all our reading, all our imagining, all our desire to see all, we have seen nothing.

I could relate to you a thousand details to explain what happened next, the thrill of every accidental touch, the sweet sympathy in every stolen glance. But this would serve no purpose but to feed a fever and might prove painful to you. (Even now, I delude myself that there still lives in your heart some shred of deeper feeling for me that could still be bruised!)

I am in love with Ariel. I never meant to fall in love with her; I could not tell you now what moment it was when this feeling came upon me. At one moment, I would have spoken of her to anyone who asked as a charming servant, educated well beyond her station, an appropriate object for pity, a proof of the injustice of her state. The next she is my very soul, and I can barely stand to speak of her at all.

I say that I love her. I do not yet dare say that she loves me.

After that first afternoon of Shakespeare, Hester became noticeably more wary of leaving me alone with the Old Man and her daughter. At first, I was insulted. Was I such a brute or curiosity that I was not to be trusted alone with a housemaid? But as the days passed with me spending every afternoon in the amiable company of Ariel and the Old Man, I began to understand. They were my respite from the Montgomery family and their endlessly active pursuits and inane conversation.

Since the coming of Naomi, the talk was all gossip, dogs, and horses. By contrast, Ariel and I talked about books and the places I had seen in Europe, Shakespeare and sea voyages and Michelangelo. She had a quick wit and a ready, musical laugh. Truth be told, she reminded me of you, Elizabeth. But because of her station, she was not so reserved as you; her enthusiasm and wonder were intoxicating. In many ways, she was like a precocious child, clever but innocent.

Most afternoons, the Old Man would doze off after his wee afternoon dram, but I would stay, and Ariel and I would read or talk on. None of my hosts saw anything strange in this; indeed, I was much praised for my kindness to the Old Man. But I didn't stay for him. I began to watch Hester like a cat at a mouse hole, waiting for the moment she would leave the room, leave Ariel and me alone.

And at last, it came. I had been reading Mr. Pope's "Rape of the Lock," and a storm had been gathering outside. It started to rain, and Hester was called to run out with the others to gather up the washing before it was soaked, leaving Ariel behind to attend Grand-Pere.

She was standing at the window, gazing out at the storm.

Lightning flashed with a loud crack of thunder just as I joined her, and she started, falling back against me. "I'm sorry," she said, recoiling from me in what seemed like real fright.

"Don't be sorry." She smelled like sun-warmed cotton and clean skin. I put a hand on her upper arm to draw her to me, and she gazed into my eyes. "If you tell me to leave you alone, I will," I promised, and I pray it was true. If she had repelled me, I pray I would have respected her wishes as I would yours or any lady's. But I confess I can't be sure.

And my chivalry was not so tested. She closed her eyes and tilted up her chin…and now she is my love.

I know you will say this is madness. I know my father will disown me. I do not even know of any place we can go where Ariel could ever be more than a servant in the eyes of the world. But in my heart, she is my wife. I will offer Montgomery any price he likes for her. I am not without my own resources. I will take her from this savage, wretched wilderness where she is a slave, to someplace beautiful where she belongs.

I do not expect you to understand. Again, if I believed you had ever returned my friendship with any more tender feeling, you would be my one regret. I hope someday you will forgive me. More than that—I hope someday you find such a love of your own. Would that not be a blissful thing, Elizabeth? The four of us together in a gondola on the canals of Venice, free at last? This is the hope I will hold until we meet again.

Yours ever in friendship,

Ezra

November 1, 1837

Elizabeth,

The town schoolteacher and librarian who agreed to act as my attorney has brought me the Bible from my room at Briarwood, a kindness that would be as nothing to me if not for your latest letter tucked inside. As I sit here now reading your beautiful declaration of love, I could weep, and I cannot but wonder what might have been had I received it sooner. But in truth, I do not think it would have made any difference.

In my heart, I know my fate was sealed the moment I set foot on the threshold of Briarwood. I am its creature, and it has waited for me for a very long time. If I have a prayer left in me, it is that you will not too much regret that you ever cared for me after you learn what I have done. I do not pretend that I am not a monster. But perhaps if you know the truth of what led me to my crimes, you can be free of me and any feeling of guilt on my behalf forever.

You will have read by now of my love for the slave girl, Ariel, and my intention to buy her, free her, and marry her. This seemed the most honorable expression of my feelings, and I expected she would agree—I had much cause to believe my love to be reciprocated. She could not have so willingly submitted to my passions without at least the hope of a binding commitment of some kind.

I was never such a fool as to believe her status as an African slave would be of no consequence. Indeed, I expected it to be the second most significant truth of our life together, coloring every other facet and second only to our love. But I did love her, and I knew she loved me, and I believed these truths to be equal to any obstacle and worthy of any sacrifice.

Ariel was not such a fool. When I asked her for her hand, she laughed at me. "Who will you pay for me, then?" she said. Montgomery, I told her. "But I am not his girl," she said. "Not his slave, no how. The Old Man is my master."

I was glad to hear this, as I had developed a sympathetic mutual understanding with the Old Man. I believed him to be my friend. I even considered sharing with him my plans before I proposed to Ariel. But when I said this to Ariel, she laughed harder, laughed and cried, too. "Sweet boy," she said, putting her hand to my cheek. "He will never let me go. And besides, I cannot leave this place."

"Not even to be with me?" My pride was wounded. "Not even to be free?"

"I cannot be free," she said. "But I will be with you here, my Ezra."

She threw her arms around my neck and held me tight, and all my anger melted away. "Tell me you are mine."

"I am yours, darling," I told her. "Always yours." In my heart, I was still certain my plan would succeed and that she would be happy. But I didn't argue the point with her anymore.

I would have spoken to the Old Man immediately, but he fell into a fever that same night. I sat up with him, hoping to catch him at a lucid moment or at least provide him with some comfort. Ariel was there in the room, and her mother, Hester, and the small boy with the fan who Ariel had told me was her half-brother, Adam. And to my surprise, Alice Rose joined us. I had never seen her visit her grandfather's room before, but she sat at his bedside all night with her chair pulled close to mine.

The Old Man never really awakened. He called out several times in French and English and once in a garbled sort of Latin which I couldn't understand but which made Alice Rose grab my hand and hold it tight. Hester crossed herself and murmured a prayer. Ariel and I looked at one another and smiled. Then she turned away to look out the window.

An hour or so before dawn, his breath became a rattle. "Go fetch Papa," Alice Rose told Ariel. "Tell him Grand-Pere is leaving us."

"What about your mother?" I asked when my love had gone.

"She won't care," Alice Rose said. Her usual gay façade had fallen, and she was more beautiful for it. But there was a meanness in her eyes and expression, a fury that looked nothing like a young girl's grief for her grandfather. "She hates the Old Man."

"Hates her own father?" I said.

She laughed, a nasty little bark. "Her father?" she said. "You mean he hasn't told you? He's Papa's father. Papa took Ma's name to get away from the scandal." The Old Man's breath was like dead leaves scratching at a window. "His plantation in Saint Domingue burned. All he had left was a trunk full of gold, Papa, and this one." She pointed at Hester, who paid her no mind but kept on bathing the Old Man's fevered brow. "Granddaddy Montgomery took him in as a partner down in Charleston and let him have Ma and the Montgomery name."

The door opened, and the man I knew as Montgomery came in with Ariel. He didn't speak to his daughter or me but went straight to his father's bedside. "Je suis ici, Papa," he said, taking the Old Man's hand.

He stayed that way in the dark for what felt like hours. The only light came from Hester's candle, and she was the only one of us who moved, tending the Old Man. Montgomery stayed standing, holding his father's hand, and I imagined I saw a look of sympathy and understanding pass between him and Hester more than once. But I was very tired and at times half-dreaming. Sometimes I thought another man had joined us, a dark figure standing behind Ariel with his hands on her shoulders. But whenever I looked again, he was gone.

Just as dawn was breaking, the Old Man died. I didn't see or hear it happen; I had dozed off. But a sob from Ariel awakened me, and when I looked up, she was crying in her mother's arms. Montgomery was kneeling beside the bed with his head down on his clasped hands. Little Adam was running out the door.

Alice Rose was still beside me, still holding my hand. Her face was pale but placid, impossible to read. "Ezra, is your father really very rich?" she asked me.

I was shocked, but I answered, "Yes."

Ellen Montgomery came in wearing her gown and nightcap, carrying a lamp. "Get up from there," she said, tugging on her husband's arm. "It isn't decent." Montgomery obeyed but said nothing. He just stood there like a lost child with tears streaming down his face. "You two," Ellen said to Hester and Ariel. "Get him ready for the undertaker. Then pack up all these books and burn them."

"You can't be serious!" I said, getting up. "His library is priceless!"

She looked at me, and at her daughter standing beside me. "Have it, then," she said. "Ship it back to England. But do it quickly. I won't have it in my house."

"Leave it, Ezra," Alice Rose said. "It doesn't matter now. Come downstairs with me and see the boys. We'll go out, go hunting or go to Charleston until this is over."

"No!" Her father seemed to awaken from his grief as if from a dream. "No one leaves the house. He must be buried properly." He sounded like the man I had known since coming to America, strong and determined. "For your mother's sake."

"I will come down soon," I said, just to placate her. But I couldn't miss the flash of fury in Ariel's eyes.

When the others had gone, I sent little Adam to fetch my own servant and some boxes. While Ariel and Hester washed and dressed the body, we packed away the books, two teams at the same work. The sun rose slowly outside the windows, lighting the room, and when I looked at the Old Man's face, it held no more horror than a figure carved from wax.

We heard a carriage outside, and my servant, Arthur, looked out the window. "Undertaker here, Mister Ezra," he said.

"All right." We had packed up all the most valuable volumes, in my estimation, the oldest and rarest. What was left would be a shame to lose if I weren't allowed to continue, but they could all be replaced. "Let's clear out of his way."

"Wait. You must take this." Ariel said. She lifted the covers at the foot of the bed, exposing the dead man's ugly, grayish-yellow feet. Between them was another book, a cracked and battered Holy Bible.

"Leave that!" Hester scolded, and little Adam's eyes went wide.

"What is that?" Arthur said. "Don't listen to these women, Mister Ezra. They think they can do hoodoo."

"You think that?" Hester hissed, making a sign at him, her hand curled into a claw. "You think it was us?"

But Ariel was looking at me. "Show me, darling," I said.

She smiled and brought me the book. "Not much, really," she said, opening it to the back. "Just one page."

She handed it over. Like most family Bibles, the back pages had been left blank by the printer to record the family history; births and marriages and deaths. The Montgomery family's version was on prominent display in the library downstairs. This one recorded a French Family, the Old Man's family, the Palissandre family. The page Ariel meant for me to see was the last and recorded the following:

Louis Palissandre: Married to Marie De Maupassant, died in

childbirth. Produced one son, ~~Louis Honore~~ CALEB MONTGOMERY

Mated to Seraphima, an African, died of fever. Produced one daughter, Hester

~~Louis Honore Palissandre~~: CALEB MONTGOMERY: Married to Ellen Montgomery. Produced two sons, Caleb and Halsted, and one daughter, Alice Rose

Mated to Hester, a mulatto. Produced one daughter, Ariel.

Halsted Montgomery:

~~Mated to Ariel, a quadroon~~

This last line was marked out several times, and below it was an upside-down cross drawn in dark brown ink that looked like blood. "Dear God," I said as I read this. "God in heaven."

"Now you see," Hester said. "Now you know." Ariel was looking at me. I could hear the voices of Ellen and the undertaker as they came up the stairs.

"Yes, I see," I said, closing the book and taking Ariel's hand. Tears came to her beautiful eyes. "Everything will be all right."

"No, it won't," she said. "Can't you see? They ain't never going to let me go."

I let go of her hand just as the door opened. Ellen Montgomery came in with Alice Rose and a man dressed in a black suit. "All right, that's enough," Ellen said to me. "You must let Mr. Harrison get on with his business now."

"Yes, of course. Arthur, take the last of these boxes to my room." I tucked the Bible under my arm. "Mrs. Montgomery, where is your husband? I need to speak with him on a matter of some urgency."

"He's not fit to see anyone," she said. "Leave him in peace."

"It's all right, Ma," Alice Rose said. She smiled at me over her mother's shoulder as if we shared a secret. "You'll find him in the library, Mr. Woodbine. Shall I go with you?"

"No." If I am truly honest, Elizabeth, I knew what she thought I wanted. Though I had never made the slightest overture to her beyond politeness no matter how often we were thrown together, Alice Rose believed I was in love with her. She believed every man she met was in love with her, that she need only to look into his eyes and pout to make him smitten past all hope of recovery. The very idea that this might not be true in my case had never entered the empty chambers of her feeble little mind. She had suggested we might marry; now she assumed I meant to ask her father for her hand. I knew it, and for the sake of convenience, I let her believe it. I returned her smile and said. "It's better that I speak with him alone."

I found the man I had known as Caleb Montgomery at his desk in the library working. Dawn was still breaking, gray light filtering through the shutters, and a single candle burned beside him. "The last of the lumber will arrive today, or I'll know why not," he said briskly without looking up from his accounts. "We'll have floors on the top two floors by the end of November; we must begin work on acquiring the machinery."

"Just as you like, sir," I said. I could hardly believe he was the same man who had wept on his knees by his father's bedside. Or the man who had raped his own half-sister to create the woman I loved. "I have come to ask you for your daughter."

This caught his attention. He looked up and smiled. "She got you at last, did she? Oh well, Ellen will be pleased."

"Not that daughter." You know my character only too well, Elizabeth. I am a coward by nature. If I were accustomed to facing off across desks against powerful men, I would never have come to America. When his brow darkened, I nearly took it back. For a single, shameful moment, I almost said I had misspoken and asked for Alice Rose after all.

But I didn't.

"Your daughter Ariel," I said, pushing on though my heart was pounding and my knees were weak. "I want her."

"You forget yourself, sir!"

"I want to marry her."

"Dear God, man! You've lost your mind!"

"I will pay you." I was ashamed to offer it, but it was the easiest way, the safest. Once we were away, I would have given Ariel her freedom, Elizabeth, I swear it. "Whatever price you like for Ariel and for Hester.

With the Old Man gone, you don't need them. I will take them far away from here, and you'll never hear from any of us again." Dreams of Africa or San Francisco or even our own Italy filled my head. "You and my father can continue your business without me. Halsted knows as much about the mill now as I do." I could see I was reaching him; the thunder was fading from his face. "Wouldn't Ellen be pleased by that, too?"

He had risen from his chair; now he sat back down. "It is hardly Ellen's business," he said. His hands shook as he drew a piece of parchment before him and started to write. "Take this to Saxonville to my attorney, John Flynn. Tell him what's needed and bring him back here to manage the papers. Halsted will go with you. He knows the way."

Within the hour, we were on the road to town. Halsted had spent a few minutes alone with his father before he met me in the hall. "I know where we're going, and I know why," he said to me there. "We don't need to talk about it."

And so we did not. We rode in silence side by side. Most of the leaves had fallen, and bare branches met in an archway over our heads. But the thick woods on either side of us crackled and whispered with life. "I am sorry about your grandfather," I said at last.

"Sorrier than me, I reckon." He spat tobacco into the road. I hadn't seen him take a drink, but I had seen him fill a silver flask at the sideboard and tuck it into his pocket. "Don't talk to me, Ezra." Calling my name, he almost sounded like a friend, but his gaze was fixed on the road ahead. "Just ride."

After another half hour of silence, I was half-dozing in the saddle when he spoke again. "Have you seen the ghost?"

I was so startled, I barely heard what he'd said. "The what?"

"Never mind." He stopped his horse and took a drink from his flask. "You'd know if you'd seen it."

"But what are you talking about?" I remembered the half-dream of the dark man standing behind Ariel.

"I said never mind!" He put the flask away and clucked to his horse. "We're almost there."

I thought about what I'd seen in his grandfather's Bible, his name linked to Ariel's but marked out with a cross in blood. I kept my peace and rode beside him into Saxonville.

We found the lawyer John Flynn in a public house having his midday meal and what was obviously not his first pint of the day. "Young Halsted!" he said, half rising from his chair. "And the very English Mr. Woodbine!" He clasped each of our hands in turn before going back to his chop. "Take a chair."

"Pa wants you at the farm," Halsted said. "The Old Man died, and Ezra wants to buy two of the Negroes." The lawyer sputtered into his mug. "Those two, yes," Halsted said. "Will you come?"

Flynn's florid face went yellow pale. "Of course," he said. "We will collect the papers from my office."

With all the preparations he had to make, we only made it back to the drive up to Briarwood just after dark. All the torches leading up the house had been lit. "All Hallow's Eve," Flynn said, taking a drink. He and Halsted had emptied one flask and started on another. I was stone-cold sober. As we passed through a thick copse of evergreen trees, I thought I saw the dark figure of a man watching from the shadows. But even now, I can't be sure.

I expected to find a wake in progress at the house, but there were no visiting carriages or servants out front despite all the torches. Alice Rose was waiting for us on the front porch, dressed in a bright pink gown. "Hurry upstairs and change," she said. "Reverend Holloway is here for dinner."

"Where's Pa?" Halsted said, getting down from his horse.

"Never mind all that," she said. "He'll see Mr. Flynn in the morning. Mr. Flynn, did you bring dinner clothes?"

"Y'all will need to excuse me, my dear," Flynn said, tipping his hat. "I think I'll go impose on my brother for the night." His brother, Simon, was the overseer at Briarwood, a bad-tempered drunk whose employment was a favor to the lawyer. "Tell your father to send for me at his leisure."

"We will," Alice Rose said. She came down the steps as he rode off toward the overseer's cabin and held out her little white hand to me. "Won't you come in, darling?"

"God's breath, Alice," Halsted said, pushing her aside as he passed on his way up the steps. "Don't be such a damned fool."

Arthur was waiting in my room with my own dinner suit freshly pressed. "When is the funeral?" I asked as he dressed me. Where is Ariel? I wanted to ask him, but I didn't dare.

"What funeral, Mister Ezra?" Arthur was a strange creature, Elizabeth. I would like to imagine a circumstance where the two of you might have become acquainted. With all your work for the abolition of slavery, you have never encountered a man like him. And I am quite certain he could never have conceived of a woman like you.

He spoke the backward patois of all the Negro slaves, but he was as efficient, as correct, as formal in his dignity as any valet in London. Placed in service in the royal household, I don't doubt he would have acquitted himself well. But there was something else that went far beyond any excellence of service. There was a power within him, felt more than seen, a silent fury that was as much a part of him as his polished ebony skin. He was unfailingly polite to me, obedient to my instructions, solicitous of my comfort. Yet I know now and knew even then he held me in contempt.

"Grand-Pere's funeral," I said, thinking he was being purposely obtuse.

"He gone, sir," he said. "The undertaker took him right after y'all left." He brushed the back of my jacket and straightened my cuffs.

"Is that not strange?" I asked him. "Do you not think that strange?"

He looked up at me, looked into my eyes for what may well have been the first time. "No, sir." His handsome face held no expression; it was like the death mask of a god. "I don't think nothing at all."

The family had gathered for dinner by the time I went downstairs, Louis-now-Caleb and the wife who had made him respectable and their fine sons and beautiful daughter. Caleb, Jr.'s wife was there, her eyes rimmed in red, clinging to her husband's arm, and Halsted's flighty little chicken of a fiancée, Naomi.

All of them seemed nervous, amateur actors unsure of their lines in some terrible play, all except Alice Rose, the prima donna of the piece. She was hanging on the arm of the Reverend Holloway when I came down, pretending to be fascinated by whatever he was saying, a dimpled simper on her face. But as soon as she saw me, she abandoned him to rush to my side.

"There you are," she said, twining both hands around my arm. She dropped her voice to an intimate murmur. "Papa says we may announce the engagement at dinner tonight if we wish."

"Engagement?" I felt like a man in a dream. "There is no engagement."

"Fine, then," she said with her prettiest pout. "You can ask me after dinner." She pressed herself against my forearm, making my flesh crawl. One more night, I told myself as I let her lead me to the dining room. One more night, then we will be away.

The dinner seemed normal enough, quiet but for a constant stream of chatter kept up between Alice Rose and Naomi. As the second course was served, we heard a horrible scream from outside. I was sure it was little Adam, Hester's youngest child, my Ariel's half-brother. Ellen Montgomery dropped her silver fork hard on her delicate china plate. "Go put a stop to that," she ordered the slave at her elbow.

"No," Caleb said, half rising from his chair. "Leave him alone."

Dessert was being cleared when the real screaming started. Through the window, we saw black figures running back and forth on the porches and heard the pounding of their feet like the terrified scuttling of rats on a burning ship. A slave woman ran into the dining room, eyes wild with fear. She ignored all of us at the table and ran to one of the Negro footman. "It done took her," she said, clutching at his arm. "She done rose up."

"Hush now," her man was saying, his eyes fixed on his master. "You can't be coming in here."

"It don't matter; can't you hear me?" the woman said, her voice rising. "Ariel is coming." At this, I stood up. "She done killed Simon Flynn." A loud bang sounded from the hall outside, the front door crashing open, cracking back against the wall. "It don't matter," the woman repeated as she slumped back against her man, her brown face going gray. "She here."

By then, all the men at the table were moving, but I was first. "Ezra, don't!" I heard Alice Rose calling behind me, but I never looked back.

My beloved was waiting in the hall just at the foot of the stairs. Her hair was loose in a wild halo, and every inch of her beautiful skin was smeared and drenched with dirt and blood. Her blouse had been ripped open, exposing one delicate breast, and her petticoat was torn straight up the front and stiff with dried, black blood. Her eyes showed white around the irises, and she was panting open-mouthed, her lips drawn back over her teeth. She was dragging a heavy axe beside her, the handle thicker than her forearm, the blade soaked in blood.

"Darling!" I cried out, running to her, taking her into my arms. She slumped against me, and the axe dropped from her grasp.

"They thought they done killed me, Ezra," she said. "That bitch… that pink, mewling bitch…she told Flynn to kill me."

"Stop this!" Caleb shouted.

Ariel screamed, and all the doors and shutters in the room slammed shut. She bowed up in my arms, and the carpet rippled like an ocean wave, knocking Caleb off his feet. "He said he would ruin me first," she said, clutching at my shirt front, leaving bloody stains —her fingernails were torn down to the quick. "He raped me, and he put things inside me, tore me up." I was crying, and my legs lost their strength. I collapsed on the stairs, still clutching her in my arms.

"Then he tied me to the post and beat me. Then she took her turn. Then when she got tired, he beat me some more. And all of them was watching, Mama and the others; they didn't do nothing, say nothing; what they going to say? They tied up too, all the time, every minute, tied and gagged and blind. But not me." She smiled. "I called to him, the dark man, and he came."

Her voice was barely louder than a whisper. "They thought I was beat to death, but he was with me. They put me in the ground and covered me up, but he was with me, in me, and we dug me back out.

He in me now, Ezra." Tears were streaming down her cheeks, but her eyes were clear and dark with rage. "Do you feel it?"

"I feel it." Her body burned as if with fever, and I could feel the power coursing through her like a current.

"He helped me kill Si Flynn," she said. "But Ezra, I so tired."

"I know, darling." I could feel the power all around me now, swarming on my skin like wasps. Looking into her beautiful eyes, I saw the dark man looking back. "I know what to do." I kissed her mouth and breathed it all inside.

The axe was an extension of my arm; I barely felt its weight. Halsted reached me first, and I buried the blade in his chest as I stood up. I should have been sickened by the blood that erupted from the wound in a fountain, horrified by the wail of pain he made. But I reveled in these things. The spirit in me drank them down like water after a desert. Caleb, Jr., grabbed for me, and I cleaved his head from his shoulders, kicking him back as he fell.

The others were screaming, running for the library, and I heard the French doors slamming shut, the shutters slamming hard into their frames, sealing everyone inside. I moved through them as a reaper moves through wheat, all the white, screaming faces, bathing in their blood, and I laughed as I did it. For it was me, Elizabeth, my rage, my desire. The dark man moved in me and gave me strength, but it was my will they should die.

The Reverend babbled prayers at me as Ellen Montgomery clung to his back. I cleaved his head still in its hat, splitting it open like a pumpkin. The crone sprang at me, hands like claws to scratch my eyes, and I bashed her skull with the flat of the blade, dropping her dead at my feet.

After that, the fury descended; all was red. The slaves were like dark shadows, watching safe and still; the others were white demons for my slaughter. I did not see a face again until Alice Rose, the last of the family, left alive. She was clawing at the shutters, sobbing like a child, her bright pink gown and golden curls splattered with blood.

"Come to me, my darling," I said, swinging the axe through empty air to hear it sing. "Are we not meant to be wed?" The blade crashed into the mantlepiece, shattering the china figure of a shepherdess, and my quarry screamed. "Look at me!" I roared, and she shook her head, curls dancing. "Look at your husband, you murderous bitch! Look at your prize!"

"Mercy!" she babbled, falling to her knees. "Mercy, please, Ezra—I love you!"

I buried the blade in her face.

From my feet, I heard a mewling sob. Halsted's pitiful little fiancée, Naomi, was huddled against the sealed window frame, her skirts bunched around her like a nest. "I told her," she babbled, her gaze fixed on the floor. "It was wrong, so wrong what they did...that poor darky girl...I couldn't bear it. I hid." She looked up at me, wild fear in her eyes. "I hid, I swear! I didn't see!"

The dark spirit that possessed me wanted me to kill her, but I wouldn't. I raised the axe, and she screamed, scrabbling like a rat. I broke through the sealed shutters on the window behind her, shattering the glass, making her a hole. "Go," I told her. "Run." I heard her escaping as I turned away, listened to her screams fading as she ran.

I let the axe drop as I shambled back out to the hall. Arthur, the man who had pretended to be my servant, stared at me in wonder. "You done it." For the first time, I saw some positive emotion in his eyes. "You killed them all."

I moved past him. The evil inside me was still strong, but my body was exhausted. I barely heard Arthur's whoop of triumph, barely noticed as the front door opened and he and the others ran out. All I wanted was Ariel.

She was dead, of course. Poor darling, she had been dead when she came out of the ground. I had left her to their mercy, but they had had no mercy to give. I lifted her broken little body in my arms and carried her up the stairs, my boots leaving bloody footprints as I went. I carried her to the Old Man's room and lay her on the bed, curling my body around her. "I won't ever leave you again," I whispered in her ear.

They found me there, and I did not resist them. The lawyer, John Flynn, has promised to post this letter to you and another to my father. In return, I have signed their confession. I did not read it. What I have written you here is the truth. I was not a faithful lover to you, Elizabeth, and for that, I am sorry. But that is my only regret.

Good-bye.

Ezra

31

Jacob slept all day. As soon as he had boarded the plane, the energy that kept him strong began to fade. As he moved further and further away from Briarwood, he felt the bond between himself and the thing that possessed him stretching and tearing like a caul. Over the course of the flight, as Serena slept beside him, his thoughts became more focused, more his own, even as he felt his body failing. When they landed, he had felt his essential "Jacob-ness" more clearly than since the night of the cross burning. But his physical body was spent.

He woke up to his daughter's voice. "Da? Are you dead?" Maggie sat on the edge of the bed. "You're going to sleep through Christmas."

He smiled at his beautiful child. "You made it." Her hair was longer than when he'd seen her last, and dyed blue-black at the roots. "How was Gstaad?"

"Shockingly Alp-y." She collapsed on his chest and hugged him tight. "I'm so glad to see you. I've been worried, and I hate to worry."

"Nothing to worry about," he promised as he kissed her hair. "Where's Serena? Have you met her yet?"

"She's in your study," she said, sitting up. "You have to come see what she's found."

Serena had shoved the sofa back against the wall and covered the rug with delicate-looking sheaths of closely-written paper. "Hey baby," she said, barely looking up as he came in. She knelt on her haunches at the edge of her creation, still dressed in her copper-colored nightie and his robe. "You're awake."

"Angel, what are you doing?" The papers were obviously letters. He recognized some of them as Elizabeth Harley's.

"Putting them all in order," she said, still focused.

"Da, she found Ezra's letters to Elizabeth," Maggie said. "Isn't that amazing? They were hidden in that old desk."

"Where did the desk come from?" Serena said. "Why is it here?" She started gathering the stacks into one.

"Viola found it," he said. "It was meant to be your Christmas present." He sat down hard on the sofa. "Stop what you're doing and come here for a second, please."

"Where did she find it?" Maggie said. "It's Elizabeth's desk, isn't it?" He had told his daughter about Ezra and Elizabeth in bits and pieces in his emails, and apparently Serena had filled her in on the rest.

"She thought it might be," Jacob said as Serena crawled over to him. He feasted his eyes on her, bathing in the sight of her as his own beloved without the filter of his passenger's obsession. "What time is it?"

"Nearly six," Maggie said. "We thought you'd slipped into a coma."

"Maggie, meet Serena," he said. "Serena, this is my daughter, Maggie."

"We've met." Maggie laughed. "Jesus, Da, are you having a stroke?"

"Are you all right?" Serena said. "Did you hear what I said?"

"I'm fine." He slid to the floor beside her. "So those are Ezra's letters?" He picked up one, and the handwriting was familiar, so much so he felt it like an electric charge running through him.

"I think so," Serena said. "It's been years since I authenticated a document this old, and we'll have to do a chemical analysis of the paper. But it looks right, and the handwriting is consistent, letter to letter, and looks appropriate to the era. And they match up perfectly with the letters from Elizabeth we already got from Miz Rae."

"Tell him about Ariel," Maggie said.

"No, not yet," Serena said. Her eyes were bright, and her hands trembled. "I want him to read it for himself."

"Read it, Da," Maggie said.

"I will. Of course I will." They were both so beautiful, the darlings of his heart. "But please, my loves, I'm starving. Can't we have dinner first?"

Serena was obviously shocked. "Sure," she said. "Of course."

"I'll make you a sandwich," Maggie said.

"No, your father's right," Serena said. "It's Christmas Eve. Let's all stop and take a breath." She kissed him and got up. "I need to get dressed."

"Just let me get my feet back under me," Jacob said. "I'll read them tonight, I promise." Once he read the letters, he would know, and once he knew, he wouldn't be able to pretend the thing inside him might be a figment of his imagination. It would all be real.

"I can't believe you can stand to wait," Maggie said. It was a story to her; she was quivering with excitement. Bless her, she was his daughter; just like him, she desperately needed to know all the gory details.

But from the expression on Serena's face, he thought she might understand his hesitation, at least a little bit. Not about the demon, not really, but that he was terrified. Had she seen a difference in him yet? Did she know he was becoming someone else? "He'll be able to focus better once we've all had something to eat," she said. "Let's make him take us someplace fabulous."

Trevor offered to cook them something, but Jacob took everyone out to the pub instead. Over steaks and too many pints, he watched Serena and fell in love with her all over again. He had expected her to be shy in Ireland, at least at first. But she blossomed, as if a weight had been lifted from her shoulders as they crossed the Atlantic. Within an hour, she had the usually-reticent Trevor talking about his mad, ancient socialite of a mother and her new beau in Argentina, and his own plans for a trip to Spain after the new year. And Maggie seemed to have taken her up as a long-lost sister. Watching the two of them laughing together brought tears to his eyes.

What do you want with her? he thought, addressing the thin, sharp sliver of *other* coiled inside his head. *What is Serena to you?*

The other didn't answer. It never answered him, though he spoke to it often in his thoughts. He wasn't even sure it heard. To the thing he carried, he was nothing but a host, and his consciousness nothing but a bug in the system.

Later at home, after Maggie and Trevor had gone to bed, he and Serena curled up on the sofa together while he read through Ezra's letters. The only real sounds were the crackling of the fire and the chimes of the mantle clock as it struck the hours. But inside his head, he could hear it all—the laughter of Alice Rose, the Old Man's labored breath. The screams of the dying. He didn't imagine these things; he remembered them. Ezra was his brother now, a conjoined twin of the mind. Reading the words he had written back home to the life he had lost, Jacob felt such pity for him, he could easily have wept. But the thing inside him felt nothing but contempt.

Serena had interspersed Elizabeth's letters with Ezra's, so the last words he read were hers. *I am writing to a dead man. I am mad.*

He handed her the final page, and she set the stack aside. "So... what do you think?"

"I think this changes everything," he said. "I think Ezra's revenge killing set off the beginnings of a slave uprising that got put down by the town."

For a moment, she looked confused. "Yes," she agreed. "It's like you said before, this makes Briarwood an extremely important historical site. If these letters are authentic, we can prove it." She took his hand. "But I meant what do you think about Ariel?"

"I think her story is the saddest, most horrible thing I ever heard," he said. "I think people need to know she existed and what happened to her."

"So you do think she was real?" she said. "Do you think she was like he described her?"

"Of course I do." The clock struck one as he took her in his arms. "Of course she was real." He kissed the top of her head, and she squeezed him tight.

"They're going to try to stop us," she said. "The town's not going to like this, and they're going to try to say it's not true."

"They can say whatever they like," he said. "We have the proof."

"It's going to be dangerous," she said. "They already tried to scare you away, remember?"

He smiled, himself and the demon inside of him in perfect accord. "Let them try."

Later, lying awake in the dark, he thought she was sleeping, then she spoke. "What about the dark man?" Her voice quavered, and he felt gooseflesh break out on her bare skin. "The one Ezra talks about, the one he wrote was inside Ariel and came inside him when she died."

"I remember." He had written about such demons all his life, so much so that being possessed by this one barely felt like a surprise.

"Do you think he was real, too?" She clutched his forearm so tightly her nails dug into his flesh.

"Nae, angel." He lied so easily, he wondered if he had help. "I don't think so."

"You don't really believe in evil spirits?"

"I believe Ezra Woodbine lost his mind." She was lying with her back to him, and he drew her closer so his chin rested on top of her head. "I think when he realized what had been done to the woman he loved, he went mad. I think he did feel an evil spirit, but I think it was really just him."

He felt her take a deep breath, then she turned to face him. "Do you ever wish you'd never heard of Briarwood?"

"No." He kissed her. "I never wish that at all."

He pulled her close again, and they talked about other things—Maggie and Christmas and what time they should call Rooster and Claudine. She finally drifted off to sleep, and he watched her, he and his demon together as one, watching their goddess in the dark.

32

The next day, the house was full for Christmas lunch, crowding the second-floor lounge and spilling down the stairs into the kitchen. In one way, this crowd of strangers overwhelmed Serena. But in another, this was the life she'd always imagined for herself, a multi-ethnic babble of accents and ideas where everyone was fascinating and treated her as if she might be, too.

As Jacob's girlfriend, she was an object of great curiosity. But unlike back home, where people would have knotted up in groups of two or three behind her back to speculate who she was and where she'd come from and what she was after from Jacob, here they walked straight up to her and asked. And no one sounded like they were accusing her of a crime; they seemed genuinely curious. And once she explained they'd met in South Carolina, that she was a librarian, that she'd once lived in Berlin and worked at a museum there, they accepted her as one of their own, or seemed to, at least. She was talking about the Hong Kong Heritage Museum with an art history professor from the local university and one of Maggie's friends, a young transgender woman studying political theory at Oxford, when Jacob walked over and kissed her.

"You'll have to come down to my office while you're here, Serena," the professor suggested. "We'll have lunch, and I can tell you all of Jacob's dirty secrets."

"That would be a very long lunch," Jacob said, laughing. "I'm not sure we'll be in Ireland that long. Serena, darling, let me steal you. I want you to meet Viola."

Jacob's research assistant was an olive-skinned woman of about his age with a steel-gray buzzcut. "It's a pleasure," she said in a crisp, English accent as Serena shook her hand. "And well done finding those letters."

"Thanks." The other woman was obviously sizing her up, and she slid an arm around Jacob. "How did you find the desk in the first place?"

"Oh, I've found out all sorts of things," Viola said. "Is there someplace we can talk?"

"Maggie and some of her friends are watching a movie in the study," Serena said. "Besides, Jacob, you probably shouldn't abandon your guests."

"Trevor can manage," Jacob said. "Come on."

He led them up through the attic and out a tall window to a tiny terrace on the roof. The weather was gray and chilly but not unpleasant; Serena had been too warm in her sweater inside. Four mismatched cushioned garden chairs filled the space, arranged around a table with an overflowing ashtray. "I come up here to smoke when I get stuck writing," Jacob said.

"You must get stuck a lot," Serena teased. "Your cardiologist would not be pleased."

"Oh, I'm sure he's turned over a new leaf," Viola said. "Clean living from now on, right, Jacob?" She sounded like she was teasing, but her gaze was sharp, studying them together. Serena got the idea that Viola might be a bit fonder of Jacob than he was of her.

"Right," he said, pulling Serena to his side and kissing her cheek. "What have you found out, Vi?"

"Ezra Woodbine was a real person, but you know that," Viola said, plopping down in a chair. "His father was a millionaire back before millionaires were really a thing." She lit a cigarette. "Do you mind?"

"Of course not," Jacob said before Serena could answer, leading her to a chair. "If he was so rich, why have I never heard of him?"

"He never did anything but make and lose money," Viola said. "He never invented anything, never built anything but textile mills, never built a bridge or endowed a church. He made a killing speculating in cotton early on, then built on that fortune over the next few decades by hiring other men and stealing their patents. He might have someday reformed and become a great man late in life like the rest of those early industrialist types, but he died in a fire at one of his mills three years after they hanged his only son and heir at Briarwood."

"You said textile mills," Jacob said, lighting one of Viola's cigarettes for himself. "And cotton." He looked over at Serena. "Think I can survive just the one?"

"That's on you," she said, making Viola laugh.

"She's not much like Gloria, is she?" Viola said.

"They have more in common than you might think," Jacob said, squeezing Serena's hand.

"But what a horrible story," Serena said, squeezing back.

"It gets worse," Viola said with a grin. "And yes, I said textiles and cotton. Apparently Mr. Woodbine, Sr., and Mr. Montgomery were business partners. Woodbine owed a fortune when he died due to a failed speculation in America—care to guess what that might have been?"

"Briarwood?" Serena said.

"From everything I can find, Montgomery built Briarwood on his own with money his wife inherited from her father. But I tracked down an old photograph of the last mill Woodbine built here in England," Viola said, opening a photo on her phone and handing it to Jacob. "Look familiar?"

"Christ in Heaven," Jacob said.

"That was completed less than a year before Woodbine sent young Ezra, fresh out of Oxford, to visit his friend Montgomery at Briarwood," Viola said.

"Show me," Serena said.

Jacob passed her the phone. "That building is nearly identical to the unfinished mill we found at Briarwood."

"The place where y'all found Davon." Looking at it, she felt sick. "It's as big as this?"

"I'd say exactly the same size, yes," Jacob said. "The bricks are a different color, but they would have been made on site."

"By the slaves," Serena said.

"Exactly," Viola said. "My theory is that Woodbine gave Montgomery the plans and probably some of the seed money to build a cotton mill at Briarwood. At that time, the cotton used in Europe was grown in the American South then sent by ship to England to be milled into fabric, which was then sent back to America as well as all over the rest of Europe. So the imported cotton was subject to major tariffs, and the price of the final products reflected that. Products produced by a mill in South Carolina on an actual cotton plantation would have had a huge advantage in both the European market and in the States. Not to mention the cost advantage of having the manufacturing work done by slave labor."

"That's why Ezra was at Briarwood," Jacob said. "Except instead of revolutionizing the textile industry for his father, he fell in love with Ariel."

"And ended up killing eight people with an axe," Serena said.

"If that's actually what happened, yeah." Viola flicked her ashes. "That name, though, Ariel. To be honest, that's the only detail from the letters you found that doesn't ring true for me. It doesn't sound like a slave woman's name."

"They couldn't all be called Prissy," Serena said, forcing herself to smile.

"Ezra mentions that the old man was interested in Shakespeare," Jacob said. "Presumably he would have had a hand in naming her."

"And it isn't an uncommon name at all in the black community around Saxon County," Serena said. "It's actually my middle name. And like Tom Stewart told us, most of the black families in the county probably started in the slave community at Briarwood."

"That makes sense, I suppose," Viola said. "In any case, Ezra's shenanigans at Briarwood apparently ruined his father. Woodbine, Sr., had been reduced to selling off his mills in pieces by the time the last one burned with him inside it. There was evidence to suggest he set the fire with all the workers inside then got trapped himself."

"Then he's still burning in hell," Jacob said."

"That would be a fair assumption, if you believe in that sort of thing," Viola said. "I didn't realize you were back to being a Catholic, Jacob." She took her phone back. "I can't find any record of what happened to his wife. But I did find Ezra's English fiancée, Elizabeth Harley. She never married. Her mother died the same year as Ezra, and her father remarried less than a year after that." She was looking through more notes on her phone. "The second wife was younger and very rich, but she and Lord Harley never had any other children. His title died with him, and the estate got bounced around various distant relatives for the next hundred years or so."

"Poor Elizabeth," Serena said, squeezing Jacob's hand.

"Dodi Fayed's dad bought the property back in the '90s and turned it into a hotel," Viola said. "It's still there and quite nice." She handed the phone to Serena so she could see a photograph of a lovely Elizabethan manor house with a modern parking lot out front. "Most of the original furnishings were sold off to an antiques dealer in London who was killed in a mugging gone wrong just a few weeks ago."

"Oh my God," Serena said.

"I managed to get in touch with his niece, who was kind enough to let me look through his records," Viola said. "She's the one who sold me the desk." She lit another cigarette and sat back in her chair. "And in the desk, you found Ezra's letters. God, Jake, what a book this is going to make."

"Not just a book," Jacob said. "This is a hugely significant historical find. We're going to turn Briarwood into a museum."

"We are?" Viola said, arching an eyebrow. "Still, the book will come first, surely. Are you doing fiction or non-fiction? Or both?"

Jacob stubbed out his own cigarette, and his pale cheeks turned pink. "I'm not really talking about it yet."

"Oh, that's nice," Viola said, laughing. "What does Gloria say? She's read some of it by now, surely."

"Has she?" Serena asked.

"Oh, you can't let yourself be bothered by that, Serena," Viola said. "Gloria reads all of Jacob's books as he's writing them, always has done." She laughed. "And the worst part is, she hates them, even the bestsellers."

"She doesn't hate them. They just upset her," Jacob said. "But she hasn't read this one. No one has." He took Serena's hand and kissed it. "Everyone will read it when it's done."

The attic window opened, and Maggie stuck her head out. "There you all are," she said. "Come down and pull a cracker like normal people, can't you, please?"

"On our way, darling," Jacob said, standing. "Come on, lovelies." Viola went through the window after Maggie, but as Serena started to climb through after her, Jacob caught her and pulled her into a kiss. She melted against him, surprised but not un-pleased, and he pushed her back against the window frame.

"Merry Christmas to you, too," she said when he let her go, feeling breathless and a little dizzy. "What inspired that?"

"You know I love you, don't you?" The look in his eyes was so desperate and sad, it scared her. "You know I would do anything for you."

"I do, yes," she said. "And I love you." She kissed him again more softly. "Is this about the thing with Gloria reading your book first? Baby, it's okay; I get it. Y'all have been together for a long time. If you need her to read it, I don't mind."

"No," he said before she had finished. "No, it's not…it's okay." He hugged her close for a moment, then drew back and smiled. "Let's go downstairs."

"Whatever you say," she said, taking his hand and following him through the window. "You know me; I never miss a chance to pull a cracker."

33

The next day Serena found herself alone on the streets of Dublin. Jacob had left early to meet with his publisher, and Maggie had gone off with friends. So rather than rattle around the empty house with Trevor asking if she needed anything every fifteen minutes, she decided to go exploring.

She took a cab to the city center with a vague idea of visiting Trinity College and seeing the Book of Kells. But she found herself wandering instead, just looking at things, getting assimilated to a whole new universe. When Jacob was with her, she was focused on him. Everything she had perceived about Ireland so far had been filtered through that shield. She was the girlfriend of a wealthy man, and she was safe and muffled. But walking among the tourists down the cobblestone streets of Temple Bar, she felt raw and naked and free. Other Black faces were scarce compared to home, but she did see them, and no one, Black or White, looked at her askance. People smiled when she met their eyes, and she smiled back.

She let herself imagine a life where she stayed here. When Jacob came to Saxonville, when she first realized their attraction was mutual, she had pushed away a fantasy that seemed grasping and wrong, a dream priced too high. In it, he rescued her from everything

—her loneliness, her debt, her role as the pitiful widow. In some ways, even the hope she allowed herself to have of Briarwood as a museum with herself as its curator was a cleaner, more acceptable version of that. In every case, the dream was tied to Briarwood.

But walking in Dublin, she could imagine something else. For the first time, she could see a future for herself and Jacob together that had no connection to the ruined plantation or its tragedy. A cold wind whipped her scarf half-off her neck, and she laughed, welcoming the chill. They didn't have to go back to Briarwood at all.

Trembling with excitement, she hurried into one of the tourist-y pubs and took a corner booth, then texted Jacob.

"Meet me at The Quay in Temple Bar when you're finished. I want to talk."

She ordered a drink and a sandwich and was picking up her phone again when it rang. "Hey, you," she said without bothering to check the number. "That was quick."

"Serena, it's Claudine." Her mother-in-law was crying.

"Oh God. It's Rooster." Her heart was pounding so hard she felt sick. "What happened?"

"Henry's fine," Claudine said. "Well ..." She couldn't tell if she laughed or sobbed. "He ain't sick."

"Claudine, what's the matter?" The waitress brought her sandwich, and she made herself smile. "Tell me what's going on."

"We got a call from that FBI agent, Harris," she said. "They're closing it down."

"Closing what down?"

"The investigation. They packed up and left."

"Are they finished? Did they finally charge—?"

"They ain't charged anybody," Claudine cut her off. "They ain't gonna charge anybody." Her tears weren't grief, Serena realized. She was raging, as furious as she'd been the day Wrenn Benson came to the house. "Harris said the investigation was a national security matter and had been declared classified."

"Classified? But that doesn't mean it just stops, does it?"

"They loaded up all their trucks and moved out," Claudine said.

"Rooster drove up there this morning, and he just called. He said that mill has been picked clean like the bodies weren't even there. I called David Duncan, and he said they're dropping all their warrants on the Benson boys and the rest of them."

"That's crazy!"

"He said it's all part of the federal investigation now and out of their jurisdiction."

"No." *It doesn't matter,* a desperate voice begged inside her head. *It doesn't have to matter. We don't have to care about this. We can stay here and be free.* "No, that doesn't make any sense."

"Serena, they took Davon," Claudine said, breaking down. "They took my baby's body as evidence, and they say they don't know when they'll release it, if they'll ever release it."

"Claudine, no..."

"You know who did this," she said. "Pink Collins and Amanda Flynn and all of them. They got it hushed up again like they always do."

"Not this time," Serena said. "Too many people saw it. We won't let this stand."

"I told Henry to get the hell out of there," Claudine said.

"That's good," Serena said. "That's real good. Y'all stay put at the beach. We'll be home soon."

She paid her check and decided to wait for Jacob outside. The crowded square, so welcoming before, had darkened with her mood. The bright blue sky had clouded over, and a sporadic, misty rain had started to fall. The holiday crowd that had seemed so friendly and relaxed now looked hurried and harassed, jostling her as they passed.

A group of carolers in Victorian costumes sang bravely on. But one of them had left the group and lay flat on his back on the cobblestones. Moving closer, she saw his eyes were closed, and he had his hands folded on his chest like a corpse in a coffin. His bright green top hat was set brim-up beside him as if for tips, and as she watched, a group of giggling teen-age girls dropped in a few coins and moved on.

She couldn't see where he was doing much worthy of tips. He was kind of cute, she supposed, with small, regular features and longish blond hair. But his costume was dirty and worn and incomplete compared to the others. He wasn't even wearing boots, she realized—his feet were bare. His cravat was missing, too, Leaning down, she saw a raw, livid bruise like a gash around his throat.

His eyes snapped open. "Serena," he rasped through his dead throat. "Help us." His eyes were blue and clouded over like the sky. "Please ..." He lifted his bare, grimy hands to reach for her. She stepped back with a shriek. He tried to sit up, and his head lolled to one side as if his neck were broken. "Let us go," he pleaded. "Angel ..."

Ezra, she thought. *That's Ezra.* His hand was almost touching hers, and she screamed, trying to run. Her boots slipped on the wet cobblestones, and she started to fall. *He's going to catch me,* she thought. She could smell the stench of him, could already feel the squish of falling into rotting flesh and bone.

Then Jacob caught her from behind. "Serena?" He was smiling. "Angel, are you all right?"

She turned back and saw the young street performer leaping up to take a bow. He wasn't blond or dressed like a caroler. His hair was black, and he was dressed and made up as a vampire, all white make-up and black goth leather. He was most definitely wearing shoes.

"I'm fine," she said to Jacob. "I guess he got me." She made herself smile at the young man and nod as he bowed to her. Several people were applauding and dropping coins into his hat. "But come on," she said to Jacob. "I need to tell you what's happening at home."

34

Flying back over the Atlantic, Jacob felt himself becoming stronger and steadily more furious. Serena had taken a sleeping pill with a vodka martini on the plane, and once they landed, he half-carried her through customs, holding her curled to his side. She fell asleep again on the drive back to Briarwood. As the car ate up the highway to home, he felt the spirit stretch and slide back into every corner of his body, mind, and soul like a fist opening and slipping into a glove. Looking over at his sleeping goddess, he had never felt more resolved. At last, their time had come.

Serena woke up from a nightmare as Jacob made the turn into Briarwood. For a moment, she thought she must still be dreaming, drifting up the long, curved drive to the house like a disembodied ghost. Then her eyes snapped into focus on Jacob. He gripped the wheel with both hands so tightly his knuckles were white, and his smile had turned his thin, handsome face into a skeleton's leer.

"Baby?" She reached out and touched his arm. "Are you okay?"

He laughed and sounded like himself again. "Of course I am." He looked at her, and his smile was fine, and the last wisps of her dream blew away. "How are you, sleepyhead?"

"Messed up," she said through a yawn. "I shouldn't have taken that pill." She stretched as the house loomed up in front of them. "What are we doing here?"

"Reese texted me that he finished everything while we were gone," he said, driving around back. "I thought we could see how it came out."

Going in through the back door, they could have been in any modern mansion with the showroom of stainless steel and marble that real estate agents called a chef's kitchen. But as soon as they stepped through the swinging door into the hallway, they found 1837.

The paneled walls had been stripped, sanded, and repainted in shades of cream and putty green. Every inch of ornate plaster molding had been restored or seamlessly reconstructed. The original brass chandeliers, black with tarnish and coated with candle wax the first time she'd seen them, had been taken apart, polished, and wired for electricity. The columns in the entrance hall had been repainted in a 19th-century-style tromp l'oeil of veined white marble, and every painting had been cleaned and rehung in its original position. The original furniture had been repaired, polished, and reupholstered in period-appropriate fabrics, and the new drapes matched the old in color and style so perfectly, they seemed to have been restored by magic. Even the new glass in the windows perfectly matched the old.

Serena walked from room to room without speaking, looking at everything and feeling slightly sick. In the dining room, the silver on the sideboard and table had been polished and put back in its original positions as if waiting to replay the last fateful dinner. "He did an miraculous job," Jacob said from behind her. "Do you see this?"

"I see it," she said. "Amazing." She thought about the ruin they had walked through the afternoon they met—had it really been only a few months ago? She remembered the empty cavern where Jacob had read the Frenchman's journal on Halloween night and the library where she went exploring with Evie.

She crossed the hall in front of Jacob and pushed open the sliding doors. For a split second, she saw them there, all the bodies freshly slaughtered, Ellen Montgomery sprawled facedown in the center of her prized Persian carpet with her head split like a pumpkin.

Then she was standing in a modern living room with plush, camel-colored sofas and a massive flat-screen TV.

"What do you think, love?" Jacob said. "Do you like it?"

"No," she said. "It's horrible. I mean, it's not; it's beautiful. But..." She turned back to him with tears in her eyes. "It's like none of it ever happened. It's like they were just erased."

"No," he protested.

"Carol Ann was right," she said. "You could have all kinds of fancy weddings here."

"No." He put his hands on her shoulders. "That's not what's going to happen, I promise. We're going to tell the truth just like I said. All this is just temporary until I finish the book."

"I don't understand."

"I'm going to live here, in this place—*we're* going to live here, if you will." In Ireland, he had seemed older and so tired, she had worried about him. But now he could have passed for her own age. His eyes were bright, and he seemed to be bursting with energy and purpose.

"I am going to write a story, but it will be the truth. And because I am who I am, people will buy it and read it. And then we'll show them the evidence, prove that it all really happened, and no one will be able to stop us. The FBI won't matter, and the stupid town won't matter. The world will know what was done here." His hands slid up to frame her face. "Everyone will know what they did to Ariel and all the others, and they'll pay, love. You'll show them the truth and avenge her."

She was still so groggy from the plane, she couldn't tell if what he said made sense or if they had both gone crazy. "You want to live at Briarwood?"

"Just until the book is finished." He kissed her forehead and let her go. "As soon as I'm done, I won't need the house for inspiration anymore. We'll rip it all apart and turn it into a museum, just like we planned." She could almost see the gears turning in his head. "And don't worry; the upstairs is very different. Henry and Reese have made it quite comfortable. We even have real bathrooms."

"I want to see it," she said.

"Upstairs? Of course."

"No." She had been thinking about this from the moment she realized they had to come back, dreading it, dreaming about it. She took his hand and closed her eyes for a moment, taking a breath before she said it. "I want to see the mill." The site had been a closed crime scene by the time she'd known it existed, so she'd never been inside. But she had imagined it, dreamed about it, dreaded it as the worst horror she could conceive. "I can't stay here until I see what it's like." *I don't have to stay here,* part of her brain protested. *This is not my husband; I can go back home to Rooster and Claudine's house.*

But how long would it be before their house sold, and what then? She couldn't afford her own place; she already had texts from her bill collectors demanding their latest payments. Didn't it make more sense to make the decision now?

"Are you sure?" Jacob said. "I don't know what the police have left there. It's probably empty, and I don't think the building is safe."

"I have to see it," she said. "You don't have to go with me if you don't want to."

"Of course I'll go with you," he said. "We'll go right now."

The FBI had cut an access road through the woods, but it surprised her how far the building was from the main house. "You and Rooster and Tom hiked all this way?" she said.

"Further," he said. "We followed the creek and came in from the other side, looking for the Frenchman's shelter."

"Did anybody ever find that?" she asked.

"No, but no one has done any more looking," he said. "Still, if it were anywhere around here, you'd think someone from the investigation would have stumbled on it by now." The road widened ahead into a red mud and gravel parking lot, and he pointed. "There it is."

The mill was just as he'd described it in Ireland, an almost-perfect replica of the photograph Viola had shown them of the Woodbine mill in England. "It's so big," Serena said. "I still can't believe this has just been sitting out here all this time, and nobody in town knew anything about it."

"Well, somebody did," he said, squeezing her hand. "But I know what you mean." She turned her face to his shoulder, and he kissed the top of her head. "Have you seen enough?"

"Of course not." She straightened up. "I want to go inside."

Plywood and yellow crime scene tape covered the loading doors. But a smaller door on the ground floor had been left standing ajar. "This is where we went in before," Jacob said. "Watch your step."

From the outside, the brick building looked finished. But inside it was a skeleton of beams and joists, the two upper stories left open except for catwalks and a bare roof. "They hadn't gotten the lumber for the final floors, remember?" Serena said. "That's what Montgomery and Ezra talked about."

"I remember," Jacob said. "It looks like they picked it pretty clean."

"Yes." The wide planks of the ground floor had been swept bare, and the smell of disinfectant lingered in the air over a deeper, older funk.

"I can't say I'm sorry," Jacob said. "I've never seen the like of it, and I hope to never again. You can't really tell now where the bodies were."

"Sure you can." She walked away from him and pointed. "Look at the beams." Every beam was marked with deep, pale grooves all the way around. "Rope marks where they left them to swing." He tried to touch her shoulder, but she shrugged him off. "So many… did you count?"

"No," he said. "I didn't, but I'm sure the FBI did."

"We have to count," she cut him off. Outside she had been near tears, but now she was just angry. She took out her phone and started snapping pictures. "Where was Davon?"

"Towards the back in the middle," he said. "I'm not sure I remember exactly."

"Show me," she said. "Try to remember, Baby, please."

"Of course." He led her through the shadowed space, holding up his phone for light. "There were bodies hanging all around here." She could hear crows squawking in the trees outside. Jacob stopped and pointed his light. "There. It was that one."

The gash in the beam looked pretty much the same as all the others. But underneath it, a faint, brown shadow of blood still stained the floor . She focused her camera, willing her hand to stop shaking, and took pictures of the stain and the beam above it. "This shit is over," she said.

"Yes," Jacob said.

"This shit will not stand." In her mind, she could see their faces, all those strong, bright, young Black men brought here to die. Their eyes watched her from the shadows. She felt their still-warm hands brushing her shoulders. "We won't let them hide this horror anymore," she promised.

"We won't," Jacob said. "*You* won't."

She took more pictures until the light from the windows started to fade, then they started back toward the house. Walking through the boggy clearing, she saw a flash of orange in the trees. Turning, still holding Jacob's hand, she saw the figure of a naked woman half-hidden in the skeleton brush. Dried red mud caked her skin, and a stream of scarlet blood flowed down her face. She raised a hand to Serena and smiled.

"What is it?" Jacob said. "What do you see?"

"Nothing," she said, turning back to him. "Let's go back to the house."

35

The Briarwood branch was still closed, so Serena went back to work at the main library in town. Sitting at her tiny corner desk in the workroom repairing picture books, she got an email in her personal account.

She looked in Tom's office, then went out to the front desk. "Hey Tricia," she asked the clerk. "Do we know where Tom is?"

"Hiding in the local history room," Tricia said without looking up from the catalog she was reading. "You need him?"

"Maybe." Tricia had worked at the library for twenty years and by all reports, had yet to read a book or break a sweat. But her uncle was minister at the First Baptist Church and a longtime member of the board.

Laurel Heath, Saxonville's not-homeless homeless man, came in from the street swathed neck to feet in scarves over a dirty coat and baggy corduroy pants. He drank deeply from the water fountain then staggered toward the couches near the magazine rack. On the way, he caught sight of Serena at the front desk and stopped. His eyes went wide, and his cracked lips broke into a shy smile. He waved, an oddly touching gesture, and she waved back. Then he limped to one of the couches and flopped across it like a beached whale. Head back, eyes closed, in less than a minute, he was snoring.

"When you find Tom, tell him Laurel's back," Tricia said. "He needs to run him out of here."

"No, leave him alone," Serena said. Laurel's mother went to Briarwood Baptist and was a good friend of Claudine's. She tried to keep Laurel at home, but she said it was impossible, that he was only happy wandering the streets of Saxonville alone. Rain or shine, cold or hot, he could be found in front of the burned-out courthouse or sitting on the sidewalk in front of Benson's Towing and Garage, a sort of living African totem. Jacob had all but stumbled over him on his morning run his first full day in Saxon County, and he said Laurel had scared him half to death, a statue come to life.

"It's freezing outside," Serena said, "and he's pitiful." Tricia snorted over her catalog. "He is, and it's not his fault. He was born that way."

"He wasn't, though," Tricia said. "When he was a little boy, he was real smart."

"Really?"

"He went to grammar school with me, and yeah, he was," she said. "He could do math better than almost anybody in the class, better than any of the White boys. And he won the spelling bee when we were in third grade."

"Was he in some kind of accident?" Serena said.

"Maybe," Tricia said. "He was out of school for a long time, and when he came back, they put him in Special Ed. I never heard about an accident, but I did hear his daddy had run off."

"That's so sad." Sometimes she thought every living soul in Saxon County must be broken. "I'm going to go find Tom."

"Y'all don't linger," Tricia said. "I'm going to lunch in five minutes."

The local history room was a glass box around four short aisles of bookshelves. Two tables with chairs sat positioned just inside the door, visible from the main library, and a microfiche machine on a cart with a rolling chair in front of it was hidden in the far back corner. That was where she found Tom, sipping from his travel mug and reading a paperback book.

"Hey," Serena said, laughing. "Tricia was right. You are hiding."

She had obviously startled him, but he smiled. "Not from you." He set the book and mug aside. "What do you need?"

"I got this email." She pulled it up on her phone. "Back before Christmas, I emailed Sandy Fletcher, the archivist down at the Charleston County Library."

"I know Sandy," he said. "She's been real sick."

"Yeah, but she's better," she said. "I emailed to ask her if they had anything on the Montgomery family or Briarwood."

"Why Charleston?" he said. "That's a hundred miles away."

"I found a notice about Caleb, Jr.'s wedding in a Charleston newspaper database—it doesn't matter," she said. With Jacob writing his book, she was hesitant to share any details about her own research, even with Tom. "The point is, I emailed her, and she finally got back to me today. She says she already sent the originals of everything they had to us on long term loan more than a year ago. She seems pretty steamed that I don't seem to know where that stuff is." She handed him her phone to show him the email.

He stared at it with an expression she couldn't remember ever seeing on his face before, a sort of angry pout. "Well, she's mistaken," he said, handing it back. "Any requests from us would have come through me, and I didn't make one."

"Are you sure?" she said, remembering how absent-minded he could be. "Like I said, this would have been more than a year ago."

"Are you calling me a liar, Serena?"

"Of course not!" They were friends. From the time she'd come back to Saxon County, he had been nothing but kind to her, he and Evie both. "I just know you have a lot of projects going, and I thought you might have forgotten."

"If I had information about Briarwood, don't you think I would share it with Jacob?" he said. "I've been bending over backwards to help him ever since he got here."

That was an overstatement, but she let it lie in the interests of peace. "Tom, if you say you don't have it, you don't have it. I'll email her back and tell her there's been a mistake."

"No, I'll email her," Tom said, getting up. "I might not be living in the big house, but I am still the director of the library."

"I beg your pardon?" From anybody else, that cheap shot would have pissed her off. From her friend, it hurt, too. "I don't know what your problem is, but you are not going to speak to me that way."

He looked stunned, like she'd slapped him out of a trance. "I didn't mean to offend you."

"Well, you did." Tears stung her eyes, but she fought them back.

"I'm sorry," he said. "Serena, I'm so sorry."

She could see he was, but that didn't make what he said go away. Was that what he really thought of her? Was everything else a lie? "Do you want to email her?" she said.

"Yes, please," he said. "I'll go email her right now. We'll track this stuff down, I promise."

Looking through the glass, she saw Jacob come in and stop at the front desk. "I need to relieve Tricia so she can go to lunch," she said. "Thank you for your help."

"Serena, wait." He started out after her, but when he saw Jacob, he veered off and went to his office.

Jacob was just asking Tricia where to find her when Serena touched his arm. "Hey Baby," she said, hugging him. "What are you doing here?"

"Are you here now?" Tricia interrupted. "I need to go."

"Sure, honey, go ahead," Serena said, moving behind the desk.

"Okay, good." With a sidelong glance at Jacob, she grabbed her purse. "Bye."

"Bye," Serena said, waving as Tricia left. "Have a good lunch."

"What a delightful woman," Jacob said, making Serena laugh. "What's wrong?"

"Nothing," Serena said. "What do you mean? She's always like that."

"Not her." He took her hand across the desk. "What's going on with Tom? I saw him scurrying off, and I can tell you're upset."

"No, I'm fine," she said. "It's no big deal. I'll tell you all about it later." She leaned over the desk and kissed him, ignoring the shocked stares of two old White ladies browsing the new releases rack. "What are you doing here? I can't go to lunch until Tricia gets back."

"I have some news." He leaned in and lowered his voice. "My Washington lawyer called. The case file on the mill is still sealed and marked as classified, and he's going to keep working on that. But he got Davon's body released."

"You're kidding!"

"Not at all. He said it should be available for transport to a local funeral home by the end of the week."

"Baby!" She ran around the desk and hugged him. "That's wonderful! Claudine will be so thrilled."

"It's a start," he said. "I thought you might want to be the one to tell her and Henry."

"Yes. I'll call them right now."

One of the old White ladies now stood at the far end of the desk. She cleared her throat. "Excuse me. Could I be checked out, please?" She was watching them with the pale, watery eyes of a scared rabbit, and her voice trembled with righteous defiance.

"Yes, ma'am," Serena said. "Of course." She had been exchanging pleasantries with this woman for years, had eaten tomatoes from her garden and bought band fruit from her grandson. But now she acted like they were strangers. *Well, fuck you very much, too,* Serena thought, but she smiled and took the woman's library card. She checked her out the latest Nora Roberts and an Amish romance novel. "Will there be anything else?"

"Thank you," the woman said, scooping up her books. Her friend didn't even come to the counter. She put the books she had selected down on a table, and the two of them marched out like they might start singing "Dixie."

"Bless their hearts," Serena said, making Jacob laugh.

"Indeed." He took her hand. "My brave, beautiful girl."

"I'll call Claudine and Rooster as soon as I get off the desk," she said. "Thank you, Jacob. Really."

He squeezed her hand. "Just tell them I said hello."

36

Amanda Flynn hadn't darkened the door of the Saxon County Library since high school. But she felt the situation required drastic measures. She walked in just at closing time still dressed for court in a suit and high heels—she had stopped by her office just long enough to fluff her hair and reapply her lipstick.

"We're closed," one of the clerks who was leaving informed her, a bovine redhead she vaguely recognized but couldn't name. "The computers are off."

"It's all right," Amanda said with a smile. "I'm not here to check out a book."

Tom stood at the front desk closing out his cash drawer. Serena Decatur was turning off the lights in the stacks. She saw Amanda, but she didn't speak, nor did she say good night to Tom—an interesting detail. They were supposed to be such pals. With her purse on her shoulder, the Black woman making Amanda's life so difficult left, no doubt headed for Briarwood.

Tom looked up, noticed her at last, and frowned. "What are you doing here?"

"We need to talk," she said. The rest of the staff was gone; their headlights swept across the glass front doors as they pulled out. "You've been dodging my calls, so I figured I'd best come over."

"I've got to get home to Evie," he said, slamming the drawer shut. "And we've got nothing to talk about."

"I disagree." She followed him back to his office, the last island of light left in the building. "We've been missing you at poker."

"I've got a baby coming; I need all my money." He put on his coat. "Besides, I get plenty of Kirk, Jr.'s winning personality when I see him on the street."

"Tom, nobody respects your last White liberal in Saxon County act more than I do," she said. "But we have a crisis, and you are just not doing your part."

"A crisis?" he said. "Is that what you'd call it?"

"The Trust has been in sticky spots before." Some of the stories her father told her about the 1960s had made her shudder. "But we've always made it through because we stick together. We watch one another's back."

"All those bodies?" he said. "Was your daddy watching Kirk Benson's back on that? Was somebody else watching somebody else's back all the way back to 1837?"

She pushed the image of the mill out of her mind the same way she had since she was eighteen years old, and Jack Flynn explained that someday she would be chairman and exactly what that meant. "That has nothing to do with the Trust."

"It has everything to do with it, and you know it!" His pale, freckled face had gone splotchy. "That's it, Amanda. I'm done. I'm out."

"Sorry, honey, but that's not how it works." She had anticipated this. Her father had foreseen it years ago when they first brought Tom on. *That one is going to give you trouble one of these old days,* he told her. *Watch him.* But Tom was the librarian; they had to take him whether they wanted him or not. Florence Creighton had gone too far around the bend by then to be of use.

More to the point, like Amanda herself and like Kirk, Jr., and like all the rest of them, Tom Stewart was of the blood. He hadn't known it until Jack Flynn told him, but Florence Creighton had been his grandmother's first cousin. He was named for his ancestor, Tom Creighton, the first librarian, the timid little schoolteacher who had acted as Ezra Woodbine's attorney and gotten a shiny new library for the town for his trouble. The Trust was in Tom's blood, whether he wanted it or not. And as always, blood would tell.

"We can put all this ugliness behind us," she said, putting a hand on his arm. "The worst is over now. Pink has done his part getting the case made classified. He was able to make the right people understand what going public with all of this would do to Saxon County, maybe to the whole state. Now that's done, nobody else has to get hurt." He gave her a look that made her take her hand away. She'd never manage him the way she did Pink Collins and Frank Sweatt. She wasn't Tom's type. So fine; he'd have to take it straight. "You have to fire Serena."

"Get out, Amanda," he said, turning off his desk lamp.

"I know you've gotten complaints about her," she said. "I've had calls from board members myself."

"I'm leaving," he said, moving past her. "Shall I lock you in?"

"Give it up, Tom. She's never going to want you." She followed him into the dark workroom. "She doesn't need you anymore. She has McGinnas." She expected a bigger reaction from this, but he just snorted.

"You and I both know firing her would be doing her a favor. She could get out of this shit job in this shit town and go back to Ireland with her rich, White boyfriend. And we can get things back to normal." Tom pretended he wasn't listening and took out his keys, but she pressed on. "But whatever," she said. "Eventually she will leave here with him, and you'll have no choice but to forget about her and make more babies with your bitchy little wife."

He grabbed her by the throat and slammed her into a bookcase, scattering books and shocking her to the core. "Don't say one word about Evie." He gripped her so tight, she could barely breathe. "Keep her name out of your fucking mouth."

"Why?" she said. She teetered on her heels, dancing on her tiptoes, but she refused to let him think she was afraid. He would let her go any minute now. And she would see that he was punished. "You're a fucking librarian, Tom. What are you going to do?"

He laughed, and his grip tightened until she saw stars. "You think I'm afraid of you, Amanda?" His face was so close to hers, she could smell the coffee on his breath. "You think I'm weak?" His mouth twisted in a madman's leer. "Ask Ontreas Clark how weak I am." He lifted her higher with strength she could never have guessed he had. Her toes barely made contact with the carpet. "Ask your daddy." She gasped, and he laughed. "Maybe you should have let old Chuck Kennedy do that autopsy."

In that moment, she was sure he meant to kill her, and for the first time in her life, she was really, truly afraid. She clawed at his fist, kicked him with all her fading strength. But he barely seemed to feel it. "Bastard," she rasped. "You bastard."

He let her go as suddenly as he had grabbed her. She crumpled, one foot slipping off her high-heeled pump and twisting her ankle. She had to grab the bookcase to keep from falling completely to the floor. "You're wrong about the worst being over, Amanda," he said, the madness fading from his eyes. "It's just getting started."

"Murderer," she said. He had killed her father. "You'll go to jail. You'll get the death penalty—I'll see to it!"

"Good night, Amanda." He sounded like a dead man called back from the grave. "It's dark in that parking lot. Let me walk you out."

37

Jacob's attorney was as good as his word. Davon Decatur's remains were released for burial five days later. Reverend Holloway and Serena put that time to good use, making plans and talking to the media. Now on the rainy Friday morning of the funeral, the highway leading to and from the Briarwood Baptist Church was lined on both sides with the parked cars of mourners, not only of Davon but of all the other young black men who had disappeared without a trace in Saxon County.

Jacob and Serena pulled out of the drive at Briarwood and followed a national news truck to the church, and they passed another one going the other way. "They can hang it up," Serena said. "The Reverend gave a statement last night, and the man from the NAACP is doing a press conference in town after the graveside. But Claudine and Henry said there'd be no cameras in the church."

"There won't be," Jacob said. Two Saxon County Sheriff's Department patrol cars sat parked with their blue lights flashing a hundred yards from the turnoff to the church, but the security guards checking people coming into the parking lot had been hired by Jacob himself. Jacob stopped the car and waved one over. "How are things?"

"Very quiet, Mr. McGinnas," the man said, nodding to Serena. "The rest of the family are already inside."

Jacob parked and jumped out first with an umbrella to shield Serena as they walked to the church. But just as they reached the stone steps, a shiny silver limousine pulled up. A Black chauffeur got out and opened the back door. He held his own umbrella over Amanda Flynn as she climbed out. She wore an impeccably tailored black suit with a skirt that nearly showed her religion, sky-high heels, and a cunning little black hat with a veil. She was followed by the doctor, Chuck Kennedy, and the banker, Frank Sweatt, both of whom had just enough decency to look embarrassed. Last out was Kirk Benson, Jr., who smirked as if he might be spoiling for a fight.

"No," Serena said, stepping out of the shelter of Jacob's umbrella to confront them. "Get out of here right now."

"My client and his friends just want to pay their respects," Amanda said. She wore heavy make-up, but Serena could just make out a faint pattern of bruises around her snow-white throat. "And express their condolences to Davon's family."

"Don't you dare say his name," Serena said. "How dare you?"

"Get back in the car, Amanda," Jacob said. "Don't make me have security drag you out of here."

"That won't be necessary." Reverend Holloway had come out the front door of the church behind them. At six-foot-four and two-hundred-fifty-pounds, he always cut an imposing figure, but in his gold and purple robes, he was resplendent. "Miss Flynn knows she's not welcome here." Other members of the congregation had filled in behind him, a wall of impassive Black faces blocking the way into their church.

"This is God's house, Amanda Flynn," the Reverend said. His always-mellifluous voice took on a deeper, richer cadence, the voice of the prophet who would not be moved. "Nothing here belongs to you. No one here is beholden to you or your friends. No one here owes y'all anything at all." The slightest suggestion of a snarl curled the corner of his mouth. "At least not anything y'all would want." A ripple of quiet agreement passed through the crowd behind him.

Looking back, Serena saw Rooster standing among them, shoulder to shoulder with two other deacons of the church. When she'd seen him that morning for the first time in weeks, she had been shocked by how thin and tired he appeared, a broken old man. But now he stood tall and proud among his brothers, his handsome face as smooth and alive with vitality as ever. *He looks so much like Trey,* she thought as tears sprang to her eyes.

"Let's go, Amanda," Chuck Kennedy said. Kirk, Jr. made a move as if to argue, and the doctor grabbed him by the upper arm and held him back. "Please forgive the intrusion, Reverend," Chuck said. "We're so sorry to have troubled you." He steered the younger man around and all but shoved him back into the limo. Frank Sweatt looked a little lost at first, then he turned and ducked in behind them.

Amanda was the last to go. She glared up at Serena, an angry challenge in her eyes. Reverend Holloway put a hand on Serena's shoulder, and she took a step back. With a final, smirking glance at Jacob, Amanda turned and got back in the car.

"Thank you," Serena said, pressing the Reverend's big hand between her own as the limo drove away.

He smiled. "Come on inside."

"I'll wait out here, love," Jacob said as the others went in. "I'll keep watch for any more trouble."

"Baby, no," she said. "You know Rooster and Claudine are glad to have you here."

"I know." He kissed her forehead. "I'll see them after. Go be with your family."

"I love you," she said.

He smiled. "I love you, too."

The service was long and rambling with lots of music and multiple speakers and much weeping and answering back. Lost in her thoughts, Serena barely heard most of it, but she felt it. She felt Claudine's hand clasping hers, their fingers intertwined. She sensed Rooster's hand on her shoulder as he sheltered them both under his arm. She experienced the love and the grief and the power of the congregation around her as a living, breathing thing that raised them up as one.

She hadn't much believed in God since she was a little girl, but she believed in this power. She was other, but she was part of these people, too.

At the end of the service, Reverend Holloway sent them out to make their way to the cemetery. As Serena walked out, the sun was shining, and she saw Jacob standing in the parking lot, leaning on Carol Ann Sweatt's white SUV, talking to her through the window.

When he realized the congregation was coming out, he stepped back, and Carol Ann waved to Serena. Even from the across the parking lot, Serena could see the other woman had been crying; there were black streaks of mascara smeared down her cheeks. But when Serena started toward them, Carol Ann waved again and drove away.

"She didn't want to intrude," Jacob said. "She just wanted to leave a ham." He held up a bag from a fancy specialty food shop in the city. "How was the service?"

"It was beautiful." Across the parking lot, Rooster and Claudine got into the back of the funeral home's ancient black limousine to make the drive across the road to the cemetery. "Put that in the car and come on." She took Jacob's free hand and held it tight. "You belong with the family."

38

That night at midnight, Jacob was still downstairs writing. Serena sat up in the dark in the brand-new four-poster bed she and Jacob now officially shared. They slept in the room where Jacob had first felt a presence, the one they suspected had once belonged to the old warlock, Palissandre, but she didn't let herself think about that.

While she waited for Jacob, she shopped on her phone for a baby gift. She and Tom were still being too careful with one another after their argument, and she hoped that the perfect present for the baby would fix it. She wanted him and Evie to know how much she appreciated them and wished their family well.

She yawned and clicked a unisex onesie with a cartoon sloth on it into her cart. She wanted to wait up for Jacob, but she was exhausted. She was just about to give up and put down the phone when she heard a car drive past the house. At first, the sound barely registered; she was used to living in town where cars drove by all night. But Briarwood was half a mile from the highway.

She stumbled out of bed, dropping her phone on the hardwood floor as she went. She reached the window just as a pair of red taillights disappeared into the woods, headed toward the mill.

She grabbed her robe and ran downstairs. "Jacob!" She found him at his desk in the old library working at the computer with headphones on his head. He jumped when she touched his shoulder and shut down his monitor—she caught a glimpse of a dense page of text. "Baby, somebody just drove by the house," she said.

He blinked at her like he didn't understand. "What?"

"A car just drove past the house headed towards the old mill." His desk faced the front windows. "Didn't you see the headlights?"

"I didn't see anything." He took off the headphones. "Are you sure you didn't dream it?"

"Jacob, somebody is down there," she said. "We need to call the police."

"I'll go check." He got up.

"No!" She stopped him. "They could be anybody, doing anything. There's no happy reason for them to be here. Baby, please, let me call the police."

He pulled her close. "It's all right, love. I'll call them right now."

By the time the patrol car showed up, she was dressed, coming down the stairs as Jacob opened the front door. "You should stay here," Jacob said. "I'll take my phone and call you as soon as we know what's going on. I'm sure it's nothing, just some drunk."

"I want to come," she said. "I'm not scared. Besides, you think I'm safer here alone?" She had been watching out the window, half-expecting to see flames in the distance, but the woods remained dark.

"Y'all should both stay here at the house," the deputy said—the name on his nametag was Travis, and he looked nervous. His partner stood behind him on the porch, obviously fascinated by his first look at the famous plantation, but Travis looked like he'd rather be pretty much anywhere else. "But if you're coming, come on."

The road was so dark, Serena began to wonder if she really had dreamed the car after all. Then they broke into the mill clearing, and she saw it, a dirty, late model hatchback. "That's Tom Stewart's car," she said. "But what's he doing out here in the middle of the night? And why didn't he stop at the house?"

"I'm sure he'll be glad to tell us," Jacob said as they got out.

They followed the deputies to the same door they had used the first time she saw the mill. Inside, it was pitch black dark. Both deputies turned on their flashlights and shone bright beams around the walls and ceiling. "Tom?" Serena called. "Tom, are you here?"

One of the beams of light found a body hanging from the ceiling. "Jesus Christ!" Travis swore, dropping his flashlight. His partner turned his light back and found Tom's face.

"No..." Serena moaned. She wanted to scream, but she couldn't make the sound come out. Tom's body swung gently back and forth, but his eyes bulged wide open, a mirror of the Black faces she saw in her imagination. She stumbled backward, and Jacob caught her. "It's the spot," she said, pointing. "He's in the same spot as Davon."

"Close your eyes," he ordered. "Don't look."

"Jesus," the deputy kept repeating, sounding near tears. "Jesus Christ."

"Don't look at him, Serena," Jacob said. His voice was calm, his grip on her arms powerful enough to keep her upright even if her legs gave out. "We're going outside."

"Call an ambulance," she said, letting him turn her away from the horror. "Get him down from there."

"The policemen will take care of that."

"Jacob, help him!" They were crossing the threshold back out into the night.

"Angel." He pulled her close. "He's past helping."

The next half hour went by her in a blur. Jacob helped her to a seat on a stump and stayed beside her until the EMTs turned up and put a blanket around her shoulders. Then he left her to go talk to the cops. Behind him, she could see the open doorway, see lights flashing inside. Someone was taking pictures.

Someone will have to tell Evie, she thought. *Dear God, what will they say?* What would she say when she saw her again? How would either of them stand it?

Gorge rose in her throat. She ran for the woods, letting the blanket fall behind her. She made it to the edge of the clearing before she couldn't hold back anymore. She grabbed some unseen bulk for support and vomited like she'd never stop.

Only when her guts were empty and sore did she realize she was leaning on Tom's car. She jumped back—this would be evidence. She wanted to believe this was murder, but knew it wasn't. There had been no other cars.

Another police car drove past, and its headlights lit up the interior of the hatchback. She saw a small, white envelope on the passenger seat, dead center, obviously placed there on purpose. The light moved so quickly that for a moment she could pretend she hadn't seen what was written on the envelope. Then she opened the car door, and the dome light showed the truth—one word. Serena.

Without thinking, she sat down on the passenger seat, opened the envelope, and read:

Dear Serena,

Please don't feel sorry for me, and please don't think this is anybody else's fault but mine. I did it, all of it. I started it, and now I'm running away the only way I know how because there's no way I can stop it. I wish I could save you, save Evie, save everybody. I wish I had never been so stupid.

I won't write much. If I try to explain everything, I'll lose my nerve. But it started with the Charleston stuff. I've left it for you at the Briarwood branch in Miz Rae's old office. Once you read it, I think you'll understand better what I did. If you don't, Jacob will. I don't imagine you or anybody else will ever really understand why. Part of it was that you were my friend and I loved you, but it wasn't good love and I wasn't a true friend. I couldn't be a true friend to you, not with the evil in my blood. None of this is your fault. Amanda Flynn thinks I've got the hots for you, but I don't; I love my wife. Please, Serena, please try to save Evie.

I killed Jack Flynn. I put poison in his boner pills. Before that, I robbed the drive-in with Ontreas Clark and those two other boys to make them trust me and want to help me. I convinced him to help me break in and burn down the courthouse. Something was hidden in the basement that I had to break open. Something I thought needed to be set free.

And I succeeded. I set it loose. I thought it would be grateful, that it would do what I wanted it to do, what I knew I would never be strong enough to do on my own. But I didn't understand, and now it's too late.

Serena, please, I'm begging you for one last favor. Please protect Evie and the baby. Don't let what's coming take them. You can keep them safe.

I'm sorry. For everything, forever, Serena, I am so very sorry.

Your loving friend,

Tom Stewart

By the time she finished reading, she trembled all over. If her stomach weren't already empty, she would have been sick again. Jacob had come back out of the mill and was obviously looking for her. She made herself get out of the car and start toward him. As soon as she started, she broke into a run. "Jacob!" The EMTs wheeled a gurney out of the mill with Tom's body covered in a sheet.

"Serena?" Jacob said, meeting her halfway. "What is it?"

"This." She held out the letter. "You have to read this."

39

Serena wanted to follow her first instinct and give the letter to the police, but Jacob said no. "Tom confesses to two serious crimes in that letter," he said.

"Three," Serena said. "Killing Flynn, burning down the courthouse, and the robbery with Ontreas Clark." She remembered Ontreas. He had been the library's work release janitor the first time he'd gone into county lock-up. As she recalled, he and Tom had gotten along very well.

"Three," Jacob agreed. "Imagine the scandal that would be if people knew. Imagine what that would do to Evie."

"But it's the truth," she said.

"And what about the information he left for you at the library?" Jacob said. "If you show the police Tom's suicide note now, the first thing they'll do is go straight to the library and confiscate that evidence, and what do you think will happen to it then? Don't you think we should at least see what it is first?"

"Maybe." Whatever the Charleston librarian had sent to Tom had driven her friend insane enough to kill. Because surely he must have been insane, delusional. Surely he couldn't really have set loose some real evil.

"Let's go to the library first," Jacob said. "We'll see what's there and make a copy of it. Then we'll show everything to Evie."

"No," she said, feeling sick again at the thought. How could she ever show that letter to Evie?

"I think we have to, love," he said. "I think what happens to that letter has to be Evie's decision. She's the one with the most to lose." He took her hand. "Don't you think she deserves at least that much consideration?"

"We can't put that on her." *She'll think it's all my fault,* she thought but couldn't say out loud.

"We'll decide after we see the evidence." He kissed her hand. "Tom wrote that letter to you and told you exactly where to find it. And he wrote that once you saw it, you would understand everything he's done. Let's go see if he was right."

The Briarwood Branch of the Saxon County Library looked like a ghost ship. The FBI and state police had taken all of their computers with them, leaving Miz Rae's prized oak tables bare and scratched and data cables dangling loose from the ceiling. The bookshelves were all still crammed into the corners and covered in plastic tarps, like the corpses of giants.

Miz Rae's office was as bare and clean as she had left it except for a short stack of papers lined up neatly on the desk. "I'll turn on the copy machine," Jacob said. "You start reading."

The top page was a letter from the Charleston County Library archivist.

Dear Mr. Stewart,

I am writing in response to your request for any information we have with regard to the family of Caleb Montgomery and for Briarwood Plantation. As I told you on the phone, I wasn't hopeful going into the search. The Montgomery family resided in Charleston County for a very short time and established few significant ties here. So I was pleasantly surprised to discover a reference to Briarwood in the papers of Dr. Jeremiah Houseman, a prominent Charleston historian and the first Black professor at St. Mary's College. In his youth, Dr. Houseman worked as an interviewer for the national WPA (Works Progress Administration) created by Franklin D. Roosevelt, interviewing former slaves for a national archive. The enclosed appears to be the transcript of an interview Dr. Houseman conducted with one Adam Palissandre in 1937. It doesn't appear to have ever been filed with the WPA; I can find no reference to it in the index. After reading it myself, I can't say I'm surprised; Dr. Houseman was a historian, not a fantasist. He kept this transcript in his personal papers, not his academic files. But you did ask for anything we had, and from your C.V., I see you have some expertise in such matters. This may be exactly what you're looking for.

Per your request, I have forwarded the original materials via interlibrary loan to be used as a primary source. However, I must ask that you treat them with all appropriate care and return them to the Charleston County Library Archives as soon as possible.

Wishing you the best of luck with your research, I remain

Yours sincerely,

Sandra Fletcher

Archivist

Charleston County Library

"Adam Palissandre," Serena said. "Palissandre was the Old Man's name, remember? And wasn't Ariel's little half brother's name Adam? But it would have to be his son or his grandson; that Adam would have been dead and gone by 1937."

"Read me the interview."

The Dark Man of Briarwood Plantation

1937

WPA – 1937 – Saxon County

Interview with Adam Palissandre

Adam Palissandre is a colored man living in a rest home in Boone,

North Carolina. He claims to have been born a slave at Briarwood Plantation in Saxon County, South Carolina, in 1833. This would make him 104 years old. From his appearance, this hardly seems likely; I would judge him to be no more than 75. But his age is hardly the most incredible element of the tale he had to tell.

Mr. Palissandre was suggested to me as a subject by his great-grandniece, Serena Clark, a friend of a friend from college. Miss Clark accompanied me on my visit, and her presence seemed to inspire some misunderstanding in Mr. Palissandre as to my reasons for interviewing him.

"She wants me to tell you about the money," he said before we even sat down. "Girl, I told you like I told your mama and your aunties and your grands, there ain't no money. Whatever money there might have ever been is long gone, and if it ain't, Flynn and his people ain't going to ever let it go. And even if they did, I wouldn't want it, and neither should you. It's blood money. It's cursed."

"Uncle Adam, this isn't anything to do with that," Miss Clark said. "This is for the government. Jerry works for the government; he's a historian. He's interviewing folks about slave times."

"The government don't care nothing about no slaves," he said. "Never did."

"Mr. Palissandre, I came to ask you about Briarwood," I said. From here forward, I will attempt to merely transcribe what he told me based on my notes. Indeed, once I mentioned Briarwood, he barely allowed me to speak.

"Briarwood ... I was born at Briarwood. When I was born, it wasn't even finished yet. The white men were living in the overseer's house, and the white women, Mrs. Montgomery and her daughter, they were staying at a hotel in town. The black folks were living in tents. They were only allowed to work building their own cabins at first light in the morning and last light at night when they weren't working on the big house or in the fields. My mama said they planted those fields with cotton before Mr. Montgomery unpacked his case.

"My daddy was not white. My mama said he was a colored field hand, 'black as the ace of spades,' she called him. By the time I came along, he was long gone, sold off or dead. Mr. Montgomery wasn't going to keep him around once he took up with Mama. My sister, Ariel's daddy was Caleb Montgomery. And my mama's daddy was the Old Man, Grand-Pere, Louis Palissandre, Caleb Montgomery's daddy, too. Do you understand what I'm saying to you? Nobody ever told me these things. I just knew them, the same as I knew my mama's face. The same as I knew Mama and Ariel were witches.

"Mama didn't talk to the Dark Man much. She had sense enough to be scared of him. But Ariel didn't have no sense at all. She let the Old Man's books and talk about the old magic get up in her head. She used to talk to the Dark Man all the time, even when he wasn't there. Mama used to beat her, trying to make her stop, but she just kept on. And Mama couldn't be mad at her. We all loved Ariel. But she loved the Dark Man best.

"When that Ezra Woodbine came, Ariel said she loved him, but Mama said that was a lie. He was like a character in one of those books come to life. He and Ariel used to read books together all the time, plays where they would take turns reading the parts. I didn't understand half of what they were talking about, but I liked to hear them, and the Old Man did, too.

"And they would f*ck, too, right there in the Old Man's room with him sleeping in the bed and Mama sewing and me working the fan. When the Old Man got so sick he didn't half know where he was any more, they f*cked all the time, on the settee and up against the wall and one time right there on the foot of the bed with that nasty Old Man just laying there, watching. Ezra would call my sister 'my darling' and talk to her in Italian like he thought she might understand him. But in the end mostly they just f*cked.

"Mama didn't never say nothing when Ezra was around, but when it was just us at home in our cabin, she would scold Ariel something fierce. But Ariel just laughed. She didn't care. At night she would go out to the woods to meet the Dark Man, and during the day she had Ezra.

"But then the Old Man died. Ezra said he was going to take Ariel away, that he was going to take all of us away, and we wouldn't be slaves anymore. I believed him; I was excited. But Mama was right; that was foolishness.

"Montgomery's white daughter, Alice Rose, she wanted Ezra for her husband. When she found out he wanted Ariel, she lost her mind. She howled and hollered, and when her mama tried to tell her how good it would be for Mama and Ariel to be out of their house, she slapped her own mama in the face. She said she was going to make Simon Flynn sell Ariel south before Ezra got back from town.

"Ariel must have lost her mind, too. She told that white girl it didn't matter if they sold her or not, that Ezra still loved her and he would find her and he wouldn't never want Alice Rose. Alice Rose slapped Ariel, too. And Ariel slapped her back.

"I didn't see what all they did to her. One of the field hands, Maidie, she scooped me up and hid with me under one of the cabins and wouldn't let me go. Mama had nursed her through a bad childbirth, and she felt like she owed her. She dragged me way back up under that cabin where couldn't nothing see us but the rats. She kept her hand over my mouth so I wouldn't call out for my mama, and I kept feeling things, little bugs and things crawling on me, and it so dark I couldn't see nothing at all. But I heard my sister screaming all day long. And I kept thinking, 'Where is the Dark Man? Why don't he save her?'

"When the screaming stopped and Maidie finally turned me loose, it was dark outside. I found my mama tied to a post near the whipping post. Right in front of her was a fresh grave—Ariel's grave. They had made Mama watch it all and left her there. I ran to her crying, but she acted like she didn't even see me or hear me. She just stood there like a statue with her hands tied behind her back. I sat on the ground at her feet and hid my face in her skirts and prayed to God to save us.

"But it wasn't God who came. We had been there a long time; the moon had come up, and the dirt on the grave started moving. The ground opened up, and my sister crawled out of it, a bloody, ugly, monstrous thing. I screamed, and the other slaves who saw it screamed and ran away, but Mama wasn't scared at all. She called Ariel by her name, and Ariel went to her and hugged her neck. But when Mama tried to tell her she needed to go on, Ariel didn't listen.

"She picked up an axe somebody had left on the ground, and when Simon Flynn came running to see what everybody was screaming about, she chopped him up in little pieces. He tried to hit her with his whip; he even tried to shoot her with his gun, but she just kept on chopping. I had never seen so much blood. Even when he was dead, she kept chopping, cutting off his arms and legs and his head. Then she went off toward the big house, still dragging that axe behind her.

"'Mama, where she going?' I said. 'What she going to do?'

"She wouldn't tell me nothing except, 'You stay here with me.' I stayed there all night, listening to the screaming and watching people running and the fires burning all around. I saw the white girl, Naomi, go running down the road, screaming and crying something about Ezra, but I never thought he could have hurt anybody. I kept watching for the Dark Man, waiting for him to show up.

"In the morning, three white men came and found my mama—Simon Flynn's brother, John, the lawyer, and Mr. Benson, the farmer who owned the next big place to Briarwood, and Osiris Collins, the white trash sharecropper who rented from Mr. Montgomery and lived down on the creek.

"'Your people tell us you can stop this,' John Flynn said. His only brother was laying there on the ground in pieces, but he never even looked.

"'Why would I want to stop it?' she said, pert as anything. And that was not my mama; she was always quiet and calm, letting them have their way. 'Y'all murdered my baby, did you not?'

"'That wasn't us,' Benson said.

"'What if we murder this baby, too?' Flynn said. He acted like he was going to grab me, but Mama looked at him hard, and he stepped back.

"'Won't make no difference,' she said. 'The devil done broke loose now. He's going to have his vengeance.'

"'But can you stop it?' Flynn said. She looked at him again and smiled.

"'What you want, Hester?' Osiris said. He knew her well, and he knew she had the gift. Him and his family used to come to our cabin all the time for medicine because they was too poor for a white doctor.

"'I want what's mine,' she said. 'I want my child. I want my home. My name is Palissandre, and everything you see belongs to me.'

"'You know that's not possible,' Benson said. 'No slave can inherit—'

"'I ain't no slave,' she said. 'Not any more. Ain't no more slaves at Briarwood.'

"'Now there's where you're wrong, Miz Hester,' Flynn said. 'Briarwood is just crawling with slaves, dead slaves when we're done if this thing keeps going on. This devil of yours, do you think he can stand up to the law? To the army? To every white man in the South? And even if he does, do you think your people can stand with him? Magic is magic, Miz Hester, but the law is the law.'

"He was smiling, real pleasant and calm, but little as I was, I saw the evil in his eyes. 'Mr. Benson is right. Right now, no slave can inherit a plantation. But that might not always be so. We could hold this place in trust for you and for your child here. And someday, if things change, you or your child or his child could claim it from us, and under the law, we wouldn't have any choice but to let y'all have it. If we can put a stop to this madness right now, I swear to you, that's what we'll do. Me and these two men here and others from the town, we will sign a pact with you, a contract, saying Briarwood and all her profits are to be held in trust for Hester Palissandre and her heirs in perpetuity. Or we can let your devil have his way, and every African man, woman, and child on this place will die, including you. Including your little boy.' I could see she was trembling, and tears had come into her eyes. 'It is unfortunate that your daughter had to die,' he said. 'But there is nothing any of us can do about that now. Better we should save the living than perish avenging the dead.'

"'I want to be free and Adam to be free,' she said. 'I want a home for us that's ours, not here, but someplace nice. Put that in your contract, too. Bring it to me, and let me read it, and if it's all right, we'll sign. Then I'll see what I can do.'

"Flynn spread his papers and inkwell on Collins's old wagon and wrote up the contract on the spot. He didn't realize Mama really could read at first; she made him change some things, and that didn't make him happy. But they got it worked out pretty quick about the time the barn started burning and the horses all came running out. By that time, some militia men had shown up. They went marching across the front lawn, shooting at every Black face they saw, and for a minute, I thought Flynn would tear up the contract.

"Then Ezra stepped out on the upstairs gallery, and the militia men started catching fire, one after the other. They went up like pine knots, exploding, and each one that went took out at least one more on either side. After that, Flynn scratched out what Mama wanted scratched out and scratched in what Mama wanted scratched in. They cut her loose, and she signed it.

"'Now stop him,' Benson said.

"Mama bent down on Ariel's grave and dug out two handfuls of red clay mud stained with my sister's blood. She sang to it and made a little man out of it, then she walked up to one of the burning soldiers and stuck it in the fire. When it was hard and its face was black, she put it in her pocket. 'Adam,' she called to me, and I took her by the hand. We walked up to the big house, me holding her hand and all those white men trailing like children behind her.

"'Ezra Woodbine!' she called out. 'Bring my child to me!'

He went back inside and came out the front door a few minutes later carrying Ariel's body in his arms. But he didn't look like Ezra anymore. He was covered in blood from head to toe, and his eyes were glowing red. But when he saw me, he smiled and winked at me just like he always had. 'It's all right, Hester,' he said. 'I killed them all.'

"'I know you did,' Mama said. 'But now you've got to stop.'

"He laughed, but it wasn't Ezra's laugh. 'You know I won't, beloved.' It wasn't Ezra's voice, either. 'I will never stop.'

"'Then you'll have to wait.' She let go of me and held up the little clay man she had made. 'Wait until you're called.' She sang out witch words none of the rest of us could understand. Ezra fell to his knees, still holding Ariel's body. He threw back his head and howled. Y'all ever heard a bull that somebody tried to slaughter when they didn't get his throat cut right? You know that noise he made right before he went to fighting, right before he gored that damned fool that cut him wrong to death? Imagine half a dozen bulls all roaring out at once, or a hundred. All that hurt and fury, all them voices crying out at once. It was like that only worse.

"And then I saw the Dark Man. He reared up out of Ezra like a snake rearing out of dead leaves, a thick, white, twisted thing twice as big as any man with eyes that burned blue fire. He swept down from the porch on burning wings that blotted out the house behind them, reaching for my mama with hands tipped in claws. I fell on the ground in a ball, and the white men behind us screamed.

"Then he was gone. All that was left was Ezra, lying broken on the steps, tangled up with Ariel. Flynn and the others grabbed him up, and I couldn't help but cry. 'It's all right, little Adam,' he told me as they dragged him off. 'I don't mind.'

"They hanged Ezra and a handful of field hands that weren't worth much money in the new mill. The rest of the slaves except for me and Mama, they split up between them or sold off. Flynn wanted to take the clay doll, but Mama gave it to Tom Creighton, the schoolmaster, and told him to put it somewhere safe. He told me later that they locked it up in a strongbox in the new courthouse after it was built, down in the basement. He was a good man, Tom.

"'John Flynn bought a house for me and Mama, and I lived there until I moved up here. Mama had three more daughters, and she named the oldest one Ariel. There's been an Ariel in every generation since. But we never got another dime from the Montgomery Trust, and to my mind, we never will."

After that he stopped talking and refused to answer any more questions.

"You said the Dark Man was a thick, white, twisted thing," I said. "The Dark Man was white?"

He looked at me like I was the one who was insane. "For sure he's white,' he said. 'What else the Devil going to be?" But that was it; he would say no more.

> The Montgomery Trust is in fact a real legal entity in the town of Saxonville. But when I tried to investigate further, the director of the trust suggested strongly that I let the matter drop. It is interesting to note that this man was a lawyer named John Flynn.

When she'd finished reading, Serena put her head down on the desk and closed her eyes. "Are you all right?" Jacob asked.

"Are you?" She was exhausted, and her brain was spinning.

"Yeah." He bent down and kissed her cheek. "Poor Tom."

She laughed through tears. "Yeah."

"He thought he could release this Dark Man by burning down the courthouse," Jacob said. "But I still don't understand why he would want to do that."

"I don't understand any of this." *Was the Dark Man real?* "I don't know what to do."

"I still say we should turn it all over to Evie and let her decide," Jacob said. "He was her husband. I would think she would have more insight into his state of mind than we do."

"That's true." She just wanted to go home and sleep and somehow not know any of this anymore. "Whatever you think, Baby."

He laughed. "I'll never hear that again." She tried to laugh, but it came out a sob. "Hey, come here." He pulled her into his arms. "Whatever else happens, you know I'll keep you safe."

"I know." What had Tom wanted? Had he seen himself as Ezra Woodbine back from the grave for vengeance? *I couldn't be a true friend to you,* he had written in his suicide note addressed to Serena. *Not with the evil in my blood.*

"Come on," Jacob said. He kissed her on top of the head. "I think it's time to go home."

40

White Saxonville outside the Montgomery Trust all agreed Tom Stewart must have left his wife in dire straits. Amanda Flynn intimated to her secretary and the ladies at the beauty parlor that she had inside information suggesting at least one other woman had been involved, and Frank Sweatt told his inner circle at the Rotary Club that he suspected drugs.

What was certain and well-known to all—and absolutely inaccurate—was that Tom and Evie's little house was upside down in its mortgage, and Evie barely made pocket money teaching little girls to dance. Tom's parents had been dead for years (and had been no great shakes when they were living, Frank Kennedy told his golf foursome). Nobody knew Evie's parents personally, but rumor was that they were retired teachers barely able to afford their tiny condo in the mountains. No doubt they would help as much as they could, but they would hardly have the room or the wherewithal to take in Evie and her baby permanently. The general consensus was that she was pitiful, and Tom ought to be burning in hell.

All of these nice White folks turned up for the funeral and went by the house to visit afterwards. Evie's parents and sister entertained them and their questions as politely as they could, but Evie herself barely spoke to anybody. As soon as she got home, she put on a pair of sweatpants and one of Tom's old flannel shirts and sat down in the den in front of the TV. People came in and expressed their condolences, and she said thank you, but she never once looked up.

By five o'clock, they thought everyone had finally gone. Her mother was making her a cup of tea, and her father had gone upstairs for a nap. Then the doorbell rang again. But this time, Evie got up and answered it herself, beating her mother to the door.

Jacob stood on the porch. "You poor sweetheart," he said as soon as he saw her, and she fell sobbing into his arms. "I'm so sorry."

"Hello," Evie's mother said, nonplussed. Evie hadn't cried to her or her father this way yet. "Evie, honey, who is this?"

"I'm Jacob McGinnas," he said, offering his hand. "I'm a friend of Tom and Evie's."

"It's all right, Mom," Evie said, composing herself. "Jacob, please come in." She looked past him toward the car. "Is Serena with you?"

"Not this time," he said. "She asked me to tell you she'll call later, but you don't have to talk if you don't want to. And if you need her for anything at all, just call."

"That's very kind, Mr. McGinnas," her mother said. "But right now, Evie's exhausted."

"I'm sure she is," he said. "I won't stay long, I promise. Or I can come back later."

"No," Evie said. "Come on, we'll talk in the den. Don't worry, Mom. It's fine." Without waiting for her mother's answer, she took Jacob's hand, led him into the den, and closed the door behind them.

"I was going to bring you a good bottle of whiskey," he said. "But Serena reminded me about the baby."

"It's probably a good thing you didn't. I'd have been tempted to risk it." Her father had lit a fire in the fireplace. She sat down in one of the two armchairs pulled up to the hearth—her chair, and Jacob sat in Tom's. "It's so nice of you to come."

"I wanted to talk to you." He took her hands. "I feel responsible for what happened to Tom."

She shook her head. "No."

"If I hadn't bought Briarwood, Tom very likely never would have gone near the place."

"Yes, he would," she said. "He had—he did. He and Jason sneaked in there years ago. They even tried to do a website." Tears spilled down her cheeks, and she let them, keeping her hands in his. "But you know that, don't you?"

"I don't know anything." He kissed her forehead. "But somehow Tom got lost, and Briarwood was part of that." He let her go. "I can't bring him back to you, but I can do what he would have wanted. I can take care of you and the baby. Whatever you need. I've already talked to the bank, and I'm setting up an account for you."

"Jacob, no," she said. "I couldn't let you do that."

"And how do you propose to stop me?" he said with a smile. "Please, love, let me do this much. Let me and Serena know you're safe."

"That's really sweet," she said. "Crazy, but sweet." She had a stack of bills on the desk that screamed at her to stop being so noble—utilities, doctor, mortgage, health insurance. She and Tom had lived paycheck to paycheck, and now his paychecks would stop. The life insurance policy provided for him by the county would barely cover the funeral costs , assuming she could convince them to pay at all because he committed suicide. There was other money, stacks of it, Montgomery Trust money that Tom had been putting into a special account ever since he took the job at the library. But standing over her husband's grave, she vowed she wouldn't touch it, no matter how much she might need it. She wouldn't owe the Trust. They would never touch her baby.

"Not so crazy," he said. "There's something I have to show you."

She read the note with tears burning her eyes. "What is he talking about?" she said. "Did you find it?"

"We went to the library." He handed over the rest of the papers, and she read Adam Palissandre's story straight through without stopping, barely breathing.

"Did he tell you about this?" Jacob asked her when she put it down.

"No." She closed her eyes. "He believed it, didn't he? He thought it was all true."

"Yes."

She opened her eyes and looked at Jacob. "Is it?"

He touched her cheek and smiled. "Does it matter?"

A shudder went through her. She thought she could even feel her baby tremble inside her. "No." She folded everything back into a sheaf, the story and the note. "It doesn't." Tom was dead, and nothing would change that. No ghost could bring him back.

"What do you want to do, Evie?" Jacob said. "Do you want me to give those papers to the police?"

She felt cold in spite of the fire. "No." She handed the papers to him. "Please no."

'It's all right." She watched as he fed them page by page into the flames. "Everything will be fine."

41

After the funeral, life settled back into a routine. Over the next two months, Jacob finished the first draft of his book and sent it off to his editor in New York, and Serena continued her research into Briarwood and her work at the library. With Tom's death, the place was in chaos, and the Board was only too happy to let Serena take charge. And if the rest of the employees had any objection, they had the good sense to keep it to themselves.

For the first time since she'd come back to South Carolina, Serena felt like she was doing the real work she'd been educated to do, and she was happy with Jacob. But she felt haunted. Living at Briarwood, she saw ghosts in every shadow. And every time she saw the burned-out shell of the Saxon County Courthouse, all she could think about was Tom.

Like the rest of the town, she drove past the ruin at least twice a day every day since it burned, but until she read Tom's note, she barely noticed it. The Saxon County Council couldn't decide if they wanted to apply for a federal historical preservation grant to restore it or bulldoze the ruin and run a bond issue to raise money for a shiny new government complex, preferably out on the bypass. Since the Council was divided almost perfectly between real estate speculators and members of the Historical Society, the debate would likely continue to rage on. And like most other residents of the County, Serena could not have cared less. But since Tom's suicide, the building itself preyed on her mind. She couldn't stop thinking about was Tom's note and the story of the red clay doll. Could it have been real? Was the doll still there?

On Ash Wednesday, Jacob flew to New York to meet with his publisher. Serena wanted to ask him not to go, but that seemed silly. He wanted her to go with him, but she felt like she couldn't abandon the library. So she drove him to the airport and kissed him good-bye and prayed Ezra Woodbine's ghost wouldn't be waiting for her at home.

That night, she worked late, avoiding the inevitable. By the time she drove of town, the sun was almost set, and the courthouse ruin looked like a background set from a B-grade horror movie, black against a pink and purple sky. Without stopping to think about it, she turned into the municipal parking lot.

The downtown backlot was apparently deserted. She got sneakers and a flashlight from her trunk and swapped out her cardigan for one of Jacob's hoodies he'd left in the back seat. She slipped her phone into one pocket and her keys into the other.

The courthouse was cordoned off by nothing but yellow caution tape. She ducked under it and ignored the "Keep Out" sign. The building wasn't even locked. The fire department had apparently broken down the back door trying to put out the blaze; it was chained shut but hanging loose on its hinges. A piece of plywood lay in the grass nearby as if someone had meant to block the doorway then gave up. She had no trouble shifting the broken door aside and slipping through the crack.

She flicked on her flashlight. She had only been inside the courthouse one time before, when she and Trey had gotten their marriage license. But even if she'd known the place, she doubted it would have felt familiar. Everything was scorched and broken. She stood in a vestibule with an elevator and a staircase leading up. Tom's letter said the doll was stored in a strongbox in the basement, but a half-melted directory on the wall didn't reference any floor below where she stood. Straight ahead of her was a door marked "Mailroom," propped half-open, and it was the only thing listed on the ground floor. On the second floor were offices for the probate court, clerk of court, and solicitor; the third floor was the courtroom and the judge's chambers; and the fourth floor was a gallery for the courtroom, and storage.

She searched the mailroom for a cellar door, but didn't find one, so she went upstairs. She heard scrabbling noises in the shadows, and shuddered. *Girl, what are you doing?* The blackened remains of a metal trashcan propped open the second floor door . The fire damage on this floor was much worse. All the glass in the office doors was shattered, and the wood frames were burned black. Peering into the probate judge's office, she saw furniture and equipment crumbling to ash. The stench of smoke was overpowering. She tried the door, and it opened. She walked through every office, shining her light, but saw no sign of any strongbox or staircase down.

On the third floor, the judge's chambers and jury rooms were more of the same. The courtroom was less burned but more dramatic with its jagged, broken ceiling open to the stars and tall windows shattered down either side. A winter's worth of rain had soaked the carpet and drapes, and the miasma of mold and rot were almost as strong as the smoke.

The wall behind the judge's bench had taken the worst of the fire up here. The paint was blackened and cracked, and the flags hung in rotten ribbons from their poles. Her flashlight beam swept over a massive oil painting that looked like a portrait painted in hell. It depicted a White man in judge's robes and an old-fashioned white wig. The edges of the image were black, and his face was bubbled and blistered from the heat. It reminded her of the portrait of June Montgomery that burned the night of the Christmas party; it could have been painted by the same artist. Even close up, she couldn't read the artist's signature through the soot. But a brass plaque mounted on the blackened frame gleamed as if freshly polished. It read, "The Honorable John Christopher Flynn: 1799-1893."

"Ain't he a devil?" The voice came from behind her, and she

screamed and dropped her light. She fell to her knees to grope for it, and a thick-fingered hand touched hers in the dark. She grabbed the light and pointed it like a weapon, and Laurel Heath appeared crouched in front of her, smiling. "What you doing in here, Miss Serena?"

"Laurel..." She climbed back to her feet on legs like water. "You scared me."

"What you looking for?" He wore a plaid bathrobe over his usual shabby clothes, and he had corduroy slippers on his feet.

"Laurel, are you living in here?" she said. "You need to go home now. It's not safe."

"Oh, I know." He took a wad of tissues out of his pocket and wiped his nose. "But he ain't here no more. You know that."

"Who?' she said.

He gave her the side eye like he knew she was putting him on. "Come on then," he said. "I'll show you."

He led her out of the courtroom and back down the stairs without waiting for her light, shuffling in his slippers but surefooted as a cat. She stumbled and lost sight of him in the hall below. "Laurel?" The door to the clerk of court's office stood open. "Where are you?" Inside the broken wooden door was a tiny lobby in front of a counter locked behind steel and bulletproof glass. But to one side, an old-fashioned vault door hung open.

"In here, Miss Serena," she heard Laurel's voice call from inside. "Come on."

Inside the vault was a sort of library full of heavy books and blackened file cabinets. She swept her light all around, startling a fat rat that fled across the tops of her sneakers. She let out a shriek and danced a little quickstep of revulsion.

"Miss Serena?" Laurel's head popped up from the floor just down the narrow aisle. "You all right?"

"Fine." Moving closer, she saw he stood on a blackened spiral staircase of cast iron and tarnished brass that led down.

"Then come on."

The cellar showed evidence of some attempt at reclamation after the fire. Plastic drop cloths covered the dirt floor, and there were several stacks of acid-free boxes labeled "Property of the University of South Carolina" with the gamecock seal. "They took everything to Columbia," she said.

"No ma'am." His eyes gleamed in the dark, and when she turned her light on his face, she saw it shone with sweat in spite of the cellar's chill. "Not everything." He pointed into a dark corner where a low sort of cavern was dug into the wall.

She had to crawl on her knees and one hand to get inside, awkward with the light. *No more rats, please, Jesus.* The sulfur and ashes smell was stronger here. The cold, damp air was so thick with it, she could barely breathe. She had a sudden, awful vision of the tunnel collapsing on top of her, the weight of the whole crumbling courthouse coming down to bury her alive. *And nobody even knows I'm here. No one would ever find me.*

Her hand bearing her weight slipped on something loose and sharp on the floor, and she came down hard on her elbow. It hurt like hell; worse, she dropped her flashlight, and it went out. "Shit!" She tried to sit up, and her head slammed into the ceiling. "Shit shit shit shit shit …" She let herself fall to her belly and fumbled the light between both hands, scrabbling at the switch.

The light flashed on. For a single moment, she was nose to nose with another woman, a woman who looked very much like her but with bloodshot eyes in a face bruised and bloodied and swollen out of shape. The other drew back her lips in a scream, and Serena screamed with her.

Then the face disappeared, and the only scream she heard was her own. Behind her, she could hear Laurel whimpering, keening like a wounded dog. But the beam of her flashlight steadied, and she saw the iron box.

The lid had been blown open and twisted back. The thing she slipped on was a shard of plastic from the explosive that had cut into her palm. She hooked her bleeding hand through what was left of the box's dirt-encrusted brass and leather handle and crawled backwards out of the hole.

Laurel crouched on his haunches in the farthest corner of the room. "It's all right," she said. "I got it." She sat down on the floor with the box between her legs and dug her phone out of her pocket. She still had a signal, and barely half an hour had passed since she'd come into the courthouse. She dialed Jacob's number and started to hit send, then stopped. Anything she told him would just freak him out, and he was all the way in New York. She'd call him later from home when she knew what she had found.

"He used to talk to me," Laurel said, his voice coming out of the shadows. "I used to hear him in the light. But he gone now." He hummed to himself for a few seconds, a snatch of an old gospel song. "But it's all right. It's going to be all right."

"Thank you, Laurel," she said. "Thank you for showing me the way."

She pushed back the broken lid and looked inside the box. The heat from the explosion had set the contents on fire. A bundle of papers still tied up in a few threads of pink ribbon was burned to crumbling scraps that disintegrated when she tried to pick them up. But underneath, she found Hester's doll. The little clay figure had shattered, the arms and legs broken off of the torso. Some of it had crumbled into bits as fine as gravel, but she could still see the features of the face scratched into the clay with some fine tool or, more likely, a fingernail. The little thing was screaming. She picked it up, and suddenly she could smell it. Under the smoke and the earthy smell of clay was something deeper and richer and infinitely less pleasant.

"Put that down, Miss Serena," Laurel said with an edge of hysteria. "Don't touch that nasty thing."

"It's all right." She set it down carefully and took off Jacob's sweatshirt. She set the little broken torso with its screaming head in the center of the shirt then added every piece she could pick up. Then she picked up the whole box and shook it to get the last dust. She tied the sweatshirt into a sack and stood up.

"It's all right now," Laurel said. "He going to show us what to do."

"Who, Laurel?" she said. "Tell me who you're talking about."

He grinned and shook his head. "Come ahead on, Miss Serena. Let's get on out of here."

He left her as soon as they were outside, singing full voice as he went off down the street. She put her bundle in the passenger seat and started the car. As she backed out, she caught a glimpse of her face in the rearview mirror. Her eyes were wide and rimmed with red, and her cheeks were smeared with ashes and red clay mud.

When she got home to Briarwood, she transferred the broken doll into a sealed plastic freezer bag and threw the sweatshirt in the wash. She put the bag in her underwear drawer and took a shower.

Just as she was getting out, the phone rang—Jacob was calling. "Hey Baby," she said as she answered. She checked her smile in the bedroom mirror.

"Where have you been?" he said. "Is everything all right?"

"Fine. I stayed at the library late and got some work done." She let the image of the doll form in her mind, a broken thing sealed up safely in a plastic bag. Then she pushed it away. "I hate it when you're not home."

42

Frank and Carol Ann Sweatt had a marvelous time in Savannah over the St. Patrick's Day weekend. They stayed with Carol Ann's brother and sister-in-law on Tybee Island, and every night they went to the riverfront and drank and danced and cut the fool like college kids. Carol Ann even flashed her tits at a car full of frat boys and brought home a fistful of beads. On the ride home Sunday night, Frank said it had been like a second honeymoon, only better.

On Monday morning, Carol Ann called Frank at the bank and asked him out to lunch. "Sugar, I would love to," he told her, "but after being out of the office on Friday, I am just swamped."

"Never mind, honey," she told him. "I'll see you at home tonight."

At lunchtime, she went by the bank, but he wasn't there. "It's so nice outside, he probably sneaked off to the golf course," his secretary told her. "You know Frank."

She smiled. "Oh yes, I do." Clutching her steering wheel so tightly her knuckles hurt, she drove out to the country club. But of course, his car wasn't there.

She went by the house and ran upstairs to his office. She opened up his secret safe under the rug behind his desk—the combination was his mother's date of birth. She took out the papers she needed and left his dirty books and picture of his college sweetheart behind. She stopped off in the den downstairs for one last item and a drink before she hit the road.

Driving through the backwoods of Saxon County, she called her own office and told Loraine to cancel her afternoon appointments. Making the turn past the "Posted: Private Hunt Club: No Trespassing!!" sign, she called her lawyer's office. Jasper Banks was still at lunch, but his secretary expected him back any minute. "That's fine," Carol Ann told her. "Tell him I'll call him back."

What Jack Flynn called a hunt club was actually a shack in the woods. She drove slowly up the rutted drive and parked where she thought she'd be just out of sight of the windows. Jack's silver sedan was parked right next to a little red sports car. "Well, all right then," she said, her last suspicion confirmed. "Here we go."

As soon as she stepped up on the porch, she heard her husband. He was caterwauling so, she could have driven a tank through the front door and they wouldn't have heard. In the bedroom through an open door, Amanda Flynn had Frank strapped up spread-eagled on the kind of rack that hunters used to drain the blood from their kills, wearing nothing but his jockey shorts. Amanda herself was done up for Halloween at Hef's house in a black leather corset and thong with a garter belt, stockings, and heels. It pleased Carol Ann to note the famous Amanda Flynn tits were finally starting to sag. Saxon County's most prominent attorney was wielding a riding crop, and an equally cheesy array of sex toys was lined up on a TV tray beside her, including a butt plug the size of a small fire hydrant.

"Great day in the morning," Carol Ann said, getting their attention. "Ain't y'all a sight?"

Jack stopped hollering and froze, his blue eyes round with shock. "Now sugar, don't get excited," he said as Amanda turned away. He had clothespins on his saggy old man nipples, and Carol Ann didn't know if that was the funniest or the most pitiful thing she had seen in her life. She started laughing so hard, she thought she might not ever stop.

"Oh, for God's sake," Amanda said. "Get out of here, Carol Ann."

Still laughing, Carol Ann reached into her purse and pulled out the gun. "Amanda, why don't you shut the fuck up?" Then she shot the bitch in the middle of her perfectly unlined forehead. At that range with that pistol, she blew the whole back of her head out and shattered the mirror behind her.

"Oh shit!" Frank screamed. She turned to him. "Sugar, baby, no!" She shot him first in the crotch of his tighty whities, then one more time in the chest.

She set the gun down on the TV tray beside the butt plug and went back out to the kitchen. She considered washing the powder off her hands, but honestly, what would be the point? She dialed Jasper's number again and told the secretary she'd hold for him to finish another call.

"Hey Carol Ann," he said when he picked up. "What's up?"

"I'm going to need you to meet me at the law enforcement center," she said. "I just killed Frank and his mistress, and I'm fixing to call the police."

43

Serena and Jacob hadn't heard about Carol Ann. They spent Serena's afternoon off from the library in Charlotte meeting with a prominent Black architect who used to be the mayor. Jacob's book was finished and with his editor, and Reverend Holloway and the FBI were close to an agreement on giving the unidentified remains from the mill a proper resting place at the Briarwood Baptist cemetery. Jacob wanted to launch the book at the groundbreaking of the new museum, so he had commissioned a design. Serena agreed with him that the architect's vision was spot-on. But she had strong objections to the name he had chosen.

"Baby, you can't be calling a serious museum the Ezra Woodbine Memorial," she said. They were making spaghetti in Briarwood's ridiculously extravagant new kitchen, and she was mincing garlic for the sauce. "The man was an axe murderer."

"The people he axe murdered had it coming, don't you think?" Jacob said. At this point he supervised from a bar stool, but he had promised to make the salad.

"Even if that's true, it's not about Ezra." She scooped up the garlic on her knife and swiped it into the meat and onions already browning on the stove. "Ezra was one ugly incident. The real story of Briarwood is all the people of color who suffered and died here, not just that night but throughout the whole history of the plantation. We have a chance to give people a full, three-dimensional understanding not only of the ugly realities of plantation culture but the campaign of terror on the Black community in the South since Reconstruction.

"Fine," he said. "The Ariel Palissandre Memorial."

"Do you want a museum or a haunted house attraction?" she said. "I definitely think the story of Ariel and Ezra should be part of it, but that's the hook, the sexy bit to get people in the door. The focus has got to be bigger than that."

"So what you're saying is you want to accomplish more than flogging my trashy horror novel," he said with a grin.

"Your novel is not trashy," she said. "At least, I don't think it is. You won't let me read it."

"I will," he said. "I just don't want to spoil the surprise. Is that okay?"

"It is." She smiled over her shoulder at him before she dumped in canned crushed tomatoes. "I think it's kind of cute."

"You know, Mrs. Decatur, I'm beginning to think you don't take me seriously."

"I do. You know I do." She turned down the flame and went over to him. "I think you're amazing. And Briarwood is yours, not mine."

"Ours," he corrected.

"If you want to call it Redneck Murder House Live, that's on you," she said, sliding her arms around him.

"Nice." He squeezed her close. "Fine then. What would you call it?"

"Briarwood Plantation," she said. "Just call it what it is."

"And what happens when some sweetie magnolia from out of town shows up wanting to get her bridal portrait taken in the front hall?" Jacob said.

"We will educate her," Serena said, giving him a poke. "But hang on. Do you hear that?" A car was coming up the drive.

The ugly brown German sedan was just pulling up out front. "Jasper Banks?" Serena said, looking out the window. "What is he doing here?"

"I couldn't say," Jacob said, looking over her shoulder. Banks was the lawyer who had handled the closings when Jacob bought Briarwood and his house in town. "But he doesn't look happy, does he?"

Jacob opened the front door as Banks came up the steps. "Evening, y'all," he said. "Mrs. Decatur, I have something for you."

"For me?" He held out a thick manila envelope, but she didn't take it. "What is it?"

"I don't know, and I don't want to know." The lawyer was always a little harried, but now he looked ready to jump out of his skin. "Carol Ann Sweatt asked me to make sure you got this, and I have done that." He held the package out to Jacob, who took pity on him and accepted it. "And now, I am out."

"Hang on," Serena said. "Why would Carol Ann send something to me?"

"Oh, good Lord. Y'all haven't heard. Carol Ann shot and killed her husband."

"Oh my God!" Serena said.

"And Amanda Flynn," Banks said. "Apparently the two of them had been an item for a while now. My paralegal says everybody knew that. I didn't know that. Did y'all know that?"

"No," Jacob said, looking like he was trying very hard not to laugh.

"I had heard a rumor," Serena said. "Jasper, did she kill them?"

"Shot them both in their love nest," he said. "I mean to say, they were at their love nest out at old Jack Flynn's hunting cabin. She shot Amanda in the head and Frank ... well, the bullet that killed him went into his chest."

"After she shot him in the love nest," Jacob said.

"I'm afraid so," Jasper said with a shudder.

"When did this happen?" Serena said, ashamed of both of them.

"Just a few hours ago. It's all over the local news; everybody in town's talking about it. You can even see pictures of the crime scene on the internet if you want to. Carol Ann took pictures with her phone and posted them up on the realty company's website before they arrested her. So far, nobody's been able to figure out how to take them down. So there's Amanda Flynn, dead in a black leather corset, right next to a listing for a three-bedroom ranch."

Jacob finally gave up and laughed. "Good for Carol Ann."

"Jacob, don't say that!" Serena said. "That's horrible!"

"Now love, come on," he said. "Can you think of anybody who deserved to be dead and naked on the internet more than Amanda Flynn?"

"Nobody deserves that," she said. "And I'm shocked at you. Nothing about this is the least bit funny."

"It's a little bit funny," Jasper said. "Especially if you knew Amanda. But you're right, Serena; it is a terrible thing. I reckon she just snapped."

"Will you be the one representing her?" Jacob said. He wasn't laughing any more, but he was still smiling.

"Oh, hell no," Jasper said. "Thank the Lord, I am not a criminal lawyer. Truth be told, I don't know what she is going to do. The police have frozen all of her and Frank's joint accounts, I'm sure, so she might not be able to afford a lawyer."

"I'll get her a lawyer," Jacob said.

Jasper looked surprised; no doubt he'd share this tidbit tomorrow at the Rotary Club's weekly meeting at the Allavance Bar & Grill. "Well, that's fine, then," he said. "Y'all have a good evening."

"Hang on," Serena said. "I still don't know why Carol Ann would send me a package."

"No more do I, and no more do I care," he said. "Look, Carol Ann brought me a lot of business over the years, and I like her. So, when she asked me to bring you this stuff, I didn't feel like I could say no. But there's a whole lot that goes on in this town that I am very careful not to know about. And I've got a powerful feeling whatever's in that envelope has something to do with it. So, as I said, I am out." He started down the steps. "Y'all know lots of lawyers. I'm sure they'll be happy to help."

As he drove away, Serena took the envelope and tore it open. She pulled out a stapled report. "The Montgomery Trust Financial Report, Third Quarter 2020." Her name, Serena Ariel Sanders Decatur, was scribbled in the margin. "I saw this on Frank's desk at the Christmas party. I was getting ready to read it when Amanda came in." She handed it to Jacob.

"Is that all there is?" he asked, scanning it.

"No." She sat down in one of the porch rockers and pulled out more papers. "This is a private investigator's report from four years ago…somebody was tracking me down; they found me in Las Vegas." She pulled out the last bundle, a thick, typewritten sheaf held together with a binder clip. "And this looks like a genealogy report. Jacob, what the hell is this?"

"Come on," he said. "Let's take it inside and read it together."

"Baby, wait." She felt like she was standing on a cliff's edge; one more step, and she'd fall. So many things were coming into focus at once, and none of them felt safe. "What did you say to Carol Ann?"

"What?" He was standing in exactly the spot where he'd been the first moment she saw him, smiling the same sexy smile. "When?"

"When I came out of Davon's funeral, you were talking to Carol Ann, and she was crying," she said. "And at the Christmas party, y'all were talking when that painting started burning. You had your hand on her back."

"At Davon's funeral, she was talking about Rooster," he said. "She's very fond of him. I think she might have a little crush." He took her hand. "I don't remember what we were talking about at the party. When the sparks caught that painting, I pretty well forgot everything else." He grinned. "But you got me, sweetheart. It's all a sham. I've just been using you to get to Carol Ann."

She laughed. "Oh, shut up."

"It's true," he insisted. "It's the stringy neck that drives me wild. You think if I pay for her lawyer, she'll let me have conjugal visits?"

"You know you're not funny," she said. "You think you're funny, but you're not."

Walking inside, holding his hand, she felt herself stepping back from the precipice. But the ground was crumbling. She felt doomed to fall.

44

Reading through the packet, Serena did not discover all of this. But she definitely got the gist.

Created in 1837 as a holding for Briarwood Plantation as a property and originally funded from the proceeds of the sale of various products, contents, and appurtenances of the same, the Montgomery Trust now held assets valued in excess of $1 billion. Amanda Flynn, the Trust's latest and final director, had been scheduled to earn approximately $3 million by year's end, and every trustee had drawn an annual salary in excess of $1 million every year for decades. The principal assets had not been touched since 1837, and no beneficiary of the Trust ever collected so much as a dime. In addition to Amanda, who was descended directly from John Flynn, the attorney who originally created the Trust, the current trustees were as follows.

Kirk Benson Junior was descended from Angus Benson, the owner of the farm closest by Briarwood at the time of the massacre. Benson purchased the lion's share of Briarwood's slaves from the Trust for pennies on the dollar and went from being a hardworking Scots-Irish farmer to a gentleman planter overnight. His son, Robert Caleb Benson, lost everything in the Civil War, including his house. Robert's son, Rob Junior, decorated veteran of the Confederate Army, became the first Grand Giant of the Saxon County province of the Ku Klux Klan, a calling impeded by neither the reduction of family circumstances nor the alcoholism which eventually killed him. From this position, he provided invaluable assistance to the Trust in years to come, a tradition carried on by his descendants to the present day. Though the family received payments from the Trust throughout their history, of particular note is the gift of the franchise for three gas stations made by the Trust to Kirk Benson in 1968, in specific appreciation for services rendered during the Civil Rights Movement.

State Senator Pinckney "Pink" Collins was five-times-great-grandson of Osiris Collins, the sharecropper. Immediately following the massacre, Osiris purchased the farm he had worked since boyhood, along with three Briarwood slaves to work it for him. Within five years, the slaves had died, and the farm failed. He moved to town, opened a tavern and dry goods store, and was elected Saxonville's mayor in 1843. He continued successfully in that position for some years, even turning a considerable profit during the War, but died of an aneurysm on hearing of Lee's surrender. He left his business concerns in the delicate hands of his daughter, Rosalie. Unlike most of her neighbors, Rosalie found a way to make Reconstruction pay, converting Osiris's tavern into a bawdy house and participating with enthusiasm in the pricing practices of the day at the dry goods store.

Some good Confederates outside the Trust were heard to grumble that she was robbing her neighbors and providing comfort to the enemy. But the Trust understood the value of her connections and business sense in providing information and ammunition to Benson and his troops, and she was a much-loved trustee to the end of her days. Her son, John Lewis Collins, attended college at Harvard and returned to South Carolina after his mother's death to marry into the Pinckney family from Charleston. Her daughter, Roberta Lee Collins, married Josiah Creighton, the grandson of another first trustee, Thomas Creighton, and was the grandmother of Florence Creighton, Saxon County librarian.

Tom Stewart, the remorseful librarian, was a descendant of this same Thomas Creighton, who had a fair bit of his own remorse. He was the local schoolmaster at the time of the murders. John Flynn roused him from his bed in the wee hours and brought him to Briarwood to act as attorney for Ezra Woodbine. "But Mr. Flynn, I'm no lawyer," he protested when they dragged him into the empty shell of the mill. "And where is the jury?"

"We are the jury," Flynn told him as Benson and Collins strung up the nooses from the beams. "You just say your piece." He was the one who brought Woodbine his Bible and his correspondence and the one who posted Ezra's last letter to Elizabeth Harley. But he took his share of the Trust's money happily enough. He moved to town and opened the Saxon County Library with books confiscated from Briarwood, including those already packed by Ezra. (The more lurid volumes he burned.) Once established, he married Osiris Collins's fourteen-year-old daughter, Sarah, his star pupil from the school.

Twenty years later, when war seemed imminent, he cashed out and took his wife and their youngest daughter, Helena, to Italy, where all three perished four years later in a house fire. His oldest son, Tom Junior, stayed behind and served honorably, losing a leg at Gettysburg. After the war, he fathered twins, Josiah, who married Roberta Collins, and Josephine, who married an adventurer named Stewart and moved with him to the West. Josephine and the cowboy were Tom Stewart's great-great-great grandparents.

Frank Sweatt, the banker, was descended from Daniel Sweatt, the brother of June Sweatt Montgomery, the wife of Caleb Montgomery Junior, who had so sympathized with Ezra on the horrors of sea travel. Young Daniel was only thirteen when his sister was murdered, and he enshrined her in his memory as an angel and the money her death brought him in his coffers as a gift from God. Upon completing his degree at The Citadel, he moved from Charleston to Saxonville and opened its first bank, an august institution which survived the war with help from Osiris Collins. He was a valued advisor and business associate of Rosalie Collins, and it was with her help that he could afford to buy the 18th-century mansion on Main Street that Carol Ann later ruined with her swimming pool.

Dr. Chuck Kennedy was a cousin of a cousin of a descendant of the brother of Naomi Kennedy, the unfortunate nitwit engaged to Halsted Montgomery. When she died of fright, her father was livid. Naomi's beauty and lamb-like nature had been intended to save her father's plantation from his creditors and pay off his gambling debts. When presented with the facts of the matter, he had been unmoved by John Flynn's arguments for calm, and demanded restitution, "or I'll bring the law from Charleston and put the match to this whole scheme; see if I won't." He too was given a share, but in spite of this, his family never prospered in wealth or numbers, and Chuck was the last drop of the blood.

In return for trapping the demon and making these White folks rich, Hester Palissandre received a modest but comfortable house in town. This house belonged to her and her descendants for the next hundred years, and was the first permanent dwelling in what became Saxonville's Black district—Rooster and Claudine Decatur's house was eventually built on the same street. Hester did not survive the Civil War, and three of her sons were lynched by the Klan on behalf of the Trust during Reconstruction, lest they get any notion of demanding their family's due.

This pattern continued through the start of the new century and the First World War. Any Palissandre who seemed likely to cause trouble—a college education, distinguished military service, a hard look at John Flynn or his son or his grandson on the street—found themselves at the Mill. The other Black folks of Saxonville understood this and tried to stay out of the way. But accidents did happen from time to time and maintained the culture of fear.

By the latter days of the Depression, a hundred years after the creation of the Trust, things had gotten so bad the last of the Palissandres pulled up stakes and left Saxon County altogether, moving across the river into Coolidge. Flynn the Third, father of Jack, grandfather of Amanda, razed their house to the ground and sold it to a Yankee who built a corner store. The name Palissandre became Sanders and did its best to blend in and disappear.This suited the Trust well and they allowed it. But Flynn kept tabs.

In the 1960s, a young doctor named Sanders moved back to Coolidge from Baltimore with his wife and baby daughter, Ariel—Serena's mother. Ariel was studying law at the University of South Carolina when her father died and she received her inheritance. Jack Flynn offered her a clerk's job in his office, but by then, she knew enough to turn him down. But she did come back to Saxonville. She took a job in the Saxon County public defender's office and married a detective from the Sheriff's Department, though she didn't take his name for herself or their daughter, Serena. The detective was inquisitive by nature, and even though Ariel told him nothing herself and advised him to leave it alone, he couldn't help noticing the dark hints and comments dropped at family gatherings. He began to make discreet inquiries. Soon after, he and Ariel were driving home from Charlotte after a concert and crashed into a tree. Seven-year-old Serena went to live with her father's Aunt Lil in Coolidge. And the Trust kept watch.

The papers Carol Ann stole from her husband's safe didn't tell this whole story, but they told enough. Four days after receiving them, Serena sat in a conference room in Jacob's lawyer's office in Charlotte with Jacob on one side and the lawyer on the other. Across the table sat Pink Collins, Chuck Kennedy, Frank Sweatt Junior, Kirk Benson Junior, and Evie Stewart, who was assumed to be carrying Tom Stewart Junior *enceinte*.

"First of all, Mrs. Decatur, let me just say congratulations," Pink Collins said. "It turns out you are a wealthy woman."

"Apparently so." She resisted the urge to reach for Jacob's hand. "No thanks to any of y'all." For the past four days, she had moved in a kind of fevered trance, bouncing back and forth between a cold kind of elation and a burning rage. The precipice had crumbled; she was falling through the drop.

"Serena, I assure you, most of us had no idea," Chuck said. He was her doctor; he had seen her in the stirrups. "Jack always told us the woman the Trust was created for died, and her relatives were scattered after the Civil War. As far as most of the trustees knew, the only reason the Trust still existed was to try to find them—to find you."

"Amanda knew," Serena said. "Frank obviously knew, and he told Carol Ann enough that she knew to tell me." She looked at Evie. "Tom Stewart knew."

"I didn't," Evie said, looking panicked, like she feared Serena would tell the others about Tom's suicide note. "I swear, I didn't know anything. I knew we had the money, but Tom never said where it came from, and he wouldn't spend a dime of it. I never even knew the Montgomery Trust existed."

"All right, Evie honey," Pink said. "That's enough." A lawyer as well as a politician, Pink chose to act as counsel for the Trust. He didn't seem to have the first notion that he was out of his depth. "Regardless of who knew what and when and why, we are willing to stipulate now that you are the sole legal beneficiary of the Trust."

"That's mighty White of you," Serena said. Jacob laughed.

"Mr. Collins, we don't need you to stipulate to anything," Jacob's lawyer said. "We have the excellent records kept by Miss Flynn and Mr. Sweatt that prove pretty conclusively that Mrs. Decatur is the rightful beneficiary. And I suspect a few subpoenas will give us a great deal more."

"Oh, sweet Jesus," Chuck Kennedy said, mopping his face with a handkerchief.

"Be assured, the truth about the Montgomery Trust is going to come out," the lawyer said. "All that's left to discuss is who all is going to jail for it."

"Jail?" Pink echoed.

"I think we can agree that at least some of the trustees committed criminal acts," the lawyer said. "I've spoken at length with law enforcement and the Solicitor's office, and they certainly think so."

"Some of the trustees," Frank Junior said, glancing over at Kirk Junior. Frank was a senior at Clemson, and he had been at private school with Kirk the Third.

"Some if not all," the lawyer said. "I would imagine who gets charged with what will depend on how cooperative the rest of you are prepared to be."

"What are you proposing?" Chuck said.

"The Trust is no more," the lawyer said. "Its purpose is moot; it will be dissolved. All assets will be turned over to Mrs. Decatur immediately, along with all documents and records pertaining to the Trust or any of its assets in the possession of the individual trustees. I'll be glad to see any trustee who contests this proposal in court."

"I think we can certainly discuss all that," Pink said. "Though I'm not sure Mrs. Decatur really understands the scope of what she's about to inherit."

"And how is that your business?" Serena said.

"That's not all," the lawyer said. "Each trustee will themselves personally make a donation equal to one-tenth of their net worth as of this moment to the Briarwood Foundation to be used to found and maintain the Briarwood Plantation Museum and History Center."

"I beg your pardon?" Chuck said.

"You've all gotten rich on the misery of Briarwood," the lawyer said. "It's time you all gave something back."

"I would think the ones of you still left would be glad enough to get out while you can," Jacob said. These were the first words he had spoken, and a strange smile played around the corners of his mouth. "You folks have been dropping like flies."

Frank Junior looked sick. "I'll do it," he said. "I won't know what my net worth is until they finish probating Daddy's estate, but I'll do it."

"We'll all do it," Chuck said, giving Pink a look that clearly told him to shut up. "We don't have any choice."

"Hang on," Kirk Junior said. He had come to the meeting dressed in his Saxon County Sheriff's Department uniform—when the feds dropped the charges against him, he had been fully reinstated as an officer of the law. "You mentioned people going to jail. If we cooperate, can we assume that's off the table?"

"Not at all," Serena said. "Every scrap of evidence we get is going to the police."

"But not to worry, Kirk," Jacob said. "Your daddy never went to jail." His smile turned diabolical. "Maybe you'll get out of it the same way."

Kirk tensed, obviously itching to leap across the table. Pink put a hand on his arm. "We agree to your proposal," he said. "I'm assuming you've got documents for all of us to sign?"

An hour later, Serena and Jacob walked out of the building into the downtown square. Skyscrapers surrounded them on every side, and Briarwood and Saxon County could have been another planet. Serena took a deep breath of fresh spring air and let it out in a long, shaky laugh.

"How are you, love?" Jacob said.

"I don't know." A hundred years of theft and murder managed with a few signatures—how was that even possible? "It was all about money. All of it, all the way back to Briarwood, everything they all did. It wasn't about anything but money." She sank down on a bench. "We weren't even people to them."

"I know." He sat down beside her. "For some people, money is the whole world."

"I guess so. That's the other thing, Jake. I have been so broke for so long…" The numbers were ridiculous, obscene. "I can pay everybody finally." For a brief, dizzy moment, she imagined just taking all the money and running, a yacht that never stopped sailing, calling in at banks around the world like ATMs whenever the mood should strike her. She could do it; no one could stop her. But then it would have all been for nothing, all that blood and pain. Jacob was saying something else, but she barely heard him. She had to make sure the world knew the truth. She had to use this money to try to make things right.

"I'm sorry, Baby," she said. "What did you say?"

"I said Briarwood belongs to you now," he said.

"No." She shook her head. "You heard the lawyer. The Trust had full power to sell the property when you bought it."

"Yes, I heard him." He took her hand. "When I told Gloria back in Dublin that I was coming to America to buy a haunted plantation, she thought I was mad."

"She wasn't wrong," she said, smiling.

"No, she wasn't," he said, returning the grin. "She asked me why I would do such a thing. I thought at the time it was for me. I thought it was for the book."

"And you've written a magnificent book," she said. "Didn't your editor say it's the best thing you've ever written?"

"She did, and I'm so grateful. But that isn't what I was meant to find at Briarwood." His hand around hers was warm and strong, and she loved him as dearly as she had ever loved another human soul. "I bought it for you." He slid off the bench to kneel before her, and a lady passing gasped and smiled and nudged her friend to look and see. "I've wanted to ask you this for a while," he said. "But I didn't want you to say no because you don't want to be rescued by a sugar daddy."

"Oh Jake..."

"My darling, prideful love, I adore you." Tears spilled from her eyes, and he looked teary, too. "And you're a damned sight richer than me now." She laughed. "Will you marry me?"

In this beautiful city under the gaze of smiling strangers, the ghosts were easy to ignore. "Yes," she told him, laughing. "Hell yes, I will." She kissed him, and the strangers broke into applause.

45

The dead make convenient scapegoats. Kirk Benson was blamed for the killing, and Jack Flynn and his dutiful daughter, Amanda, got the blame for the cover-up. Kirk Junior was charged under the federal hate crimes statute but only as an accessory; he was released on bond and was waiting for trial and still hoping this whole thing might blow over. Pink Collins issued a statement, brilliantly constructed by an intern in his office, expressing shock and outrage and offering full support to all the victims and their families and announcing the sizeable donations to the Briarwood Foundation by all surviving members of the Trust. Frank Junior went back to school and graduated and waited for his mother's trial. Chuck Kennedy retired and moved to Arizona. Serena threw Evie a baby shower to show her all was forgiven.

The money paid the architect, and plans for the Briarwood Plantation Museum and History Center were going well. The house would be kept mostly intact but with exhibits, galleries, and classrooms. The mill was being converted into a memorial for the dead; Black artists from around the world had been invited to submit proposals with the final selection to be announced at the groundbreaking ceremony in June.

Serena had officially resigned from the library and hired a staff of half a dozen to help her get started, and every day of that spring was full of work that felt important. For the first time in a long time, she felt as if she were doing exactly what she had been born to do. She was the phoenix rising from Briarwood's ashes. And whenever she caught a glimpse in the corner of her eye of something or someone who ought not to be there, she turned her head away.

Jacob seemed happy, too. His book was scheduled to officially be released in the fall, but he intended to do a brief reading from it as part of the groundbreaking ceremony, and the cover art would be prominently displayed. They would open the house and grounds for walking tours at four that afternoon, with speeches to begin on the front lawn at six. Poets, activists, and historians were all scheduled to appear. Pink Collins would open the festivities by expressing support for the project on behalf of his constituents, and Reverend Holloway would close with prayer.

Serena woke up that morning at dawn too excited to sleep. Leaving Jacob still snoring, she slipped a secret item from her purse and went to the bathroom. She had been dreading her period all week; she'd had it for every other major event of her life, including her first wedding. But when it hadn't shown up, she realized it hadn't for months. That was when she'd bought the pregnancy test.

Positive. She stared at the stick and giggled. She was going to have Jacob's baby. They had agreed to wait to plan a wedding until after the groundbreaking, but she reckoned they'd better hurry up.

She set the test on the edge of the sink and washed her hands, then went to wake up Jacob.

Another woman was sleeping in her place. She was so startled that at first she couldn't speak. The strange woman was very like her in size and build and coloring, but obviously younger. She was also obviously naked under the thin white sheet, curled on her side with her clouds of hair spread across Serena's pillow. Her eyes were open, but she didn't seem to notice Serena at all. She gazed at Jacob and reached out to caress his cheek.

"Hey!" Serena said. At the sound of her voice, the girl smiled. She brushed her fingertips across Jacob's mouth as if to feel his breath. "Stop that!"

The girl turned and climbed out of the bed. She looked enough like Serena to have been her younger sister. But her body was leaner, more delicate, and scarred—an initial P had been burned into her hip. As she moved closer, she changed. Bruises blossomed on her skin, and ugly gashes opened in her flesh. Her eyes closed, and her expression twisted as if in agony while blood gushed down her thighs.

"Ariel." Serena's voice turned to a dry whisper scratching her throat. "No…you don't have to be here anymore." The ghost opened her eyes, and her lips drew back in a grimace. Her face was swollen and bruised, and one of her teeth was broken to a bloody stump. "I'm so sorry," Serena said through tears. "But it's over now. Everybody knows the truth." The ghost sneered, turning away. "It's over."

The ghost sank to her knees on the floor beside Jacob, who still hadn't stirred. She leaned close and kissed his lips. Serena started forward, then stopped. Jacob was changing, too. His wavy black hair faded to blond, and his face grew younger, the face of the ghost she had seen in Dublin; Ezra Woodbine. But he didn't stop. His shoulders thickened, and his hair and beard grew long and red—the Frenchman from the woods. "Stop it." He was still changing, still growing, a massive, monstrous thing with hands like talons and its face hidden against the pillow.

"I said stop!" She pushed past Ariel's ghost and grabbed Jacob by the shoulders. The girl dissipated around her like a cloud of mist. And in that moment, she knew.

"What?" Jacob said, waking up. "What is it?" He looked and sounded like her Jake again. But she knew he was something else. Looking into his eyes, she couldn't pretend any more. She had known it for months, even before they went to Ireland. That night at Carol Ann Sweatt's party, watching his face as he watched the painting burn. She had seen the Dark Man.

"Angel?" he said, taking hold of her wrist. She hugged him, fighting tears. "What is it?" he said, holding her close.

"You were snoring," she said. "Rattling the windows." She drew back when she could smile. "Go back to sleep."

"Where are you going?" he said as she got up and started getting dressed.

"I have to go out for a while," she said. "I'll be back soon." He sat up, and she sat down on the bed beside him. "I love you."

A week ago, they had slow-danced in the upstairs ballroom; just the two of them, claiming Briarwood for their own. But it wasn't theirs, not really. She had learned so much, but she knew there was more. One more piece of the puzzle that had always been hers, the thing she had hidden away. She had tried so hard to ignore it, to pretend it didn't matter. To build a life with this man, her man, separate from everything else. But she knew now, that wasn't possible. "You know that, right?"

"I do." He took her hand and pressed a kiss to the pulse at her wrist. "But come back to bed and show me."

"I can't." She made herself laugh when she wanted to cry. "But I'll be back." She bent and kissed him again with her eyes closed. "Go back to sleep."

"Five more minutes." He rolled over and buried his head under his pillow.

Once she finished dressing, she took the bag with the remains of the little clay man out of her underwear drawer and tucked it into her purse, glancing back over her shoulder as she did it to make sure Jacob was really asleep. She didn't know that she'd need that little bag of broken clay and blood, but she didn't know she wouldn't, and she wanted to be prepared. Checking her face one last time in the bathroom mirror, she saw the pregnancy test. After a moment, she picked that up, too, wrapped it in toilet paper and tucked it in beside the witch's totem. These were her choices, life and death, the promise of the future or the deep, dark magic of the past. She snapped the purse shut, put the strap over her shoulder, and headed out the door.

46

Jacob lay awake listening with his eyes closed until Serena left the bedroom. Then he got up and stood at the window to watch her drive away. As she disappeared into the trees, a truck drove in the other way. Soon armies of people would be swarming over the house and grounds, preparing for tonight.

He put on his running clothes and headed downstairs. Serena's assistant, Chloe, was already in the kitchen drinking coffee and going over something on her tablet. "Good morning," she said when he came in. "It's the big day, right?"

"It is." He took his morning pills with juice from the refrigerator.

"Is Herself up and around yet?" Chloe had a thick Georgia accent, but she couldn't resist "speaking Irish" to him, a habit he found at turns amusing and annoying.

"Already up and out," he said. "She said she had to go out for a while. I was hoping you'd know where she went."

She consulted her phone. "There's nothing on her schedule. I know she wanted to get her hair done early, but her stylist wasn't available. Maybe he changed his mind."

"That makes sense. Thanks."

"Have a good run!" she called as he went out the back door.

The morning was perfect for a run, misty and blessedly cool. But he went to the garage and got into his truck instead. He waved to the crew getting started on the front lawn and drove into the woods.

A quarter mile in, he veered off the machine-cut trail into the boggy brush. Another half-mile, and he had to stop or risk getting stuck. He hiked the last bit with a sledgehammer slung over his shoulder.

The stone hovel still hunkered by the stream, so covered in moss no one passing would ever have seen it. The thatched roof the Frenchmen put on it had long since rotted away, but there were tatters of an olive-green tarpaulin. One of old Kirk Benson's Klansmen had tied it there back in the Sixties. He had discovered the place by accident during a lynching, and he'd thought it might make a good hunting camp. His bones were still in the hovel, picked clean inside the rotting ribbons of his clothes.

Jacob took the sledgehammer inside. The stone hearth was carved with runes his inside self knew well, the spells and sigils that had held him to this place since before human beings could write. After so long, their magic was soaked deep into the sinews of the earth herself; the worn stones were symbols more than truth. It wasn't the runes that held him here now, and only blood could set him free. But he raised his hammer and shattered them anyway, one after another. When the hearth was rubble, he started on the walls until all that was left was a cairn of broken rocks tossed over a dead man's bones.

47

Serena hadn't seen her Aunt Lillian's house since she left it for college, or spoken to Aunt Lillian in person since the day of her first wedding. But when she called, her aunt didn't sound surprised and told her to come on over.

The little frame house had a fresh coat of white paint and new blue shutters—"To keep the haints out," her aunt always said of the old ones. The chain link fence around the front yard was still the same and still covered in the same red roses. Serena had been cared for in this house, but she hadn't been loved. As a little girl, she worried about that all the time, wondering what she'd done wrong, what was missing from her that Aunt Lil expected. But sometime in her first year of graduate school, around the same time she met Trey, she had figured out how to think it didn't matter.

The front door opened as soon as she pulled up, and Aunt Lil waited for her inside the screen, arms crossed, dressed in a pink housecoat and slippers as familiar as the roses on the fence. "Hey, Aunt Lil," she said as she got out. "Did I wake you up?"

"You know I don't never sleep." She opened the screen door. "You look good, Serena. Your fancy man must be keeping you up good."

"He's not my fancy man, Aunt Lil." This was so expected, she barely took offense. "Jacob is my fiancé. And I'm keeping myself up, thank you."

"Oh, that's right. You're a rich woman now." She went back to the kitchen to her coffee and her cigarette, leaving Serena to follow or not as it pleased her. "You come here to give me a check?"

"You can have a check if you need one." This woman had managed to spend most of Serena's inheritance before the girl's eighteenth birthday, including her college fund. Because of Lillian, Serena had spent four years waiting tables and making do with borrowed books. "But I came to get my mama's things."

"You mean that old box she left you? Why you think I've still got that?" She lit another cigarette. "You told me to burn it."

"But you didn't." She had been sixteen, and Lil told her it was the Devil's box, full of dark magic. "You're too scared of haints for that." She had never been afraid of Lil, exactly, just wary of her. Now the old woman just made Serena feel tired. "Where is it?"

"I ain't seen it for years," Lil said, avoiding her gaze. "But you might find it up in the attic."

The attic "stairs" were a rickety ladder that folded down in the hallway. Just at the top were stacks of boxes of old clothes and Christmas decorations. But shoved into the farthest corner, behind a dress form wearing her old prom dress, Serena found a cardboard carton with her mother's name written on top. Inside were homemade mix tapes from the 80s and love letters from Serena's daddy and her mother's letter sweater with a musical note on it from high school chorus. Taking this out, she felt swaddled in grief, as if no time had passed since the night they died, and she was still a little orphan girl. There was a photo album, too, but she didn't dare open it. *Later,* she promised, setting it aside.

At the bottom was a cedar box carved and painted. The paint flaked away in spots, and the finish had worn off at the corners, but it was still a beautiful object. Someone had obviously taken great care to make it. At the center of a wreath of flowers was carved the same little figure she had seen on the stone in the prayer garden at the Briarwood Baptist Church, the tiny woman with her fan: Oshun.

The box was locked, but she found the heavy brass key in an envelope underneath it marked "Serena Ariel" in her mother's handwriting, still familiar after all these years. Serena still signed her first name exactly this way; if she let herself, she could still remember sitting at the kitchen table, the feel of Mama's hand around hers as she taught her how to shape the letters. The glue on the envelope had turned brittle with time, and the flap opened without a tear.

The key turned in the lock like it had just been oiled. She opened the lid and smelled the cedar. The only thing inside was a little handmade, leather bound book. More doves and a heart were tooled into the leather. Inside the front cover she found a single long, curly lock of brown hair, and a single word written on the frontispiece: Ariel. She tucked the lock of hair into the envelope with her mama's writing on it and turned the page to read.

My darling one—

I do not ask forgiveness. Not of you or of the ones who will come after you. But they will know the truth of how you were taken from me, and you will be avenged.

My mother was a priestess of the Yoruba, a sorceress of great power. My father believed himself to be a wizard of an ancient line. They drove him from his home in France for witchcraft, chased from his estates by an angry mob with only what wealth he could carry. When he saw my mother on the auction block in Saint-Domingue and heard the curses she sang out on her captors, he knew what she was even without understanding the words. He spent the last coins in his pockets to make her his own. She hated him always, but this was of no concern to him. I do not believe he would have wanted her love or anyone's love, really, though my brother and I did love him. But that comes later.

He was obsessed with the idea of reviving his great bloodline. With my mother's body as his crucible, he intended to create a wizard so powerful, none would ever dare oppose him. He admired my mother for hating him. He gave her a new name, Seraphima, his idea of a joke, and against her hate, they made me. He was not so unhappy that I was a girl; he thought I would be the first of many. But my mother was wiser in such things than he; she knew how to kill his seed inside her.

He took a white wife, a French woman with no brothers whose father had once been a pirate. From her inheritance, he built his first plantation, and from her body, he took his son, my brother, Louis Honore. The Frenchwoman died when Louis Honore was only three years old, and though I was only six, I became like his mother. My own mother would not touch him, and after she saw I loved him, she rarely cared to touch me, either. She turned deeper and deeper into her magic, and Louis Honore and I clung to one another as orphans together. I loved him, and he loved me.

My father taught us poetry and mathematics and the sorcery of Europe. My brother and I studied side by side, and I was the cleverer pupil. But my mother taught me the magic of the Yoruba. From her, I learned the names of the Orishas and their powers and how to recognize them in the mortal world, how to see through their disguises. She taught me how to bargain with the spirits who served them, how to promise little to gain much. By the time I was twelve years old, I could see spirits everywhere. I would try to point them out to Louis Honore, but he thought I was lying to make fun of him for being not as clever as me.

"There is nothing there, Hester," he would say with a water sprite all but dancing on his shoulder in the bath. "You are very wicked." Finally, I stopped trying to show him anything at all.

Eshu Elegba was my mother's favorite god, the trickster and the gateway between worlds. She told me Eshu was in love with her. She said his love was the source of her great power and his jealousy the reason she had been captured as a slave. "Eshu sees the great wrong that has been done to me," she said. "He will regret punishing me. He will be sorry he let them take me, and someday he will avenge me."

When I was fourteen years old and my brother was eleven, my father told us we must lay together to make a child. "Your son shall be my sorcerer," he said. "I will be the grandfather of God." My mother fought him, but she could not protect me any more than she had ever been able to protect herself. I am ashamed to write that she was more bothered than me. Louis Honore was a sweet, pretty child, and we loved one another very much. It sickened me to lie with my brother, but I pretended it did not so he wouldn't be so afraid.

My mother killed my brother's seed with magic the same as she had my father's in herself, but this time, my father found out. His wrath was so great, he had her whipped. She called on the Orishas, and the other slaves rose up in her defense. They feared my mother's power more than my father's wrath. Finally, he wrung her neck with his bare hands, hoping to prove to the people that she could do nothing against him. But this only incensed them more.

I was so afraid, I called out to my mother's gods, to the Orishas. I asked Eshu to take me to the afterlife. I wanted to ask them to avenge my mother, but I was afraid they would hurt Louis Honore or my father. I loved my father in spite of what he was and the evil he had done. So I pleaded for death, for escape.

That was when I knew the Orishas not as my mother in her fury thought she knew them but as they are, true gods who live outside the bounds of time. Instead of Eshu, Oshun, the river goddess, came to me and comforted me and protected me until the storm had passed. With my first mother gone, I became as the daughter of the goddess. I pledged myself and my daughters to her. You are her child, my Ariel of the days to come, as much as you are mine, and she is the source of the best of your power. Call on her, and she will make you strong.

The plantation was destroyed, and once again my father was forced to flee, this time with his children. He was very weak; the white man's sorcery required all his strength, and he had used all the magic he could muster to escape. But he was cunning. He booked us passage on a ship to Jamaica, and before long he established another plantation there.

He was more careful in Jamaica. He did not have my mother

anymore, and he was afraid to use magic of his own, so he did not prosper quite so well as he had in Saint-Domingue. But he was patient. When Louis Honore was seventeen, our father met a Scotsman named Hamish Montgomery who had a fortune and a daughter, Ellen. Father bewitched Hamish with magic, and Louis Honore bewitched Ellen with himself. Soon Louis Honore and Ellen were married, and Hamish was dead. Louis Honore Palissandre became Caleb Montgomery, taking his dead father-in-law's name as well as his fortune. And I became nothing at all.

We moved to North Carolina where Ellen's family lived, and I was nothing but my father's slave girl. I was miserably jealous, especially when Ellen had her sons, but my father told me never mind. He must surely have known all those years I had kept myself from having my brother's baby, and he knew jealousy could do his work for him better than his magic. Finally, because I was so jealous and so alone, I prayed to Oshun and let myself have you, my Ariel. Again, my father had hoped for a wizard, and again he was disappointed. He named you for a spirit from a book, the slave of a great wizard. But I knew from the first moment I saw you that you had great power of your own.

Over time, my father weakened, and my brother became master of our house. His wife despised us, but she did not dare defy her husband. She put us to work in the apartments of her father-in-law and tried to forget we were there.

When we came to Briarwood, we both perceived the Dark Man as soon as we arrived. He saw our power and called to us from the woods, do you remember? You were still so much a child. I write now to those who will come after. Know that he is a beautiful, terrible thing that is drawn to the old magic like a moth to a flame. And Ariel, my Ariel, was drawn to him.

At that same time, my father, who feared that he would die before he made his God, demanded that my Ariel be given over to Ellen's son. I said no; I told my brother we must say no, that this madness must stop. But he would not defy our father. Ellen liked it no better than I did, and to her my brother made concession. He would send her second son and leave the first untouched.

I hated him for this. I hated that he would not defy a sick old man for me or for our child, and I hated that he would placate his wife and treat me like a slave. I closed my heart against him and his house, and I called Eshu Elegba.

And the Dark Man came. He told me he was Eshu, come at last to avenge our pain. He said that with my mortal magic, he could be born into the world to save us all. I knew he was a trickster, and I was afraid. But my daughter was braver and not so wise. She became his witch completely. With his help, she grew more powerful in the dark art than I or even my mother had ever been, so powerful the other slaves feared her even though she was just a girl. With his dark magic, she bewitched and defied the boy my father wanted for her and drove him mad.

But my daughter didn't know how to help her spirit take a mortal form, and I refused to help her. Watching the power he gave her, I could see he was no god. He was a demon, not Eshu, not an Orisha at all. He did not strive for balance; he yearned for chaos for its own sake. I tried to explain this to Ariel, but she wouldn't listen. Would you, my love?

Then Ezra Woodbine came. At first I thought Ariel only meant to taunt him as she had the other one. I saw nothing special in him. But Ariel did. She truly loved him; she even tried to defy the Dark Man for his sake. But she was his witch, and the demon would not be denied.

And Louis Honore and his white family made it so easy for him, being so heartless and cruel. They were demons, too, weak, white demons, petty and selfish, even my brother. They murdered you, beloved! He let them murder you, his own child! My child! That jealous white bitch murdered my child, my sorceress, as if she were nothing! As I watched them, yes, I called on the Dark Man. I let him take your broken little body. And when he took Ezra, I was glad.

But I could not let him kill them all. Forgive me, beloved, but I was afraid. If he were truly free, no mortal could oppose him, and his rage would devour the world. Someone trapped him on this land, some power more ancient than the stars meant this place to be his prison. The land itself is what holds him, and I used it to bind him in the doll.

But I didn't destroy him. In the moment of his binding, I realized I could release him not the way he wanted but as nothing, break him apart in bits so small the air would carry him to all the corners of the world, and he would be so weak he could never remake himself. The Orishas had given me this power just as his gods had once had the power to bind him to the land at Briarwood.

But I know the wickedness of these white men who have given me this contract, and I know their promises can never be trusted. I will leave this demon trapped but strong. I will make another Ariel, not from my dead brother but from a man beloved of the Orishas as I am. We will found a great bloodline of our own, and this demon will be our legacy. This lawyer Flynn has told me that one day my people will be free. He doesn't believe it, but I know it is so. In those days of freedom, my daughter, my Ariel of the future, take your legacy and make the choice. Take vengeance, or vanquish him forever.

In all things and in all ways, know that you are loved. Your ancestors are righteous, and they bless your path.

Your mother,

Hester Palissandre

Serena closed the box. *None of this is real,* she thought, pressing a hand to her belly where a child grew, a real child, her child and Jacob's. *This is fear and rage and superstition, a fairy tale made up by a woman who had lost her mind with grief.* But it wasn't. She knew it wasn't. She had seen the ghosts. She had felt the presence of the Dark Man everywhere at Briarwood. She had seen him in her lover's eyes.

Under the box she found a fan. Not some ancient ceremonial object, just a funeral home fan, a piece of cardboard with a picture of Black Jesus on one side and an ad for the funeral home on the other. She had a vague recollection of being handed one just like this at her parents' funeral, maybe this very one.

Aunt Lil's voice came up through the hole in the floor. "Girl, you gonna spend the night up there?"

"No, ma'am." She wiped away her tears. "I'm coming."

On her way out the front door, she saw a plaque hanging on the wall, the Serenity Prayer. *Grant me the Serenity to accept the things I cannot change, courage to change the things I can, and the wisdom to know the difference.* "Aunt Lil, what if the end of the world was coming? Judgment Day," she said. "Would you try to stop it?"

"Girl, how am I going to stop Judgment Day?"

"But what if there was a chance you could?" She turned to look back at her aunt and saw fear in her eyes. "Would you try? Or would you just let it happen?"

For a long moment, Lil didn't answer, and their eyes stayed locked. Then her aunt turned away. "Go on out of here, Serena, and stop blaspheming in my house," she said. "God's will be done."

48

By mid-afternoon, the house and grounds at Briarwood buzzed with people getting ready for the ceremony. Jacob came downstairs to find a woman he had never seen before standing frozen in the front hallway with a vase of flowers in her arms. "Sorry," she said when she saw him. "But it's beautiful, isn't it? Can you imagine what it must have been like when it was new?"

"I can," he said with his most charming author photo smile. "But I'm a professional."

At Serena's insistence, the library would be off-limits to guests and hadn't been touched. But he found more flowers on his desk beside a wrapped package. The card was from his American editor: *Congratulations! Isn't it beautiful?*

It was his new book, and it was. The cover art was a painting of Briarwood as he had first seen her, a malevolent beauty in ruins. Dark clouds above the house almost but not quite formed a face. The title, embossed in a gothic calligraphy specifically designed for this cover, was *Freedom*.

Holding it at last, he felt dizzy. He had to sit down. He knew it was his best work, his great masterpiece. The devil had delivered on his promise. He opened it up to the dedication. He had never had one before, not even for Gloria, just a page of acknowledgements. But this one read, "For Serena … beloved and muse." He ran a fingertip over the text and smiled. She had texted just before he came downstairs to say she was on her way back. She would be home soon.

Another wave of weakness passed over him, settling in his chest this time. Almost without thinking, he reached for the bottle of nitroglycerin in his desk drawer. Then he stopped. Through the French doors, he could see the platform raised on the front lawn and all the empty chairs set up before it, rows and rows of them. In a couple of hours, they would all be full. He felt the thing inside him smile in satisfaction, so much a part of him now, the hungry joy felt almost like his own.

"You did it," he said aloud. "You gave me what I asked for." The sliding doors to the library were closed; anyone passing would think he was on the phone. "Aren't you going to congratulate me? Gloat? Speak to me at all?"

Why should I speak to you? The voice was his own, his diction, his accent, and to him it sounded like it was speaking out loud. But his lips weren't moving. *I am you.*

"No," he said. "You're something else." He had thought this over very carefully over the past few months, wondering if perhaps this presence he felt was some sort of fugue inside his own brain, a symptom of some illness. "You were here when I got here. You came from Briarwood."

The voice laughed. *Not even close. I came from the other side of all that is, closer to where you started than here. But yes, I am something else. I am everything else. I am everything.*

He had thought this over, too, what questions he would ask if he ever coaxed the thing to speak. But he had only half-believed it was real, like God or Santa Claus, a thing imagined in detail but never seen. "If that were true, you wouldn't need me."

I will be everything, then. And for that, I thank you. You will be everything. We will be one.

"But what do you want?"

What you want. Love. The goddess.

"Serena?"

It laughed again. *Serena, yes. All the Serenas. All the Hesters. All the Ariels. My goddess who has always been and now shall always be. She is mine, and I will avenge her.*

"I don't understand."

You have been a good vessel, the best in all this time. I should have chosen a poet from the first. I have strength; you have given me knowledge. You have given me a soul.

"You say Serena is a goddess. Is that poetry?" The pain had started in his chest, a heavy ache.

That is truth. We found her, all of us, sailed our ships over the edge and found her world. But she loved me above the others, so they cursed her. They brought me to this wilderness, thinking she would never find me. But I will break their curse, and they will pay.

"Who?" He clenched his fist around the bottle of medicine.

I will have my goddess, and I will be everything. You will be everything. We will be one.

"Sounds good."

One final laugh that faded away like distant thunder. But the thing was still there, still inside him, reading all his thoughts.

He put the nitroglycerin away.

49

Serena got caught behind a line of pulpwood trucks coming back from Coolidge, so she didn't pass through Saxonville on her way back to Briarwood until almost five o'clock. She considered pulling over to text Jacob again but decided against it. In the time it would take her to park and text, she could drive most of the way there.

She still had no clear idea what she meant to do. She had decided not to decide until she got back to Briarwood and Jacob was with her. Until she looked into his eyes, she wouldn't know what she could stand to do. Tears blurred her vision, and just as she was heading around the last long bend in the highway before the turnoff, she reached up to wiped them away.

The man stood directly in the center of the road—Laurel Heath. She swerved hard to miss him and felt her right front tire leave the pavement and sink into the mud. The car flipped over and kept rolling across an open field of weeds. The last thing she saw before she blacked out was the steeple of the Briarwood Baptist Church.

She woke up to a voice calling her name. "Serena? Miss Serena?" Kirk Benson the Third was on his hands and knees in the mud beside her upside-down car. "Are you all right?"

"Yeah..." She had been wearing her seatbeat, and her airbag had deployed. "I think so." Though badly shaken and disoriented, she felt as if she'd been unconscious for a while. Through the broken windshield, she could see the sun had sunk almost to the horizon.

"The door is stuck," Kirk said. "But it looks like you still have power. Can you reach the control for the window?" The car was still running, she realized, and her window was open a crack.

"I think so." She couldn't even begin to process why Kirk should be there. And Laurel—what the hell had Laurel Heath been doing walking down the middle of the road miles from town? Where was he now? She reached for the window control and felt a sharp pain in her shoulder. Gritting her teeth, she touched the button. She pushed the wrong way first and started closing the window, and a wave of panic made her feel faint. Then she pulled it together, pushed the other way, and the window opened.

"That's good," the boy said. "I'm going to reach in there and try to unfasten your seatbelt, all right?"

"Okay." She braced herself. "Thanks, Kirk."

"Kirk, you dumb son of a bitch!" a voice called from nearby. "Leave it and come on!"

"Just hang on!" he yelled back over his shoulder.

"We ain't waiting," another voice answered, moving away.

"Who is that?" Serena asked, more to distract herself from the pain in her shoulder than because she cared.

"Just some boys. Don't worry about them." He slid one arm around her back and fumbled with the other hand around her hip. "Here we go. I got it." He unclipped the seatbelt, and she slumped against him, crying out in pain. "It's all right. I got you," he said. "I'm going to pull you out."

She wrapped her arms around him and tried to push as he pulled, but she was stuck. "My foot's pinned under the dash." Nothing felt broken, but something was holding her fast. "Do I smell gas?"

"That ain't the car," he said. The field where she crashed belonged to the Briarwood Baptist Church and abutted their cemetery. Looking past his shoulder, she could see a cross burning in the churchyard. "Don't worry about that," Kirk said.

"Boy, what are y'all doing out here?" she asked, feeling sick.

"It ain't nothing," he said. "Just messing around with those graves and raising some hell. Everybody's up at that thing y'all are having at the plantation; ain't nobody going to get hurt."

"Kirk, no." The other boys were whooping and hollering in the distance. "It's not nothing—"

"Just keep wiggling your foot so we can get you out of there," he cut her off, and she realized he was crying. "I ain't going to let anybody hurt you, Miss Serena, I swear it."

"Okay." She didn't have any choice but to trust him. She braced her left foot on the floor and turned her right until she felt her ankle pop. Tears came to her eyes, it hurt so bad, but she was free. "Pull me out."

He dragged her through the car window, falling backward so she was sprawled on his lap. "Anything broken, you think?" he said, his voice cracking as he extricated himself.

"My ankle might be sprained, and the seatbelt got my shoulder." Out of the car, she could see his friends in the cemetery waving their Confederate flag and kicking at the tombstones. How long would it be until somebody got the bright idea to set fire to the church? "Kirk Benson, what are you doing?" she said. "Is this you?"

"I don't know," he said. "You don't know—you don't know me!" He took off his denim jacket and put it around her shoulders. "Now come on, let's get you home." He hoisted her to her feet. "How's the ankle?"

"It hurts, but it's all right. I can walk on it." She let go of him, ready to bear her own weight.

"How come you to run off the road?" he said, leading her toward his truck.

"Laurel Heath was standing in the middle of the road when I came around the curve," she said.

"All the way out here?" he said. Like the rest of Saxonville, he knew exactly who she meant.

"Hey Benson, you pussy!" one of his friends yelled. "Don't you and your girlfriend want to come play?"

"Come on," he said, taking her arm to help her quicken her pace.

Just as he was opening the truck door for her, a low, powerful rumble shook the ground under their feet. The hooting and hollering from the boys in the cemetery changed to screams. Kirk faced the cemetery, and his pale face turned whiter. It had started. She might be too late. In that moment, she knew her intention, and it made her feel sick. "Get in the truck," she ordered. She grabbed his shirt front. "Kirk, get in the truck."

"Miss Serena, look," he said, pointing over her shoulder, but she didn't want to look.

"Kirk Benson, you mind me," she said. "Get your lily-White ass in this truck."

His eyes met hers, wide with terror. "Yes, ma'am."

50

On the front lawn of Briarwood, Pink Collins was giving a speech. "There are those among us who would say we don't need a museum." McGinnas and his girlfriend could call Briarwood a museum all they wanted. It was a plantation, and today it was in its full glory. The perfectly-manicured grass glowed the vivid green only seen on June afternoons in the South. The azaleas banked against the porch were past their bloom, but the magnolias that lined the drive were bursting with white blossoms, and purple wisteria dripped from the branches of the live oak trees. The air was thick with the scent of the grass and the flowers, and now as the afternoon gave way to evening, birds and insects were just beginning to call out from the woods, adding sweet music of their own.

But not even nature could compete with the beauty of the house itself, restored to gleaming white perfection, a monument to all that had once been graceful and good in this great land, all that their world could have been. Standing on the dais in front of it looking down over the crowd, Pink thought he knew how Caleb Montgomery must have felt when Briarwood was new, standing in this same spot, surveying his domain.

"They say there's no need to remember our past, that looking back can only hurt us," he went on, reading from the teleprompter. The guest of honor wasn't even on the dais to spoil the effect. Apparently Serena Decatur had decided she had to get her hair done for the occasion and hadn't made it back in time for the opening address. ("Typical," his late mama's voice said inside his head when McGinnas told him.) But her fiancé had assured him she wouldn't mind and that she was on her way. "They say our bridges have already been mended, that by raising this monument, we risk new hurt from a grievous wound long healed."

A grumble of dissent and disbelief went through the crowd, started by the Blacks, no doubt. It was a good-sized crowd, though, he had to admit, and there was press from as far away as Raleigh and Charleston. McGinnas and his people had gotten the word out. Scoring the opening address had been an unexpected coup.

Three months ago sitting in that lawyer's office in Charlotte, he certainly never would have expected to be standing here now. But in the chaos that followed that meeting, Pink had done what he always did, what had made him such a success in the first place, what his sainted mama had taught him to do when he was still wearing short pants to Sunday school. Pink had played ball. He had been first in line to denounce the Montgomery Trust in the press, the first one to write his check to the new Foundation. He had made a motion on the Senate floor to recognize the new Museum as a shining symbol of South Carolina's multicultural future, a phoenix from the ashes of the past. He had played the part so well, there was even talk now of his running for governor next term, and maybe even President after that.

McGinnas himself had called him and invited him to make this speech. "I can't think of anyone better suited to it," he said in that Irish brogue of his, friendly as could be. Talking to him that day, Pink got the idea he might be getting a little tired of his angry Black woman and her politics already, that a day might come in the not-so-distant future when he was ready to sell off and go back to Ireland. Standing on that dais, Pink could imagine retiring here himself someday, the grand old man of the South.

"To those people, I would say shame on you." He raised his voice slightly, going into his big build. His granddaddy on his mother's side had been an itinerant preacher in the hills of Virginia, and he had inherited his gift for oratory. "I say there is every need." He saw a light-skinned Black lady in the front row nodding in agreement. "I say that our wounds are still bleeding; that our bridges are on fire!" From deep in the crowd, he got an "Amen." He had them; they were his. "I say in the words of the great statesman Winston Churchill, those who cannot remember the past are doomed to repeat it!"

From behind him, McGinnas said, "Santayana." He was still sitting down and spoke quietly, but the microphone picked up his voice and carried it over the crowd. "Churchill didn't say that. It was a Spanish-American philosopher named George Santayana—or at least that was his name in English." The Irishman smiled, perfectly pleasant, perfectly at his ease. "And he didn't say doomed. He said condemned."

"Thank you, Mr. McGinnas," Pink said. He was able to smile as he imagined firing the idiot who had written this bullshit speech. "I did not know that."

"Mr. Collins!" The voice came from the back of the crowd, moving closer. "Mr. Pink Collins!" The speaker was Laurel Heath, the village idiot. Pink knew his name; he had a vague idea he knew more, that there was some connection between them, but in that moment he couldn't imagine what it could be. Heath was what Pink thought of as a waste of humanity, a Black-skinned tramp. He was disgustingly dirty; even from this distance, Pink could smell him, sweat and urine and filth so old it all blended together into a general sickening stench. His clothes were filthy, too, mismatched and ill-fitting. His jacket was too tight, but his pants were so loose they sagged around his hips and under his bulging belly. His Black face was greasy with sweat and marked with a pale pink scar that made his thick lower lip turn down at the corner, and one of his eyes was lazy with a drooping lid and clouded over with a cataract. He shuffled down the aisle, huffing and panting like he'd run for miles. He stopped, barely ten feet from the stage, and pointed at Pink. "You killed my daddy!"

The moment called for quick thinking and superior statesmanship. Senator Collins said, "What?"

"You killed my daddy, Mr. Collins," Laurel said. "You and Benson and Dr. Kennedy and all the rest of them White boys. Y'all remember that? I wasn't but ten years old." He pulled a gun out of the pocket of his jacket, and someone screamed. "Mama didn't want him to go out. When Kirk Benson called him in the middle of the night and told him to go down to the gas station and get the wrecker and bring it out here, she begged Daddy not to do it. But he told her he wasn't worried, that he was Kirk's best mechanic. But I could tell he was scared." He held the gun limp-wristed in his right hand, and used the same hand to wipe away a tear. But when Kirk Junior, who sat down front, moved to grab him, Laurel snapped back to attention and pointed the gun at his face.

"No, sir," he said. "Y'all going to listen to me now." He had started to tremble, then his gaze met Jacob's, and he smiled. "I hid in the back of the wrecker truck where Daddy couldn't see me," he said, steady again. "Dr. Kennedy's old Cadillac car had got stuck in the mud out there by the mill—y'all remember that old gold Cadillac he used to drive? Kirk told Daddy to hitch it up to the wrecker and pull it out, then he could go on back home. Daddy didn't say nothing to none of y'all. I was laying there hid in the back of the truck under an old blanket, and I didn't hear Daddy say nothing. But I heard old Kirk say,'Y'all really want to see it? Y'all really want to see how it works?' When Daddy got that car out of the mud and unhitched it, y'all grabbed him up and dragged him in that mill. You strung him up, and you hurt him, and it wasn't for no reason." His speech was putting Pink's to shame. The crowd was hanging on his every word. "He didn't do nothing. Y'all was just bored, and he was there, and you killed him."

Pink did remember that night, vaguely—they had all been so drunk. They were all young then; he hadn't even run for office yet. They'd been playing poker, and Kirk had been bragging about how he was the only one doing real work for the Trust, telling the rest of them they were a bunch of pussies. Chuck Kennedy took offense and said he wanted to see the mill, like he didn't believe it was real. "Sir, if something happened to your father, I am so sorry," Pink said.

McGinnas was actually smiling, the bastard. "But I assure you, I had nothing to do with it."

"I seen you," Laurel said. "Y'all knew I seen you. I heard my daddy screaming, and I sneaked up and peeked in through the door. I seen it when you knocked that box out from under him. I heard y'all laughing at the noises he made and the way he was kicking his feet. Kirk said y'all should have made bets on how long he would dance, and you laughed fit to bust." He pointed the gun straight at Pink. "You fell out on the ground, you was laughing so hard. You remember that?"

"No," Pink said, though of course he did. "Please…"

"And you saw me," Laurel said. "Kirk was the one who ran me down, and he wanted to string me up, too. But Dr. Kennedy said there wasn't no more time for that. So Kirk threw me down on the ground, and all of y'all went to beating on me. You beat me and kicked me in the head 'til you thought you had killed me, too. But I lived." Security guards closed in, but with the gunman so close to the dais, they moved slowly, trying to escape his notice and protect the crowd. "As soon as y'all were gone, I started crawling toward the road," Laurel said. "I knew wouldn't nobody come looking for me up here at Briarwood, not even my own mama. That's how come me to hear the Dark Man. He talked to me all that long night and through the morning while I crawled through them woods." He looked up at Jacob. "And he's been talking to me ever since, ain't he, Mr. Ezra?" he said. "He told me he was coming back. All these years he whispered to me, all them nights in the dark, telling me to be patient, to just wait. So I waited. But now I don't have to wait no more."

"Please, don't hurt him," Reverend Holloway said, rising from his own seat on the dais. Laurel had been part of his flock since he'd first come to Briarwood Baptist, and he wasn't talking to him; he was talking to the security guards. "He doesn't know what he's doing. Laurel, son, come on away from there."

"He promised me revenge," Laurel said. "Ain't that right, Mr. Ezra?" Without waiting for an answer, he fired. Once, twice, three times, like a string of firecrackers. Pink Collins dropped dead as a stone.

"Don't touch him!" Jacob's voice roared over the screams of the crowd as he stood up. "Leave him be." The onrushing security guards stopped and stared at him, confused.

"He had it coming," Jacob said, stepping over Pink's body to move to the front of the stage. "You've all had it coming for such a long time." One of the security guards started toward the stage, and Jacob raised a hand. A hot blast of wind rose up around him, ruffling his hair before it swept over the first few rows of the crowd. The guard was lifted off his feet and shaken the way a dog might shake a rat. First he screamed, then a *crack* split the air; he went silent, and his lifeless body dropped at Laurel's feet.

"The Dark Man!" Laurel said, laughing and brandishing his gun. People screamed and ran, knocking over the neat rows of folding chairs and pushing and clawing their way past one another. One of the cameramen from the local TV station had moved to the middle of the center aisle to capture all the gory details as soon as Laurel pulled his gun. A wave of people from the front rows plowed straight over him, knocking his camera out of his hands then trampling him as he dove to retrieve it. Rooster Decatur put one arm around his wife and drew her close as they kept their seats. She hid her face against his chest as he pushed people back with his free arm, the two of them making a little island in the middle of the chaos. Kirk Benson, Jr., dressed as always in his Sheriff's deputy's uniform, had drawn his gun and was considering firing into the air or maybe straight into the mob.

But as the crowd ran clear of the columns and bunting erected to mark the audience area and saw what was coming up the lawn behind them, they all stopped running. Like a wave that began at the front of the pack and rolled backward, they crashed into one another and froze, then screamed even louder.

Shining figures came out of the trees from every side, up the drive and out of the woods, heading toward the house. At their center, they were corpses, the rotting flesh of black men murdered on this land, some fresh and still recognizable, some no more than bones. At the front of the pack walked Oscar Heath, father of Laurel, still wearing the rags of his Benson's Towing workshirt. A past preacher from Briarwood Baptist from the early 1960s staggered dead-eyed near the center of the first wave, the oozing outline of the cross branded into his flesh still visible on his chest. There were hundreds of them, each one unique, the tattered bits of clothing they wore telling the tale of generation after generation of senseless slaughter, from slave days to the present. They seemed incapable of speech, but a single basso note rumbled from them all as if they moaned together in a single voice.

But worse than the moan was the fire. Each man radiated a hellish green fire that licked and writhed around him, shrieking as it burned, an eerie umbilical stretching from the farm in rural South Carolina to the depths of Hell. The grass burned to ash as they passed over it, and the flames raced over the ground to build a wall of fire around the crowd, stinking of sulfur as it hissed and keened. One of the security guards tried to push through the wall, and the flames consumed him in an instant. He screamed out in agony just once before his body fell, and those closest to him recoiled and shrieked in horror. The next moment, his corpse, in its own robes of green fire, rose to join the deathly throng, his voice joining the chorus.

"Condemned," Jacob said, in a voice not his own, a voice older than Briarwood, older than America. Jacob spoke, but it was the Dark Man who said, "And judgment has come."

Kirk the Third slammed on brakes as soon as he saw the ghosts. "Oh shit… Miss Serena, are you seeing this?" His friends from the cemetery marched past his truck with the others, their torn, bloodied corpses bathed in the hellish green light. "Oh Jesus …"

"Keep driving," Serena said, clutching his arm. 'Drive right up to the edge of the fire."

"Are you crazy?"

"Just do it!" He put the truck in gear and drove forward. "Just stay with me," she said. There were hundreds of the burning ghosts, more than she could count, many more than the little cemetery at the church could have possibly held. "Where are they all coming from?"

The ground opened up ahead of them with an ugly cracking sound, and more ghosts crawled out of the gap. These were skeletons, but the glowing spirits around them wore the clothes and ornaments of the Catawba and Cherokee nations. They had no real, solid faces, no mouths, no throats, but the same low moan radiated from them, the bass note below the fire's screams.

"I've got to stop," Kirk said, bawling like a baby. His blandly handsome White face was blotched with red and streaked with tears, and his blue eyes were wide with terror. "I'm going to run them over; I've got to stop."

"You can't hurt them anymore," she said. "Drive up to the wall of fire."

He did it, wiping his eyes on his sleeve; with her hand on his arm, she felt him trembling. The ghosts gave way before them, opening a path. "Okay," he said as tongues of fire licked the front of the truck. "Now what?"

"We've got to get out."

As soon as she opened the door, she heard Jacob's voice roaring out over the crowd, over the moans of the ghosts and the unearthly shrieking of the flames. "Look at the evil you have done on this land," he said. "On every land you touch! You are a scourge! A plague!" But she couldn't see him past the fire and the spirits.

"Come on," Kirk said. He lifted her up on the tailgate, and together they climbed to the top of the cab. Her ankle hurt like hell, and she leaned on the weeping boy, letting him haul her up.

The ghosts had surrounded the crowd and stopped. Jacob stood in front of the podium. Pink Collins lay on the platform behind him, dead—a pool of blood spreading from his body. Reverend Holloway herded the rest of the speakers, Black and White, to the end of the dais behind Jacob. As she watched, the preacher put himself between the others and Jacob, and the others sank to their knees, sheep huddled behind their shepherd.

She searched the crowd and found Claudine and Rooster still seated two rows back from the front. Rooster was watching Jacob, but Claudine was staring at something off to the right, utterly transfixed. Serena followed her gaze and found Davon among the army of ghosts, his arms raised, his mouth open, silently screaming for justice.

Kirk Benson Junior suddenly stood up on a chair at the edge of the crowd, waving his pistol in the air. "Fuck this shit!" he shouted. "Fuck all of y'all! I am not afraid of you!"

"Daddy, no!" Kirk the Third screamed from beside Serena. But the ghosts drowned out his voice . In a single moment, their moan became a roar. The people in the crowd put their hands over their ears and wept as the spirits cried out as one in a deafening voice like a howling wind, centuries of agony swept up in a single sound. Kirk Junior was swept down from the chair and snatched up in a dozen pairs of ghostly arms.

"Daddy!" The last son of Angus Benson screamed, and Serena grabbed the boy and held him back with all her strength as the horde of justice-starved spirits ripped his father to pieces. The body had barely fallen when it rose back up, another spirit in the throng.

"Stop it!" Serena shouted, and like Jacob's, her voice carried like magic over the din. "Jacob, stop!"

The ghosts fell back into their eerie moan, swaying back and forth as if they starved for more blood. "They aren't worthy of your pity, my love," Jacob said. His voice was the same as always, with the lovely Irish lilt that never failed to make her heart beat faster, even now when it was beating out of her chest. But the words didn't come from her Jake. She could hear the echo of the fire's screams behind them, a reverberation from the pits of Hell. "Let them die."

"Who?" she demanded. "Who are you going to kill? Everybody? Why?"

"Justice," he said, laughing. "Justice for us, and for your people." He wasn't speaking English, she suddenly realized. It was obvious from Kirk's face beside her that he couldn't understand a word either of them said. "I will avenge you, beloved, and we will be together. You will set me free."

"I never made that deal." She suddenly realized two of the ghosts were moving against the tide, moving towards her, one from either side. The rest of the ghosts were men, but these were women. "What are you?" she shouted at Jacob. "Why are you trapped here?"

The first woman ghost had reached the truck. The earthly flesh at her center was no more than crumbled bone, and the spirit around it was naked and caked with crackling mud. Her long black hair fell past her hips. "He is an evil one," she said, clambering over the front of the truck. "A thunder spirit."

"You're the Frenchman's captive," Serena said.

"He is a demon," the second ghost said. When Serena had seen her before inside the house, she had seemed alive, a thing of living flesh and blood. Now she was like the others, a burning shape around a center of decay. Ariel. "He lies."

"He is holding you here," Serena said. "All of you." She held out her hands, and the ghosts took them, holding her in their own circle of flame, blue instead of green, singing instead of screaming.

"I am your slave," Jacob shouted. "I will be your savior!"

Serena looked down at the chaos before her, this hellscape of the living and the dead. "I don't need you," she said. "I don't *want* you." She saw Reverend Hollaway on the platform ready to defend his flock, defiant before the demon. His hands were raised to heaven, and his lips moved in prayer. She saw Claudine with her hands clasped below her chin and her eyes closed and Rooster with his arms around his wife and his gaze fixed on the spirit of his son. She saw her people standing tall, shoulder to shoulder, together, not just the ones trapped here now or the ones who had died here at Briarwood, but the ones who had lived, who had risen above this evil to survive and bring her here. "*We* don't need you."

"The Creator turns his face from you," the Cherokee spirit, Chitsa, called out. "Kalona Ayeliski, begone!" The ghosts had stopped moving again, poised at the edge of the crowd. Other voices from the spirits joined Chitsa's chant, repeating her words.

"In the holy name of Jesus Christ, we cast you out!" Reverend Holloway shouted, and his people all cried, "Amen!"

"My mother Yemoja rebukes you!" Ariel called out. "My father Olorun casts you out!" Other ghosts took up this chant in the ancient language of their people, and some of the living did, too.

"Amen!" she heard Rooster's voice rise above the others.

"Amen!" Kirk the Third said, huddled on his knees beside her, choked with tears. "God forgive me all my sins, amen!"

Serena felt the living power of her people flowing through her, the blood of her ancestors burning inside her, pushing back against the darkness. She climbed down from the truck and moved through the clamoring crowd, the living and the dead, floating on the power of their voices and their will. When she reached the wall of fire, she raised her hand, and it parted before her, blue light pushing back green flame. Most of the White folks still cringed in terror, but some few had stood and added their voices to the throng. She climbed the steps of the platform.

"I am not yours," she said. Behind her lover's eyes, she saw the other raging thing, the Dark Man, the demon. How many centuries had he been trapped here? How twisted and broken would his devil's heart be now? She felt herself two people at once, herself and another as ancient and heartsick as the demon. "I never was."

"You're wrong, beloved." His smile was terrifying; but it was his tears that tore at her heart. "I will never let you go."

"In the name of Yemoja and Oya and all of the gods of my blood, I defy you," she said in a language she hadn't known she knew and a voice that wasn't all hers. She held up the broken pieces of her great ancestor's totem.

"No," Jacob said, shaking his head, and thunder rolled across the sky. But it wasn't Jacob. She could see Jacob looking through the demon, and her heart ached for him. But she had to be strong.

"In the name of Osun, I break our bond," she said, crumbling the clay between her hands as rain started to fall.

"No!" the demon roared as Jacob collapsed to the platform and Serena fell to her knees beside him. It reached up from Jacob's fallen body, trying to escape, but Jacob was the host it had chosen, and Serena's magic refused to let it go. The spirit they called the Dark Man was a beautiful, terrible thing, not dark at all, but glowing white. She pressed down on Jacob's chest, pushing back his shirt, and the red, wet clay smeared on his white skin. The demon grabbed her arm, and one of his talons carved a deep gash in her flesh. Her blood flowed down her arm, mixing with the clay and adding her power to that of her ancestors, of the ghosts around her, of the living town that she was now, and forever, a part of. The demon writhed beneath her, wrapping her in its tentacles, fighting to rip free. But she held him in the broken, dying body of her mortal lover. Through her tears, she said, "By the blood of my heart, I release you."

The thunder crashed so loud it shook the earth. Lightning split the sky. The demon screamed through Jacob's throat as he dissolved, and Serena cried out with him, the sound of his agony breaking her heart. But both of their voices were drowned out by the dead. They roared out once in triumph and the green fire dissolved. The old ones crumbled to dust and blew away on the wind. The fresh corpses fell to the earth, bloody and broken, their souls free.

For one sweet moment, she saw her Jake looking up her. He smiled, and just for that moment, she was back in time on their first day, the first time their eyes met on the front porch of Briarwood when he'd smiled at her and offered her his hand. Her favorite author in the flesh. She took his hand now and held it, smiling back. "My angel," he whispered, that little brogue and the smile in his eyes pure Jacob. Then he let out a long, slow breath, and like all the others, he was gone.

EPILOGUE

Four years later.

Serena drove the rental car up the long drive behind one school bus and passed another one heading back the other way. "Look, Ezra," she heard Maggie say from the back seat. "Look at all the kids. Wave! Let's wave!"

The bus turned off, following a sign for the Mill Memorial. She smiled, driving on to the house.

Miz Rae was on the front porch waiting for them. "Finally," she said, coming down the steps as Serena unbuckled Ezra from his rocket seat. "Did y'all forget the way?"

"We stopped off to eat," Serena said. She handed Ezra to his big sister and hugged Miz Rae tight. "We knew y'all would be busy." Her old boss looked like a new woman. The pencil skirt and sweater set had been replaced by a stylish bohemian tunic over perfectly tailored pants, and the heels on her boots were higher than Serena's. Her carefully relaxed bob was gone, too, replaced by a luxuriant mass of silver braids.

"Hello," Maggie said. "It's so nice to meet you finally. I'm Maggie, by the way."

"No," Rae said. "I never would have guessed it." She shook Maggie's hand. "You look so much like your father."

"Thanks," Maggie said. Jacob's daughter even had his wicked smile. "And this is Ezra."

Serena's three-year-old son regarded Rae with Jacob's eyes. Then he let go of his sister's hand to run and hug her.

"Come on, sweet boy," Rae said, scooping him up. "I've got something for you."

Inside, the house had been transformed just as Serena envisioned. The front hall was now a reception area for the museum, with desks for registration and signs for all the exhibits. The dining room was a bookstore and gift shop—the framed certificates for Serena's Pulitzer and Jacob's Booker Prize hung discreetly on the wall on either side of the double doors. Serena went in and found Miz Regina behind the counter, ringing up a copy of Jacob's book and a brightly-colored handwoven blanket for a young White couple. The couple obviously recognized Serena, but she ignored them, pretending to be engrossed in a pottery display until they left.

"Hey, darling," Regina said, coming out from behind the counter to hug her. "It's so good to have you home."

Outside in the hall, Ezra held his sister's hand and gazed up at a painting of a girl who looked like his mother. Maggie wasn't paying him any attention; she was talking to the lady with the braids. But the girl in the painting was watching him; he could see the smile in her eyes. He knew her name was Ariel.

Guess what, he told her, whispering in his mind, knowing she would hear him. *I can do magic, too.*

THE END

ACKNOWLEDGMENTS

Acknowledgements

Thanks and thunderous applause to my amazing editor, John Hartness, and the conclave of brilliant weirdos that is the Falstaff Books family. I could never have made it through the process of writing this story if y'all hadn't been lifting me up. Marcia Addison of Stark State College and Tally Johnson of the Chester County Library helped me hugely with both the real history and realistic protocols for historians. If I get it wrong, blame me, but whatever I got right is thanks to them. Ditto author and critic John T. Allen who gifted me with an amazing representation read on the final manuscript. He saw what I couldn't see, and I will be forever grateful for his insights and suggestions. I was particularly blessed with brainstormers and beta readers on this one, especially fellow authors Nicole Givens Kurtz and Alexandra Christian and attorney Michael Lifsey. Their insights were also invaluable, especially when they told me what I didn't really want to hear. And finally, endless thanks to my beautiful family not only for their support on this book and every book but for just getting me through the past year. I love you all very, very much.

ABOUT THE AUTHOR

Lucy Blue lives in a decrepit old house in a small town in South Carolina with her husband, artist and game designer Justin Glanville, and her Jack Russell terrier, Luke. She is a graduate of Winthrop University and the South Carolina Governor's School for the Arts.

ALSO BY LUCY BLUE

Also by this author

At Falstaff Crush

Guinevere's Revenge: A Stella Hart Mystery

The Passion of Miss Cuthbert: A Stella Hart Mystery

Misguided Angel

Bury Me Not

Eat the Peach

American Starlet

Winter Knight

At Pocket Books

My Demon's Kiss

The Devil's Knight

Dark Angel

At Pocket Books as Jayel Wylie

A Falcon's Heart

This Dangerous Magic

Wicked Charms

As one-half of the collaboration known as Anne Hathaway-Nayne

Forever Knight: These Our Revels

FRIENDS OF FALSTAFF

Thank You to All our Falstaff Books Patrons, who get extra digital content each month! To be featured here and see what other great rewards we offer, go to www.patreon.com/falstaffbooks.

PATRONS

Dino Hicks
John Hooks
John Kilgallon
Larissa Lichty
Travis & Casey Schilling
Staci-Leigh Santore
Sheryl R. Hayes
Scott Norris
Samuel Montgomery-Blinn
Junkle

www.ingramcontent.com/pod-product-compliance
Lightning Source LLC
Chambersburg PA
CBHW050510110726
47899CB00005B/1399
9781645541240